Not All Of Me Is Dust

Not All Of Me Is Dust

Frances Maureen Richardson

In memory of
Gladys Garner Leithauser

Gladys died before I finished this novel, but it was her belief in me that gave birth to it, saw it through the rough days, and, at last, brought it to fulfillment.

For Rachel, Sara, and Zoe

Throughout history, humankind has told two stories:
the story of a lost ship sailing the Mediterranean seas in
quest of a beloved isle,
and the story of a god who allows himself to be crucified on Golgotha.

— JORGE LUIS BORGES, *THE GOSPEL ACCORDING TO MARK*

The elderly Jesuit had broken off his narrative and, with his guest, paused to watch the closing of the day, for the evening air was aglow. The sun burned in the beautiful shadowed firs along the shore and, far out on the lake, the water, burnished bronze and copper, seemed to be on fire. In the distance a wood thrush called and, somewhere beyond the forested hills, its flutelike note either echoed or was answered by a fainter call and, farther off, by another, fainter still.

The old priest was reliving memories for his guest, and now, with the dying autumnal day and the distant call of a bird, there rose before his eyes young men's impassioned faces and there came to his ears young men's eager voices, and for a moment he sat with his eyes half-closed, as if to hold the vision in.

He was a tall, gaunt old man with a stately bearing, and something of the Biblical patriarch about him: the long, elegant nose bent at the bridge, the strong chin that stood out from his jaw like a ledge, the thatch of silver-white hair brushed straight back and slightly wild. As he dreamed under the silvery tufts of his brows, his eyelids drooped like folded wings lowered over a nest, but when he looked up, his shining eyes again impaled the visitor, and his voice invoked the memory in warm, rich tones:

"It was my last year as dean of theology. They were the members of an exceptional class, who wanted to think in high, imaginative ways.

"Peter Moore, the most analytical intellect among them, became the youngest dean in the province's history;

"Alan Black is an associate professor of humanities;

"Matthew O'Malley..." He murmured the name softly and tremulously. "Oh, Matthew broke my heart," he said, and in the dry, throaty inflection of his voice could be heard a weight other than his age.

"Charles Cullen is with the Jesuit Refugee Service in Guatemala, and writes and lectures on Mayan culture."

The speaker broke off again, and the listener, who had asked to hear the story, understood the reason for the pause.

"And Stephen Engle…At the time, Stephen was, in many ways, the most memorable one of all."

The Jesuit gazed at his guest with searching eyes and a note of wonder came into his voice.

"Yet who could have foreseen for what he would be remembered?"

—⁜—

Not All Of Me Is Dust

Part One

Home is where one starts from.
As we grow older the world becomes stranger,
the pattern more complicated. . .

— T. S. ELIOT, *FOUR QUARTETS*

I

When the skater reached center ice, snow was falling softly through the air. She pulled up and stood, attentive, looking at the sky. Until a moment ago, she had been tracing circles and loops on the frozen surface of a country pond. Then the sky had clouded over and the snow predicted for early evening had begun to fall, steadily and evenly, the air, too, having stilled.

She shifted about on her skates, shivering a little, getting her second wind. It was growing late and she had been skating for over an hour, but she wanted to circle the pond one more time. Out of personal dedication, she slipped through the veil of white and glided again out over the ice.

She was young and alone and caught up in wonder at the vast and freer plane that she had stepped upon, at once released and held, enchantress and captive at the same time. She was on a country pond, beautifully asymmetrical with its long, curved wooded shore, groves of pine and spruce, tangled willows, and a second pond, remote and misted over, that lay like a mirror image beyond it.

The girl worked up speed and struck out for the opposite shore. Lost for a while in the veils of snow, all at once where the shoreline bent, she swept back, coming from the other direction. Like the sibilant endings of words in a conversation the ear cannot quite catch, her skates scratched lightly over the ice—*hush hush hush*—and beauty flowed from her, shining in her hair, her eyes, the smile that curved her lips.

Her father watched her from the shore, trying to keep warm by walking back and forth and rubbing his hands together vigorously.

Lawrence Engle was a man in his mid-forties, tall and dignified, with symmetrical features and prematurely graying hair, a professor of humanities, and a widower due to the death of his wife two years earlier.

He called from the shore, "Kathleen!" His voice was swallowed up in the air so that the girl couldn't hear it. But she had seen him, and she waved her arm to say she was coming in.

The dark-haired young woman skating lightly and effortlessly toward her father was striking, a willowy eighteen-year-old with a classically oval face, warm brown eyes with long eyelashes, and lips deeply indented at the corners, a quality that gave her smile the dreamy, introspective sweetness of a sketch by Leonardo. Only one of the great sorrows that were to mark her life had yet befallen her. She was, on this wintry, snow-swept day, at the peak of her beauty and promise.

Her father met her on the shore, taking hold of one red-mittened hand and pulling her in.

"How long was I out there?" she asked, getting her breath.

"Had to be over an hour."

"It seemed like ten minutes," Kathleen said, laughing.

Sitting on a frozen patch of snowbank, she unlaced her skates, slipped them off, and quickly replaced them with ankle-high boots she took from a blue canvas duffel bag. She tucked her skates inside the bag, zipped it shut, brushed a long, damp strand of hair from her face, and reached up to take her father's hand.

In the waning half-light, father and daughter made their way across a frozen field and up a steep incline to the paved road where a gray Buick was parked. At the top of the incline, Kathleen turned suddenly.

"Did you forget something?" her father asked.

"No, I have everything," Kathleen said, glancing round. The look of wanting in her eyes had been for the ice.

Those who knew her felt it ironic that a girl who craved social activity the way Kathleen did would choose as her hobby a solitary pursuit.

Kathleen's passion for the sport had evolved over the years. When she was a child she had loved skating for the speed; as she grew into her teens, she was drawn to it by the beauty. Now, at eighteen, a motherless young adult, she found the sense of being in control, of being absolute master of the surface of a world, fulfilled her as nothing else was able to do.

—⁂—

From the study window, beside the fire snapping in the grate, Lawrence Engle looked out at the street. His six-year-old daughter, Clare, was skipping up the walk, engrossed with springing from one side of the pavement to the other. The hood of her pink snowsuit had fallen off and her fawn-colored hair, tumbling out, hung in ringlets around her brow. Her small mouth was opened in a sustained, joyful *O*. She reached the front porch, jumped up the steps, and, spraying slush in every direction, shrieked with delight.

A few yards behind her walked a tall, slender teenage boy in a black leather jacket, carrying a guitar case by his side and wearing an expression of thoughtful absorption. When he heard his sister's gleeful squeals he looked at her and laughed.

"Nature has been kind to Stephen," Lawrence Engle had remarked to his wife one evening in the month before her death.

Everything about their middle child—his thick brown hair, worn slightly long in a style that brought to mind an artist or poet, the sculpted lines of his brow and cheekbones, the clear dark eyes that stored everything—gave indication of the handsome features that would distinguish him in adulthood.

"More than nature," Elizabeth Engle had corrected gently, her gaze passing, loving and sustained, from son to father, then returning to linger long upon the son, beyond the window, out of reach. "Stephen has been touched by grace."

—⁂—

An aura of mystery surrounded Elizabeth Engle's death. In the early evening of May 7, 1964, she had suddenly, without explanation, left home. At 11:20 p.m. she reached the end of the two-lane road that followed the shoreline of the county's large inland lake. Disoriented by the darkness and the bends and curves of the road, she pulled out onto the highway and immediately into the path of an oncoming truck. It was the last act of her life. Her aorta was almost severed in the crash.

Outside the emergency room she lay alone on a stretcher near a wall. As her husband and children watched, a nurse took her away. En route to radiology she died.

Why she had left home, where she had gone, who remembered seeing her: these questions went unanswered.

Cultured, warm, and outgoing, Lawrence and Elizabeth Engle had lived a quiet, unpretentious life centered on intellectual activities, their many friends, and their three children. Each year they hosted at least one foreign exchange student, and Kathleen at sixteen had been preparing to spend her junior year studying in France. But with her mother's death, everything changed.

For months afterward, Kathleen withdrew into her moods and shut others out. She refused to talk about her mother's death, tried to repress her feelings, struggled to force happiness out of every situation, and, except when she was skating, feared being alone.

Stephen, too, retreated into his inner life. Learning a coping skill he would make permanently his own, he turned to literature for strength, searching for writers who portrayed men and women struck by tragedy, who had endured, unbroken. But he also reached out to the external world. While Kathleen would not discuss their loss, Stephen wanted to talk about it, and he found a confidant in his father.

Occasionally, it was the son who looked after the father.

On many nights after his children had gone to bed, Lawrence Engle spent hours reading in his study. Sometimes he played old recordings that had belonged to his father, Irish airs sung by the tenor John McCormack. His favorite was the same one his father had loved, though he had come to an understanding of it at a younger age than his father had. The record was very old and its quality was poor, but the pure tone of the voice and the plaintive note and the awareness of evanescence came through in spite of the defects:

> *Oh! The days of the Kerry dancing,*
> *Oh! The ring of the pipers' tune,*
> *Oh! For one of those hours of gladness:*
> *Gone! Alas! Like our youth, too soon,*
> *Oh! To think of it!*
> *Oh! To dream of it!*
> *Fills my heart with tears.*
> *Silent now is the wild and lonely glen*
> *Where the bright glad laugh will echo ne'er again.*
> *Only dreaming of days gone by*
> *In my heart I hear*
> *Loving voices of old companions*
> *Stealing out of the past once more,*
> *And the sound of the dear old music*
> *Soft and sweet as in days of yore.*
> *Oh! To think of it!*
> *Oh! To dream of it!*
> *Fills my heart with tears.*
> *Oh! The days of the Kerry dancing,*
> *Oh! The ring of the pipers' tune,*
> *Oh! For one of those hours of gladness:*
> *Gone! Alas! Like our youth, too soon.*

Often when Stephen woke during the night he would see the light on in the study. Going downstairs, he would find his father asleep in his leather armchair. Stephen would wake him and the two would sit and talk for a while. Then they would climb the stairs together—the son going first, pausing on every other step to turn round to speak to his father, who moved with the manner of a man who has forgotten the reason for the journey.

The Engle family home was a two-story brick colonial painted white, with ivy-covered walls and a black-shingled roof with two chimneys. A pair of lofty maples and a great sycamore grew on its broad lawn, bald where the trees cast their long shadows. To the left of the front door was a Japanese maple with slender branched leaves that flushed dull wine red in summer and in autumn flamed bright crimson. To the far right stood a gnarled oak with a knotted trunk and lengthy branches, one of which stretched perpendicular to the ground and wrapped like an arm around the side of the house. Where this bough bent, a child's wooden swing hung from the tree.

These features—the whitewashed brick, the latticework of ivy, the magnificent old trees, the long shadows, the stepping-stone walkway spiked by wayward blades of grass—gave the house a particularly time-less and poetic look. It stood, the last house on a cul de sac at the end of Oldbrook Road, a shaded street of dignified Georgian colonials built before World War Two, each with tall, multipaned windows and cen-tered doors of paneled oak.

In spring, lilacs and orange blossoms formed flowery walls along the lot lines, their perfume pervading the walks. Throughout summer, Oldbrook Road was a cool street of beautiful green shadows. Mourning doves called their sorrowful *hoo-oo, hoo, hoo, hoo* within the leaves and cardinals flashed amid conifers in backyard gardens. By mid-October, the majestic maples that stretched from block to block glowed with the prismatic brilliance of stained-glass windows. In the winter, Oldbrook Road, adrift in snow, had the look of a still-life landscape; day and night pillars of smoke drifted slowly upward through the great bare trees.

It was a quiet street, for all its children were grown but one: the dreaming little girl in the Engle house.

Clare was a precocious, touching child. She asked countless questions.

"Where is my mother?" With God, among the stars in heaven, she was told.

"Was she high enough," Clare wondered, "to see the years ahead?" And what was it about the stars that they could hold on to her mother forever, but she and Kathleen and Stephen could not?

—⁂—

At sixteen, and for seven years after, Kathleen became the surrogate mother of her small sister. It was she who fixed Clare's breakfast each morning, who knelt beside Clare's bed each night and taught the child her prayers, who brushed and braided Clare's hair, dressed her each morning and got her ready for school.

But it was not she who shared Clare's confidences; they were given to another. Painstaking and particular, Kathleen insisted on her way of doing things and, if disagreed with, was easily upset. Imaginative and lively, needing to be loved and to feel approved of, Clare felt constrained and misunderstood, and the sisters often clashed.

But with her brother, all was different for Clare. It was Stephen who talked with her as if she were a grown-up, who gave her a dictionary and thesaurus of her own, who taught her to carry note cards and a pen in her pocket wherever she went.

"Write down the descriptions of sounds you like, sights you want to remember," he told her. "You don't have to be sure of the words—just write down the thought as it strikes you right then."

And, "Read, Clare, read. Fill your mind with the beauty of words…"

Thus, she fell in love with language.

Each day after school, when her homework and chores were done, Clare climbed onto the cushioned window seat at the end of the second-floor hall with her favorite books. There she stayed, reading, until supper. Dusk would come on, the light would dim, and the branches of the great trees would trace mysterious shadows on the walls, but Clare sat, somewhere else, turning page after page, absorbing a world.

What rose in her mind were images of ancient Rome, of lantern light dancing on limestone walls, of luminous young women emerging from the shadows to relive their stories:

> *Listen to me, daughter;*
> *See and bend your ear.*
> *Forget your people and your father's house,*
> *For the king has greatly desired your beauty.*

The virgin martyrs of the first three centuries after Christ: Lucy, thrown into flames before dying by the sword; twelve-year-old Agnes, stabbed through the heart; Catherine, bound upon the horrid revolving wheel of knives and hooks which, miraculously, shattered at her touch. And Cecilia.

In the second century AD, when Marcus Aurelius was emperor of Rome and Christianity was declared illegal throughout the land, the beautiful young noblewoman Cecilia was among those discovered to be a Christian. Arrested by the Roman guard, she was condemned to death by beheading.

As she knelt before him with bowed head, the executioner struck his blade three times against her neck; incredibly, Cecilia survived. Because Roman law forbade a fourth blow, her life was "spared," and the young woman was left to bleed to death in the public square, in the place where she had fallen.

In the basilica where her body is interred, a life-size marble statue of Cecilia depicts her at the moment of her death: lying on her side, her face averted from the world, the index finger of her left hand extended to attest to the one true God, the thumb, index, and middle fingers of her right hand held out to signify Father, Son, and Holy Spirit. In both life and death, Cecilia bore witness to her faith.

Some nights, when Lawrence Engle looked in on his younger daughter, he found her sleeping, curled up on her side, the pure small oval of her face pressed down into her pillow, her arms stretched out, several fingers of one soft, limp hand extended. He smiled, thinking she had nodded off while counting something to herself. He could not know that in her dreams Clare had become Cecilia.

—⁂—

At ten, Clare entered the fifth grade. On her first day, she and her class-mates signed up for the school library's sole copy of the book whose stories had been passed down to them by students in the upper grades. A small gray book, an old and tattered hardcover with a loosened spine, *The History of the North American Martyrs* told the experiences of Isaac Jogues, Jean de Brébeuf, Gabriel Lalemant, and their companions, the French Jesuit missionaries put to death by the Iroquois in the seventeenth century.

In late October, Clare's name came to the top of the "reserved" list. On that warm, windy autumn afternoon, Clare claimed the *history* and hurried home to the window seat, her heart thumping like it did at Christmas.

Before opening the book, she sat with it in her lap and looked for a few minutes at the threadbare cover and nearly effaced letters of the title, treasuring the feeling of anticipation. Then she began reading the most consequential book of her life.

Scores of small, eager hands had dog-eared the pages that recounted the most appalling tortures. Each chapter, utterly real in its descriptions of the missionaries' sufferings, was more gruesome than the one before it:

Famine was ravaging their fields and, in the false belief that the Jesuits harbored an evil spirit, the Iroquois blamed the missionaries for the failure of the crops...

Upon his return from France, Father Jogues was once more taken prisoner. Once more, he was tortured, his body burned with torches and hot coals, his fingers severed with clam shells, strips of flesh cut from his arms and neck...

While the council of chiefs decided his fate, members of the Bear Clan secreted Isaac Jogues away and beheaded him. His body they threw into the Mohawk River, his head they placed upon a pole facing the Jesuit mission at Quebec...

As she plunged into the astonishing stories, Clare had no way of knowing that, at that very moment, another member of her family was also focusing on the Jesuits. She would not learn of it until a future day, in the following spring. Now she was caught up in another world, one of incredible courage and unspeakable cruelty, where life was strange and fraught with danger, and men were fated for brutal death.

For Clare and her classmates, the feelings of horror and revulsion aroused by the vivid accounts of the martyrs' deaths were the most achingly physical sensations they had ever known. And for Clare, in those hours of intense reading, another awareness was dawning. On a higher level, a question was forming: along with the torment they had endured—Isaac Jogues and his companions and, before them, Lucy, Agnes, Catherine, and Cecilia—they had experienced something else, an even whiter heat than pain. That had to have been true, or they could not have gone on.

And Clare wondered: What was its name?

II

They were a family bound together by love and need and an imponderable loss. There was an unspoken solidarity among them, a deep trust in and loyalty to one another. As time passed, Lawrence Engle's quiet, reflective way of life deepened. His bearing became even more reserved, characterized by a vague, indefinable sense of mourning. He lost touch with the social contacts he and his wife had developed together. When he felt the need for companionship, he sought out the priests in the parish, and one or two of them became his frequent dinner guests.

His chief concern was the well-being of his children. With a father's discernment he realized that his son was self-directed and would succeed at whatever he set out to accomplish, but that Kathleen was self-doubting and would be easily discouraged.

Brother and sister resembled each other so closely that often those who did not know them mistakenly called them "the twins." But the resemblance was physical only. At school, Kathleen was a preoccupied, indifferent, uninspired learner. By contrast, Stephen distinguished himself: he was a thoughtful, attentive, dazzling student. Socially, with her bright, assertive smile, Kathleen was lighthearted, poised, and outgoing, while Stephen was quiet, modest, even shy.

Both said *should* often. Kathleen used the controlling *should*:

"You should have known…"

"You should have gone…"

"You shouldn't have done…"

Stephen spoke the creative *should*:

"You should have great dreams."

"You should imagine what could be."

"You shouldn't be bound by what is."

After graduation, Kathleen, at her father's urging, entered Loyola University, a liberal arts college run by the Jesuit order. For the first four months she studied languages. At the end of the term, she changed her major to speech, and in her sophomore year she transferred to education. Her junior year passed in the same irresolute way. Finally, at the start of her senior year, she came to her father in tears to tell him that she intended to leave school.

"No," he replied gently, "every woman needs a marketable skill." And the second time, understanding his daughter's aspirations, "No, your husband will want his wife to be a college graduate." And so she persevered.

Although Stephen was a year younger than his sister, he was accelerated a grade in high school and graduated with her in 1967, the valedictorian of their class. He entered college with Kathleen and together they drove to and from school in a used 1957 blue-and-white Chevrolet.

Stephen considered studying architecture or psychology but, unsure of the direction he wanted to take with his life, he decided to enroll in English studies. But his restlessness was different from Kathleen's.

He found nothing in his studies that could satisfy him. He was indifferent to material goods and absorbed by ideas, by the concepts of time and timelessness, and by thoughts of the imperishable. In his reading he searched for unified patterns, for beauty and truth. He questioned the purpose of existence and sought to understand human nature in light of its highest possibilities. And then, one afternoon early in his senior year, he stopped at the Jesuit residence hall and asked to talk with a priest in order to learn what it meant to be called to the life of a Jesuit.

—◊◊◊—

Stephen graduated from Loyola in May 1971, at the height of the Vietnam War. Like countless other graduates, he immediately registered for the draft. On the Saturday in late June when he received the news he had drawn a high number in the lottery, he sought out his father.

Stephen found him sitting alone on the steps of the front porch, gazing at a thunderhead towering over the line of trees that led up the street from the cul de sac. Its upper limits seeming boundless, the great cloud massed higher and higher, beautifying the entire afternoon with its dominance of the sky.

For over an hour father and son talked together, Lawrence Engle looking straight in front of him, listening as Stephen described the decision he had made. At one point he ran his hand over his head, touching a bald spot in the back. He smiled.

"I'm losing more of my hair. I should be the one to go into religious life—tonsured, a monk." He nodded firmly to himself. "The Jesuits." He turned to his son.

"Can you make the vow of celibacy, Stephen? With all that it implies? For a lifetime?"

"Yes, I believe I can. I'm committed, Dad."

"What concerns me," Lawrence Engle advised gently, "isn't how the strictures of that vow will affect you now, when you're young and idealistic and full of enthusiasm. What concerns me is how they'll wear on you over the years. There are needs apart from the physical. I'm thinking of the emotional loneliness of the celibate life." Lawrence Engle leaned an elbow on his knee, his hand pressed against his cheek, and gazed into Stephen's eyes.

"You remember your grandparents," he went on, "and how as they grew older they even came to resemble each other…how the intimacy they shared increased over the years, and strengthened and comforted them in their old age.

"And I think of you—when you're that age," he said, lightly touching Stephen's shoulder, "and how being alone will be very, very hard on you."

They were silent again. Then Stephen said:

"Dad, having found this…No, that's not accurate. Ever since I've felt myself called to this, I've known there would be no other way in life for me, but this."

Stephen intentionally repeated the word *this*, knowing his father would understand that in doing so he was giving it more than usual significance, that he was referring to it as a mystery of faith. That meaning silenced opposition.

Lawrence Engle took out a small pocket handkerchief, carefully unfolded it, and held it against his eyes. "If I told you that my allergies have suddenly started up, would you believe me?"

Stephen shook his head, laughing softly. "No, Dad."

Lawrence Engle leaned over and for a long moment embraced the most gifted of his three children. Then he stood, adjusted his shirt, walked down the steps, and with a slow, steady tread crossed the lawn to meditate on the day and its significance.

Stephen watched him walk away, one of the most private of men, and wondered if, when his father had remarked on the loneliness of age, he'd been aware of whom it was he had, in fact, been speaking.

—⁂—

They decided to tell Kathleen and Clare the next evening.

It was an evening in June, luminous and warm. The white blossoms and dark boughs of the cherry laurel glowed against the faded violet sky that attended dusk in late spring. All about the lawn the great maples raised their tender new leaves heavenward in what seemed a gesture of Nunc Dimittus. But the air had the heavy feel that comes just before a storm and, forever after, when Clare thought back on the events of that day, they merged in her memory with rain.

After dinner, while they were still gathered about the table, Lawrence Engle looked thoughtfully at his daughters and, laying his hand on his son's arm, said, "Stephen has something to share with us."

Kathleen and Clare looked across the table at Stephen. His even calm did not reveal it, but he was deeply moved, carefully making eye contact with each of his sisters as he spoke.

"For the past year," he said, "I've been considering the priesthood."

Kathleen caught her breath. Clare sat paralyzed.

"I looked at various possibilities," Stephen went on, "and the one that kept coming back, always with more certainty, is the one I've decided on." He glanced at his father. Then he said, "I'm going to enter the Jesuits."

Clare twisted in her seat, the color draining from her face, a wave of nausea passing through her body. She asked in a small, shattered voice, "The Jesuits?"

Again Isaac Jogues was taken prisoner by the Iroquois, and his fate imperiled...The head of the Tortoise family argued that Father Jogues brought peace and wanted only to serve, but others cried, "Blackrobe is an evil spirit. Kill him!"...While the chiefs debated the Jesuit's future, members of the Bear family slipped away from the group. They led Isaac Jogues, his hands bound behind him, into a small, coarse tent, bent him over the flickering flames of a night fire, and beheaded him. His headless body was thrown into the Mohawk River, and his head put on a pole facing toward Quebec...

"The Jesuits?" Clare, remembering, asked again.

"We have the Jesuits at Loyola," Kathleen said in the brisk, matter-of-fact tone Clare felt her sister used when she wished to indicate that her way of thinking settled an issue.

Stephen started to say something. Clare turned her head to look at him, miserable.

"The Jesuits have found a way of looking at the world that I realize is what I've been searching for," Stephen said. Then, speaking to Clare as he had always done, as though she were his equal in age, he became confidential: "It's important to me to have a life of the mind. And I want to share that enthusiasm. I want to help develop the minds of others."

Kathleen leaned forward to touch her brother's hand. "I think it's wonderful."

Clare looked to her father, who was watching her with an empathetic smile. The tears that had been welling up in her eyes were beginning to make their descent.

"Stephen's very levelheaded, Clare. He's ready to make a decision like this."

Clare was about to blurt out, "What about me?" but she saw a look on Kathleen's face that said she ought not to do it. Instead, she got up quickly, circled the table, threw her small, thin arms around Stephen's neck, and hung on, crying bitterly.

Kathleen exclaimed audibly, but Stephen, glancing at her, said, "She's all right. We need to talk alone." He brought his mouth close to Clare's ear. "It's not going to rain for a while. Let's go for a walk."

Clare shook her head. She couldn't pretend; she didn't want to be brave. "I have something to do," she said. She had nothing to do; a perverse sense of power coursed through her body: the impulse to reject. Yet Stephen seemed not to interpret her objection as a rebuff. She remained clinging to him until he patted her several times on the back to let her know he wished to stand, and then took her by the wrists and gently released her grip. He pulled out his handkerchief and gave it to her so that she could wipe her eyes.

"I'm going out to the car," Stephen said. "I'll be back in a few minutes. Then I'd like to go for a walk. I wish you'd come with me."

Without replying, Clare covered her face with the handkerchief, turned and ran from the room, into the hall and up the stairs, to her room. Once there, she fell, disconsolate, onto her bed. She was convinced that she was going to have to bear her suffering alone, that no one understood the depth of her feeling, not even her brother, whom she had once believed was the most sensitive member of the family.

Her hands gripping her pillow hard, she lay for long moments, sobbing uncontrollably. She missed the light tap on her door. Totally absorbed in her misery, she was picturing the future. Stephen had left home to enter the Jesuits and grief over his departure was about to cost her her life. She would be dying here, in her bed. "There are only moments left," a male voice, a doctor, was whispering. "If only someone had understood the child's pain..."

Then, as she was about to take her last breath, Stephen would arrive. He would plead with her to speak to him, but in her weakened condition she would be unable to talk—only to listen. Realizing the grief he had caused, Stephen would tear his cassock—as they did to their garments in the Old and New Testaments—and admit how selfish he'd been. Overcome with anguish, he would fold her in his arms and beg her to forgive him for going off to care for others and leaving her to become ill and die at such a young age. And he would suffer, suffer, suffer, suffer, as she was suffering now.

But what was that? The front door closing. She dried her eyes on the backs of her hands and, jumping up, ran to the window and pressed her face against the pane. Stephen. He had reached the street. And what was he doing? Whistling.

A whistle so pure and piercing and joyous.

A whistle that went right up to the stars.

—◊◊◊—

The next day, Stephen rose ahead of the others and left on an errand before eight. And so it was with her father that Clare went for a walk in early afternoon.

It had rained overnight; in places the branches still dripped. The softened air was heavy with the scent of lilacs. Delphinium, just coming into bloom, were tall along the hedges.

Clare walked with her head down, listening to her father's deep, even voice. Her father took her hand, squeezing it so she would know he was aware of what she was going through. He explained to her that Stephen could have gone away to college after high school, but had chosen to stay at home and attend Loyola, largely because he felt a responsibility to his family, and to her in particular.

"Your brother has years of serious study ahead of him. It will be hard for him, too, to be separated from his family. It will be even harder if he thinks we're unhappy. So I want you to try your very best to be unselfish. Let him know you're proud of him and that you believe he can make this commitment. Don't let him leave having to cope with the thought that you're at home grieving."

"I promise."

—ɯ—

Slowly life changed. Clare no longer read about the North American martyrs. The stories had lost their fascination; in fact, they had come to represent a world—the world of the Jesuits—from which she was excluded.

She tiptoed around the house, following Stephen at a distance, like a detached shadow. In contrast to the free and decisive way her brother moved about as he prepared to enter into his new life, she felt trapped and powerless in her childhood, her unhappiness deepened by the need to conceal it. Her religion came under scrutiny. She wondered: In the homes of Lutherans or Methodists or Episcopalians, were there tragedies of separation like this? Stephen was the one to whom she had always turned for advice, and she needed to ask him.

She found him in his room, clearing his desk. On a chair near a window lay an empty suitcase with the lid raised.

"Do you have any books about Protestant religions?" she asked from the doorway.

Stephen set a notebook filled with papers down on the desk and looked at her, smiling. "Hi. No, I don't have anything here. I can bring some books home from the library for you. Are you doing a report of some kind?"

"No," Clare said, staring at the floor. "It's for my personal study."

Stephen gazed at the tender, young face with its downcast eyes.

"I see. Come in."

Clare took a step and stood just inside the door.

Going to a cardboard box by his bed, Stephen bent over and searched through it. After a few moments he pulled out a slender book in a blue-and-green binding.

"I was planning to give this to you later," he said, "but maybe you'd like to have it now." He walked across the room to her. When she didn't lift her head or say anything, he went on, "It's one of my favorite books: *The Collected Works of Gerard Manley Hopkins.* He's the only priest—a Jesuit—buried in Poets' Corner in Westminster Abbey, right between Tennyson and Browning. A few years from now, when you study English literature, you'll learn those names. I'd like to talk with you about the book then."

Moments passed. Then a small voice came from the lowered head. "Would you sign it?"

"Sure. What would you like me to say?"

Finally, shyly, Clare raised her eyes and looked at him. Her answer was a near whisper:

"'To Clare, with love. From Stephen.'"

Stephen went to his desk and picked up a pen. In his vertical, artistic script he wrote:

"To Clare. Whom I love. Stephen"

He walked slowly through the house for the last time, like a visitor or a stranger among them, entering each room, absorbing it with his hands and eyes. He touched pictures, bookcases, tables, chairs, portals of doors, his own room last of all, with a long, slow, meditative casting of the eyes. And then he released: like a skier out of the chute, like a rush of wings, visibly, palpably, he let go. He turned and, without breaking stride, barely touching the rail, he ran down the stairs and out the front door. He joined Kathleen on the lawn; they put their arms around each other's shoulders and, turning their heads, faced their father, who was preparing to take their last picture together as mere brother and sister. It was accepted that he would not be back, that he would not waver, that his life as he had lived it here with them had ended.

Clasping and unclasping her hands, Clare watched and prepared for the event about to occur. She mustn't cry now. *Stephen, if they throw me into flames, if they put me to the sword, if the Iroquois rip my heart out, I will not cry now.*

He knelt before her on the grass and hugged her fiercely. She felt his arms around her shaking. He said:

"Stay close to Dad and Kathleen, Clare.
Come to see me when you can.
Pray for me, darling."
Once more, the rush of wings.

—⚊⚊—

In the evening in spring and summer, Stephen's room, facing west, filled with long shadows for hours; the moon and early stars were first seen from its windows.

It was evening now and Clare stood in the doorway and slowly looked about her, the way Stephen had done mere hours before. How natural it all seemed. The scuffed black guitar case was propped up in the corner by the bed. A dark leather jacket showed through the half-open closet door. Silver medals fastened to a plaque mounted on the wall and framed black-and-white photographs of a high school swimming team hung beside the maple dresser. A bookcase built between the windows contained *A Farewell to Arms, The Scarlet and the Black, Dubliners, The Sound and the Fury,* a complete set of Shakespeare. The aquarium with silver-and-black angelfish, their laterally compressed bodies moving back and forth in slow, undulating arcs, was freshly attended to and left for her, if she wished to have it.

The room had lacked neatness and order while he had lived there; it had been restless with life and thought.

How unnatural it all seemed.

Stephen was gone.

For weeks afterward, Clare fantasized that some reversal might occur, and Stephen would be allowed to come home, to walk through the front door as he had always walked and, taking the stairs two steps at a time, return to his room. Then at night, before the house fell silent, from her room she would hear again the blissful sound of his footfall past her door. Thoughts like these produced a deep sense of betrayal, and Clare knew that she would have to give them up. But, for a while at least, she let herself drift off to sleep with her guilty, secret dream.

—◊◊—

Two weeks later, Clare returned to school. She loved school and had always been eager to get back to it. It was never necessary to set an alarm for her or to call her. She was invariably the first one up, rushing through breakfast, slipping on her jacket and book bag, kissing her father good-bye, hopping onto her bicycle and riding the mile and a half to the parish school of Saint Thérèse of Lisieux.

But this year she had to drag herself back. She dreaded being asked about Stephen, hated the thought of mentioning the Jesuits. And something else had changed. To the pain of Stephen's leaving was added the jolt of learning that Sister Borgia Marie, the teacher she'd looked forward to having, had transferred to a different school over the summer and another nun would be teaching sixth grade.

As Clare entered the classroom that September morning, she saw, standing in the front of the room among a group of softly laughing girls, a middle-aged nun with rosy cheeks, a round, buxom figure, and unfashionably gray hair. Her manner was poised and attentive, a rare quality of listening deeply. She had a gentle, kind face with fine cross-stitches of wrinkles, a hushed, warm, expressive voice, a very gracious glance, and a lovely wink that told even the rowdiest boys that she understood them.

Her name was Sister Mary Bernard; she had taught school for many years, though usually in the upper grades, and students said of her: "It was impossible not to love her."

—— *~~* ——

The school year settled into its familiar routine. As the weeks passed, Sister Mary Bernard found her gaze turning again and again to the quiet girl with the fawn-colored hair who sat in the third seat in the row of desks along the side blackboard.

Sister Mary Bernard observed an imaginative, sensitive young girl, an eleven-year-old who carried with her and read the Jesuit magazine *America*; a precocious, vulnerable young girl whose homework, when it was completed, was beautifully written in meticulous detail; an entrenched daydreamer with too-thoughtful eyes and a distracted glance, whose work often went undone.

Long before they became consciously aware of it, both Clare and Sister Mary Bernard knew intuitively that they were going to be close, each catching sight of something undefinable in the other's eyes. It was simply a matter of beginning.

—— *~~* ——

Everything stood out in stark relief in November. Clouds were mightier: silver and smoke or dark and heavy-laden. Snow fell through the air cleanly and beautifully, like poetic lines, and the empty spaces of sky were like caesuras. Years later, when she had fulfilled her dream of becoming a writer, Clare wrote a poem in which she said that November had about it the feel of one's last hour, when one notices everything: that clarity, that quickening, when one knows one must let go. But her reflections on November began here, as a child, the first November that Stephen was gone.

—⁂—

"Such lovely work…when it's done…"

Returning an assignment to Clare on a day in mid-November when school was over and they were alone in the room together, Sister Mary Bernard opened the conversation this way:

The nun walked around the table where Clare was sitting and took a seat in the chair across from her. She thought for a moment and then she asked in her warm, hushed voice, "What's he like, your dad?"

And in the deserted classroom, while snowflakes were falling through the air outside the window, Clare talked haltingly about her father, who was "loving and kind, funny and wise…But, at other times, when he's reading late at night, or walking alone in the garden, he seems so lonely. He's thinking about my mother, I know."

"Do you remember your mother?"

"I remember her leaning over to hug me," Clare said softly. "She was all hug, if you know what I mean."

Eyes bright, the nun nodded.

"When I was a child," Clare continued, and Sister Mary Bernard suppressed a smile, "I liked to crawl into a chair after someone had been sitting in it so that I could feel the warmth. When I told my father, he said that was my mother's presence among us. That warmth in the chair…"

Clare's voice trailed off. Then she said, tentatively, "My sister, Kathleen, became my substitute mother…"

"What a big responsibility for her!"

Clare's mouth twisted a little at the corners. She had a somewhat different perspective, but knew that she should not say this. Instead she offered, very quietly, "Kathleen doesn't mean to be strict…"

"Perhaps," Sister Mary Bernard said, "she's a little overburdened?" She winked at Clare to convey her understanding.

There was a silence then.

Kindly, Sister Mary Bernard urged, "Go on. Isn't there someone else?"

Clare drew in her breath. "My brother, Stephen," she said, her small hand brushing her hair back nervously, her hazel eyes glancing up shyly from beneath fair lashes. "Do you know him?"

"No, but I've heard about him."

Dry-eyed, in a voice barely audible, Clare told the nun about Stephen's decision to enter the Jesuits, his leaving home, her heartbreak, and her self-reproach.

"I'm so ashamed of how selfish I've been. But I miss him so much. I want him to be happy, but I'm not…" She pressed her hands against her chest and went on, "I'm not brave enough to wish he'd stay."

Sister Mary Bernard listened seriously, her eyes following every word. She waited until Clare had finished speaking. Then she leaned forward and said very tenderly:

"How tragic those feelings are. How you've had to struggle. But I will tell you that what you've experienced is only the beginning of a story, a story that will have many beautiful, surprising turns. All that you've described to me takes place in Chapter One, 'The Departure.' It will be followed by many more chapters: 'The Visit,' when Stephen comes home for the first time, and another one a little farther on that I like especially, 'The Friendship'—for you and your brother are going to be great friends throughout your lives."

"How can you tell?"

"Is he intelligent and sensitive and kind? Others have described him to me that way."

"Yes."

"Well, that's the way you are, too. And since you and Stephen are so much alike, you'll always be close to each other." Sister Mary Bernard paused. Then she asked, "Do you know what a soul mate is?"

"No, I don't think so."

"A soul mate is someone who is so close to you that he or she is thinking the very same thoughts you are, even if you're not together. It's the highest form of friendship. And I think that you and your brother could be soul mates someday. When you see him, just ask him if I'm not right."

The remark affected Clare so deeply that her lips trembled and she had to struggle to hold back tears.

"Thank you, Sister. That gives me something to live for."

She felt in her uniform pockets and took out a white handkerchief, opened it, and blotted her eyes, while Sister Mary Bernard, who valued bravery and understood its many forms, smiled fondly.

III

Soul of Christ, sanctify me.
Body of Christ, save me.
Blood of Christ, inebriate me.
Water from the side of Christ, save me.
Passion of Christ, strengthen me…

— FROM THE "ANIMA CHRISTI" BY IGNATIUS LOYOLA

Born in Spain in 1491, a contemporary of Leonardo da Vinci, Christopher Columbus, and Henry VIII, Ignatius of the family of Loyola came of age in stirring times and imagined earning glory as a knight.

His dream was smashed, literally, when, at the ill-fated battle against the French for the fortress of Pamplona, a cannonball shattered his right leg.

Naturally active and outgoing, Ignatius was quickly bored with a lengthy rehabilitation that kept him immobilized in solitude. Turning to reading, he found the only books available to him were religious works: a life of Christ and *The Lives of the Saints*.

But something in those pages awakened his soul, for a changed man emerged from the long convalescence: a man of prayer, a servant to the sick, a beggar living on alms, and a pilgrim, first to Rome, then to the Holy Land.

As his spiritual life deepened, Ignatius resolved to study for the priesthood, humbly learning Latin among schoolchildren to prepare for the university.

Intelligent, charismatic, committed to the highest ideals, Ignatius drew like-minded young men to join him in following Christ. In time, he and his companions decided to take vows of poverty and chastity. But they would not live in a monastery apart from the world; they would live on the streets among the forgotten poor. Together they would combine the active with the contemplative life; together they would form a society, the Society of Jesus.

—m—

Stephen had entered the Society during a period of crisis. The changes brought about by the cultural revolution of the 1960s affected American religious communities like atmospheric pressure acting upon a sensitive barometer: admissions to novitiates fell to numbers never seen before; the departure of candidates for the priesthood and ordained priests rose in disturbing increments.

When Stephen took his first vows at the end of the two-year novitiate, only five out of an original class of twelve remained. But they were an unusually gifted and fiercely bonded five.

Alan Black was a former doctoral student in fine arts. He was tall and athletically built, with a long, thin face, a classic Greek nose, and large, deep-set eyes with dark hollows underneath that gave him a weary, melancholy look. Yet a sly show of wit, followed by a rich, hearty laugh, completely altered the impression, and revealed his true personality: brilliant, garrulous, and irrepressibly good natured.

A small man physically, with alert gray eyes and a fine, intelligent face, Peter Moore was a year out of law school. He was a precocious student, having studied engineering before committing himself to law, and then, at twenty-five, to the Jesuits.

Charles Cullen was a boyish-looking young man with a high-cheek-boned face with red patches, animated brown eyes, and an unruly cow-lick in his wavy blond hair. Lacking the linguistic talents his classmates possessed in abundance, he sometimes struggled with his theological studies. However, the empathy with which he understood another's point of view, the soft-spoken, thoughtful way he engaged in conversation, showed the intuitive, intrapersonal intelligence that would one day make him a discerning spiritual director.

Gentle, impressionable, unreservedly Irish, Matthew O'Malley had been a campus minister at Fordham University. During the novitiate he became Stephen's close friend and confidant. At six feet four, Matthew was the tallest of the young men, had very fair, freckled skin and thick, sandy brown hair, which in ten years would become a white storm out of season. His pale coloring and open face with its glow of enthusiasm presented a striking contrast to Stephen's dark hair and eyes and air of quiet reserve.

They needed each other's differences. Matthew was drawn by Stephen's intellect and creativity; Stephen found his friend the person with whom he could completely relax and feel emotionally at home. And they understood each other's aspirations. Both thirsted for ideal ways of doing things, hungered to make a better world.

—m—

On the path leading to ordination, Stephen met, at separate points in time, two men whose personalities and influence were legendary among the men in the classes ahead of him.

His spiritual director, Anthony Valerian, was sixty-four when Stephen got to know him, a tall ascetic with wisps of graying hair, gaunt features, watery brown eyes, and skin ruddy and withered as the leaves on a dogwood tree in autumn. Mentally, he had the rare beauty of character that can effect a change in others, enabling them to feel ennobled in his presence. Remembering Valerian in later years, Stephen, who flowered under his direction, thought of lines from D. H. Lawrence describing the scene in which the philosopher Maximus encountered a divinity in human form:

> *I said to him: And what*
> *is your name?*
> *He looked at me without answer,*
> *but such a loveliness entered*
> *me…*

Valerian placed a book in Stephen's hands, the book that would influence Stephen as long as he lived: *Man's Search for Meaning* by Viktor Frankl. Stephen found in Frankl's writings the conclusions that were to shape his adult mind and thought. Stephen wrote in his notes:

> *The extraordinary collection of insights that came to Frankl was not the result of months spent in scholarly contemplation, but a deeply spiritual series of convictions drawn immediately from life experience—the death camp of Auschwitz.*

At the start, upon his arrival at Auschwitz, he was faced with the uncertainty that this life held meaning any longer, with no child to survive him, with his "spiritual child," the manuscript of his first book vanished, hidden in the coat he was forced to surrender. He describes the moment when the meaning of life suddenly became clear to him: Given the clothes of an inmate who had died in the gas chamber, he found in the pocket of the coat a single page of paper; it contained the great Jewish prayer "Shema Israel." Frankl's interpretation: Even as he'd felt that his life had been deprived of meaning, he was challenged anew, not to write his thoughts, but to live them…

Amid mental anguish and physical deprivation he discovered that the intensification of the inner life can enable one to surmount an external world that seeks to degrade one; that even when a man has everything stripped away from him, still he has left his core, his soul, and there the inner resource Frankl calls "the last of the human freedoms-to choose one's attitude in any given set of circumstances, to choose one's own way."

—⁂—

A picture of Joseph Edmund, the dean of academics, hung in the hallway outside the juniorate library. Taken years earlier in Rome, the photograph showed Edmund standing amid a group of Jesuits surrounding Pope Pius XII. The pope's profile was to the camera. Edmund faced him in the left foreground: a large man with strong features, dark blond hair, and a short, elegantly trimmed beard. In the photograph he appeared to be listening intently to something Pius XII was saying, tilting his head to one side, smiling with half-closed eyes in a look meant to curry favor, an obsequious expression that made him unrecognizable to those who knew him in later years.

Older now, and clean-shaven, his long face, asymmetrical as most faces are, was more pronounced than usual in its divisions: the right side handsome, brooding, introspective; the left side, with the eye slightly raised, supercilious, sardonic, shallow. His full mouth, sensual in its curvature, pitiless in its line, characteristically wore a faintly amused smile, the amalgam of irony and scorn. Edmund read and wrote in French, Spanish, and German, and could converse in Latin. His intolerance of mediocrity was widely known.

Charles Cullen, who struggled to keep up with his classmates, became a frequent whipping boy. Stephen, too, suffered under the dean's supervision, though he excelled in the very field that had been Edmund's province. The older Jesuit considered sensitivity in a man an affectation. He interpreted Stephen's reserve as arrogance, Stephen's tendency to think on a high conceptual level a false air; and in Stephen's silences, the dean read resentment of himself.

"You're a good student, Mr. Engle, a good student," Edmund said to Stephen in private one day. "But you give yourself the air of an Augustine or an Aquinas, and in that league you are not."

Another day, while returning written assignments, Edmund commented on Stephen's paper in front of the four other young men.

"I had several problems with this paper, Mr. Engle. The insights were romantic and commonplace, not the developed thought of the serious scholar."

Stephen sat motionless, his face reddening; cut to the quick, he said nothing.

Later that afternoon, crossing the quadrangle, Matthew caught up with Stephen. They walked for a few moments without talking. Then Matthew said:

"I have an opinion what's going on with Edmund."

Stephen glanced at him. "I need to find a way to communicate with him."

"I think Edmund is jealous of you. He finds the abilities of a younger man threatening."

"No...I don't think that's what it is."

"What then?"

"I think someone crushed him—or tried to crush him—once, and now he identifies with that kind of psychological power. Rejection is strength."

Matthew thought a moment. Then he dropped his voice into his chest and, imitating the dean's haughty, ironic tone, he said, "Do we have here another one of your romantic, commonplace insights, Mr. Engle?"

Stephen looked down and nodded his head, smiling faintly. "He knows where to stick the knife."

In order to withstand the repeated barbs and criticisms directed his way, Stephen withdrew into his inner life and adopted a defensive posture of formal politeness that never left him during those years, and which he never entirely lost for the rest of his life.

Long after he had left the formative years behind him and become an ordained priest, Stephen thought back on that period, asking himself whether either his spiritual director or the dean of academics had truly been as remarkable a man as he remembered, or had the polarity of the men's natures and his own youth at the time led him to exaggerate their qualities out of relation to reality? And always, he came away with the same answer.

"No, they really had been just that way: Valerian had been that noble a human being. And Edmund—" But he would not allow himself even in his thinking to finish the thought. The man was gone, but the memory of the pain he had meted out was forever too deep to fade.

—⚇—

Clare entered eighth grade with more than a student's usual delight at being only one year away from high school. That September Sister Mary Bernard had been assigned to teach eighth grade, and again Clare would be her student. Clare supposed, and was right, that the year would be a chance to deepen the bond between teacher and student. But the best day of that school year would be the last.

The seven girls were seated around the table in their green-and-blue plaid uniforms, their hands folded politely in front of them, their feet neatly crosed at the ankles, their pleated skirts properly pulled over their knees. At the end of the table Clare, one of the seven, sat, tense and moved, studying the face of Sister Mary Bernard, who was sitting in their midst. She knew that to many, Sister Mary Bernard would seem unprepossessing, with her worn skin and faded eyes. But to Clare the lines that creased the nun's features were as delciate as watermark designs, the pale eyes with their flecks of white as lovely as opals. Everything about Sister Mary Bernard was soft and kind and incomparably gracious.

The nun smiled at the girls fondly and began to thank them, her special helpers, for their efforts during their eighth-grade year. She addressed each one individually with words she had carefully prepared:

Alice, commended for her sense of responsibility and the lovely smile that lifted countless spirits. Carolyn, for her resourcefulness and readiness to tutor younger students. Barbara, who was so generous with compliments, and accepted criticism with such grace. Betsy, whose academic work was the best in the class, always done to perfection. Mary Elizabeth, who did things in such modest, unselfish ways. Helen, whose honesty and truthfulness were an example to everyone. And Clare.

There was a brief pause. Then Sister Mary Bernard said, "There's nothing I can put into words about you, Clare. You are too special."

Clare closed her eyes just for a moment to let the incredible warmth fill her. She would hoard those words all her life. They touched her, flowed over her like a sacrament. In imagination her lips shaped a word, newly minted, never before spoken, clear as a bell tone, and she said it silently to herself: Mother.

—⁂—

In the summer of 1975, Kathleen was married in the beautiful Gothic church of Saint Thérèse of Lisieux, where she had been baptized and where she made her first communion. Don Shearer had fallen in love with her when they were in the seventh grade; though Kathleen barely noticed him in high school, he had continued to adore her from afar. With his upturned nose and rounded cheeks, his guileless, unaffected manner, with the way his mouth hung a little open when he saw her, he seemed still a boy. Then he had gone east, to Yale.

On a December evening in 1974, Kathleen set out to do Christmas shopping. Her arms filled with boxes, the strap of her purse slipping from her shoulder, she was making her way down the aisle of a men's clothing store, wondering how she would manage the door, when a young man in a tan gabardine trench coat stepped out of the crowd and pulled it open for her. She didn't recognize him at first. The courteous stranger was no longer the slack-jawed, baby-faced teenager she remembered, but a self-possessed young professional with taut, clear features and thoughtful blue eyes who, having gone out on a last-minute errand, had purely by chance met her again.

Six years had passed since they had seen each other last, but in the instant that he said her name and Kathleen returned his glance with the reserved, hauntingly sweet smile so reminiscent of a Leonardo, Don Shearer knew that he still loved her and that he would always love her.

He began to call her, and she responded enthusiastically. They went out to dinner, to films, took long drives, played tennis at the country club to which Don's parents belonged, and walked the shoreline along the lake where Kathleen had skated as a child. Little by little they opened their hearts to each other. Within weeks they were inseparable. By the end of April, Don asked Kathleen to marry him.

The only child of a distinguished attorney, Don Shearer was one of those young men who, owing to education and family background, would have every door in life opened for him, and Kathleen, radiant, eager, was ready to go through each one with him.

They bought a home in the Dunham Lake district, a sought-after subdivision created in a setting noted for its wild, intact beauty. From the road the property looked undeveloped. Hawks traced spirals over the twisted birches and towering firs. Foxes appeared in the shadows at dusk. Now and then a car turned into a driveway that wound back to a house hidden in the trees.

Set back on its secluded lot, the home selected by the young Shearers was, like each of the area's homes, uniquely styled, with varied rooflines and high gables. A low stone wall and flower beds bordered the lawn on the left and on the right; where the driveway made its first turn, a solitary gingko tree stood.

From the window of their second-floor bedroom Kathleen could see, through a copse of firs and pines to the south, the shores of Dunham Lake. It was a gorgeous landscape of dense green woods, deep, vivid blue water, and high, overarching sky, a scene transformed with the seasons like an ever-changing oil painting.

Her marriage to Don Shearer enabled Kathleen to create a secure, trustworthy world. At first hesitatingly, then with full confidence, she set out to entertain the bright young people of the area. The same desperate need to force happiness that had characterized her as a teenager after the death of her mother was still present in much of her activity, though if someone had made such a comment to her, Kathleen would have strongly denied it.

When, in one of his letters to her, Stephen quoted Augustine's description of peace, "the tranquility of order," Kathleen felt she was seeing her experience captured in words, believing she had realized all three: peace, tranquility, and perfect order.

—⁓—

They were alone in the house in those years, Clare and her father. Lawrence Engle never remarried, but his reserve did not prevent him from opening his home to Clare and her friends. Yet, though she was outgoing and full of life, Clare, like her father, cherished privacy. A love of solitude was one of the gifts her father had given her.

After dark on most nights, she went to her room to read or write in her diary. At ten, she turned out the light, propped her head on her pillows, pulled the comforter up to her chin, and lay still, looking out the window, eyes full of wonder.

In late spring, her window was open and the curtains pulled back. The nights were dark and very still. Lights from the street did not reach round to the back of the house, but the moon stood just over the window, and its pale light passing through the branches of the sycamore made shadows stir among the leaves. There was a promise of adventure in the leaf shadows, and there was the suggestion of faces, remembered or only dreamed of.

"Every year, at the beginning of winter, male white-tailed deer lose their antlers..."

It was her Grandfather Shannon's voice, the rough, gravelly voice that sounded as if Demosthenes had swallowed the stones, coming back to her on a warm spring night when she was thirteen. Grandpa Shannon, who had died when she was eight, was the only one of her grandparents she had known. He had had a deep love of nature and an abhorrence of violence. When he went hunting for deer, it was in order to claim a different kind of trophy: he hunted for tines.

"If you walk along deer trails in the woods in the early spring," Grandpa Shannon would go on, his voice becoming more and more gravelly, "and if you have an observant eye, you just might be able to spot, in the dust and leaves of the forest floor, or on the bottom of a dry creek bed, the rack left behind by a stag when it passed through the brush."

At times, in her dreams, Clare found herself near a wooded grove of sweet-smelling cedars on a cool, misty morning in early spring. Fragile lanes of sunlight revealed the forest floor where the first blades of new grass were pushing up through earth still hardened from the winter cold. Paying careful attention, she spied a dull gray object which, had she not been knowledgeable, she might have passed by. It looked like a stick jutting out of the brush, but when light touched it, as if by magic, it turned into a tine.

Sometimes she saw her grandfather walking the forest paths, his back stooped, his eyes glistening, as he leaned over, delighted, to pick up in his weathered hands the magnificent headpiece shed by a stag. These dreams, recurring, integrated all the elements of herself; they became symbols of love, of discovery, of reunion and longing.

One night she had a different dream. Again she saw the woods described by her grandfather, the dust and leaves of the forest floor, the dry creek bed. But other things had changed. White flakes fell through the air; like torn gray sleeves, stratus clouds stretched across the tops of denuded trees. The time of year was autumn.

And though she was by herself, she was not alone. A male white-tailed deer had stepped out from the trees and come to a standstill a few yards away from her near the creek bed's edge. It was wounded. Blood flowed from the left side of its neck and, streaming down its chest, pooled on the ground beneath its hooves, staining the grass dull rust.

The deer's proud head with its large, panicked eyes seemed to be staring through her, beyond her, at the ashen sky, as if seeing into another world.

Clare tasted the wet snow upon her tongue, smelled the cold, raw air, heard through the deep silence of the forest an ominous sound, like the snapping of branches, and she so clearly saw the stag—beautiful and noble and doomed—that she started awake, and burst into tears.

Occurring only once, this dream, too, became a sign, though of what she was not sure.

IV

In the spring of 1979, after eight years of formation, Stephen and his four classmates, having completed philosophy studies, entered the school of theology to prepare for ordination.

Floorboards creaked at the quick, authoritative step and the seated young men abruptly stood. A stately, immaculately groomed Jesuit in a black cassock strode vigorously into the classroom and went to the lectern.

His large, severe features—the long, elegant nose, bent at the bridge; the strong chin that jutted out from his jaw like a ledge; the startling blue, translucent eyes; the thatch of silver hair combed back and slightly wild—lent him the air of a biblical patriarch. He was Gerald Kaestner, the rector of theology, and a Jesuit for over fifty years.

He began without formalities to speak in a resounding baritone: "And so, you are nearing ordination…"

Stephen and his companion—Peter, Alan, Charles, and Matthew—were listening and taking notes. They were in a second-floor classroom that overlooked the lake in the woods. It was a long room with walls bare except for a large wooden crucifix and six time-scarred desks in front of which the lectern stood. In one corner was a plain gray metal file cabinet, the only other appointment.

The rector paused for a moment to acknowledge the closing of the day, for the evening air was aglow. The sun was burning in the beautiful shadowed firs along the shore, and far out on the lake, the water, burnished gold and copper, seemed to be on fire. From a distance a wood thrush called, and somewhere, beyond a forested hill, its flutelike note either echoed or was answered by a fainter call and farther off, by another, fainter still.

Kaestner's eyelids drooped like folded wings lowered over a nest as he dreamed under the silver-white tufts of his brows, but when he looked up, his piercing blue eyes impaled his listeners and his voice invoked attention in warm, rich tones: "You are called to be men for others, after the One who was the man for others. And what can we say of Him, in the idiom of our times?

"He set out at age thirty or thereabouts, as you will be doing. When He chose those whom He wished to accompany Him, He didn't select from among the distinguished men of his day, but picked instead a rather ragtag bunch…"

The rector broke off and gave the five seminarians a meaningful look.

"His pattern," he added dryly.

The young men laughed.

Kaestner gazed off into space again. Then he looked back at them intently.

"If it's true that the entire psychological spectrum of trust is seeded in our first human bond, then we know He bonded mightily with his mother, for He was grounded in trust. Out of that bond came His extraordinary ability to accept others unconditionally and His capacity for deep and sustained relationships.

"What caused people to follow Jesus of Nazareth was an impression on the level of feeling and intuition. They may have met Him only once, yet so moving was the encounter that many left everything behind to go after Him. On that basis, all the rest of Christianity developed:

"Christianity is about the pursuit of that man."

Kaestner concluded his line of thought. He glanced beyond the window at the gathering dusk for a minute, and then he looked back at his audience. Within the room all was hushed, with the silence just before an arrow flies—only breath drawn, the rest of the air still. Stephen and his classmates sat wholly focused, caught up in the rector's words.

Kaestner, seeing them, understood. He knew they were members of an exceptional class who wanted to think in high, imaginative ways. With his eyes fixed steadily on them, he spoke slowly in a rising voice:

"Death says, 'this far and no farther,' to every finite possibility. But once in our history, there came a human life so beautiful and heroic that God remembered it, and called it back, and willed it always to be."

Kaestner paused. Then he said:

"Cognizant of this meaning, refusing to be deflected by anything less than total commitment to Christ, the first Cistercian monks prayed: 'When I fall, let me fall as flame.'"

As he said those words, Gerald Kaestner was standing in front of Stephen's desk, his elevated thoughts unfolding in front of Stephen's imagining eyes. Stephen could not take his gaze away from the rector of theology. He knew, as did the others—Peter, Alan, Charles, and Matthew—that for them the scene beyond the window would never again be merely of sky and lake and wooded shore. Always it would be wedded to the image of Gerald Kaestner, the severe features of his remarkable face, the vibrant timbre of his eloquent voice, his urgent summons to the heroic life.

—ᴍ—

"Are there others who think the same thoughts?" Clare asked herself. "Who seem not to have a place in this world?"

On a beautiful June day, in the summer after graduation from high school, Clare drove out to Dunham Lake. She had been that way countless times over the years, but never alone, as now. The drive was a pilgrimage to what in her mind was a sacred site, the scene of her mother's accident.

She parked by the side of the road and walked to an unmarked intersection, knelt at the spot and laid flowers on the grass, a homemade bouquet of pink-and-white begonias. Afterward, she climbed down to a grassy spot on the bank of the lake. Not in the Engle family, but there, by the lake, she felt close to her mother.

That summer, Clare was undergoing an intense inner struggle to know herself and what she wanted to do in life.

Raised on stories of the saints, told from her earliest years that God had created her for a purpose that only she could fulfill, that her soul was a veritable breath of God, Clare was more a child of the forties or fifties than the seventies: she had grown up in love with the thought of becoming a saint. She did not want to marry as her mother and Kathleen had done. If you wish to become a perfect Christian, she reasoned, you go all the way: she wanted to become a nun.

She had thought that after she graduated from high school she would follow Sister Mary Bernard and enter the Sisters of the Sacred Heart. But when Stephen joined their father in advising her to attend college for at least two years before making a commitment, she had agreed to wait. Meanwhile, in the summer of 1979, she made pilgrimages to Dunham Lake to feel close to her mother.

All around her the earth brimmed with life. Yellow daylilies, gone wild, rose out of flowering drifts of uncut grass. Small dark barn swallows darted low over the ground with sweet, twittering cries. Far out on the lake, on water the wind carved bark-like, the solitary figure of a man on the foredeck of a sailboat was hauling up the spinnaker.

Clare sat with her legs stretched out before her and her hair tossed back, the delicate sails of her imagination unfurling. Strange and beautiful feelings were stirring within her, and she felt the throb of the old longings, too. A breeze blew through the stand of copper beeches on the slope above her and she could hear the hushed breathing leaves seem to whisper words: listen…mystic…infinite…

"Infinite…" She held the word on her tongue, saying it over and over again softly, so that it sounded familiar and strange at the same time. "Infinite…Why is it that everything in us longs for the infinite, and yet all we can know—and then for such a short time—is the finite?

"Are there others who think the same thoughts, who seem not to have a place in this world?"

Later that summer, Clare received a note from Sister Mary Bernard and learned that the nun who had seemed to her like a second mother would not be returning to Saint Thérèse parish in the fall. Instead, she was moving to the motherhouse of the Sisters of the Sacred Heart to take up a new assignment, as Mistress of Novices.

Clare, when she read about the appointment, felt that her questions had been answered, and that her belief in signs and inspirations was being borne out.

V

One evening in late May of 1981, Stephen walked across the flagstone terrace of the commons and stood at the head of a series of narrow stone steps, gazing at the grounds. They lay as numinous as in an exquisite dream, or in a painting by Corot: the formal gardens, the dark spruce woods, the great oaks and dawn redwoods, the old willows, the flash of silver in the middle distance where the lake sparkled like cut glass between the trees.

He had to look at everything harder, more intensely now that this serene and ordered world was about to go into the past. Here, in late spring, when it seemed that dusk held back its presence so as not to disrupt the delicate poise between light and shadow, when the sweet scents of grass and earth commingled with the drift of air borne from off the water, when the light that fell on the lake itself silvered, "like shining from shook foil": this was the way he wanted to remember the scene for as long as he lived.

Somewhere a door closed. Voices came from a walk beyond the arborvitae to the right. Stephen turned around and smiled at the approaching group: Peter, Alan, Charles, and Matthew, walking across the terrace toward him. When they had exchanged greetings, the five young men descended the narrow steps to take the path that ran down to the lake.

These were treasured hours, the walks a custom from their novitiate days. Inseparable friends by now, the young Jesuits talked over everything; like brothers, they confided in, empathized with, supported, and challenged one another.

Stephen, Alan, and Peter had come out of adolescent worlds where they were the most gifted among their peers. Although Matthew and Charles preferred the active life to the life of the mind, they were readers and imaginative thinkers, too, and eager to be drawn into the intense intellectual exchanges of the others.

Now the five were continuing a discussion begun earlier in the week. Charles was attempting to come to terms with decisions made by the Jesuit Jim Carney, whose autobiography he had just finished reading. They all knew to some extent the details of Carney's life as a Jesuit, but Charles had been the most affected by the story.

In 1961, when he was in his late thirties, Jim Carney had requested and received permission to live in Honduras, among the poor people of the villages. Once at home in that country, he became a tireless advocate for social justice.

Expelled to neighboring Nicaragua by the Honduran authorities, Carney remained committed to the people he'd known in the villages, and resolved to return to them. When at last he reentered Honduras, he joined members of the Honduran underground resistance as their chaplain.

As his ties to the resistance movement became increasingly consequential, Carney made a startling decision. He asked his Jesuit superiors to release him from his vows so that his actions wouldn't have a negative impact on the Society.

When he'd read Carney's autobiography, Charles had experienced the rush of excitement one feels in encountering a person destined for a life beyond ordinary expectations. Relating his admiration for the former Jesuit to his Irish predilection for poetic insight, Charles was convinced he understood what motivated Carney in each moment of crisis: the anguished impulses of an unconditional heart.

Now, turning to his classmates, Charles said, "Carney embodies the heart of liberation theology: the radical living out of the Gospel...seeing Christ in the poor and oppressed..."

"Carney lives on the edge," Matthew answered emphatically. "What men could be, if they would."

Stephen, Alan, and Peter walked along behind, listening, taken up with the thoughts voiced by the two "activists" in their midst. The five young men walked for a while in silence. Each of them was penetrated by a sense that he mattered at his own special moment in history and that what happened to him, because of his calling to be a Jesuit, happened not only for his own sake, but also for a larger purpose.

In less than three years, in September 1983, the resistance group to which Jim Carney belonged would be annihilated in a series of ferocious battles with the military, the few survivors tortured and left to starve in a pit deep in the earth; and Jim Carney would vanish forever into the tangled wild of the Honduran jungle.

But in the spring of 1981, the five young Jesuits had no way of knowing about that future event and Carney's tragic fate, and they went on discussing their views of liberation theology, which were the idealistic impressions of youth: enthralled by heroic concepts, unsure of the practical applications.

They came to a place where the path divided into two narrow lanes. To the right, it sloped upward into aisles of oak and dawn redwood, and to a wooded hill beyond; to the left, it meandered through a pine woods down to the water's edge.

They turned to the left, to walk down to the lake. The conversation evolved to larger themes, from the poor and oppressed people of Honduras to the poor and oppressed people of all nations and all times, and to the Gospel of Christ.

"From the very start," Peter said, "when Christianity was new in the world, it has been a sign of contradiction, its message of hope coming out of a culture where the daily story was of oppression, violence, suffering, and death. And each generation is confronted with that sign, and chooses to accept or reject it—just as those living in the time of Christ chose to accept or reject Him."

Alan said, "Dostoyevsky epitomizes the history of nonbelief when, in *The Brothers Karamazov*, he has Ivan Karamazov, the rationalist, ponder human suffering and reject the Gospel vision. Today that voice belongs to the existentialist, to secular man, disposed to doubt and impervious to persuasion."

Matthew, turning on the path, said, "I know what agnostic existentialism denies. But what does it offer us, in the dark hours?"

Peter said, "The premise that human greatness lies in the individual's capacity to find meaning in life in spite of an ultimately tragic fate."

They were leaving the pine woods. The spring sky that had been obscured by the trees opened up. High, bright stars shone overhead. Beyond an arc of dark firs, a brilliant full moon was passing over the lake.

"Ultimately tragic..." Matthew said softly. He tipped back his head to look at the sky. "No, it can't be."

He paused and then he went on in a more impassioned voice, saying that he refused to accept reasoning he believed was defeatist, and stressing that, even if he didn't have his Christian faith, he would search to find something more, something that hinted at a higher purpose.

"Viktor Frankl found that possible even in Auschwitz," Stephen said.

"It occurred to me over and over—as I read his descriptions of prisoners who survived the deprivation of the death camp by deepening their inner lives—how in that stark existence people could realize the ideal we strive for in religious life: the progressive interiorization of the soul."

The path had brought them close to the lake, not far from the mossy bank; twenty feet away, the silver reflection of the moon shivered on the black water.

"Frankl illustrates his thought with living examples," Stephen continued. "Some incredibly moving, others startlingly insightful, all charged with the recognition of Providence, like the event he called his deepest experience at Auschwitz.

"As part of the dehumanizing process, guards took his clothes from him when he arrived at the camp, exchanging them for rags of an inmate who had died in the gas chamber. In relinquishing his clothes, Frankl also lost the manuscript of his first book, his 'spiritual child.' But in the pocket of the new coat he found a sheet of paper, torn from the Hebrew prayer book, and containing the 'Shema Israel.' He felt God had spoken directly to him.

"And another incident a few days after his release, when he was walking in the open countryside, and the words 'I called to the Lord from my narrow prison and He answered me in the freedom of space' suddenly pierced his heart and sent him to his knees," Stephen said at the end, very quietly.

No one spoke; no one wanted to speak. The tranquil night, the moonlit path, the fresh scent of the pine wood, the shining water—all these seemed one with the beauty of those thoughts. When conversation began again, that elusive symmetry would shatter.

Stephen reached the foot of the path first, and turned to face the others. He could not recall a time when he had felt more invigorated: to be absorbed by such lofty ideas, among such like-minded, high-minded friends, under a night sky so immense, bright, and still that it seemed to hold the promise of some imminent disclosure.

As he stood looking slowly from one friend to another, Stephen was unaware of how his classmates perceived him when they looked back: that they recognized there are those few who respond more imaginatively and creatively to life than others do, that he was one of that number and, therefore, the one whom they all sought to emulate.

When Kathleen heard footsteps, she looked toward the door. Confused, she raised herself on her elbow and tried to sit up, the loose sleeve of her hospital gown falling from her shoulder.

Don reached her in three strides. She came into his arms, and he sat down beside her and rocked her gently.

She asked him, "Did you see her again?"

"Yes." He adjusted her gown. "After they brought you here…I talked with the doctor…I asked to see her…"

"She was so perfectly formed…I don't understand…why? Oh, God, why?" Kathleen said, and searched his eyes; she took his face in her hands and whispered passionately, "Promise me we'll never forget her."

"I promise you." He kissed her palms. "We'll never, never forget her."

VI

Earlier that same day, miles away, a young woman stepped onto the small concrete porch of a white-frame bungalow. She was about twenty-two, with straight, shoulder-length blond hair and thoughtful blue-gray eyes.

The house she had arrived at, its paint peeling under the eaves and its corroding gutters sprouting tiny trees, looked long neglected, though little different from the other houses on the street.

The girl rapped lightly on the door and then let herself in, as if it was something she was used to doing.

She came into a small, stale-smelling room. The shades on all the windows were drawn, though the sun was on the other side of the house. The room was lit only by the bluish light emanating from a television screen. Shadows from the street outside made asymmetrical lakes move regularly across the uncarpeted floor. A days-old newspaper and an empty coffee mug sat on a dark mahogany end table finely coated with dust. The television was set against the near wall, an armchair, a rocking chair, and a chenille sofa grouped around it.

A middle-aged woman was sitting on the sofa. She had long, thin features and limp hair bleached platinum. She was wearing a loose, flowered dress and blue bedroom slippers, and her whole being—face, hands, body, the soul that showed through heavy-lidded eyes—seemed to have taken on the dull, somber character of her surroundings.

When the girl came toward her, she looked away from the television, gave a slight wave, and asked in a voice edged with derision:

"What brings you back so soon?"

Accustomed to the woman's ways, still the girl tensed as she responded, "How are you, Mother?"

The older woman's mood changed. She motioned to a chair and sighed resignedly. "Oh, I don't know…"

The girl crossed the floor and sat down in the armchair, the woman's lowered glance following her. They did not kiss or embrace as mothers and daughters do.

As the girl's eyes adjusted to the dimness, she looked around, her gaze lingering on the drawn curtains, the layers of dust, the side table marred by cup stains, and, across from her, the wan, impassive face with its inaccessible emotions.

There was a bond of pain between the two women whose existence was unknown to the outer world and to which they never referred. Instead, they spoke haltingly, awkwardly, of superficial, commonplace things: the unusually warm spring weather, the continuing decline of the neighborhood, the paint peeling off the eaves above the porch, the drunken neighbor who played his radio loudly into the night.

When there was a silence, the girl reached for a navy blue cloth tote bag she had with her and took a sheaf of papers from it.

"Mother…" she said, and hesitated. Then, "Mother, I've brought my final exam in American literature to show you. Our professor liked it so much he read it to the class. Would you like to see it?"

With an indifference that masked a subtler intention, the older woman gestured toward the table where the newspaper and the cup were.

"Leave it on the table," she said. "I'll look at it later."

Her daughter lowered her eyes against the rebuff. They sat quietly for a minute, the girl holding the papers in her lap.

Then the older woman suddenly leaned forward and asked intently, "How's your aunt Jo?"

The girl looked up, surprised. "She's fine. She's gotten her CPA."

"Are you happier living with her than you were living in your own home?"

The girl did not answer at first. Unconsciously, she looked toward the hall, in the direction of a bedroom in the back of the house, out of view. As her glance traveled along the walls, a feeling of despondency penetrated her like the chill of a winter rain. Remembering that room brought back the image of the child she once had been, the frightened, isolated child over whom the frail woman on the sofa had wielded total power; and instinct told her that, were it not for her self-imposed separation, she could become that child again.

"It...works out better this way, Mother."

"Better for who? I hate being alone."

"I can come back to see you again soon."

The older woman picked up the remote control for the television, turned up the volume, and sat and stared at the screen. Her face, lit by the flickering light, was like a cold, far-off moon.

The show was a rerun from the 1950s. For several minutes mother and daughter watched it in silence. Then the girl made another attempt at conversation.

"Donna Reed is pretty, isn't she?"

Her mother turned her head. She gave the girl a steady, knowing look. "A lot prettier than Mary Ainsley will ever be."

The girl heard the malice in the voice. Making herself get up, she walked over to the window and drew back the curtain and looked out.

The grass had been slow to green up; it was dry, flattened, and gray in places where snow had lain in the winter. To the right, the interwoven mesh of a chain-link fence glistened in the slanting light of the afternoon sun. A black squirrel with a rust-colored tail scampered by. There were cars passing on the street and, somewhere in the distance, children squealing with delight.

The girl returned to the chair to collect her things, quietly slipping the paper on American literature back into her tote bag. Then she walked toward the door, heading back to another life.

It was a ritual that occurred between the two women: the inflicting of a wound, the silent acceptance, then separation.

"Where are you going, Mary?"

"I have to leave, Mother."

That was part of the ritual, too: the mother, assigning guilt; the daughter, withdrawing in pain.

At the door, Mary Ainsley paused for a moment, her hand on the knob, looking back into the darkened room.

By the way she departed—with a tentative, lingering glance, with the infinitely careful closing of the door—one could tell what leave-takings meant to her.

VII

*Jesus walked by the Sea of Galilee as the
fishermen were casting their nets. He called
Simon and his brother Andrew and James,
son of Zebedee, and his brother John, and
they left everything and followed him.*

— MARK 1:16

Ordination day was one of those high moments of which all who were present—even as they were living through it—felt the significance. It was beautiful and sunlit, so characteristic of a June day, yet completely set apart. Its images—the great raised stand-alone stone altar and the life-size crucifix suspended from the wall above it; the brilliant assembly of white-robed Jesuits; the candidates, the five young men clothed in white garments; the white-mitered bishop walking in solemnity behind them—all these evoked, for the families watching from the pews, an intense sense of the sacred.

—⁓—

The lector stood up to read from the First Book of Samuel:

"Samuel was sleeping in the temple of the Lord where the ark of God was. The Lord called to Samuel, who answered, 'Here I am.' He ran to Eli and said, 'Here I am. You called me.'

'I did not call you,' Eli said. 'Go back to sleep.' So he went back to sleep. Again the Lord called Samuel, who rose and went to Eli.

'Here I am,' he said, 'You called me.'

But Eli answered, 'I did not call you, my son. Go back to sleep.' The Lord called Samuel again, for the third time.

Getting up and going to Eli, he said, 'Here I am. You called me.'

Then Eli understood that the Lord was calling the youth. So he said to Samuel, 'Go to sleep, and if you are called, reply, "Speak, Lord, for your servant is listening…"'"

—∽—

Clare was in such an elated mood that she had to struggle to keep her composure. Nearly twenty-one, she was grown in the understanding of herself, a young woman of keen sensibility, susceptible to idealistic impressions. So she knew she must be mistaken, that her imagination had beguiled her. It could not have happened, that at one instant during the reading—the third call of Samuel—a shaft of light had thrust out from the high vaulted ceiling and fallen on Stephen, touched his left shoulder, gleamed on his face. Stephen alone. A spear of light, at just that instant.

She smiled inwardly at her adolescent hero worship. Her imagination had deceived her. How Stephen would tease her, if he knew…

—∽—

From somewhere behind them and high above, a glowing baritone intoned in Greek:

"Kyrie, eleison…"

The candidates knelt as the Litany of the Saints began, and prostrated themselves before the altar.

The priests and people knelt and prayed, "*Christie, eleison,*" and the cantor in return intoned, "*Christie, eleison...*"

The voices went on and on, rising and falling, chanting phrase after phrase, calling out to all the angels and saints to pray with them and for them.

The candidates knelt again. In silence the bishop laid his hands on the head of each and, invoking the Holy Spirit, said the prayer of consecration.

—⚏—

First Stephen embraced his father; then, holding on to him, drew Kathleen close. Clare was standing transfixed when she felt a man's hand take her by the arm and pull her against his side. As if he were unreal, she reached out to touch her brother. Forever fastened in her memory of this day—his stiff white collar, the thin fabric of his cassock, and his arm, tight, encircling her. Then Stephen turned his head to her and smiled, such a smile! Exhilaration, love, joy, relief; Clare jumped to the heroic: a beatific smile.

She would remember of that moment that time did not move. She would believe that, for each of them, all journeys would be departures from that center, all existence lived in its wake, all progress, a seeking to return.

VIII

*Moreover, between us and you
a great chasm is established to
prevent anyone from crossing who
might wish to go from our side
to yours, or from your side to ours.*

— LUKE 16:26

What Stephen noticed first was how thin the children were, playing in the sullen quiet of the narrow, treeless streets, darting between the dusty hulks of parked cars, pausing at the curb to look with solemn eyes at the gray sedan with its two black-clad occupants as it slowed, nearing the corner.

Stephen was riding with his new superior to the church and school that would be his first mission, out of the downtown area, into the inner city. The car drove along streets with turn-of-the-century stone mansions, through an underpass, past open fields, past tumbledown bungalows set forward on shallow lots with narrow alleys running behind, past traditional white-frame houses that had something worn-down and grief-stricken about them, like withered faces stained with the crack lines from a thousand tears.

Ahead, the twin spires of a church rose over the low rooftops and in another minute one could see the old redbrick buildings that were the church and rectory and school of Saint Aloysius Gonzaga standing austerely in a field apart, as if they were on an ice floe that had broken away from the land.

At the wheel, the older Jesuit stopped the car and shut off the ignition. For a moment he looked ahead in silence. Then he said, "In the 1920s, when the parish was prosperous, the people wanted their church constructed with Old World craftsmanship. The result is this remarkable example of French Gothic architecture." He smiled ruefully. "With the decline of the inner city in the late sixties, the parish, too, deteriorated...but before all that, Saint Aloysius, in the 1840s, was a small chapel at the edge of the woods, with a few homes scattered about and a dirt road into town."

The senior Jesuit was Eugene Dowd, a man in his late sixties, tall, dignified, very spare, with a high, polished forehead, a long, aquiline nose, and intelligent green eyes. Intellectual, with an intensely practical mind, he was a smart, worldly priest, as at home on the streets as in the classroom, and highly attuned to the needs of others. In his vocation as a Jesuit he had been a professor of Latin and the romance languages, Master of Novices, and Provincial Superior. But he was never interested in titles; in his heart he had longed always to serve as a simple parish priest. When retirement neared and his activities diminished, he was granted his wish, and assigned to be the pastor of the inner-city parish of Saint Aloysius Gonzaga.

In the lingering light of a late-August evening, he parked the car on the small lot that joined the church and the Jesuit residence. There was no one else about. The teenage boys who played basketball at the hoop at the end of the lot had finished their game and gone on.

Going in by the front entrance, up a broken concrete walk, the men climbed deep stairs to a canopied porch. Eugene Dowd was fumbling in a pocket and starting to say that he had misplaced his key when the door was unexpectedly flung open.

Short and portly, her round cheeks pinked by lines and wrinkles, Helen Blaney, the rectory's housekeeper, stood haloed by the ceiling light in a narrow, wall-papered foyer. Her smiling glance went to Eugene Dowd, then to Stephen.

"Will you look at this now! We needed someone to make heads roll, and they've sent us a patrician child! Come in, Fathers."

—⁂—

Two other members of the staff had arrived only minutes before. They were turning on lights and bickering over something when Stephen came in. The first to quit the argument and walk over to him was the associate pastor, Daryl Lewis. A connoisseur of art and holder of two master's degrees—one in history and one in fine arts—Lewis nevertheless made a poor impression at first. His build was coarse: a large head atop a stumpy, massive torso; a pockmarked face with a double roll of chins; black, ungovernable hair streaked with gray; and stubby, short-fingered hands shaded in a way that made them seem permanently soiled. Offering Mass, he was heavy-footed and lumbering, his strained movements accompanied by audible grunts and gasps. But when he stepped into the pulpit, his entire being transmuted into something wholly different, fresh, and original, the voice resonant and richly cadenced, the words steeped in erudition.

Over time, his reputation had grown into a kind of renown. On the Sundays when Lewis offered the late Mass, professional men and women from the suburbs slipped into the worn, creaking pews to look past the ungainly appearance in exchange for what they recognized was genuine intellectual discourse, delivered in that distinct, vibrant voice.

The other Jesuit—a tall, gaunt Ichabod Crane of a man, with small, heavy-lidded eyes close set in a long, stony face—came over to Stephen and Lewis self-consciously and with evident agitation. Terry Rhodes had had a difficult and unhappy life. When he was eleven, his parents had divorced. Abandoned by his father, dominated by his mother, Rhodes grew up as a timid and anxious loner, saved from an empty existence by a fertile and inventive mind. He attended a Jesuit high school and, at twenty, applied to join the Society, drawn to men whom he could call Father. His mother would not hear of his becoming a priest, and threatened suicide. Rhodes stood up to her and she disowned him. Her rages continued throughout his novitiate and formative years. Then, after a chaotic pattern of short-lived reunions and long separations, she suffered a stroke suddenly and died estranged from her son.

Years passed. Terry Rhodes matured into an accomplished research biologist and able teacher; alongside all this, negative emotions characteristic of his mother also evolved: he grew suspicious, guarded, testy, and compulsive. His fixations showed in random, startling ways. He fasted unless, under obedience, he was required to eat; he fussed over cleanliness; and he was abstemious about his vow of poverty, shunning a briefcase and luggage and carrying his things in paper bags. Eugene Dowd viewed this last behavior with mild irony.

"Terry may make it to heaven before the rest of us, but we'll all beat him to Chicago if a bag breaks," he once commented drily.

A fifth Jesuit lived at Saint Aloysius, in retirement. Mark Anders was a frail, stately old man with sensitive blue eyes, soft, thinning white hair, and a long, modeled nose like that of the Christ in a Byzantine icon. Illness and age had ravaged his once-handsome features; his head shook a little; and he lived in a Monet world, the world of macular degeneration, where everything is seen through a haze. His character was exceptionally beautiful.

"You're living with a saint, Stephen," Eugene Dowd counseled. "Learn from him." Another time he said, "Mark has liver cancer, in remission. There are days when he's very frail. Will you look after him?"

"Of course," Stephen said. "It would be my privilege."

Thus Stephen gained the friendship of Mark Anders.

—⟋⟍—

The next morning before offering Mass, Stephen left the Jesuit residence alone; he wanted to walk through the neighborhoods. It was very early—the streetlights were still on and there was scarcely any traffic. He walked down a street that went in the direction opposite from the way he and Eugene Dowd had come the day before, past the same kind of small-frame bungalows.

Dark alleys at the backs of houses were alive with secret scurrying among the filth. Like blackened tea leaves, debris settled in the murky gutters. A man sat curled up in the entrance to a storefront church with "Jesus Saves" on the placard above the door, his coat drawn up over his head like a cowl. From far off came the long, drawn-out wail of a siren.

Where once a downtown area had stood, tall tenements sprang up out of the shadows like barren cliffs, their contours fringed with pink. Light seeped into the sky above the line of rooftops; frail and indistinct, the moon shied away. Morning was breaking over the east end as if an artist had sketched the scene on torn paper in graphite, and for the dawn added pale seams of color.

The streets ahead still lay in shadow. Blocking the first rays of light, a three-story building stood along half a city block. Closed for many years, abandoned, the structure that had once been a fine department store was a grim ruin now, its ornate facade defaced and unrestored. On a second-story ledge a large bird, a crow, had alighted. It perched there, its head cocked, like a symbol of ill fortune.

Stephen, passing, stopped and looked up at the scene. It was his nature to see a pattern in things, and at that moment, these images— the derelict building with its dark, gaping windows and scarred facade; the lonely figure huddled in a doorway somewhere behind him; the hard streets; the pervading air of depression—evoked the opening lines from a parable in the Gospel of Luke, "The Gospel of the Outcast":

There was a rich man who dressed in purple garments and fine linen and dined sumptuously each day. Lying at his door was a poor man named Lazarus, covered with sores, who would gladly have eaten his fill of the scraps that fell from the rich man's table...

—⁂—

"Come in, Stephen," Eugene Dowd said, smiling and pushing back his chair. "How are you getting along?"

Stephen stepped into his superior's darkish office. Having come to pick up a book, he found Eugene Dowd glad for the opportunity to talk.

The cranberry-red room with its quiet good taste and lack of clutter reflected a mind given to the inner life. There was an orderly desk with a reading lamp, a typewriter on a little table, two straight-back chairs, a glass-fronted bookcase along one wall, an icon of Christ the Teacher above it. On the short wall across from the desk, a worn plaque, its outer mat torn in one corner—unrepaired one might surmise, for the sake of a story it held—read: "God, whom I do not know, but whose I am." Dag Hammarskjöld.

From the window one could look across the walk and up the private drive to the north tower of the church. The lawn was sparse there, the grass gone to clover. In a background filled with shadows, evening sunlight touched a solitary pine.

Seated at his desk, his chin on his hand, Eugene Dowd chatted quietly, drawing Stephen out. From the start, the senior Jesuit felt that in the thirty-one-year-old Stephen Engle he had found someone almost like a son, a young man only just ordained but who knew philosophy and the classics, enjoyed one-on-one debate, and could more than hold his own.

"You're idealistic," he said, deep into the conversation, "a dreamer with a poetic bent." Dowd lit a cigar and went on, with warmth in his voice to make clear his comment was not critical, "I'm somewhat wary of poets and mystics."

"Why is that, Father?"

"Because with them everything is intuitive and subjective. Rudolf Otto was right when he said the rational and nonrational must intersect, or you end up with fanaticism."

Dowd was quiet a minute. He looked out into the yard and up the private road to the church. Then he glanced at Stephen and said, "I've seen those men and women absorbed in their own private attempts to reach God, indifferent to the human need around them.

"'Mysticism can never be selfish preoccupation with one's little ego; it must be an opening to other people and to the universe.' The quotation is from *The Cloud of Unknowing*. I may be skeptical of mystics, but I've read them."

Stephen thought for a moment. Then he asked, "Have you read Hopkins?"

"Yes, with great admiration. But Hopkins was a square peg in a round hole. Though clearly gifted and saintly, he was often unhappy and subject to depression."

Eugene Dowd thought, as he looked at Stephen, of the young Gerard Manley Hopkins. Not long after ordination to the priesthood, Hopkins had left the beauty of North Wales to serve in the dockyard slums of Liverpool. The dreariness of the setting weighed heavily on the sensitive young Jesuit. During the years he spent in Liverpool, he suffered emotionally, and his creative imagination withered.

"Tell me whom you read, Stephen," Dowd requested, resting his cigar. "What matters to you? Whom do you love and seek out?"

In answer, Stephen thought first of certain poets.

"Yeats, of course," he said. "Eliot...Wordsworth...Blake...the Russian Osip Mandelstam. Among writers of fiction, I like Faulkner because of his insight into the human heart. I like Chekhov for the same reason."

"What do you make of Joyce?"

"Joyce..." Stephen echoed. He shook his head slightly and ran his hand along the back of his neck. Thoughtfully, he said, "If you look past his antipathy for the Jesuits and his repudiation of the Church..."

Eugene Dowd chuckled.

"No," Stephen said with feeling, "I'm not being facetious." And he began painstakingly to explain how, as a graduate student enthralled by language, he had struggled to come to terms with James Joyce. His way had been to see Joyce as archetype, the artist as rebel. He explained his perspective.

"The choices Joyce made cause us to ask ultimate questions: What course does one take when the accepted traditions of culture clash with one's vision of the world? Are there times when a daring leap of the imagination calls for a break with the established patterns of society?"

Eugene Dowd, meditatively resting his index finger against his temple, asked, "Are you perhaps reducing religious faith to merely a social construct?"

"No. I'm saying that the workings of the Spirit are deeper and more intricate than we know.

"When, for example, in *A Portrait of the Artist as a Young Man*, Stephen Dedalus says, 'I will not serve that in which I no longer believe, whether it call itself my home, my fatherland, or my church,'" Stephen went on, quoting Joyce's words, "we're hearing a strange reversal of Francis of Assisi's declaration to the court in which he severed all worldly bonds, including his status as son: 'No longer will I say, my father, Peter Bernardone, but rather, Our Father Who art in heaven.'

"Each man—Francis and Joyce—was 'throwing it all away' for the sake of an inner vision."

Stephen paused, his eyes, in which shone an appeal for understanding not evident in his words, searching Eugene Dowd's eyes.

"That Joyce didn't return to the Church in later years, yes, that troubles me. But to my mind, for the young man he was in that hour of crisis, remaining Catholic was not possible."

Eugene Dowd, who had been listening intently, put down his cigar and looked off into space for a moment. Then he gazed at Stephen.

"I think you are breathtakingly tolerant," he said.

—⚏—

Stephen lay, his hand beneath his neck, listening to the silence of the streets. Discordant images rose in his mind. The silence of the city was different from the silence of the grounds of the Jesuit seminary:

not contemplation, but suspense; not Eliot's "lucid stillness," but murmurs, undertones, intimations of violence. He listened, detecting movement.

In a distant alley a metal lid had struck the pavement and was rolling around among the giant bins of trash.

Dogs. Originating as strays of various breeds, through rapid inbreeding they had become compacted into a generic marauder that ran the streets at night in droves. Lean as rope, ears hanging low on wide backskulls, eyes glinting red and rapacious, jaws malevolently grinning, they moved swiftly and efficiently, more dangerous than rats.

Stephen turned his head to read the green dial of the clock on the desk. Twelve thirty. He had the 7:00 a.m. Mass. He willed himself to sleep.

—m—

Stephen, watching her from the doorway, said, "I have such admiration for the work you do."

Margaret Strand looked at him and smiled. "I'm just an ordinary old broad, Father."

She was a buxom, middle-aged woman with a furrowed, heart-shaped face, short, sandy brown hair, green eyes, and a smiling, generous mouth. Or, Stephen wondered about this radiant last feature, was it an average mouth, and the smile so generous? She lived an hour's drive away in an affluent suburb, and both times Stephen had seen her she had come to Saint Aloysius to tutor students who were reading below grade level. Now on a rainy autumn afternoon when classes had ended for the day, he had run into her again as she sat at a long rectangular table crowded with textbooks in a deserted high school classroom, searching in her tote bag for her keys.

"There's nothing ordinary about the work you do," Stephen said.

"Are you trying to butter me up for some job?"

Laughing, Stephen put up his hands in mock surrender. He walked into the room and over to where she was sitting. "No," he said. "Unalloyed appreciation."

Margaret Strand looked for a few moments about the room. Remembrance came into her eyes. She said:

"I've been volunteering here for six years, and the place just seems to get more run-down and poorer. I have memories of it that go back decades.

"Fifty years ago, my grandparents belonged to this parish. They lived in an upstairs flat about a mile from here. When I was a child my mother and I used to take the streetcar to visit them." She smiled at Stephen in an aside. "You're too young to have known streetcars.

"My grandparents were immigrants from Italy. My grandmother was a short, plump woman with very rosy cheeks and bright, dark eyes. My grandfather worked as a night guard for the railroad until he lost both legs to diabetes. Neither of them spoke English very well. When we visited, my mother talked with them in Italian. Their flat was so simple, so modest. It smelled of lint and old blankets, like a sealed-up linen closet. As a child I thought it was enchanted. How else could you explain the mysterious language, the seclusion, the unchanging pattern of life? Within those walls, everything had stopped."

Margaret Strand turned her eyes to the window in silence. After a minute she said, "My grandparents clung to the ways they had known in Europe. A child doesn't see the pathos of it—how these people were never going to fit in. How they would live out their lives on the margins of life. How the Church would give them the only sense of belonging they would ever have."

She looked at Stephen as if she were about to go on, but was silent again. A tenderness suffused her features, the look that comes over one when all of love is gathered into a single glance. It was as if her grandparents had somehow regained corporeality and were with her in the room, and she was seeing them afresh, but as a woman now, a middle-aged woman to whom the years had given understanding, a sense of context.

Quietly, Margaret Strand went on, "The streetcar tracks were torn up and laid over with pavement a long time ago. My grandparents have been gone for more than thirty years. Who they were, in terms of their dreams and struggles, is unknown to me.

"Not long ago, I read an article about anthropologists who had located an ancient well used at one time for religious rites by the Mayans. At the bottom of the well the group uncovered precious jewels and, here and there among the relics, the skeletons of young girls who had been offered as sacrifices to please a Mayan god.

"As they stood amid the ruins, it wasn't hard for those in the party to be wholly absorbed and carried back over the centuries, imagining the sights and sounds that once came from that place.

"I think of that story and remember my grandparents...We bear within us our own historical remains, traces of those who went before us and now lie at the bottom of our memory well. Were they once beautiful? Once strong? Once brave? The answers are their indecipherable secrets..."

Margaret Strand broke off and looked over at Stephen. She said, "Thank you, Father. You've been very patient, listening to me ramble on."

"Thank you, Margaret."

"For what?"

"For sharing those thoughts. They're beautiful and very moving."

Margaret Strand answered with a dismissive wave of her hand.

"I know," Stephen said with a grin, "here comes the disclaimer. But I mean this very sincerely: thank you."

Margaret Strand began rummaging again through her leather tote bag. She found a small white handkerchief, brought it out, and pressed it briefly to her eyes. Then she looked some more and at last found her car keys. When she stood, Stephen walked with her to the door. In the doorway, before they stepped into the hall, she smiled the generous smile that was distinctively hers and patted him on the arm.

"You're such a sweetheart to listen."

—m—

In the shadow of an empty storefront, unobserved by passersby, four teenage boys were standing, flicking cigarette butts onto the walk and looking from one another to the light at the intersection. Halfway down the block, a young girl stepped out of another storefront and walked at an angle across the street.

Waiting at the corner for the light to turn, Stephen was unaware of her, until a soft hand slipped into his and a gentle voice addressed him:

"Hello, Father."

She was a pretty girl, not more than sixteen, with a delicately boned face and long blond hair as fine as corn silk. The only flaw in the pale yellow vision she created was the faint stain of cigarettes on the small, even teeth showing between her bright coral lips.

As Stephen opened his mouth to reply, she let go of his hand and ran off, hurrying to the opposite corner. At the curb, within sight of the covey of boys, she turned round. Her hair tossing about like fluttering candlelight, her face in three-quarter profile a mocking smile of ravaged innocence, she made an obscene gesture with a finger of one hand.

Stephen looked down. His watch was gone.

—❦—

The days following the last Sunday in October were shortened. Daylight saving time had ended. The clocks were set back an hour; dusk fell at six. When families sat down for dinner the streetlights were already on.

Going into the Jesuit residence in the afternoon on the second of November, Stephen found himself alone. The other priests were in the church, hearing confessions for the feast of All Souls. He turned to go back out the door when a sound in the hall stopped him.

Where the staircase curved, on the first landing, Mark Anders was standing, breathless, supporting himself with one hand on the banister and groping with the other for the wall.

Stephen dropped his briefcase and rushed up the stairs to help him. "Father, here—" He gripped the old man's arm, surprised by that first touch how frail it was—the black sleeve encasing it seeming to have more substance. It took the two of them almost fifteen minutes to climb the stairs and walk the short length of the hall, with Anders taking long pauses to recover his strength. Inside the room, as the elderly priest faded, Stephen guided him to the bed and helped him to lie down. He pulled the covers up around the thin shoulders, tucking them in, and then opened the wobbly window a crack so that the cool autumn air might clear the stale odor of the overheated room.

Looking back from the door, he saw Anders's eyes shining in the semidarkness.

Stephen brought dinner on a tray to Anders's room one weekend evening, helped the old Jesuit to the table, and afterward stayed to read to him.

The room was small, with a dark hardwood floor. In places the ceiling was peeling from leaks in valleys in the roof. The only window was badly warped. Books were stacked neatly on a table by the window, the kind of thick-lensed hand magnifier those with macular degeneration use lying alongside. A high-backed chair stood next to the table, and when Stephen came he brought in another from the hall.

"What would you like to hear, Father?" Stephen asked that late November night as intermittent raindrops scratched against the window like mice running in a wall. Mark Anders was not feeling well and had spent most of the day sleeping. He was enlivened when Stephen came.

"Julian of Norwich, please, if you would."

Stephen went over to the table to the books and read the titles and the authors' names. *What riches*, he thought.

At hand were Rudolf Otto's *The Idea of the Holy*, an anthology of the writings of John Henry Newman, several volumes of Karl Rahner's *Theological Investigations*, and Chesterton's masterwork, *The Everlasting Man*. From among the assortment, Stephen took a dark green hardcover with a gray ribbon bookmark sewed into its binding, *Julian of Norwich: Showings.*

He returned to the bed where Mark Anders lay propped up by pillows, his hands, corded with protuberant blue veins, folded loosely on his chest. Stephen sat down on a chair beside him. Smiling, he said:

"These are mystical writings, Father. I'm not sure Eugene would approve."

"Maybe," Anders said with a conspiratorial wink, "we should bring in a chair for him so that he can listen, too."

—⁓—

One night Stephen confided, "I would like to deepen my faith, Father."

They were sitting at the table within a pool of lamplight, quietly talking. Outside the window, snow was falling. The wind had picked up, whirling clouds of dust and snow about the yard. A solitary branch knocked against the glass. Mark Anders leaned forward and said:

"Then you must pray, 'He must increase; I must decrease.'" In his quiet, serious voice, the elderly priest told Stephen about the years when he had served as a missionary in Peru. He spoke of the beauty and simplicity of the people, and of the need. He talked, too, about men whom he had known personally, the Jesuits who had been murdered in Zimbabwe, and, movingly, he recounted the story of their deaths.

Stephen sat listening, totally absorbed. In Mark Anders he saw a living exemplar of a pure and selfless human being. He had come to understand why the older Jesuit would not complain of physical discomfort or ask to be exempted from a life lived in common with its attendant pressures. Anders had transcended his seeming ineffectiveness. The waves of pain that doubled him over, the nausea that would not let him keep food down, the fatigue that left him dependent on the charity of others—these were his silent offerings, the intercessory prayers he made for the sake of the Jesuit missions. Mark Anders had discovered a way to lay down his life.

Daryl Lewis had given him a small print of Velázquez's "Christ on the Cross," and in the hours when he could not sleep for pain, the old priest lay lost in contemplation of the face of the dying Son of God.

One night Stephen found the print where Anders had used it to mark the place in a book. Turning it over, he found five words penciled on the back. In a careful, even hand, Mark Anders had written: "O My One Thing Necessary."

Sitting on the other side of the table, the elderly Jesuit, neatly buttoned into his black soutane, strands of white hair fallen into his eyes, had nodded off to sleep and was snoring softly. Stephen set the book to one side and studied the print and the invocation on its reverse side. The prayer was stark and strange. Had Anders reworked Henri Nouwen's phrase, "One necessary thing," or was the choice of words coincidental, the old priest's unconventional, personal thought?

Out of deference, Stephen would not ask. With characteristic idealism, he committed to memory the haunting image of the crucified Christ by Velázquez and the elevated affirmation of faith Mark Anders had written on the back.

In future years, long after Mark Anders had died, Stephen came upon various interpretations of the "Anima Christi." And each time he remembered, with an unexpected pang, the little room with the window that never opened right because its frame was warped. He remembered the peeling ceiling and the table with its treasure trove of books, the pool of yellow lamplight, and, in the midst of all, the aged face with its humble look of love.

Mark Anders, with a text of devastating simplicity, had paralleled the insight of Ignatius of Loyola.

—∽—

One evening at the end of November, Eugene Dowd, Daryl Lewis, and Terry Rhodes were sitting at the table in the dining room, eating supper and talking. Outside, a chill wind blew. It had stopped raining; a luminous, nearly full moon rose in the dark, starless sky.

Stephen, having first looked in on Mark Anders, arrived when the others were halfway through the meal. He paused to speak to Eugene Dowd and, nodding in greeting to Lewis and Rhodes, took the seat at the end of the table. Lewis passed him a casserole dish and he poured himself a cup of coffee from a carafe that had been set out for supper.

He did not take part in the conversation at first. His attention was drawn elsewhere—to the window at his right. It overlooked the long curve of the drive, now covered with wet leaves, and the part of the deserted street where a traffic light rocked unsteadily in the wind. From where he sat, Stephen could see the moon rising between the church spires, and moonlight glistening on the shards of wet pavement. There was no more beautiful sight, he thought, nor one with deeper meaning, than light shining in the darkness.

Suddenly, he realized that Terry Rhodes had raised his voice.

At the other end of the table, the discussion had become more intense. Eugene Dowd was sitting at the head of the table, his head bent to one side, his index finger tracing an abstract pattern on the tablecloth, listening attentively. On his left, straight-backed and stout, a white dinner napkin bunched into his collar, Daryl Lewis sat ponderously in his chair, sipping coffee from a mug and eating mashed potatoes and a slice of roast beef in the European manner, knife in his right, fork in his left, tines down. Every now and then he glanced up at Terry Rhodes, who sat facing him across the table.

Rhodes was seated with his blue-veined, long-fingered hands folded tightly in his lap, his gray, thinning hair combed precisely so that it lay across his scalp like lines of iron filings. He had been carrying the conversation, enlarging on particular themes: the tragedy of human existence, the frustration of irreparable wrongs, and the intransigence of the youth of Saint Aloysius.

He had just punctuated his opinion with an exclamation. There was a pause for a moment. Then Eugene Dowd leaned slightly forward to say with total focus:

"We work in an area where the successes are going to be small. Sometimes, I think our efforts can be compared to those of archaeologists: years are spent on seemingly fruitless endeavors, and only once in a while does one see a breakthrough. But the work matters—it makes a difference."

Rhodes passed his fingers along the stem of his unused spoon once, then again, and yet again, as if it were a talisman. Determined, he murmured his dissent. "I can't pretend to see promise where there is none. I can't pretend to see breakthroughs when the sense of despair is palpable. 'When every door and window remains shut...when the whole world has become an inn for the night.'"

Daryl Lewis slowly wiped his mouth with his napkin, a smile playing about his lips. "That's Kafka, isn't it?"

"Yes. And if you're familiar with Kafka, you know how perceptive he was about the human condition. He understood the dark hours; he understood suffering. He was a prophet of twentieth-century alienation and despair."

No one there disputed Kafka's genius, but Eugene Dowd, to make a different point, remarked:

"Kafka was Jewish. Somehow, I associate the Jewish mind-set with hope and determined resistance."

"Kafka was more sensitive than most to the anxiety that permeates the modern world."

Lewis rested his elbows on the table, loosely clasped his large, thick hands together, and said in his rich baritone:

"Kafka was one of those people who, if you happen to see him coming, you find yourself wishing you could think of an errand that would take you to the other side of the street, dreading having to meet him and having to ask the requisite 'How are you?' Imagine the lugubrious exchange:

"I am without soul or significance. My life has no meaning. My will is not my own. 'I am here; more than that I do not know. Further than that I cannot go.'" Lewis laughed heartily and looked around. "And how are you?"

A muscle at the corner of Terry Rhodes's mouth twitched. "I'll thank you, Daryl, not to mock one of literature's great minds."

Daryl Lewis smiled pleasantly. "The mood was getting a little heavy, Terry. That's all."

"The people of this parish would understand Kafka's writing about cold, ineluctable fate. This whole area seems to have come out of one of his novels."

"Christ has come to this place, Terry," Eugene Dowd said quietly.

"And been unappreciated."

Eugene Dowd, absently touching the temple of his steel-framed glasses, looked thoughtfully at Rhodes and said in an even softer voice, "I mean that we are here in this place to make Christ present."

"Yes, that's what we believe. But in these surroundings, reality has a different feel. What expectations can those who live here nurture? Think what it must be like, the sense of being unaccepted..."

Eugene Dowd leaned forward and pressed his index finger against the cloth. "But they *are* accepted somewhere. They're accepted *here*. And because they are, some of these young people will have a chance at a brighter future."

Rhodes stared at him sideways. Speaking in an impulsive outburst, he all but shouted, "But what of the rest? The merely average...what happens to them? We speak of the presence of God, but what about the nonpresence? Kafka challenges us to think. He questions the silence of God. Even Karl Rahner has said that the experience of loneliness and darkness is the real argument against Christianity."

"And gone on to say that it's easier to let oneself fall into the abyss of despair than into the mystery of God, but not more courageous—or more true," Eugene Dowd returned at once.

A cold, haughty note came into Terry Rhodes's voice. "It takes a certain kind of courage to strive alone, against the prevailing wisdom, knowing one's efforts are not understood."

Eugene Dowd, realizing to whom Rhodes was in fact referring, sighed resignedly and glanced away into the darkness beyond the window.

Rain had begun again; he could hear it clinking in the gutters on the roof. The thought struck him that the rain might leave the air charged with negative ions, an atmosphere that could allow Terry Rhodes to be enveloped in a layer of well-being.

Turning back to his colleagues, Dowd looked down the table, gazing thoughtfully at the one who had not taken part in the conversation. He said, "Stephen, I'd be interested in your view on all this."

Stephen, having finished dinner, had pushed back his chair and been listening to the discussion in silence. He did not answer at first, disinclined to differ with Terry Rhodes, whose long, solemn face with its dark hollows and sunken cheeks was suddenly turned inquisitively toward him. Eye contact was essential with this most apprehensive of men; Stephen was alert to that. He said:

"I've read Kafka with great admiration. He's never trivial or superficial. He goes directly to essential things. Ultimately, the question he raises…it seems to me…is whether or not our trust in transcendent reality is justified." Stephen added, with deference:

"Terry, would you be offended if I said that Kafka implies no? But we in this room have staked our lives on the opposite: that the story of Jesus is true."

From under lowered brows, Terry Rhodes looked at him unblinkingly. He said, "No, Stephen. I'm not offended." Then he folded his unsoiled napkin, placed it to the left of his plate, and rose from his seat. With great deliberation, he straightened his chair, adjusting and readjusting the legs, so that they aligned with the squares of the beige-and-brown floor tiles, his attention fixed on the act as if it were the most serious work in the world. Nodding politely to each of his colleagues in parting, he turned and walked toward the open door in the stiff, awkward way that was his alone—tall, gaunt body slanting slightly to one side, left shoulder held higher than the right—bumping against the door frame as he passed into the darkened hall. Catching Stephen's glance, Eugene Dowd shook his head and made a move of his hand to indicate that Stephen should let the matter go. Then for a long moment he let his gaze linger on his young associate, as if he were committing the scene to memory.

—⁓—

It began with aimless walking.

That fall, Tim Carruthers, the youngest child and only son of a postman and his wife, had returned to school changed. The once lively, chatty, conscientious teenager had become impassive, distant, indifferent to his classmates and his studies. But the most conspicuous behavior was the walking.

By late October he came to school less and less frequently, cutting classes to roam the streets. Shopkeepers and passersby noticed him in the middle of the day. With his hands shoved deeply into his pockets, his jacket undone, he dreamed away the afternoons peering into storefront windows, or tramped in the knee-high weeds along the railroad tracks collecting stones and bottle caps while talking excitedly to himself.

As his disorientation deepened, his appearance altered. The soft young mouth hanging open as if in continual surprise, the flaxen hair falling like a snowdrift across his sunken features, the dark around his eyes—all this gave him the sad, untended look of a lost, abandoned thing.

Then one Friday in mid-November, Tim stood up unexpectedly to address his fellow students in chemistry class. His thoughts swirling, he strained confusedly for words, but he was certain: voices in his mind were warning him that the solutions Father Terry Rhodes had assigned for study contained an imperceptible form of arsenic trioxide that could poison them all. Breathless, he announced his findings to his astonished classmates and to Father Rhodes, who was aghast.

And tragedy pressed his family to the ground.

In a closed-door meeting the following week, a somber Eugene Dowd told his staff:

"Tim is suffering from schizophrenia. The antipsychotic drugs used to treat that illness offer only limited recovery. Tim won't be returning to school…I don't know if he'll ever be able to return…His parents are in shock; they need to know we're here for them."

—⁓—

"Leah Carruthers would like to see you," Helen Blaney told Stephen from the door of his office.

"Is she on the phone?"

"No. She's here. Should I tell her to come in?"

"No. I'll go out to her."

Stephen found Leah Carruthers standing alone in the rectory's small beige parlor. She was a slightly built, middle-aged woman in an old blue woolen coat. Her straight brown hair was brushed back off thin shoulders, her eyes were big and luminous, her face lined but still pretty. When she smiled, she raised a hand to her mouth out of shyness.

"Father, I'm sorry I didn't call you first. I was out driving, and I wondered—if you weren't busy—if you would have time to talk to me?" Her voice was soft and high-pitched and rose at the end of a sentence, like a child's.

"Mrs. Carruthers. Come back to my office, please. I'm glad you came, just the way you did."

Stephen led her down a narrow hall, past half-open doors with tiny plaques: Father Dowd, Father Lewis, Father Rhodes. At his own door he stepped aside so that she could enter his office before him.

Leah Carruthers drifted across the room, demurely drinking in her surroundings: a small room with a bay window and books lying everywhere. The window looked out on the snow-covered walk between the rectory and the church, a walk she had never seen before. Stephen took a chair out from behind the desk and set it by the window for her, then he brought over the room's other chair for himself. They sat facing each other as they talked, Leah Carruthers with her blue woolen coat wrapped about her shoulders.

"Father," she said, "Timmy—when he was Timmy—told me that you were his favorite teacher, because you are so kind. And so I've come to ask you a favor…"

Stephen could hear the weight of emotion in the quiet, lilting voice. "Of course. Anything."

"There's a story I have to tell someone." She looked long and solemnly out the window. Then she said, "I've had a troubled marriage, Father. My husband has a temper. He drinks too much." Her eyes sought the floor. "Sometimes he's hit me."

Stephen, wondering, asked, "Did you ever go for counseling?"

"Yes. James, my husband, agreed to go with me to talk to Father Dowd. We went three times, but then we stopped going. James didn't see eye to eye with Father Dowd. Once, I was describing a situation to Father Dowd and James interrupted to correct me—it was for the fourth or fifth time, I think—and Father Dowd stood up and said, 'Mr. Carruthers, would you shut up!' My husband was so dumbfounded to hear a priest talk that way he didn't say another word the rest of the hour."

Stephen smiled inwardly. "Father Dowd is direct," he said.

Leah Carruthers shifted on her chair. Talking seemed to relax her. She went on in a calmer voice, recalling another incident from the past: "One day, Father Dowd saw me alone after Mass and said to me, 'Now, don't you worry. If it comes to a divorce, I'll help you to get an annulment afterward.'

"And I said, 'Oh, Father, I know how the Vatican discourages all these annulments.' And he said, 'You just come to see me. You're too young to go through life alone.'"

Stephen laughed quietly. "You're going to enable me to open a dossier on Father Dowd."

Leah Carruthers laughed in her shy way, her head tilted downward, her hand fluttering up to her mouth.

There was a long silence, then Leah Carruthers went on softly, "I've stayed in my marriage for the sake of my children. We have eight, you know…My dream was that, after they grew up, I'd be able to begin a new life, on my own. But I had to make sure my children would be safe and self-sufficient, especially Timmy, who is the youngest and most sensitive one."

She was quiet a moment, drawing back into the thin comfort of her coat. Tears came into her eyes.

"This is my story, Father. When I was a child, my family was very poor. My clothes were old-fashioned and, because I was small and skinny, they often bagged on me. I took it very hard. To escape, I turned to fairy tales. Everything was so perfect in a fairy tale. Homely little girls like me…"

Stephen raised his hand in a gesture of dissent, but Leah Carruthers shook her head.

"No, Father. I'm not feeling sorry for myself. I'm just being honest. I was a plain-looking little girl.

"But in a fairy tale a plain girl could, by magic, become a beautiful princess. A poor child, by finding a coin or a bean or a slipper, could become someone special. Some nights I'd look out of my bedroom window and see the moonlight glistening on the roof of my father's car in the driveway below me, and it seemed to me for an instant that the car had become Cinderella's carriage. The birds and crickets and frogs alive in the bushes seemed to speak a magic language all their own. And I belonged to that world. It delivered me."

Leah looked down at the floor again. "I haven't thought of fairy tales very often since," she said. "Except for one. Even when I was a child, it seemed different from other fairy tales, darker and more cruel. Now it's the one that haunts me, because it came true in my life. It's called 'The Wild Swans.'" Slowly, she raised her eyes. "Do you know it, Father?"

"No, I'm sorry. I don't."

"It's a story about a princess and her struggle to save her eleven brothers. It's part of a larger story, but the meaningful part for me. A witch had put the brothers under a spell and turned them into swans. When they took flight and vanished, the princess was frantic. She searched everywhere for them. Time went on, the months passed, she wandered over half the kingdom, but she couldn't find them.

"Then, one day, her fairy godmother appeared to her, telling her there was a way she could rescue her brothers. But the task would be a difficult, painful one. She would have to gather stinging nettles and trample them into flax with her feet. Out of the flax she was to weave eleven long-sleeved shirts. Then, when the swans returned, she would throw the shirts over them, one by one, and the spell would be broken. But there was a condition: if she failed to complete the mission, her brothers would be doomed to remain swans forever.

"And so, the princess prepared. She went into the woods and gathered the nettles and concealed them in her cloak, and hurried back to the castle. Alone in her bedchamber, she went to work. Her hands stung, her feet burned and bled, but she kept on in spite of the pain and her wounds."

Listening to the story line, Stephen was struck by the allusions to Christianity: the loss of original integrity, the eleven, redemptive love, the piercing of hands and feet, the garment which, like the baptismal robe, confers new life.

When Leah Carruthers had reached the critical point in the narrative, a note of anguish came into her soft, childlike voice:

"The princess worked through the night. By a heroic effort and after much suffering, she had completed ten of the shirts and was finishing the eleventh one. It was nearly dawn and she heard the wing beats of the swans. She ran to the window with the shirts. As each swan flew by the tower, she threw a shirt over it. At once, that brother stood beside her, turned back into a handsome prince again. All of them were restored—all except the youngest brother. The princess hadn't been able to finish his shirt in time, so she had to throw it over him with one arm unfinished, which meant that arm would remain a swan's wing forever. The youngest brother would never be whole, like the others. He would be damaged…

"And so, you see, Father…Timmy…" In an unbearable moment of pain, Leah Carruthers put out a trembling hand and gestured feebly, like someone drowning who has no fight left and, before going down, waves despairingly toward the shore.

Stephen, penetrated with compassion, looked upon her grief-stricken face, the ruins of her eyes, the small, nervous hands, which in imagination he saw nettle-plaiting, and he struggled for words.

A conventional phrase offered itself to his mind: We don't know why God allows the innocent to suffer…But he set it aside.

"Leah," he said, his eyes locking with hers, "I understand. And I promise you, I will never forget you, nor Timmy. Your courage, this story."

—⁂—

The first heavy snowfall that winter began at noon on Christmas Day. By nightfall, nearly a foot of snow covered the city, and the inconsequential streets surrounding the parish buildings of Saint Aloysius had transformed into glistening avenues of white.

At nine, Stephen came out of the rectory and shoveled a footpath to the church. He was the only priest on assignment that night. Mark Anders had been in and out of the hospital throughout December, battling pneumonia, and when, three days earlier, his condition had relapsed, he had been admitted again. The other Jesuits had left for the evening and would not be back until morning.

When Stephen had cleared a path he walked over to the church. He climbed up the flight of steps, opened the heavy door, and, stamping his feet to clean them of snow, stepped inside. Near the back wall he paused.

Long shadows enveloped the nave from wall to wall, shrouding the statues recessed in wells at the sides of the altar. The great stained-glass windows encircling the apse had vanished, also lost in shadow. Within the sanctuary the marble altar rose, stark and magnificent. To one side, the sanctuary lamp glowed with a hazy ruby light, the only light to pierce the darkness.

He had been ordained less than a year and that morning he had offered his first Mass of Christmas Day, but this night he had come back, a Catholic alone on Christmas, needing to be in a Catholic church.

Now as Stephen stood and looked around, he saw across a distance, to a Christmas spent in darkness, in poverty, in abandonment, in a cold stall, and in imagination he heard on the air the pure, austere tones of the entrance antiphon for the Mass of Christmas Day:

Puer natus est...
Unto us a child is born,
unto us a son is given...

He knelt down, losing himself to a profound sense of the eternal in time.

—⁂—

On December 28, Kathleen gave birth to twins—in spite of all her precautions, regardless of the best medical care—a stillborn boy and girl. Born six weeks prematurely, on the feast of the Holy Innocents, the infants were christened Stephen and Nicole.

The feast of Saint Stephen, December 26, was Stephen's birthday. He had arrived at the Shearers' on the twenty-seventh to spend the weekend with Don and Kathleen and, by accident, was there to baptize his small namesake.

—⚬—

On a wintry morning in mid-January, when Stephen had been back at Saint Aloysius for a week, Eugene Dowd made a request of him. An elderly widow, housebound and living alone, had asked for a priest to come to hear her confession.

Three miles from the Jesuit residence, in the former parish of Saint Christopher's, poverty wore a distinctive face. The area that had once set the standard for elegant living was now a faded relic. Broken shells of cars, stripped of wheels and tires, corroded at curbside. Rats lapped water from the gutters at dawn. Now and then, solitary aged figures in heavy woolen coats moved among the stately ruins like survivors who were making their way home in the aftermath of war.

In the same period in which Rome had determined that the venerable Saint Christopher had in fact not existed, the church had been closed due to dwindling membership. Its building was converted into a seniors' center, the bewildered faithful were assigned to Saint Aloysius, and the parish bearing his name followed the saint into the past.

As he entered the area for the first time, Stephen was struck by its strange, ethereal beauty. Snow had fallen throughout the night and a white mist still permeated the air, making everything appear silvery and secret and inaccessible. Three-story houses seemed to rise out of a seascape, as if sponged on the stone-gray sky. Ice-covered side streets, resembling frozen streams, receded into fog. A fine haze caught on the branches of boxwood hedges like a film of cobwebs, or moved, wraith-like, along the walks.

Stephen parked in the middle of the block and walked up the street, checking the addresses against a card he carried with him. At the foot of one long drive he found the home he wanted, its number discernible on a mossy boulder landscapers had laid long ago.

Set far back on expansive grounds, half-hidden from view by a great blue spruce, the house was a classic English Tudor with a steeply gabled roof and stucco outer walls with dark wood beams. A brick walk wound up to three wide flagstone steps that dipped in the middle, worn down with age. Silhouetted in black near the front door, a solitary apple tree spread out twined braches. Within, the house appeared silent, perhaps uninhabited, but at one window a curtain moved a little, and a small white head showed fleetingly through the dotted voile. Before Stephen could ring the bell, a bolt unlatched, and the door was opened by the owner of the house.

Colette Green stood, trim and dignified, in her doorway, a diminutive woman, past ninety, with alert blue eyes, pure white hair, and skin as fragile as tissue. Her voice was warm, raspy, and unhesitating:

"Oh, Father Engle! You came!"

Entering and closing the door behind him, Stephen came into a faded blue, once-pretty foyer. "I'm pleased to be here, Mrs. Green."

Colette Green went ahead of him into a step-down living room, clapping her hands together, as much for warmth as from delight. The house was cold.

She said, "I told Father Dowd, 'Send the young, good-looking one, not that dour Father Rhodes.'"

"Very few get to see the committed teacher Father Rhodes is in the classroom," Stephen offered politely.

"Now, don't go defending him," Colette Green said, shaking her finger in mock scolding. "When something's wrong, it's wrong, and there's something amiss with that man. He was born without the smile gene."

Stephen smiled. "That's clever," he said, glancing around, the redirection of his eyes a well-mannered attempt to change the subject.

"Ah, you've been too schooled in loyalty," Colette Green said brightly. Then, "Won't you have some tea? I started it before you came. Sit down, please. I'll be only a minute."

Satisfied that she had voiced her opinion—her displeasure with Father Rhodes and her enchantment with Father Engle—she hurried from the room.

While he waited for her, Stephen sat down in one of a pair of antique channel-back chairs and looked about, thinking of what this home must have been in decades past. He was in an immaculately preserved living room whose coved cathedral ceiling, ornate chandelier, and sweeping staircase survived in elegant defiance of the outer world. A threadbare Oriental rug, its tree of life pattern nearly effaced by wear, lay on the oak herringbone floor. Yellowing pictures of religious art were fastened tenuously on pale blue walls. Over a high-back sofa hung the portrait of a middle-aged man with a high white collar, a slight mustache, and a beard like a soft fog.

The only other picture in the room was a photograph in a silver frame that stood on a nearby side table. Sepia-colored, printed on poor quality paper, the photograph showed a nun standing in what appeared to be a deeply shadowed archway. The nun's square, handsome face, stiffly bound by a starched white headpiece, looked slightly to the right of the viewer. Black hollows in the grainy paper gave an illusion of depth to the background, beautifying the strong planes of the nun's face, but withholding her eyes.

Colette Green came back into the room carrying a silver tray with a silver tea service and two blue-and-white Wedgwood china cups.

"Do you know why I asked you to come, Father?" she asked, setting the tray down on a central coffee table. She handed Stephen an intact cup and kept the flawed one for herself, the chip in the blue china turned discreetly inward. "Oh, I know I told Father Dowd that I needed someone to hear my confession, but that was a fib."

She seated herself on the high-backed sofa and, sipping her tea, smiled impishly. "What I really need is someone to help me write my obituary."

Stephen sat back a bit, laughing.

"I've been working on it for weeks." Colette Green eagerly set down her cup, opened a drawer in the table beside her, and picked up a small notepad, plainly having had it ready if circumstances were right.

"I have it right here."

She gave Stephen a glance and, seeing that he listened, she turned to the first page and read:

"'For sixty-seven years she lived in her lovely old home, forty-nine of them as a widow…She was a former teacher…a lifelong member of the altar society…'"

Colette Green dropped the pad into her lap dramatically and, leaning forward, said unhappily, "I don't recognize myself, Father. That's not me—so ordinary and dull."

Removing several sheets from the pad, she smiled sweetly and almost shyly, like a child entreating a parent, and asked, "If I tell you other descriptions I've written, would you help me make them suitable for print?"

Stephen set down his cup and took the pad from her. "All right." He patted his pockets in search of something with which to write, and retrieved a ballpoint pen from the breast pocket of his jacket.

Colette Green watched him, nervously fingering the paper that lay in her lap. When Stephen looked up, she began to read again in a soft, confidential voice.

"'She was a lover of sunsets and storms.' Do you like that?"

"Yes. It's wonderful."

"'She dearly loved the Catholic Church, but because of her outspoken views, probably belonged in some heretical group.'"

Stephen wrote with head down-turned, smiling.

"'She lived alone and, little by little, saw her world diminish, but she was without self-pity, and *she was a survivor*.'" Till that point the elderly widow had been speaking almost hushedly, but on the last four words her tone elevated and strengthened.

Stephen stopped writing and gave her a thoughtful glance, but Colette Green, wholly immersed in her thoughts, had interrupted herself to change course.

"'She had weaknesses. She had a sharp tongue, and she was envious of women with slender waistlines because she was thick-waisted, and didn't look pretty in dresses.'"

Colette was silent a long moment. Then she said, "'When she was a child, she wanted to be a nun. But when she grew older and came to realize her nature was too independent, the dream died. Still, all of her life she regretted not having tried.'"

Stephen, unaware, let his eyes wander to the sepia-colored picture in the silver frame.

Following his glance, Colette Green asked very softly, "Isn't she lovely?"

"Yes, she is."

"That's Mère Marie de la Sacre Coeur."

"Mother Mary of the Sacred Heart," Stephen said quietly, translating.

"God love you! You know French!" Colette Green said delightedly. "I was born in Montreal, you see, and raised by nuns in convent." She leaned forward suddenly and asked eagerly, "Do you think you could help me to recall the Litany of Our Blessed Mother that the nuns used to sing in choir?"

"I can try."

Colette Green sat with uplifted chin and clasped hands and began to enunciate with restrained emotion:

"Holy Mary, Mother of God..."

"*Sainte Marie, Mère de Dieu,*" Stephen interpreted in reply.

"Cause of our joy..."

"*Cause de notre joie.*"

"Tower of ivory..."

"*Tour d'ivoire.*"

"Gate of heaven...morning star..."

Colette Green went on, her voice trailing off until it could barely be heard.

"It's been eighty-six years, Father. I was an orphan in a Benedictine convent school in Quebec—not because my parents were dead, mind you—but because their lives were chaotic. When they went their separate ways, my mother thought it best to leave me with the nuns.

"And Mère Marie saved my life. I was just a little bit of a thing, and she would take me aside and talk with me in her beautifully accented voice, and build me up.

"Entire scenes from my childhood fell away like rotted wood, and new sets went up"—frail hands formed tent shapes in the air—"with new scenes, and a new script, and new possibilities. Mère Marie created a new world for me."

Colette Green paused and lowered her eyes. Then she said, "When I married, I came to this country. But I always intended to go back one day, to see Mère Marie and tell her how much she had mattered in my life, that her words to me had been pure gold. But I never did go back…and then, one day—it's been almost fifty years now—I learned she'd died."

Colette Green looked away, gazing humbly at the strangely beautiful face in the silver frame. When she turned back to Stephen, a mist covered her eyes.

"These days, I sit and think about her and try to remember the things she told me, but the words are blurred now.

"She affected my life more deeply than anyone I ever met, and yet, when I try to recall her words, I can't."

Colette Green looked confusedly at Stephen. "Can you help me?" she asked. "What do you think they were?"

Stephen hesitated, unsure how to respond. But before he could say anything, the elderly widow went on:

"I can see her so plainly." Colette Green inclined her head to one side, her gaze lost in contemplation of some distant point. "She was always immaculate and her lips were naturally pink, and when she walked, she made quick little taps with her heels."

Colette Green sighed a little. She laid her head back against the sofa. More to herself than to Stephen, she murmured:

"I don't remember her words now, only that they were beautiful…"

Stephen kept the notes he'd made that morning, and added the name of Colette Green to the list of parishioners with whom he would maintain regular contact. But as it turned out, he did not see her again.

Later that same day an attentive neighbor looked in on the elderly widow. Five hours had passed since Stephen had left and now there was no answer to the doorbell. Remembering that a key was kept under the mat, the neighbor retrieved it, and let himself in. From the foyer he could see the shadowy depth of the living room, then the small figure curled up asleep on the sofa, the thin afghan she'd used as a cover fallen to the floor. How chilled she would have been, had she not slipped away an hour before.

The following Sunday, the Saint Aloysius parish bulletin published her obituary:

> *Colette Green*
> *A lover of sunsets and storms, of the spoken word,*
> *of all beautiful forms;*
> *A Christian existentialist in her belief in the*
> *potential of the human mind and through her*
> *conscious participation in the life of the church,*
> *even when this commitment led her to dissent;*
> *One who believed, as saints and poets do, that true freedom*
> *is found on the high interior plain of the spirit.*
> *Widow of Michael Green.*
> *Idealist, survivor, teacher, friend.*
> *Died January 12*

—⟋⟍—

The bus first passed Children's Hospital and then the broad towers of the medical center, moving steadily along a congested downtown street. Stephen, seated on the aisle toward the rear, watched a city block pass by, like a film unrolling in slow motion: a grocery, a liquor store behind barred doors, a pawnshop, a drugstore with obscene graffiti scrawled on its walls in red block letters—*some vandal's cubist period*, he thought whenever he saw it.

The bus ground to a halt in midblock. Stephen got up from his seat, briefcase in hand, and went out through the side exit door. The fresh early air fanned his face. The day was cold, bright, and windy, the sun blazing through swift-moving clouds. From curbside Stephen looked toward the gray concrete building on the opposite corner. Then he stepped into the street. In the next instant he felt a staggering blow, tried to take a step, stumbled sideways, and fell to the pavement.

Swerving to the left, maneuvering through jumbled traffic, the driver of a maroon Chevrolet drove on, all the while searching for Stephen in the rearview mirror. The car's other occupant, a young woman who had been feeling on the floor for a dropped earring, quickly straightened up and, looking round, exclaimed with fear in her voice:

"What was that?"

"I almost hit a priest." The driver struck a thick fist on the steering wheel. "Damn it! He had his head in the clouds. He wasn't looking where he was going."

The driver swore again and cast another swift glance in the mirror, but a sudden shift in traffic obscured his view. Thinking that luck—or fate—was with him, he continued on.

But Stephen had been hit. For thirty seconds, perhaps a full minute, he lay on his side next to the curb, breathing heavily. Several bystanders rushed to his aid. A woman in a green woolen coat leaned over and spoke to him. A heavyset man took his arm as he tried to stand. Someone insisted they should call for an ambulance. But Stephen, who in another minute was on his feet, assured them he was all right. He felt a little unsteady was all, though his right eye was tender and beginning to swell, the knee of his right pant leg had ripped open, and a smear of filth from the street streaked his right shoulder and lay like a misplaced military stripe along his sleeve.

As his briefcase struck the pavement, it had sprung open, and disgorged its contents. Newspapers, arranged in neat piles—a two-week collection of sports pages—broke loose and were taken up by the wind.

Some fluttered down the street with the waddling gambol of ducks; others flattened against building walls; a scattered few blew past the gunmetal-gray building on the corner opposite where, unperceived by the outer world, which saw only the plaque reading "Berchmans' Health Clinic,"in a room plain as a monastic cell, waited a slender, adolescent boy with an uncomprehending stare, who was the subject of Stephen's visit. Tim Carruthers would notice no difference in his former teacher, who arrived on time but looking like the victim of a mugging.

—⚏—

Mark Anders's stay at Saint Aloysius was nearing an end. His recent medical tests showed his condition worsening. His colleagues could tell that his health was declining by his lessening appetite, by his new, excessive need for sleep, by his increasingly faltering step. In June he would move to Colombiere Center outside of Detroit, the home for ailing and elderly Jesuits.

Stephen, after officiating at a wedding one Friday, went upstairs to read to him.

He paused at the half-open door, knocked and waited a moment, then entered and walked to the bed where Mark Anders lay. The old priest seemed to be asleep, the covers pulled up to his chin, his head tipped back, his mouth hanging open a little.

The room was close and overly warm; a harsh smell of disinfectant mingled with the sour odor of sickness. Stephen went to the window, undid the catch, and, pressing against the frame, worked the window open.

It was a beautiful spring evening, after a rain. Washed clear of color, the sky was a pale, watery gray. A transparent three-quarter moon had risen above the church tower. In the delicate lacework of its greening branches, a solitary birch bore the promise of summer. The air was soft, scented with bark.

Quietly, Stephen brought the chair he was used to sitting in over to the bedside. Anders stirred, still asleep, and Stephen noticed his look.

Though nothing about the room had changed, its occupant was fading, unmistakably, and Stephen felt within himself the awareness, instinctive and elemental, of finality.

"Hello, Stephen."

The words were indistinct. Stephen had to lean forward to catch them. He said, "I'm sorry if I woke you, Father."

"No. I've been expecting you to come." Anders tried awkwardly to move and Stephen eased him back onto his pillows. He took the old man's wrist, as he did each night, to feel his pulse.

Mark Anders craned his neck a little. His eyes as serene and soft as a child's, he asked, "Is it evening yet?"

"Yes. It'll be dark soon. May I get you anything?"

"Could we resume our reading?"

Stephen smiled in agreement. "Do you want me to go on from where we left off?" He'd been reading from Joyce's *Dubliners*, and had come to *Ivy Day in the Committee Room.*

"No. Tonight I'd like to hear the Psalms. Would you mind? I was reading them earlier and left the Old Testament on the table. I think I marked the place."

"I'll get it," Stephen said, going to the window.

Standing at the table, looking for the book, he didn't pay attention to the grounds outside, until he heard what sounded like a woman's soft laughter.

From the window he could see the parking lot between the church and the school. A car had pulled in and was parked in the well of shadow along the wall of the school, its lights extinguished. Someone stirred within it. Stephen glimpsed the nape of a man's neck moving across the dark rectangle of the window and the man's back arching suddenly and rocking to and fro, and then he heard the woman's soft laughter again.

Affected, he looked away. The frank carnality of the scene startled and unsettled him. To collect himself he turned and directed his attention to the aged figure lying gray and frail in the narrow bed. From the books spread on the table he took the thick volume with a black leather cover. He returned to the bedside, seated himself, and leaned forward and flicked on the wall light switch. Opening to a place in the Old Testament Anders had marked with a frayed Christmas card, he began to read aloud:

"'In every age, O Lord, you have been our refuge. You turn man back to dust, saying, "Return, O children of men. For a thousand years in your sight are as yesterday, now that it is past, or as a watch of the night. You make an end of them in their sleep; the next morning they are like the changing grass, which at dawn springs up anew, but by evening wilts and fades…'"

—⁂—

On Saturday afternoons only a handful of parishioners came to confession at Saint Aloysius, where a priest was present from three to four, the four Jesuits who were in good health alternating with one another.

As Stephen left the confessional on the last Saturday in May, he saw Eugene Dowd standing in the sanctuary, nodding his head not in greeting, but in summons. There was no mistaking his solemn self-containment—the bearing of one who brings fateful news.

In silence the two men stepped outside and walked along the pot-holed street together, bits of concrete cracking under their feet. At the curb, before starting up the walk, Stephen paused and stared overhead, his gaze held for a moment by the window of the corner room on the second floor. Then he turned his head and looked at Eugene Dowd with an unguarded expression of affection.

"I think that, after my father's…and one other's…Mark's will be the most profound influence on my life," he said in a voice taut with controlled emotion.

And Eugene Dowd, understanding that Stephen wanted him to know he was the other, put his hand on the young Jesuit's shoulder and smiled wordlessly.

—⁂—

Summer was cruel to the streets. If elsewhere it brought radiant dawns, luxuriant days, glowing sunsets, and a profusion of growing things, to the streets it brought hard, unforgiving light, interminable heat, sultry air, and invasions of flies.

When, in later years, Stephen thought back on that summer, he connected it with a specific sound, a background noise, methodical and quotidian—the sound of paper flapping in the heavy air. In memory he would walk again through the dusty streets, feel the heat of the afternoon sun upon his back, once more see the elderly poor cloistered on their porches, and hear, with instant clarity, the even, rhythmic waving of their homemade paper fans.

—⁂—

Summer was uneventful in the Jesuit residence, except for a day in mid-June when assignments for the school year beginning in September were given out. Eugene Dowd learned that June that he would be welcoming two new associates. Daryl Lewis was leaving, having been appointed to serve in administration at Fordham University. Stephen was leaving as well, to pursue a doctorate in English literature. Terry Rhodes had been reassigned to teach physics and chemistry at Saint Aloysius.

Having hoped for a transfer to a more distinguished post, convinced now more than ever that his superiors intended to bury him permanently at this remote corner of the province, Rhodes was bitter and defensive. The seeming unfairness of his situation gnawed at him, intensifying his feelings of inferiority, a self-perception he believed was also the unspoken judgment of the community. After nursing his frustration in private for days, he at last voiced it to Eugene Dowd in a long, indignant lament that could be heard even through closed doors. Afterward, Rhodes retreated to his room and avoided contact with his colleagues for the rest of the day.

—⁂—

After offering the early Mass on weekdays, Stephen usually sat in a front pew to read his breviary. When he'd finished, he'd leave the pew and walk down the center aisle to the outer door; by then the body of the church was empty.

But this morning Terry Rhodes knelt in one of the pews at the back, his head sunk into his shoulders, his shoulders hunched high. He seemed not to see Stephen, or made as if he did not. Stephen caught sight of him and, changing direction, made his way through a center row of pews, walked down the side aisle, and paused a few steps in front of him.

Rhodes did not move or speak but continued to stare ahead intently until, realizing that Stephen remained standing in front of him, he looked up, puzzled and irritable. All of his suppressed frustrations—the years of rejection by a critical, punitive mother; the thwarted idealism which had long ago permutated into cynicism; the disappointments in prayer; the loneliness; the seemingly irrelevant place he held in the community to which he had devoted his life—all this burned in Terry Rhodes's embittered eyes, and he glared at Stephen wordlessly, as if to ask: "Why are you stopping here? What do you want, you who have been blessed with everything? You, who are everyone's favorite? You, who are headed for the kind of life I've hungered for, but will never have?"

"Terry." Stephen, leaning forward slightly, put his hand on Rhodes's shoulder and looked directly into his eyes. In the low, urgent tone his voice took on when he was moved, he said, "Terry, pray for me, please."

Terry Rhodes shifted on the kneeler and glanced hard at Stephen. Stephen's manner showed such deference and his gaze expressed such a certainty that Rhodes had something valuable to offer him, that the older Jesuit was softened and prompted to say:

"I'll pray for you, Stephen."

"I'm grateful for that. Thank you."

Stephen patted Rhodes's shoulder for a moment and then moved away.

Rhodes heard the great outer door open; after that he heard Stephen's footsteps sound on the stairs. The door slowly closed and Stephen's steps died away. A great silence came over the church. Alone now, Terry Rhodes continued to kneel in the pew, staring ahead at the altar, his face a pale plaster cast that was beginning to crack.

—⚏—

In mid-August Daryl Lewis and Stephen left Saint Aloysius for the Jesuit provincial house, Eugene Dowd accompanying them.

Lewis drove slowly through the empty streets in the early morning of a wet summer day. In unspoken agreement with the others, he took a roundabout route, slowing down at certain corners so that for a minute longer he and Stephen could take in the surroundings.

Stephen, swiveling in his seat, gazed through the rain-streaked window at the neighborhoods receding into the distance: the little white-frame houses, the broken fences, the boarded-up storefronts, the crossbreed dogs wandering about, the run-down tenements—there, in a second-floor window, a crock of red geraniums—the desolate, deserted streets in a summer rain, when the very air seemed to lean toward the car, yearning for a breeze to deliver it elsewhere. And just as had happened on the morning after his arrival when, as a stranger to the parish, he had walked these streets for the first time, lines from Luke's parable of the rich man and Lazarus rose in his mind:

> *Moreover, between us and you*
> *a great chasm is established to*
> *prevent anyone from crossing who*
> *might wish to go from our side*
> *to yours, or from your side to ours.*

IX

*And Clare entered
the monastery of Saint Damiano,
and there she put down the anchor of her soul...*

— FROM THE RULE OF THE POOR CLARE NUNS

In the moment that she heard Francis speak of the love of Christ crucified, Clare of Assisi knew where her destiny lay.

She was beautiful, high-spirited, to the manor born, and committed by her father to a marriage that would unite two ancient and distinguished families. But none of that had meaning for her anymore, after she met Francis.

On the night of Palm Sunday in the year 1212, Clare, aided by a sympathetic aunt, left her father's house in secret and came to make her home in the chapel and house of the old mission at Saint Damiano. Together with Francis, she founded a new religious order, born of idealism and dedicated to a radical living-out of the Gospels.

No one would trade clothes with a beggar or kiss a leper's hand. But Francis of Assisi did. And Clare was his soul mate. Embracing poverty as the means to identify with Christ, the Poor Clare nuns cared for the sick, the aged, the marginalized; they produced what they needed to eat and, if they couldn't support themselves in this way, they begged for their sustenance.

The story of Clare of Assisi lived on in the Catholic imagination, renewed again and again down through the centuries, in distant, diverse lands, with other names, other faces.

Because of it, Clare Engle now had come to live among the Sisters of the Sacred Heart, believing with all her soul that this was the setting she had been born for.

The motherhouse, with its broad wings and three stories, was a gray world of cool stone walls, great silvery columns, and cavernous corridors that bent away into shadow: a gray world fixed in surroundings of exquisite natural beauty. Behind the main building a lawn serene as if never stepped on stretched for a mile to where wildflowers blew beside a country road. To the left of the motherhouse grew an apple orchard; its fieldstone wall had half collapsed and all along it ivy and wild roses spilled in from the meadow beyond.

Clare's room was on the second floor, a sunlit cubicle with a small dresser and a narrow bed. It didn't have a mirror, but it had something which to Clare mattered more—a window with one of the best views the motherhouse had to offer.

From that window she could look down on the fountain in the cloister garden below, or out across the grounds to where a single aged tree stood, bent and stark, like a Chinese ideograph sketched among the orchard's grasses.

From that window she could hear the horn of a train sounding in the distance. And she could hear birds singing all about her in the autumn dusk—the loud "weep" note of a robin, the harsh voice incongruous with the flitting chickadee, and from time to time, a string of liquid, musical phrases softer than a robin's coming from one of the beautiful old trees along the cloister walk.

Clare opened her whole soul to the experience. *And there she put down the anchor of her soul.* The words of Clare of Assisi came naturally to her. She thought, *And so it will be with me.*

But not everything was what she had expected. Having imagined the postulancy would be a sorority-like setting of girls like herself, Clare was surprised to learn that there were only two other entrants, and both were older than she.

Regina Palm was a heavyset woman with a broad face, a large, high-bridged nose, and a frank, clear gaze. She spoke in a polite, businesslike manner with a quiet, girlish voice that seemed to belong to a smaller, younger woman. An only child, she had been an excellent student and, after graduating from college, had begun law school. But in her first year, her mother was diagnosed with cancer, and Regina left school and returned home. When, a year later, her father suffered a stroke, she became his caregiver, too. After her parents died, Regina, who never complained of all that life had denied her, gave away her small inheritance and, at age thirty-four, entered the convent.

The other entrant, twenty-eight-year-old Allyson Martin, was a beautiful, nervous girl with long auburn hair and a bitten thumbnail. Engaged to be married at twenty-four, she had survived the auto accident that had taken the life of her fiancé. Shattered by the experience, Allyson, the daughter of an alcoholic father and an emotionally distant mother, had had no one to turn to. For the first time since childhood she began to think of being a nun, and this time she had not pushed the thought away.

Clare, Regina, and Allyson spent six months as postulants, or candidates, for religious life. Then they were admitted into the community, and received the brown habit and white veil of a novice.

Like most young women, they had romantic notions of religious life. Grounding them in reality was what the novitiate was for. For two years they lived in a cloister-like setting, learning what would be expected of them as women religious, the discipline of the life.

They learned how to sit with ankles crossed and hands folded, slow their walk, keep silent, and control their glance so as not to be distracted by activity to their right or left. Never were they to take the last piece and always were they to take the smallest piece of anything presented to them, a practice which could have comical consequences if they were offered the same dish at once.

Novices learned that time was structured in a new way. The prayers and psalms of the Divine office, sung in the choir seven times a day, defined the passage of day and night. Rising before dawn, the community sang Matins and Lauds, and then attended Mass. Afterward, the novices studied and did menial chores, the day unfolding according to the dictum of Saint Benedict, founder of monastic life: *ora et labora*, prayer and work. Silence was suspended at three and at seven, the hours of recreation. Television precluded, conversation was lively, cherished.

The life was simple, austere, unvaried in its outward form, spiritually intense. Its regimen could produce boredom, frustration, depression, fatigue, and agonizing questions about the value of one's vocation. But far from wilting under the demands of the life, Clare thrived. She found that it was in awakening in the solitude of her room, or meditating in the long daytime silences that she felt fully alive.

She was determined to take herself always to the limit and, continuing a pattern begun in childhood, collected in a notebook words and phrases directed toward that end. She memorized lines of Augustine's, altering them in her mind to include the feminine:

Give me a man in love;
he knows what I mean.
Give me one who yearns;
give me one who is hungry;
give me one far away in
this desert, who is thirsty
and sighs for the spring
of the Eternal Country.
Give me that sort of man;
he knows what I mean...

And continually, she asked herself, When does the hard part begin?

There was, as in all religious communities, a strict separation between novices and professed sisters. In the greenhouse environment, which the novitiate was, only those religious who were exemplars of the Rule were permitted to come into contact with young women in their formative years.

Here, in this enclosed world, a world they both understood and now shared, Clare and Sister Mary Bernard were reunited, and the older nun, as Mistress of Novices, bore officially the title that Clare for years had given her in her heart and at last could openly express, the name of "Mother."

Mother Mary Bernard was the ideal choice to guide young women: the understatement of inner beauty, a character of such selflessness that she could suppress her own personality in order to focus totally on those entrusted to her care. Like haiku of the highest order, she was the start-ing point; the novices' work was to form themselves in the image of spiritual maturity that she disclosed.

When Mother Mary Bernard herself looked at Clare, she discovered what she had expected to find: a bright, single-minded young woman of twenty-one, intellectually advanced, but emotionally naive. No one was more pleased by Clare's dedication and adaptability for the life, even though, in order not to show favoritism, the mistress of novices treated her former student no differently than she did the others, and was, at times, even a little cool toward her. But the pleasure and love shone in her eyes and, under her direction, Clare flowered.

Mother Mary Bernard's concern was for the years ahead. She recog-nized in Clare a young woman who needed an obstacle, who needed to sacrifice in order to thrive, who needed, even, to live in a counterculture, as had her childhood heroes, the early Christian martyrs. An environ-ment that suited the novice now might later give her little room to grow. Providing that room would be a challenge for her future superiors.

—⚭—

Years later, Clare happened upon a photograph that someone had taken of her on the day of her first profession. She saw a young woman in a brown habit with a close-fitting black veil standing under the elms on a spring afternoon, a slender, gangly young woman, body pulled up like a dancer's, almost on tiptoe, her eyes wide and shining, smiling at someone offstage and now long forgotten. And in the background, slightly out of focus, that was her father, talking with Stephen; yes, it was Stephen, seen purely by accident, his back turned to the camera, walking to the car with their father. Her father and Stephen, held there however tangentially; and she, in the foreground, in that instant, forgetful of them. How happy she had been, they all had been, and how untroubled, that day in early spring.

—m—

That year, Stephen was nearing the end of his graduate studies at Columbia and living in a brownstone near the university campus, the building one of narrow stairways, dim halls, and small, modest rooms, with his in the attic. The inner life of study and research invigorated him so thoroughly that on most days he made the six-floor climb with little effort, pausing only, if at night the stairs were dark, to tighten the flickering lightbulb on the third-floor landing.

Though months at a time were spent in bone-chilling cold, in later years, when Stephen thought back on that period in his life, it seemed to him to have been a springtime of the soul. With characteristic intensity he lived for his studies, disciplining his hours so that the bulk of them could be given to work. He chose for the subject of his doctoral dissertation the nature of symbol in the creative process, developing a theme of Carl Jung's, that water is the symbol for the unconscious mind. In his introduction he wrote:

"A correspondence exists between what water is—amorphous, dark, and mysterious—and what I know my own psyche is."

He read and reread preeminent writers, assimilating knowledge, sensing new levels of awareness, reflecting, imagining, making rough drafts, and writing and rewriting. He drew on Auden's essay, "The Mirror and the Sea" and selected from Joyce the passage:

His soul was swooning into some new world, fantastic, dim, uncertain as under sea...

And from Pablo Neruda:

Night and the water seem one; it washes the sky, enters our dreams with the immediate burst of its presence...

His adviser, Karl Mack, was a scholar of considerable note, a short, thickset man in late middle age with great force of personality. His memorable features—his shock of unruly brown hair, his thick, expressive eyebrows, his deep frown lines of concentration—put one in mind of Beethoven.

From the beginning he understood that in Stephen he had an exceptional student who needed special mentoring. On many nights, Mack, in a rumpled green tweed jacket, a pipe in the corner of his mouth, sat bent over a desk strewn with papers, listening, silent with admiration, as Stephen paced the floor, absently stroking the back of his neck and turning often with intent dark eyes to look questioningly at his kindly confidant.

"These concepts aren't just abstract ideas," Stephen said, pausing in midstride, "but images that come to life in my mind. I see it this way so clearly...Yes, some on the doctoral committee will disagree with my methodology, but I can combine lyricism with analytical criticism. I can meet their objections."

Thus, his summation ended with a reflection on the creative process in the form of a poem that depicted beauty created out of chaos by the structures of the human mind. With water as his metaphor, Stephen wrote of disorder, struggle, and calm; of turbulence, surcease, and the gifts the unconscious mind gives up, unbidden:

Tomorrow, the sea will be a
dreamer again,
And loose a thousand visions
from her hands...

Stephen titled his dissertation *Analogue: The Sea*. With its publication the following year, word that an academic star had been born reached the campus of the Jesuit college where he would begin his teaching assignment. With deft, soft-spoken explanations of his research and a poet's insight into symbolism, he seemed the model of a self-assured young scholar. However, Stephen was unprepared for the recognition. He felt that his thesis was an incomplete work and that another, more mature writer could have given proper expression to the elegance of the conception. Ill at ease in his new surroundings, he wrote to Eugene Dowd:

"The humble parish of Saint Aloysius, far removed from and seldom regarded by middle-class society, is, in spirit, closer to the life of the Gospels than the academic world of which I am now a part. I miss the streets, the sounds, the faces of the children, the unhurried coming to the communion rail of the elderly on dark winter mornings, the simple, unpretentious way of life..."

And then he answered a letter from his father, which ended:

"It's been too long. Come home. I need to see you, Stephen."

X

Silent now is the wild and lonely glen…

— FROM "THE KERRY DANCE"

It was not every day that a member of the family received his doctorate, and Lawrence Engle wanted to give a dinner party in honor of his son.

Recovered from the loss of her twins three and a half years earlier, enlivened by the thought of a festive occasion, Kathleen offered to be the hostess of the party, and planned it for the Saturday at the end of August.

She and Don arrived at her father's house in early afternoon that day, their arms laden with groceries. While she prepared dinner, Kathleen banished her husband and father to the study where they watched baseball on television and waited good-naturedly to be allowed to help.

Fresh flowers were delivered at four, and vases throughout the house were filled with masses of white—snapdragons, roses, and chrysanthemums. On the dining room table a bowl of white roses and trailing ivy became the centerpiece. Kathleen used a turquoise cloth on the table and lit tall white candles to softly illuminate the room. Waterford goblets and white china bordered with raised blue flowers were set at each place. Amid them, Elizabeth Engle's sterling shimmered.

When, at six, the doorbell rang and the front door opened, Lawrence Engle and Don went at once to greet Stephen, who had come into the hall with another Jesuit.

"Stephen, let me look at you," Lawrence Engle said, taking his son by the arm and then embracing him with great emotion.

"Dad...Dad," Stephen said in a whisper, and hugged his father tightly. Then, turning from his father to his companion, "Dad...Don, you know Matthew..."

"Of course. Matthew, you're a member of this family, too."

Kathleen came in from the dining room.

"Oh, Stephen!" she said with a cry. "It's been so long!" Putting her arms around her brother's shoulders, she embraced him for a long moment until, remembering decorum, she stepped back and stretched out her hand to her guest. "Matthew. How wonderful you could come." She smiled up at the young Jesuit, her eyes shining.

Matthew was tall, at least six feet four, athletic and handsome, with prematurely graying hair and a warm, expressive smile. "It's good to be here," he said. "Like home." Everyone went into the study, where Lawrence Engle served Stephen and Matthew wine and he and Don had martinis.

Kathleen watched them from the doorway. *What a good-looking group we make*, she thought. She had changed out of a blouse and jeans into a dress of rose silk and put on a single strand of white pearls. Her father and Don were attired almost identically in navy blazers, gray slacks, and dark blue-and-red-striped ties; the two Jesuits were dressed for any occasion, anywhere in the world.

Dinner was a small feast—wild mushroom soup, tenderloin of beef, whipped potatoes, asparagus with hollandaise the way her mother used to make it, fruit, cheeses, red wine; for dessert, fresh strawberries with whipped cream, her father's favorite. Throughout the meal Kathleen sat, glowing, while "her men," as she thought of them, lavished praise on her. The dining room resonated with the tinkling of crystal, the ring of laughter and bright conversation.

At one point, Stephen turned to his father and remarked that Matthew had a natural gift for music. "He's never had a lesson," Stephen said. "He improvises completely by ear."

Lawrence Engle listened quietly, but an entire thought process passed across his face. After a moment's hesitation, he said to the young Jesuit seated at his right:

"Our piano hasn't been used in years, Matthew. Would you consider playing for us?"

Kathleen quickly glanced at Stephen to catch his eye, but he was looking at Matthew and didn't notice her. She lowered her head and thought excitedly to herself. What a step this was for their father! How healthy it would be for him to dismantle what, over time, had all but become a shrine. And who better than Matthew to play the piano for the first time after all these years?

Everyone moved across the hall to the living room when dinner was over. Lawrence Engle had changed very little in this room in the twenty years since his wife's death, and everything in it still reflected her taste. It was a warm, spacious room of beige and cream and soft blues, paled by age, with a bay window that looked out on maple trees and shaded lawn, a worn white sofa, a love seat, wing chairs, the elegant black of a grand piano at the far end.

Elizabeth Engle had been the only member of the family who played the piano; after her death it had been closed and its surfaces used as settings for pictures in remembrance of her.

The photographs showed her during the years of her marriage. On her honeymoon, a very slender young woman with a shy tilt to her head that suggested reserve, and a whimsical curve to her mouth that hinted at playfulness. At thirty, not a beautiful face but an appealing one—the expression eager, bright, and direct. At forty, a radiant mother, holding two-year-old Clare on her lap, Kathleen and Stephen, lanky young teenagers with dark, shining eyes and self-conscious smiles standing on either side.

The largest photograph was an eight-by-ten portrait that had been made for her forty-second birthday and was the last picture taken of her. Wearing a white silk blouse and pearl earrings, she sat resting her head against her joined hands in three-quarter profile. Her sharp, fine-boned features, shot in soft focus, appeared more idealized than they had been in life, the cheeks rounded, the skin poreless and fair. Her hazel eyes, made golden brown by the photographer's retouch, gazed past the viewer, into some unseen distance. So moving was the effect that Elizabeth Engle seemed more a mystic absorbed in prayer than a vivacious wife and mother.

Now Kathleen and Stephen collected the pictures and relocated them around the room. Picking up his mother's last portrait, Stephen took out his pocket handkerchief and gently polished the glass. Then he set the photograph on the table beside the sofa, centering it so that it was the first picture one saw upon entering the room. Some few feet away, Matthew stood admiring the piano.

"A Steinway. What a beautiful instrument." He ran his fingers lightly over the keyboard and, striking a chord, glanced at Lawrence Engle. He smiled. "It's a little out of tune," he said. "But never mind."

Matthew settled himself on the bench. His hands moved skillfully over the keys. In a pure, resonant voice he sang:

> "O Danny boy,
> The pipes, the pipes are
> calling..."

"Why, you're a tenor, too!" Kathleen exclaimed.

"Think what Broadway missed!" Don said with a laugh.

Matthew, half turned on the bench, sat picking out a melodic line with the fingers of one hand and speaking in a mock Irish brogue to a delighted Kathleen:

> "There's a tear in your eye
> And I'm wondering why,
> For it never should be there
> at all!

With such pow'r in your smile,
Sure a stone you'd beguile,
So there's never a tear drop
should fall
You should laugh all the while
And all other time smile,
And now, smile a smile for me…"

Swinging round, Matthew began to pound the keys vigorously and deftly work the pedals with his foot as he sang in a clear, lilting voice:

"When Irish eyes are smiling,
Sure, it's like a morn
in spring!
In the lilt of Irish
laughter
You can hear the
angels sing!"

Kathleen, holding her husband's hand, glanced toward the archway, where her father and brother stood listening. Lawrence Engle was standing to Stephen's left, leaning one shoulder against the wall, and something in his expression drew her attention to him and away from the music. *How alike they are*, she thought: the same modest demeanor, the same dark good looks—though the austere, nearly perfect facial symmetry of the father softened to a more sensitive finish in the son.

Lawrence Engle met his daughter's gaze just then, and his look was unmistakable: it was the look he gave to one he cherished—a banked intensity in the eyes, a reserved and tender smile, an almost imperceptible nod of the head, which acknowledged, "Yes, you've caught me gazing at you with open adoration."

Why, she thought, *it's almost as if I'm seeing him after a long separation. How handsome he is still. How gentle his eyes. But how tired the brow. I must tell you more often, how dear you are to me, Dad.*

Matthew was calling for them to join him in singing the final chorus. They sang it, Kathleen and Don and Matthew together, and as the song ended, Kathleen, wanting to hold on to the joyous mood, urged Matthew to play it one more time. Afterward, breathless and happy, she outdid both men in holding on to the words: *sure they steal your heart away.*

But Matthew was just now hitting his stride. Running his hands over the keys with a trill and giving a look toward the archway, he called out:

"Have Stephen come here."

Kathleen chuckled at Stephen's reserve as he walked the few steps to the piano, inclining his head a little, a smile breaking at the corners of his lips. A glance to her left, and Kathleen saw their father's face brighten as she stood with her husband on one side and her brother on the other, all three with their arms linked, holding each other.

"This was Father Stephen Engle's favorite request during our seminary days," Matthew said, looking back over his shoulder with a wink at Kathleen. Then briskly he began to play a spirited rendition of the drinking song from the operetta, "The Student Prince."

"And to think it was I who let this fellow into the house," Stephen said, laughing.

Matthew played "The Harp that Once Through Tara's Hall," "The Green Isle of Erin," and "Believe Me, if All Those Endearing Young Charms," while Kathleen and Don and Stephen sang softly in pure, muted voices.

During one of the pauses, Kathleen leaned forward and smiled at her father. "What would you like to hear, Dad?"

"Oh...I don't know, honey...maybe 'The Kerry Dance...'"

"'The Kerry Dance'..." Matthew said, reflecting. Tentatively, he picked out a few notes, trying to recall the correct musical phrase. He sat for a moment and concentrated. Then he said, "I have it."

Matthew leaned over the keyboard and began to play the haunting chords and to sing in a changed voice of heartache and longing:

> "Only dreaming of days gone by,
> In my heart I hear
> Loving voices of old companions
> Stealing out of the dear old music,
> Soft and sweet as in days of yore…"

Kathleen saw it first: a slight start that registered only at the fringe of awareness. Then, suddenly, knowing, she looked toward her father and felt her throat close.

Lawrence Engle was pressing his hands against his chest staring, not at her, but down, at the place where Stephen had been standing. In another instant, his legs gave way, and he fell heavily to the floor. Kathleen took hold of Stephen's arm and gave her brother such a violent shove in their father's direction that he stumbled and would have fallen if he had not caught himself with one hand.

Things happened too fast then. All around her vague figures passed back and forth. Men rushing. Voices calling. The world, moving away from her. At once wanting to know and fearing to know, Kathleen stepped toward her father.

He lay on his back at the entrance to the living room, his face ashen, his eyes wide with shock and pain. Stephen was on his knees beside him. He looked up and spoke to her.

"Kathleen. He's alive. He's had a heart attack. But he's alive. He has a pulse."

Don was kneeling opposite Stephen. She watched her husband performing CPR on her father, pressing down on his chest and then allowing it to rebound and then pressing down again, quickly, rhythmically, counting to one hundred, his words clipped, almost inaudible.

At the front door, Matthew stood staring out into the darkness of the street, waiting for the ambulance he had called for, a rosary dangling from his hands, his lips perceptibly moving.

All this happened in a short span of time, less than ten minutes. But to Kathleen it was as if a moment stretched on for hours. She seemed to stand at a remove, in a dream state in which time was suspended and nothing was real. Pale and shattered, she turned to look back into the living room, which had been the setting of such happiness. And then a chill ran through her, bringing her back to reality with a start.

Forgotten on a side table, stilled within the borders of her silver frame, her head resting on her hands in an attitude of unnatural repose, silent, serene, rapt with attention, Elizabeth Engle looked on.

—*m*—

Lawrence Engle lived until noon the next day, drifting in and out of consciousness, his son and daughter by his bedside in the cardiac care unit of the hospital to which the paramedics had brought him. Near dawn, he received the last sacraments of the Catholic Church for the second time, Stephen having administered them for the first time the night before. In late morning, the cardiologist Don Shearer had asked for appeared at the door of the room, a middle-aged man with a thoughtful face and a clear, direct gaze, tall and very thin, in a long white coat that accented his thinness. With a calm nod he signaled to Stephen, who alone realized he had come.

They met in the hall near the nurses' station, in the privacy of a window alcove. The doctor stood with his back to the light. He took out a pen, saying, "I need to show you where we're at."

On the top page of his clipboard he drew a rudimentary heart with valves and ventricles and arteries like tiny roots, and then at the lower right of the sketch, he traced a large spot.

He said, "Here you can see the clot, and how it's cut off blood flow to the heart. In these shaded areas, the heart muscle is dying."

The doctor paused to give Stephen a studied, unmistakable look. For a moment, neither man moved. They stood, each respectful of the other's world, each searching the other's face as if asking for an insight which, if shared, might alter fate.

Stephen was the first to speak, saying with effort, "I understand. Thank you for coming in on a Sunday. Please—know how grateful we are."

He walked down the corridor, reentered the room, and stepped around the white curtain that screened the bed where his father lay. At the foot of the bed, beside the room's lone window, Kathleen was dozing in the glow of late summer sunlight, her head bowed, her long hair loosened and falling like dark feathers. Her cream-colored heels, the left toe badly scuffed, lay scrambled beneath the hanging bed clothes. Stephen stood for a minute with his hand resting on her shoulder, thinking. He gave her down-turned head a long, considered glance, then he left her and went to their father.

He bent over and kissed his father's eyes, pressed his lips against his father's ear and said softly, "Thank you, Dad." It was in that moment that he heard other voices, saw other faces, disclosed, at a distance.

The boy of seven.

"All of the leaves are gone off our red maple, Mom."

"Why, they are!"

"Do you think the maple tree cried last night when the wind came through and blew off all its leaves?"

"Oh, Stephen, you're such a little poet!"

"Is death a bad thing?"

"No, honey." Soft hand rumpling his hair. "Stars die. Leaves on the trees die. Humans die. God, who is all-good and all-loving, wouldn't have made things that way if there wasn't something wonderful on the other side of death."

"What's dying like?"

Soft mouth against his cheek. "The wisest words I've ever read say that dying is like falling asleep in the arms of God."

Stephen felt a slight tug, a release, felt his father slip and fall softly away. He made the sign of the cross on his father's forehead and then, stepping back, he turned to his sister and said:

"Kathleen...he's gone...Kathleen."

"Oh, no!"

Kathleen got to her feet, stumbled over the shoes lying by the bed, and sank almost to her knees.

"Oh, Daddy, please don't go! Please don't go!"

Stephen caught her before she fell. "Kathleen." He raised her up and held her. "He knew we were here."

Kathleen buried her face in the black cloth of his suit jacket, shuddering. "Stephen, he suffered so."

"No, no, he didn't."

"He suffered so," she cried like a child.

—m—

"I didn't know on the day I made my first vows that it would be his last spring."

Clare, accompanied by two finally professed nuns, came home to see her father buried. When the car she was riding in turned into the drive of the family home on Oldbrook Road, the front door of the house opened and Kathleen and Stephen came out together.

In a black knit suit, her face colorless without makeup, Kathleen seemed frail and haggard, anxiety apparent in her oblique, fitful glances. Stephen, too, was changed. Without his Roman collar on, his hair tousled and soft, his face drawn from grief and lack of sleep, he looked at once more boyish and far older than his thirty-six years.

Beautiful, brave, and broken, they stood side by side on the front steps of the old two-story house, as if cast out, the gods of her childhood.

For the first time in her life, Clare felt herself their equal: an adult, who no longer needed to be understood and comforted, but one like them, who shared their sorrow and who could herself understand and comfort. This new sense of place in her family braced and fortified her outwardly, while inwardly she was torn by conflicting emotions.

She was at once a grown woman and a grieving child, yearning to recover the past, longing to return to the day of her first vows, to that final spring, when blossoms had told of recurring life and not of flowering graves; and she was an aspiring writer, determined to set down every detail of the events surrounding her father's death. However, in later years, these days would seem fluid and dreamlike, like images from an impressionistic painting, since reality had been blurred and intensified by great feeling.

—⁂—

The day of the funeral was a warm, overcast autumn day. Outside the Engle family home, scarlet leaves fell through the air. Blue jays hopped from branch to branch in the maple trees. Within the house, white bedsheets were spread on tables and chairs. Less than a mile away, mourners filed into the beautiful Gothic church of Saint Thérèse of Lisieux, where Lawrence and Elizabeth Engle had been married and where their children had been baptized and gone to school.

Because of his retiring lifestyle, Lawrence Engle had few friends remaining in later years. Several colleagues came from Loyola where he had been a professor, and many Jesuits were present, some who had known him professionally; others who were attending out of respect for his son.

One of these Jesuits Clare recognized at once, though she was meeting him for the first time. Eugene Dowd was an aging intellectual with a dignified stature and somewhat severe features, and a direct, penetrating gaze that intimidated her a little. He was one of three Jesuits, each dressed in a white chasuble with a high, wide cowl, who were concelebrating the funeral Mass.

A fourth priest, also wearing white vestments, sat alone on a wooden bench at the left of the altar, all eyes turned toward him. After the Gospel reading he stood and walked to the high lectern. In a low, beautifully schooled voice he quoted the lines:

"That best portion of a good man's life, his little, nameless, unremembered acts of kindness and love…"

Stephen had begun the eulogy for his father.

"Words from Wordsworth's 'Lines Composed Above Tintern Abbey,' words that describe our father, as if written for him. Such was his decency, his forbearance, his love…

"Forty-one years ago, a modest, even reticent, Lawrence Engle fell in love with a fiery, tender young woman named Beth Shannon and, from that moment until the day she died and further, until his own death twenty-one years later, he loved her dearly.

"He lived out the promise of the Irish air, 'Believe Me, if All Those Endearing Young Charms':

'It is not while beauty and youth are thine own
and thy cheek unprofaned by a tear
that the fervor and faith of a soul can be known…
No, the heart that has truly loved never forgets,
but as truly loves on till the close…'"

Stephen broke off and, looking to his left, sought the first row of pews, and met his sisters' eyes.

"For Kathleen, Clare, and myself," he affirmed simply, "theirs was the model of Christian marriage."

—⚭—

May choirs of angels escort
you into paradise
And at your arrival,
May the martyrs receive and
welcome you,
And lead you to the Holy City,
Jerusalem.

With the singing of the hymn "In Paradise," the funeral Mass ended.

Lawrence Engle would be laid to rest next to his wife in the century-old Gate of Heaven cemetery, once the Catholic graveyard for the entire county. To Kathleen would fall the responsibility of selling the family home and, with her husband's help (Lawrence Engle had named Don Shearer his executor), putting her father's affairs in order. Stephen was starting out for the university later that day, and Clare for the Juniorate. The adult Engle children were taking their leave of one another and, though for fear of grieving the others not one of them spoke of the strain of this parting, all felt it.

Evening was falling when the car returning to the motherhouse turned onto the highway. Seated alone in the back, freed from the need to enter into conversation, overcome with fatigue, Clare drifted off to sleep. From time to time she opened her eyes and stared absently through the window. To the left, she could see the sun spreading like a port wine stain upon the horizon, and the gray tiers of nimbostratus clouds that screened it like the fingers of a soft-gloved hand. The evening sky, drained of its color, mirrored her tiredness and, more than any human companion, relieved her sense of isolation. She laid her head against the seat back. The droning road, a loose tire thumping in the trunk, and soon, a drumming rain were lulling her back to sleep. And there was another reverberation, one she could not place.

Somewhere a door was swinging gently on its hinges, closing slowly. Its far-off thudding made a succession of soft, dull sounds, like that of objects lightly falling. It echoed the rhythmic pulsations she detected all about her, though it was separate from rain or road or tire.

She fell into a deeper sleep and the image came clearly into focus.

The front door of the Engle family home, lightly swinging in the wind, was closing by its own momentum: closing on the dreaming face of her beloved father; closing on the old two-story house in whose rooms she had stood for the last time that morning; closing, finally and irretrievably, on her childhood.

Clare shivered slightly in her sleep, tears of which she was unaware running down her cheeks.

Autumn Maple

What cry went forth last night,
Inaudible to me?
For this morning you stand
Before the opened window—shorn,
And, surely,
Such beauty was not torn from you
In silence.

— STEPHEN ENGLE, SJ
FOR MY FATHER

Part Two

Give me a man in love; he knows what I mean.
Give me one who yearns; give me one who is hungry;
Give me one far away in this desert, who is thirsty
and sighs for the spring of the Eternal Country.
Give me that sort of man; he knows what I mean.

— Saint Augustine

XI

When Stephen returned to the university, classes for the fall term had already begun.

On that first morning back, a soft golden September day, he paused on the steps of the liberal arts building and stood for a few minutes, taking in his surroundings.

It was an enclosed campus, evocative of an Old World village with its trees, its towers, and its winding lanes. To the right, long shadows fell through the arboretum, a double lane of lofty maples that formed a vast walled park along the edge of the grounds. To the left, the chapel bell tower rose, gray and otherworldly, behind a screen of dark firs. All around were ivy-covered buildings, with an old brick walk bordered with dark green boxwood running among them. Where the walk curved, a low footbridge over a pond at the south end of the college appeared through dogwood, beech, and cherry trees.

Inside the ivy-covered walls was another environment, the inspired world of literature, timeless and imperishable, which Stephen knew and hungered to impart.

He would be teaching two sections of "A Survey of English Literature" to freshmen, then a survey of American literature to freshmen and sophomores, and a course for upperclassmen and graduate students, "Theology of the Imagination." Because this last class allowed him a sweeping choice of subject matter and the clear potential for creativity, it would immediately become his favorite. For reading material he drew upon the resources that had been essential to his boyhood.

These were his love of words and his search for meaning in the central struggle of his youth—his striving to cope with the death of his mother.

The second-floor classroom assigned to him was long and narrow, with tall casement windows on one side and rows of desks grouped casually about the floor. A small steel desk by the window held several books: *Dubliners, The Collected Poems of W. B. Yeats, T. S. Eliot: The Complete Poems and Plays*, William James's *The Varieties of Religious Experience*, Cleanth Brooks's *The Well Wrought Urn*, and a collection of John Updike's short stories.

Later, on that warm morning in September, Stephen stood at the desk by the window, considering how to respond to one of his students. A young man had asked him to say something about why certain works of literature are regarded as classics, and endure, while others, though popular in their time, eventually are seen as lacking lasting significance, and fade.

After a long pause, Stephen turned away from the window. He walked over to where the young man sat and stood beside him. Nodding his head in understanding, he replied, "I think it has to do with authenticity.

"So much in our culture seems intent on making life something other than it is—by this I mean the avoidance of suffering and the denial of death. Great literature deals with these issues without equivocation."

Stephen went back to his desk and from the books assembled there, picked out a thick paperback, the collection of short stories. Looking around at the class, he went on:

"And so, when we read a story like John Updike's 'Pigeon Feathers,' we can identify with David, the young protagonist, who refuses to be deterred from coming to terms with the issue of death.

"Out of her own quiet despair, David's mother asks her son why this life isn't enough for him, while the worn pages of the family Bible mutely tell of his deceased grandfather's search for a higher purpose to human existence."

When, as a grief-stricken teenager, he had read the story and come upon David for the first time, something had been wrung from the young Stephen Engle, which, for a moment, showed itself by a slight tremor in the voice of the man. Pausing to collect himself, Stephen replaced the book on the desk, then he went on more evenly:

"Civilization has advanced to the doorstep of the twenty-first century and yet its sorrows remain the same as those of all preceding ages: the infinite divisions of the human heart, the tragic loss of young and gifted life, the worldly success of some of the least desirable of men, while countless others die impoverished, with what they might have been lost to history.

"Well, imagination, imagination in the sense Coleridge understood it—as the supreme creative faculty—enables us to transcend the forces that would seek to diminish us and to dream of existence in terms of its highest possibilities.

"Whether he meant them straightforwardly or in irony, two lines written by the Russian poet Alexander Puskhin are freighted with this meaning:

Not all of me is dust.
Within my song, safe from the worm, my spirit will survive.

The young people listened, rapt and moved by Stephen's passion for literature and his empathy for them.

These qualities of Stephen's—utter sincerity, coupled with an unselfish concern for those entrusted to him—were what allowed him, a young man honor-bound to a vow of chastity, to stay inviolate. By the end of his first year, he was thought of as at once the most approachable member of the staff, and the least accessible. He politely kept his personal life private. His students sensed intuitively his need to protect himself; not one of the women tried to bridge the psychological distance he maintained, though many silently fell in love with him.

—ⱳ—

She dwelt among the untrodden ways
Beside the springs of Dove,

A maid whom there were none to praise
And very few to love...

She was chalked in pastels, a slender young woman with long fair hair, pale, almost ivory skin, and intelligent blue-gray eyes that held an indefinable quality, akin to sensitivity, but more touching.

She sat in the back of the room in one of the seats nearest the door, and often she was the last student to arrive for class and among the first to leave. Until she approached Stephen as he sat at his desk one day in the autumn of 1986, his second year at the university.

"Father Engle..."

At the softly inflected enunciation of his name, Stephen looked up.

"Mary Ainsley," he said, smiling.

She spoke in a clear, quiet voice that had a slight quaver. "I have the idea for my master's thesis, but I don't have an adviser. Would you consider helping me?"

Stephen paused to think. "You might be better served by a more experienced member of the faculty, Mary," he said, declining the request, but in the tone of a man amenable to changing his mind.

"Father, when you speak to the class about the creative imagination...how it can enable us to transcend forces that might seek to diminish us..." She broke off. Then, coloring slightly, she went on:

"Those words resonate deeply with me."

Stephen stood and walked around his desk, pausing in the aisle a few feet away from her.

He said, "I'd like to hear your idea."

Mary sat down at one of the student desks and Stephen pulled a chair over for himself and sat down facing her. In her soft, serious voice, the young woman spoke from notes written in beautiful cursive on pages worn and curled at the edges, which she kept in a plump blue notebook now opened on the desk before her.

"Theories about the origin of language differ fundamentally. Cardinal Newman believed that thought and speech are inseparable. Many authorities hold that thought occasions language; and, conversely, some scholars propose that it's language that initiates thought.

"When, for example, the primitive person, or the young child, concentrates his entire self upon an object, he is lifted out of himself, creating out of the object a temporary god. In that moment, language arises."

Tense, the young woman paused and glanced at Stephen, who sat listening to her with intent, thoughtful eyes.

Mary continued, "The great Jesuit theologian Karl Rahner held that the poet restores to language the quality of immediacy, from which words have been cut off by what he described as the diminution of primordial words into utility words."

Stephen asked, "How would you distinguish one from the other?"

"Using the diamond as a metaphor," Mary said, citing Rahner's own writings as an illustration, "a utility word would be the diamond that is utilized as an industrial tool—for abrasives and glass-cutting, for example—while a primordial word is the precious stone, an object of contemplation, evoking wonder."

Mary sat back, her expression changing. The anxiety that had strained her features during her presentation fell away. Caught up in thought, she said:

"Do you know the beautiful line, 'Poems are gifts given to the attentive'? The words of poems are primordial words; if we pay attention, they allow us to see more deeply into reality." She paused, then added, "For my thesis, I'd like to examine the restorative power of poetic words."

Stephen did not respond at once. He was moved to say a world of things in reply, but for the time being, he decided to make only a brief comment.

"I think it sounds like an excellent project..."

"Would you consider being my adviser, Father?"

"Yes, I would," he said, rising. "I look forward to it."

Mary smiled, a flush of color spreading over her cheeks.

Struck by her obvious giftedness, Stephen stood to talk with her for a while, asking her what she had studied as an undergraduate, complimenting her on her grasp of Rahner's work, encouraging her to share her insights with the class.

Mary, thanking him, told him that she had majored in humanities, with an emphasis on the classics, and hoped to teach at the college level someday. Shyness in group settings was a trait she was trying to overcome, and still needed to work on.

When Stephen left the room, she was sitting again at one of the student desks, crossing out and adding words to her notes.

—⚏—

Overnight, golden October turned into leaden November. Along the walks, snowflakes blew like scattered ashes; a chill mist hung low over the pond at the south end of the college. Autumn by the calendar, yet winter had come.

Mary Ainsley edged her way in through the great door of the liberal arts building, shaking her fine pale hair loose from the shaggy dark hood of her parka and stamping her booted feet on the polished floor. She had come for her weekly appointment on her master's thesis, the fourth of such meetings.

Stephen's office, which he shared with a member of the staff who was on sabbatical, was a scholar's retreat, a quiet, sunlit room, three walls lined ceiling to floor with books. A few framed portraits, tinted a watery gray, hung on the window wall. They depicted the founder of the Society of Jesus, Ignatius of Loyola, and the Jesuit poets Gerard Manley Hopkins and Edmund Campion. Stephen's desk, centered in front of the long wall, faced the window and looked out through trees to the north end of the campus.

A great elm stood immense as a wall to the far left of the window. Waiting for Stephen, Mary watched a stiff wind punish the great tree.

As the last of its brown leaves scattered, several sparrows could be seen, bunched together and trembling, like small, drab scraps of cloth caught upon the swaying branches. The scene attracted the young woman's notice, not only because she was usually alive to visual images but also because that particular image—of birds cloistered within the branches of a great tree—held for her a personal meaning.

At his desk, Stephen sat looking over the outline of her thesis. When Mary turned around, he glanced up.

"This is excellent," he said. "Thorough and concise. Beautiful work." He rearranged the pages. "Have you considered including Hopkins?"

Mary sat down on the chair by the desk, the parka drawn about her shoulders. "I'd thought of introducing him, but I find his work difficult."

"You can't not use him, for all he'll give you."

Mary's eyes went to the nearby portrait of Gerard Manley Hopkins: a young, sad face, lean and angular, with a prominent, high-bridged nose and intense, vulnerable eyes. Never in robust health, Hopkins had died of typhoid fever when he was only forty-four.

His poetic vocation had evolved in an unusual way. Hopkins had written poetry as a young student.

However, when he entered the novitiate of the Society of Jesus, he made the extraordinary sacrifice of burning everything he'd written up until then; more, he resolved not to write poetry again, unless under obedience.

He did not write poetry, but he did keep a journal in which he set down his reflections on his daily experiences, on art, on nature, or on whatever struck him especially.

And during the seven years of his self-imposed silence, Hopkins became conscious of a fresh, original rhythm that was stirring in his mind, straining for expression. Then, unexpectedly, *The London Times* reported the story of the wreck of the German ship *The Deutschland* and the deaths of many of its passengers, five of whom were nuns. The superior at Saint Beuno's College, where Hopkins was a student, asked him to write about the tragedy. As soon as Hopkins relinquished his silence and set to work on the poem, he found his voice.

His genius was not fully understood during his lifetime. Only in later years did the Jesuits realize that the most gifted English poet of his generation had lived among them.

Stephen opened the top drawer of his desk and brought out a slender blue book with gilt edging: *The Poems and Prose of Gerard Manley Hopkins*, given to him at his ordination by his father. Turning it so that its title faced out, he handed the book across the desk.

"When you read him, think of Chaucer. Hopkins's work has a musical accent, going from strong beat to strong beat. Hopkins called it 'sprung rhythm,' scanning by stresses instead of by syllables."

Astonished by the gesture, not sure if Stephen meant that she should take the book, Mary sat uncertainly.

"It's yours for as long as you'd like," Stephen said.

Mary accepted the book, running her fingers lightly, deferentially, over the cover. "Thank you, Father. I'll return it quickly."

"There's no reason to hurry," Stephen said, smiling.

Slipping into her parka, zipping it, Mary lowered her head for a moment. She was turning a thought over in her mind. A painful secret weighed on her heart, a story she had never shared with anyone. Her teacher—who was also a confessor—had just shown her a high degree of trust. Looking up at him, she said:

"Father, for many years, I've kept a journal. Someday—if I can make it as good as I want it to be—I'd like to shape it into a book. Do you think...would you ever have time to read and evaluate it?"

Stephen, hearing the slight trembling of her voice, said, "I'm sure I would." He stood at his desk and began to fill a briefcase with papers. "I can't say how soon I'll be able to get to it, but yes, of course I would."

Stephen went to the door with her and, as they walked out into the hall, he asked, "Do you have a title for the book?"

"I've thought of several. At different times, one has more appeal than the others. If I were to decide today, I would use the title *Half-Hidden from the Eye*."

"From the Wordsworth poem?"

"Yes."

"Can you give me your journal for the Thanksgiving holiday?"

—⟊—

Stephen found the journal on his desk on Monday of the following week. Two weeks later, during the break for Thanksgiving, he kept his commitment to Mary Ainsley.

In late morning on the quiet Friday after the holiday, he went alone to his office and, taking out the journal and setting his other work aside, sat down at his desk to read.

Like all of the young woman's other compositions, the journal was written in small, beautiful cursive. Certain sections had such a polished feel that it was evident they had been reworked many times. Some passages had the quiet, reflective character of decanted sunlight, as if the author had distanced herself from the emotions tied to their memories; others indicated the terse restraint of a young woman unaccustomed to voicing her private thoughts. Most were unsettling. All held him.

This journal, begun when I was twelve and revised over the years, was intended to be a form of therapy (though I didn't know that term then), a record of my experiences growing up. I wanted to write out certain retrospections to make sense of them, while I was still young enough to remember things as they were, before my memories blurred and faded out, like a trail of footprints covered over with snow. And, perhaps, if my effort grew into the larger work I could imagine, I could encourage others who, like myself, have known traumatic childhoods.

For what I'm evoking is not an impersonal case study, but a living record of flesh-and-blood people, whose lives were entwined and held fast, not by love, but by pain.

Today, I imagine that I'm standing near a pool of water and looking down into the reflection of my life. Outwardly, the waters seem serene, but a slight disturbance and the accumulations of the past stir, and then, to the surface come the ugly stores. In my writing, I am plucking out, first, this marring piece, then the next, then the next, until I reach a state of inner peace where I can say, in the words of a Chinese poet:

> Down in my heart
> I have always been as pure
> As this limpid water is

My mother named me after her mother "in order to make things right," she said, but what that statement meant I never learned.

I remember my grandmother when she lived in her little bungalow with the enclosed front porch and the pointy roof; and later, when she moved to a one-room apartment at the Salvation Army home, taking with her the little radio that played only when it was upside down.

By then she had aged beyond her years. Tiny, frail, missing her teeth, she had lost all beauty, and she knew it, too. No longer was she the dark, pretty girl whose face shone in the oval frame amid the photographs and pill bottles beside her bed, but someone more like a gnome, with her projecting underjaw and the smile of which she was ashamed, only a fold across her face, like the pretend mouth children make with the index finger and thumb of their hands. But my grandmother's eyes were still lovely, and keen.

What went wrong between her and my mother? In the years I saw them together, childhood years, their communication was carried on, not in the rapid French in which they conversed, but in the *glances they exchanged in silence. And no one else was admitted to that secret dialogue.*

I was six when my father left for Vietnam, where he was killed the following year; but he and my mother had separated many times before that last parting...

Sunlight plays, dappled and tender, on the step where last I saw my father stand in the strange green clothes that meant to me then only that he was going away. When he bent over me, the sun behind him made a halo around his face. "I will come back for you, Mary," he said...

Whether her moods were the reason for my father's repeated leaving, or whether his departures were what caused her to descend into deepening despair, I will never know, but after he left for the final time, something unhinged my mother.

She had always walked on an edge, a little different from other people, suspicious, distrustful, more vulnerable to the ups and downs of everyday life. But then her moods became unpredictable, and darkened. From depression, from apathy, she passed to destruction—and she turned against me...

When what I did upset her—if I broke something or forgot something, or if I were awkward or slow—she lashed out, threw things, broke things, screamed she would kill herself, because of me.

What made my mother fly into rages, and scream that she wanted to die? For, in one way or another, she was always dying, it seemed: the illnesses that turned out not to be illnesses, the threats of suicide...

I was not allowed to cry; the only one with the need to cry, my mother said, was she. And so I tried to stop crying. I learned to make my face very stiff and my inner self very still.

She said that I acted only to get attention. And so, I tried to be very quiet and stay in the background, so that no one would notice me. As the months turned into years, her paranoia worsened; she pulled the shades in all the rooms: the neighbors, she murmured, *were watching her. Her hostility toward me grew; sometimes she locked me out of the house: I was the one, she swore, who was turning everyone against her.*

She gave me a warning: I was to tell no one about what happened in our house. I never did.

Just as happens when storm clouds discharge their burden and rumble away, periods of normalcy would come, the dark moods would vanish, and my mother would return to herself. She would draw a funny face on the shell of the soft-boiled egg in my little cup; take down from the closet shelf and share with me the box of photographs of herself, of her parents, of their home in Maine when she was very small…

When she was her normal self, my mother seemed fragile and defenseless, and I wanted to protect her. She evoked "The notion of some infinitely gentle/infinitely suffering thing," as T. S. Eliot once wrote.

My mother was an anemone, a flower of sensitive beauty. Like the wood anemone, she needed protection from the wind and sun. With its solitary white blossoms, born on weak stalks, the flower, like my mother, was made for the shelter of the wild garden.

But there are two anemones. The other is a creature that only resembles a flower. It also is beautiful, with arms like waving petals. There on the sea floor it lifts those arms in a continual invitation to embrace, and then trap.

And the pain of my childhood was the need to inhale the flower and to beware of the creature that only eats and eats.

When he read these lines, Stephen pressed his face into his hands and shook his head in disbelief.

I grew into an extremely shy and sensitive child, longing to take part in life, fearing I would never be able to.

Can a small child feel despair? Yes.

When I read descriptions of cold wastelands where the lives of prisoners drain away in a silent effacement of the spirit, I know, I remember those places.

I channeled all of my dreams and aspirations into intellectual pursuits. Maybe I left parts of myself behind in childhood, but other parts grew, grew into adulthood. They are the parts that will survive.

What saved me was my love of language. I clasped words to myself like strange, exquisite birds and withdrew with them into my inner world. There they warmed me, there they sang to me, and there their singing fed my dreaming. Even today, on a lost limb of childhood, they perch in delighted song. But I am free now, and the words, in all their tremulous beauty, are mine to release or mine to call home.

Here the journal ended.

—✄—

"Have a seat, Mary," Stephen said, indicating the chair he had placed beside his desk for her. After the young woman sat down, he took out the journal and said:

"Thank you for entrusting me with this extraordinary memoir. Many passages are beautiful and extremely moving. Some parts are very painful to read. I marvel at how you survived. You're a kind of miracle."

With great tact he asked her, was her mother still living? If she was, what was their relationship like now? Was there anyone to help her with her college expenses?

"Yes, my mother's still living. I left home when I was seventeen. I hadn't planned to, but one day, in one of those strange moods that came over her, my mother locked me out. I didn't know what to do. I ended up taking the bus to the home of my great-aunt, my father's aunt Jo. She took me in and for three years I lived with her."

Mary looked off into the distance for a moment. Then she said, "I see my mother once in a while. I don't know how to help her. Her animosity toward me is fierce.

"I paid for college with scholarships and grants. After graduation, I worked for five years to earn the money for graduate school. That's why I'm older than most of the other students."

"Your journal...the phrase from Wordsworth?"

"I thought of *Half-Hidden from the Eye* because that's the way troubled relationships are. At times, someone—a teacher, a relative, a neighbor—may sense something is amiss: a bruised eye, an overly delicate sensibility, a more than ordinary sadness about a child..." Mary paused for a long moment with her eyes downcast, but Stephen did not interrupt her silence.

She continued, "I want to say that in cases like that I wish someone would act, become involved. And yet, a part of me feels like I'm committing a kind of betrayal: in writing about my childhood, in going into details with you, am I being disloyal?"

"No. Your writing is exactly as you described it, a form of therapy. The same is true of our conversation here."

Stephen asked her whether she knew that counseling was available on campus, so that she didn't have to carry around memories he was certain must be overwhelmingly stressful at times. With personal conviction, he explained his belief that grieving for a loss was important, even the loss of something one has never known, and surely, she needed to grieve for the childhood denied to her.

Mary sat beside the desk, listening with total attentiveness. But there was a moment when she stopped hearing Stephen's words and became absorbed with another flow of thought. She reflected that Stephen did not talk about himself at all. She wondered whom he talked with when he was lonely or discouraged. She wondered who cared about him when he was tired or ill. Her heart had begun a long, slow turning.

—m—

The seminar in Yeats ended in mid-December. For her final paper in the course Mary wrote on Yeats's poem "An Irish Airman Foresees His

Death." Afterward, Stephen asked her if he could make a copy of her essay for his files. "Passion in a Cold Light" stood out because of its pointedness and directness, and because of the power of its conclusion:

The poem reiterates Yeats's high and lonely melody, his desire to escape the ravages of this world, his belief in a calling that led him far from the crowd, literally 'above it.' Imagination has in a sense made him a 'blessed-cursed' figure. Cursed, because alone; blessed, because it is the faculty of imagination which frees him from being 'blinded by death.' The world as imagination sees it is the lasting world...The last lines sing of the world of impermanence, which poetry transcends because it endures.

—∾—

It was an afternoon in mid-January, white, with numbing cold; the winter sun hung low in the sky, pale as an early moon. Catching an angle of light, the snow-laden branches of trees shone like mother-of-pearl.

At his desk, Stephen sat concentrating on the rough draft of a short story just now given to him. Sitting across from him, the spare light touching her, Mary read Wallace Stevens to divert her thoughts.

When Stephen had finished the first chapter, he turned back to glance at the opening paragraph again:

"As soon as Laura entered the room, she turned off the light and hurried to the window. One hand holding back the curtain, she stared out across the road. How tense it was, waiting for the storm to begin. The lightning over the mountains thrilled her. It spread like the branched extensions of a nerve cell, from the empyrean to the horizon—taut, living, supernaturally white. *The finger of God*, she thought."

Looking up from that line, Stephen said, "I like the two levels of tension—one within nature, one within the human psyche—and the metaphor of the dendrite very much." He collected the manuscript pages, arranged them and, half rising, handed them to Mary across the desk.

"Won't you show your work to someone who teaches creative writing?"

Mary shook her head. "Thank you, but no, I can't...not yet."

"Would you like me to do it?"

"No, thank you, I wouldn't...I don't have the courage...Writing isn't my hobby. It's my heart...my spirit. I've staked everything on it. To approach it as a course of study...no, I couldn't..." Wanting to explain further, but not quite knowing what to say, she concluded her thought in the only way she could at that moment, with a shy tilt of her head, a graceful, artless shrug, a poignancy in her eyes that said, "I'm sorry. Just now, words fail me. Please understand."

And Stephen, moved by what he considered an incredible misstatement—that she lacked courage—comprehended that look.

"Show your writing to me then," he said. "And when you give me permission, I'd like to share it with someone I have in mind."

In the failing winter light Stephen watched her, thinking. How still she was. He felt like someone who had wandered into a strange wood and come upon a rare and delicate flower on the forest floor, its beauty unfolding in secret and out of season. For a brief, privileged moment, while she was his student, he was the first to glimpse the promise that others would recognize in time.

He said, "Writing can be your life's work, if that's what you want."

Mary was quiet for a moment. Then she said, "To study great literature...to live, attempting to reach that height—if just once—that's what I wish for."

Stephen looked at her, deeply affected. Never had he experienced with anyone such a sense of peace and completion as the deep and wordless understanding of each other that flowed between himself and Mary Ainsley in that moment.

—〰—

More and more they were being drawn together by their scholarly dedication to excellence in literature and in life, and protected—for a time—by a refined inner sense of each other's autonomy and by the unspoken boundaries that defined and constrained them.

With Mary Ainsley, Stephen was experiencing his first deep friendship with a woman who was his intellectual equal. The young woman's lack of self-pity for the deprivations of her childhood, the eagerness and facility with which she learned, the originality of her thought, the trusting gaze of her clear blue-gray eyes—all of these affected him profoundly, recalling to his mind words from Eliot's "Preludes," which Mary herself, referring to her mother, had used in her journal:

> *The notion of some infinitely*
> *gentle*
> *Infinitely suffering thing.*

—⚏—

"When you think of Hopkins and Joyce," Mary said one day, "Hopkins, a Jesuit, and Joyce, taught by Jesuits, each believing in the power of language to astonish, to reveal beauty. Isn't it ironic that Hopkins imagined an Incarnational view of the world that enabled him to unite physical and spiritual beauty, but when Joyce came to be at peace with mortal beauty, his faith passed away?"

Stephen, for some reason feeling strangely disconcerted by the thought, hesitated before answering, "Yes…yes, it is."

—⚏—

Spring returned to the campus. Outside Stephen's office, mourning doves, nesting in a crevice in the eaves, filled the early hours with a soft, recurring *coo-roo*. The new leaves of the elm hung before the pane, delicate as tatting. Like fragrant perfume, the scent of lilacs came up from the grounds below.

Mary, struggling with her deepening love for Stephen and the inconceivability of sharing her thoughts with anyone, found a confidante in nature. Fragile, liquid, blue-gray, mute: spring that year seemed to mirror her inner world.

At the same time she was experiencing a rush of creative thought, discovering that, without trying for it, she could write at the height of her ability. Never before had words and images come to her more naturally.

Once, having spent most of the night working on the final draft of her thesis, she had two separate and wholly different poems come to her, fully formed, suddenly, the next morning. Meeting with Stephen later that day, Mary submitted the draft and gave him a copy of the first poem.

> *Masses of birds*
> *The wild, uncomprehending*
> *Thoughts of my childhood.*
> *Now, with an autumnal instinct,*
> *They have found direction:*
> *And oh!*
> *What flight!*

Stephen returned it to her a few days later. Across the bottom of the page he had written: "Beautiful. Both the words and the event they celebrate."

Torn by conscience, convinced she was seeing things that weren't there, unwilling to tell Stephen of her feelings and thus distress him, Mary struggled with the second poem and, in the end, destroyed it.

> *As expected, I found lilacs*
> *Newly blooming;*
> *For these I've spent the morning*
> *And have gathered in an armload.*
> *Your face, open just now*
> *And waiting,*

More vulnerable to cold:
I rush, having been unaware
Love would show itself today.

Mary sat on the edge of her bed, staring at the torn scraps of paper that had been her poem. Outside the window of her small apartment, rain was falling in a drizzle so fine one could see it only where it fell against the light of the streetlamps. Beyond the arboretum the chapel bell tower rose, barely discernible, against a black ground of firs; far to the right the long low profile of the law library disappeared into shadow. She had never felt more alone.

She would never get over him, never forget him. His memory would live on in her mind until the end of her life, in eternal springtime. But now the hour had come when she could bear her inner conflict no longer.

Mary decided she must leave the university. She would write Stephen a letter afterward, telling him what he had meant to her and explaining why she had gone away. But when she began to think about the letter, she felt that to part from him that way would be cowardly and unworthy of the bond of trust between them. No, she would tell him about her decision to leave school in person, trying her utmost not to let him know how hard all of this would be for her.

Stephen became aware that someone was standing in the doorway and looked up from his desk. The afternoon sun cast its light through the window, directed its light in a stream toward the door. She stood, diaphanous and fair, her hair sifted by sunlight, saying to him:

"May I talk with you, Stephen?"

Stephen got to his feet. "I can't right now, Mary," he said. "I have to finish this project by four." He glanced at his watch. "It's three ten now." He hesitated. Then he said, "I'll be free tomorrow at this time."

He stood behind his desk, his hands resting on the papers strewn there, and looked at her. More with eyes than voice he said, "I'm sorry."

Mary turned away to walk slowly back to the juncture of the main hall. She could think of no place to go. She wanted only to return to a time when she had felt nothing at all.

A secretary from the front office—a plump, tidy woman in a blue suit and thick black shoes like the ones the nuns wore—came into the corridor and addressed her.

Holding out a boxed set of books, she asked, "Would you take this back to Stephen Engle for me?"

"I don't think he wants to be disturbed," Mary said, reluctant to return to the room she had just left.

The secretary laid a dimpled hand on Mary's arm. "Just knock on the door and leave it on a chair," she said with a smile. "He's been asking about these books for weeks."

Carrying the box, Mary retraced her steps to Stephen's office. To her surprise, the room was empty when she arrived. Books, papers were still spread out upon the desk, but Stephen was gone. The two offices she had just passed were unoccupied; the only other door, at the end of the hall, led outside.

The bell in the chapel bell tower was striking 3:30 as Stephen crossed the quadrangle and entered the arboretum. He stood, tense and moved, looking down The Nuns' Walk. The broad corridor of stately maples was deserted at that hour. Everything seemed pristine, ethereal—the long shadows, the sunlight spilling like sprays of wisteria amid the dark branches, the whisper of the air in the upper aisles of leaves—an intact beauty, "pure with the passing of saints through a wood."

He had never made a decision more painful than the one he had reached now. He loved her, and he would not let that love be diminished or profaned by considering it a weakness or a temptation. They had not sought each other out; had they worked among a thousand, among ten thousand, they would have been drawn to each other.

But they could not continue to work together. He would ask one of his colleagues to be her adviser. Her life would go on, like a road turning off in the distance and becoming lost to sight, and he would have no part in it. That could not matter. What mattered was that she fulfill her promise as a writer, and that she someday have a home, a family, and a husband who could give himself wholly to her.

His need was to protect her from the trauma of yet another loss in life, knowing how much this parting would cost her, and him.

These were the thoughts he turned over and over in his mind, walking slowly now, on the wooded lane.

—⁂—

The next day, Stephen was waiting in the doorway of his office when Mary arrived. He seemed to her thoughtful and more tired than usual, though his eyes had the same alert, patient focus, and he gazed at her warmly.

He told her, "I've blocked out an hour of time and let the front office know I don't want to be disturbed."

Stephen turned to go into the room, but Mary hesitated and still stood in the doorway.

He walked back to her. "What's wrong, Mary?"

"Stephen...I..." She stepped to her right, swaying a little. Her head brushed the wall. She was suddenly so weary words wouldn't come. At last she said:

"I won't be able to finish my thesis...not this year."

Years earlier, as a child denied the right to express her feelings, she had learned to shelter her inner life with the tremulous external poise she strained for now, looking away shyly, a hand rising up to her eyes.

"I have to withdraw from the university."

"Withdraw? I don't understand." Yet even as he said this, Stephen realized that he understood completely. He gestured to her. "This isn't the place to talk. Let's go inside."

But Mary, afraid to go into the room with him, wanted to say everything she had prepared in her mind, there, in the hall.

"Please…I can't…" The self-restraint she had counted on was failing her. "I don't know what else I can do." The words came out shattered. "I've fallen in love with you, Stephen."

She was standing with her back to him, just outside the entrance to the office. A few steps away, Stephen saw her shoulders quiver and knew that she was crying. He reached out his hand, then quickly dropped it.

"Look at me, Mary," he said.

"I can't…I'm so sorry…I shouldn't have come here…I should have written you…"

"Look at me, Mary."

She turned around in the doorway.

Through her tears their eyes met, and in Stephen's glance Mary Ainsley saw a tenderness she could not misunderstand. Without saying anything more, Stephen motioned her inside and closed the door behind him.

—⁂—

It was midmorning, the next day. Stephen entered the faculty office and went to the mailbox wall. His box was empty, except for a slip of blue paper. Before he could stop himself, he let out a groan. Ainsley, Mary E. withdrew from the university.

—⁂—

She dwelt among the untrodden ways
Beside the streams of Dove,
A maid whom there was none to praise
And very few to love:
A violet by a mossy stone,
Half-hidden from the eye!

Fair as a star, when only one
Is shining in the sky.
She lived unknown, and few could know
When Lucy ceased to be:
But she is in her grave, and, oh,
The difference to me!

———

During the consultation the older Jesuit sat with his back to the window, his head bent to one side, one arm extended on the desk in front of him. From time to time as he listened he made a note on a sheet of paper in a large, even hand. Then he would look up again, focused. His eyes were soft and thoughtful through the lenses of his wire-framed glasses; his smile was wry and quiet. The Reverend James McCullough, S.J., was a tall, well-built man in his seventies, with a full head of white hair, heavy white eyebrows, and a firmly modeled cleft chin; now semiretired, he had been a professor of psychology and religion.

Across the desk from him, in the shadow of a moving grillwork of leaves, Stephen was seated. His face was candid, serious, intent, now engraved by light, now darkened by shadow and broken into shards. He was speaking very determinedly in a quiet voice.

"I think of her alone, her plans for her thesis ended, her life turned upside down...I'm responsible for that." He looked down at the floor. "She came from an emotionally deprived background...trusted me. I should have seen what was happening and prevented it."

"How old is she?"

"Twenty-eight," Stephen said.

"You aren't her parent, you know." McCullough cleared his throat and was quiet a minute. Then he said, "What you failed to see was your own vulnerability to someone so much like yourself."

Stephen, looking up, queried with his eyes.

"Oh, not in your backgrounds, certainly," McCullough said. He sat forward and leaned his arms on the desk, wanting to be understood. "But as I listened to you sketch a portrait of a sensitive, gifted student, committed to excellence, already demonstrating significant achievement, I could imagine I was also hearing someone else describing Stephen Engle to me.

"Add to that mix your protective instincts for a young woman you view as fragile and defenseless...well..." He sat back in his chair and gave Stephen a sympathetic smile. "It's a difficult struggle, isn't it?"

"Yes, Father, it is."

"What would help?"

Stephen stroked the back of his neck. "Work."

"How many classes are you teaching?"

"Four."

"Does studying a language interest you?"

The remark stirred a warm memory, the remembrance of Eugene Dowd. "Greek," Stephen said. "I could study Greek, with the intention of teaching it someday." After a pause, he added, "And I can work on another degree."

"That would be a heavy load, Stephen."

"It's what I need to do."

"Then it's what you should do."

His chair scraping on the hardwood floor, McCullough stood. He asked confidentially:

"Can you manage this?"

"With time, yes."

Stephen rose and went to the window and stood looking out, resting his eyes on something lambent and lovely, overhanging the pane. All the while they had been talking it had been there, impinging on his consciousness; now he took it in fully.

The long, arching branch of a great maple, transformed by the rains of late May, its tender, newly formed leaves glistening in the late-afternoon sun, seemed to him in that moment to be the likeness of the lost limb of childhood on which a dream-stricken young girl had once placed for safekeeping the secret poems of her soul; and he stood, transfixed, unable to take his eyes away from the scene.

At last, controlling himself, he turned back to McCullough.

"But the worry's a different thing," he said, his voice catching on the words. "I'll always worry about her."

XII

For Stephen, a new period in his life was beginning, months characterized by a deepening asceticism and a commitment to scholarship that was exceptional even for him. Unexpectedly, the sense of delight a teacher finds in witnessing a surprising advance in the development of a talented student came to him again—this time from a familiar source.

Dear Clare,

On my desk is a copy of Christian Comment, *opened to an article on the Jesuit martyr Edmund Campion. I was so impressed with the quality of the writing that, after I'd finished reading, I looked back to learn the name of the author. When I saw "Sister Clare Engle," I nearly fell out of my chair. Congratulations! It's a very fine article.*

You even mentioned that Shakespeare made use of Campion's History of Ireland. *Much has been written about Campion's genius, but that connection is seldom noted.*

I want to compliment you on using a light hand in describing his martyrdom. It has always seemed to me tragically ironic that a man with one of the finest intellects of his time was the victim of such butchery. "His eloquence died on the air, his genius was quenched in his blood…" Your wonderful quote from Hopkins.

Great work! I hope there'll be more.

Yours,
Stephen

Dear Stephen,

Thank you for your letter of encouragement. I'd hoped you would come across the article on your own and wondered if you'd like it. I'm going to be doing an entire series of articles on martyrs, so you may be seeing more.

Stephen, I'm the youngest sister in the history of the community, and the only temporarily professed ever to have something published professionally. I trace my success back to you, my first teacher, who impressed on me the importance of reading, and building a vocabulary, and daring to dream.

With Love,
Clare

Stephen went over the letter several times, smiling as he read; then he folded it, returned it to its envelope, and placed the envelope within the pages of his copy of *Poems and Prose of Gerard Manley Hopkins*.

—⁓—

But, unknown to Stephen, Clare was not thriving.

Soon after entering the Juniorate she had decided that after she had taken her final vows she would dedicate herself to the contemplative life. To her delight, her classmate Allyson Martin felt the same pull to the cloister and a life lived "without compromise."

Both young women aspired to bring to fruition in contemplation what one realizes through a great and serious love: the ascension from self-absorption to selflessness.

But they were still temporarily professed sisters and, together with seven other Juniors in the classes ahead of them, were under the direction of the Junior Mistress.

Authority in religious communities is centered in the Superior General and emanates downward, not unlike higher and lower rank in the military. At the motherhouse of the Sisters of the Sacred Heart, three women held positions of leadership.

First and most evident of these was Reverend Mother, a thoughtful, highly refined woman, tall and striking, but past eighty and in declining health. Another was the Mistress of Novices, Clare's adored Mother Mary Bernard. Each of these women used her influence for the spiritual good of the community; neither sought power for its own sake.

The third, Mother Helena, had been a superior in various houses of the community for twenty years before she returned to the Motherhouse as Mistress of Juniors. Short and heavyset, with a puffy, pear-shaped face, pale, near-sighted eyes, a small sensual mouth, and an indistinct chin that receded into fleshy jowls, she was a singularly ungainly woman. Her attractiveness was in the force of her personality. She had great intelligence and great charm and therefore great charisma, which blinded many to her capricious, autocratic side.

With uncanny intuition and a particular instinct for the vulnerable, Mother Helena had perfected the ability to draw impressionable young women to her and make herself indispensable in their lives.

"Lean on me; let it be my problem, too," she coaxed in a lovely trill when, in a moment of need, a Junior sister came to her for counsel. "Trust me, and you will see the kind of nun I can make." And, opening her heavy arms, making a show of affection, she turned her cheek for her young charge to kiss, in this way requiring the Junior sister to affirm her acquiescence.

Deep-seated, troubling inadequacies concealed themselves in these effusive displays, and it was to assuage them that Mother Helena encouraged dependency in others. Her needy appetites protruded into the flesh — the pale, fleshy hands, the sensual mouth, the rounded torso, its abdomen hillocky and high, the heavy step accompanied by audible, deeply drawn breaths, as if the Junior Mistress, in merely crossing a room, were scaling a flight of stairs.

She was egoism clothed in the disguise of magnanimity, and she hoarded her young charges like someone who has an exclusive cache from which she secretly eats at night. It was Mother Helena's pattern to choose certain sisters to be her favorites and, selectively, to slight others. Shy, lovely, timid Allyson Martin she singled out to be her protégé; Regina Palm, with her awkward, mannish ways, she ignored; Clare she rejected.

Clare, who looked on professed nuns as if they were living exemplars of perfection, and had perceived Mother Helena as understanding and generous, was stunned and dismayed.

The rejection was subtle and arbitrary and therefore more cruel. Clare had no defenses against it. Nothing she could do would please the Junior Mistress, who seemed to misinterpret her intentions at every turn.

Like her father, like Stephen, Clare kept pain to herself; like a good religious, she accepted hardship as a trial, and as an opportunity—if one were willing to pay the inner cost—to identify with Christ. And so, for a long time she did not think she should speak of her troubled relationship with the Junior Mistress to Mother Mary Bernard; and then, before she could bring herself to do so, fate intervened.

One night in late July, 1987, Mother Mary Bernard was alone in her room when she suffered a massive stroke and died. The next morning one of the novices found her lying on the floor at the foot of her bed, her arm straining for, but failing to reach, the half-open door. Whether the stroke had caused her to collapse, or whether the Mistress of Novices had fallen, and the fall had brought on the stroke, was unknown.

Unlike the time of her father's death, when she had shared the devastating loss with her brother and sister, Clare endured this death by herself, grieving terribly.

—⁂—

By tradition, Mother Mary Bernard lay in state in a simple pine box, in the brown habit and black veil of a professed nun, a black wooden rosary intertwined around her fingers. The great front parlor where she lay had been darkened, its fringed red draperies drawn against the heat. On a prie-dieu at each end of the coffin, an elderly nun knelt, praying aloud, the aged voices merging in a low, discordant, ceaseless incantation of the rosary.

A long procession of nuns was making its way into the parlor. One by one, each member of the community filed past the coffin, paused for a moment to pray for the repose of the soul of the deceased, then walked the length of the room through a set of French doors, and stepped out into the marble corridor that went back to the cloister.

Struggling to compose herself, Clare waited near the end of the line until, through the glass of the first set of French doors, she sighted the coffin and caught a glimpse of the face she longed to, dreaded to see. She was acutely aware of sounds all about her—the shuffling of feet, someone clearing her throat, whispering, snatches of a conversation. The noises got on her nerves, made her fear that, distracted, she might miss the only moment she would have at Mother Mary Bernard's side. To relieve her anxiety, she lowered her head and talked quietly to herself.

If only everyone else could pass by the coffin and leave her alone for a few minutes to say good-bye properly, to thank Mother Mary Bernard, to tell her: "I will love you always and never, never forget you. In my mind, you are pure gold." To tell her: "No, you were not my real mother. You were more. You were my true mother…"

She had reached the catafalque with the coffin on it. She took one step, then another, and stood alone in front of the coffin, made the sign of the cross, braced herself, and looked down.

In the past, when other nuns had lain in state in this parlor, Clare had been disconcerted to observe how dying had altered their expressions, conferring a startling sameness and divesting them of individuality in death. But the barrenness of Mother Mary Bernard's features shocked her.

A grim, resolute line replaced the sweet, expressive turn of the mouth, creased with wrinkles that ran off the lips into the face, embedding themselves like scars upon the flesh. The slender, agile hands, interlaced with a rosary, were folded in an unnatural repose. Now that the tension of life was over, the muscles of the dead nun's face had slackened, flattened out, and lost all vitality, as if Mother Mary Bernard had released a great sigh and, in that instant, been arrested for all time.

In the days when she had been a young nun laughing under the elms, had there been any suspicion of these gray lips, these gray lids, these gray hands?

Clare could look no more and yet would look forever. The incessant droning of the incongruous voices, the darkened room with its stale odors, the seemingly indifferent stares of the other nuns—all these impaled her heightened senses. She was a solitary observer, looking on a scene that others, comprehending, could contain; she could only behold and endure, and her vulnerability frightened her. And then she had passed.

—⚭—

In the week following Mother Mary Bernard's death, Clare had one of the intensely lifelike dreams to which she was given.

Mother Mary Bernard, restored to the time when she had been a teacher at Saint Thérèse of Lisieux, wearing a simple blue dress, her unfashionably gray hair gathered into a neat chignon, was sitting alone at a table in vague sunlight, erect and strong, a small book with a yellow binding lying in her lap. Her lips parted upward in a beautiful smile when Clare appeared in the doorway.

Clare crossed the floor and eased herself onto a chair, overcome with joyful confusion.

Again the radiant, opal eyes engaged her; again the warm, hushed voice entreated, "What's he like, your dad?"

And it all rushed back to her, exactly how it was—the long-ago November afternoon, the empty classroom, snow falling softly outside the window, and, in front of her, that wonderful, worn face, knowing.

"Go on. Isn't there someone else?"

"Oh, yes!" Clare answered, the word coming out tremulously. "You! How hard it is, Mother! I pray for acceptance, but I'm handling things badly." She dropped her head into her hands and cried. "I was always so confident. But in a time of crisis, I'm not brave. I'm not strong. I'm weak, and I doubt..." She looked up at Mother Mary Bernard.

The nun did not say anything, but gazed at Clare with a look of pro-found tenderness. Lifting the opened book she held in her slender hands, warm and pink again with life, she held it out for Clare to take. With trembling hands, Clare accepted it. The page Mother Mary Bernard had offered her contained lines from the writings of Julian of Norwich:

See, I am God: see, I am in all things:
See, I do all things: see, I never lift my
hands off my work, nor ever shall...
All shall be well and all manner of things
shall be well.

—⁕—

But Clare continued to struggle. In the fall of 1987—two months after the death of Mother Mary Bernard—she fell ill with mononucleosis. For five days she lay weak and feverish in the infirmary. When her health improved, she returned to her room and convalesced there. Yet for months after her fever and sore throat had abated, she was still plagued with headaches, nausea, and fatigue. For the first time in her life dis-couraging easily, she hungered for the Junior Mistress's reassurance. But Mother Helena continued to treat her with the same air of disregard.

The role of outcast, of child held in disfavor, bewildered and frus-trated Clare. Lonely, apprehensive, having no one to turn to, she strug-gled through the winter, through Lent, to Easter, then to mid-June, and the eight-day retreat before final profession. Prayer and her studies—the everyday rituals of religious life—these sustained her. But by mid-June, her disappointingly slow recovery from mononucleosis, Mother Helena's disapproval of her, and the loss of Mother Mary Bernard had brought her to a point she would once have believed impossible. She had begun to doubt her vocation.

—⁕—

On an afternoon in mid-June, at the end of the eight-day retreat, Clare sat alone in the second-floor hall of the motherhouse.

Each sister about to make her final profession was required to have an interview with the Junior Mistress. Allyson Martin had met with Mother Helena two days earlier. On the last day of the retreat, the Junior Mistress had scheduled appointments with Clare and Regina Palm, talking to Regina first. Over an hour had passed since the door had closed behind them.

Clare sat trying to concentrate her thoughts, but was unable to. The air in the hall was warm and close. A claustrophobic feeling, heightened by the prolonged delay, made her feel tense and light-headed. Nothing was as it should be. She had looked forward to this week as the happiest of her life; instead, she dreaded the isolation of the long, silent days strangely drained of meaning. Only by strength of will would she get past them.

She raised her head and looked about her. The hall was gray and high-ceilinged. To the left, a series of doors lined the walls, the last door on the far left, the Junior Mistress's; to the right, a great window stood at the head of a wide staircase that went down to the first floor. From there one could see the approach to the motherhouse and the corridor of great elms that stretched in a long, dark sweep to the perimeter wall where wildflowers blew along a country road.

Maybe it happened when she was focusing on her coming talk with the Junior Mistress and she hadn't noticed, she wasn't sure, but the overcast had ended. The great leaden bank of clouds in the sky to the west had parted and the brightening sun was glistening like strewn diamonds in the trees along the drive. Looking on, Clare yearned suddenly to get up, to throw off the weight of ill health and disillusion and run toward that breaking light opening out and spreading over the earth like a grace. Mother Helena's door opened. Regina Palm came out and headed up the hall with lowered eyes, rubbing the bridge of her nose in a gesture of self-comfort. Clare saw her face.

Conversation during the week of retreat was not permitted. Wanting to reach Regina, Clare leaned forward, and in a warm, intense whisper said the only words the Rule allowed:

"Praised be Jesus and Mary!"

The greeting seemed to revive Regina's spirits. She raised her eyes and gave the traditional response in an emotional voice, giving herself away, her insecurity, her gratitude.

"Now and forever, Sister."

Regina continued walking toward the stairs, but even more slowly, wanting to see what Clare was doing. Clare stood and went toward the half-open door.

Calm, stately, her corpulent figure starkly obvious in the small, shadowy room, Mother Helena was sitting to one side of her desk, gazing ahead with total absorption.

"Come in, Sister," she called. "There's no need to knock."

Clare took a step forward, then hesitated, checked in the doorway by that focused stare. The Junior Mistress looked at her pleasantly and nodded her head a little. Without saying anything, with her glance alone, she had established control. Clare entered the room and closed the door politely.

"Hello, Mother."

"How are you feeling, Sister?"

"Fine, thank you, Mother," Clare said, coloring slightly. It was impossible, remembering how often she had heard Mother Helena comment cynically on "sisters known by their illnesses," not to detect another level of meaning in the question.

Mother Helena indicated a chair and invited Clare to sit and, after a moment's pause, made the sign of the cross, and invoked the Holy Spirit:

"Come, Holy Spirit, fill the
hearts of Thy faithful..."

Clare murmured the words in unison with her.

The Junior Mistress began to speak about final profession, the seriousness of the commitment, human frailty, the need to die to self. Then, less businesslike, but still somewhat detached, she said:

"You've expressed an interest in the contemplative life."

"Yes, Mother."

"Only a few sisters decide to take that step. What is it that draws you?"

"I want to live a life without compromise…"

"The sisters who teach, who nurse, those who work with the poor and the aged, don't do that?"

"Yes, of course they do. I mean—" Clare had heard the note of reproach and she faltered. But silence was tense and uncertain. She began again, saying very seriously:

"I would like to live by a stricter observance of the Rule. To devote one's life to prayer, to the study of Scripture and the works of the great spiritual writers seems to me to be a beautiful, purposeful existence."

Focusing on someone who was absent, someone who had believed in her unconditionally, Clare drew on a memory that moved her deeply.

"Mother Mary Bernard taught me to love the writings of Julian of Norwich," she said softly.

"That's very advanced reading. What have you learned?"

"That Julian perceived God as Mother, far in advance of twentieth-century feminism," Clare answered, encouraged. "That Julian's theme—that God is all-encompassing love—is rooted in Scripture."

Dealt with as a child by both her father and Stephen as though her confidences were treasured notes which, if missed, might be lost irretrievably, Clare had grown up speaking in a slow, earnest way that conveyed to the listener her words were to be taken with utmost seriousness. The characteristic had charmed Mother Mary Bernard, who had perceived it as an outgrowth of trust. It annoyed Mother Helena, who saw the trait as evidence of the self-absorption of a hothouse plant, who needed to be coddled and fawned over by others.

Continuing in that same meditative voice, Clare said, "Because of her insights, Julian struggled with the issue of sin and damnation. She couldn't accept the idea of wrath in God, whom she defined as unconditional love."

Aware that a silence had fallen, Clare asked, out of politeness, "What do you think of her, Mother?"

The Junior Mistress smiled carefully. "Oh, my spiritual director hasn't yet recommended Julian to me."

Clare dropped her eyes.

Mother Helena said, "I've always mistrusted those sisters who seem so much 'deeper' than others."

Clare said nothing.

"You have a need to be noticed, don't you, Sister?"

"No," Clare said in surprise.

"Oh, but I think you do."

Clare shook her head forcefully in denial. "I see myself as no more important and no less important than any other member of the community."

"I think differently. Aren't you, in fact, self-important, playing a part in a drama, a drama in which the rest of us serve as backdrop and whose heroine is yourself?"

"No, Mother!" Clare said with a soft cry.

The Junior Mistress went on, as if she hadn't heard, in a voice prolonged with honeyed leisureliness:

"Articles published when you're in the Juniorate ... a Novice Mistress who made life replete with favors..."

Knowing that, in spite of how difficult this woman was, she needed to be understood by her, Clare struggled to control herself. She was groping for words that could show how deeply sincere she was, but Mother Helena spoke again.

"And then, there's the matter of the missed vow class."

"Oh," Clare said, caught off guard. She had intended to acknowledge her mistake. She had known she should have done so since the day in the previous week when she had failed to read the notices on the bulletin board outside the refectory, and missed the announcement about the vow class.

She asked for pardon, growing anxious that whatever she said would be inadequate. "I forgot to check the bulletin board that day, Mother. I am very sorry. It won't happen again."

"I don't think you forgot, Sister. I think you felt you were above it."

Mother Helena looked steadily at Clare and with short, fleshy fingers kneaded the black rosary that hung from her belt.

"On the one hand, you're a young woman who thinks the ordinary life of the community isn't demanding enough for her rarefied spiritual taste; on the other, you're a spoiled, pampered girl who decides which aspects of religious life she'll honor and which she'll disregard."

Clare sat very still, the color gone from her face.

"I don't recommend final profession for you at this time, Sister," Mother Helena said. "I believe you need another year under my direction…a year in which to determine your suitability for community life."

Shaken by the abruptness of the judgment, struggling to cope with its implications, Clare stared at her superior in disbelief. Mother Helena's face was hard and unmoved. The eyes that had read Teilhard de Chardin's promise that one day all of humanity would come to love with Christlike love and then, "for the second time in human history, man will have discovered fire," were cold and loveless.

The interview had come to an end; the Junior Mistress told Clare that she could go. From the doorway, Clare, afraid she could not control tears, still out of respect, stopped and glanced back; Mother Helena, seeing that she paused, returned the look, her lips curved pink and full in a remote, enigmatic smile.

—⁓—

Something tender and broken, like a young tree bent, like the crushed petals of an opening flower, had come to a standstill in the darkened hall beside the scriptorium: Clare Engle, with no place to go.

She had not been able to eat her evening meal. She had needed to find a place where she could be alone, and all the rooms in the mother-house were filled with sisters home on retreat, except this one.

She sat down at a table by the door and glanced about. This special world. In later years, when Clare thought back on the beauty of the cloister, she would see this room as it was now, in the copper glow of the last hour of daylight. Things appeared different in that glow—perfect, rounded out.

To one side of the door, in partial shadow, stood a black wood grandfather clock, wound down and stopped, its hands fixed at noon. The shelves of books along the walls had been neatly put in order for the night, but two books still were out. They were on a table close by. A copy of the New Testament lay opened to the Gospel of Matthew, a companion volume set to one side. Someone had begun to compose a paper on the Synoptic Gospels; she could make out the headings of the outline that the writer had made.

On the wall facing the window, sunlight falling full upon it, hung a print of Caravaggio's second "Supper at Emmaus," the work of the art-ist's mature years.

Jesus, with the shadow of suffering in his meditating face, is raising his hand in blessing over the meal. Flanking him on either side, their hair tousled, their skin blackened and hardened by a life lived out-of-doors, the two disciples, Cleophas and the mysterious "another," sit in wonderment, having just recognized the Risen Lord in "the breaking of the bread." In the background, at the right, the innkeeper stands, impressed, uncertain, but open to suggestion; and, at the far right, phys-ically within the circle of onlookers but mentally apart, is an old servant woman, her head bowed and her face ravaged by age and want, one of those poor whom life had tossed aside, too worn down now to believe in miracles, though one is happening in her presence.

Clare had always been affected by the painting and its gifted, com-plicated artist, but in that moment she was penetrated anew. Depicted as an ordinary man, limned in dark earth tones, mysteriously introspective, this was not the Christ of Luke but of Caravaggio, an image of deeply moving solitude.

Clare was unable just then to comprehend all that had occurred or all that she was feeling within. As a young girl she had been drawn to the convent and had not imagined any other life. No matter what else had beckoned to her, no matter that some may have questioned her decision, she had never wavered or lost her resolve: she would emulate the saints of the books of her childhood. Mother Mary Bernard, with her sensitive intuition, had understood those youthful hopes and ideals, but from the day of her death, Clare's life had fallen to pieces.

She would leave the convent not knowing what she wanted to become, knowing only that she did not want the life held out to her by Mother Helena.

One day, when the present crisis had passed, she would tell Stephen all that had happened, and the full story behind her decision to leave, but that would occur many months later. Now she needed the strength that silence alone could offer her.

And she was consoled by something else, something she had not grasped until that hour. The dream she had had, in which Mother Mary Bernard had shown her lines from Julian of Norwich, the dream that had comforted her when she had needed comforting so badly, had taken on a new meaning. We are always working toward the future. Leaving the convent did not mean life was over; a new existence lay before her. Mother Mary Bernard had known.

—⁂—

In June 1988, after five and a half years spent in the convent, Clare set out to find her place in the world. At twenty-seven, she was an attractive but not remarkable-looking girl, more and more resembling her mother, with her mother's same vitality and inner glow. She had the clear, direct gaze of one used to searching great distances, a sea captain's eyes, or an aviator's. Endowed with extraordinary candor, innocent but stern, intense, almost a little fierce, those eyes revealed a young woman who would always make life something larger—more desperate, more noble, more tragic—than reality offered.

She was tall and willowy, with a small, straight nose and a slender, graceful mouth disposed to squeal with laughter or seal in repose; she had a windswept, careless look, her sandy hair short and boyish after wearing the veil of a nun, and an expression at once tender and severe— opposite forms of one attribute: her unrelenting hunger for perfection.

In the first week that she was on her own, Clare began to look for a job and contacted *Christian Comment*, which had published her series of articles on martyrs. The managing editor remembered her work and recommended her to fill an opening as a staff assistant in the news division.

Her first assignments included doing background research for senior reporters and writing filler stories that were often shelved. But Clare was happy simply to be moving in the company of people who wrote for a profession; she couldn't believe she was being paid for doing work so natural to her.

Her small desk was in a corner across the aisle from a large plate-glass window that overlooked an industrial park. The view was flat and banal. On humid afternoons in spring and summer, the bloated red sun hung over the smokestacks like the inflated dot on the improvised letter "i" a child makes when she is first learning to print. Tall columns of smoke rose eternally along the rooftops, a mirage of dark pillars in the deep yellow sky. The nearby streets were hard corridors. A bus line ran past the front door two stories below. Every forty minutes one of the behemoths charged around the corner from out of nowhere, and the sudden sighing of the air brakes, carried upward, could be heard even through the sealed windows. Clare, looking out, timed her watch to it.

Her career at *Christian Comment* soon became her entire world, as the convent had been before it. Her colleagues teased her about being a woman with a past—they meant the convent—and quietly admired a dedication to writing they sensed was deeper than their own.

Kathleen, again assuming the role of surrogate mother, became her guide back to the outer world. She bought Clare a wardrobe of suits for work, helped her find an apartment, furnished it for her, and provided six months' rent in advance. Brought close by the death of their father, the two women were for a time inseparable, going everywhere together in Kathleen's sleek gray Mercedes. But Clare did not aspire to the social world of country club luncheons and parties that were Kathleen's life-blood and, after a while, the sisters went their separate ways, though they always stayed in touch.

Clare's refuge, her solace, her strength, were her books. She explored Japanese haiku and Russian poetry, reading over and over the works of Bashō and Buson, of Akhmatova, Mandelstam, and Brodsky, and, in studying the latter poets, became entranced by a culture where poetry mattered so much that men and women went to prison or died for its sake.

In her hours of reading, Clare continued to challenge herself, teaching herself by working and reworking her sentences, learning from the writing of authors she loved and wanted to emulate. Sitting at the round table in her little kitchen in an old sweatshirt and jeans, her soft, earnest face bathed in the pale yellow light of the low chandelier, she would spend hours deciphering and developing her notes, often forgetting what hour it was, or even if she had eaten dinner.

She had a line she wanted to build a story around; the line contained a metaphor that would support a story: somewhere, an as yet undefined young woman was singing. Her voice had a thrilling emotional character and Clare, imagining she could hear it, had written the words, "elevating the golden chalice of her voice to a soaring height." If nothing had come of them yet, still, Clare was on her way.

Her yearning had been to live for something beautiful and lasting and greater than self, and she realized now that writing, which involved a commitment to the inner life and called upon her to spend herself for excellence, could become that all-consuming passion, a cloister of the heart.

XIII

On the second Monday in October, Don Shearer was going down the drive when he saw the first leaves of the gingko tree fall. Within the space of a single hour they would all drop. He stopped the car for a moment and sat, watching; then, remembering where he had to be that morning, he started up again and drove on. At the end of the lawn, before the drive turned into the trees, he glanced back for a last time.

The road ahead of him curved for two miles beneath gently stirring shadows, passing by a wood. Now it wound through a birch forest and was showered by leaves, falling like golden rain. The day was mild and gray. There was a stillness in the trees and a lovely candor to the air, and over everything had come the sense of autumn.

Forty minutes later, he passed through a heavy glass door and entered the spacious suite of interconnected offices of the law firm where he was a partner. His secretary was sitting at a desk outside his office, writing memos when he came in. Julia Brys was a small, delicately boned woman in her late fifties, with eyes a little wider apart than most eyes are, and long brown hair brushed into a taut chignon.

"You look ready to take on the world this morning," she said, handing him her memos.

Don laughed. "Let's hope that look doesn't evaporate in the first five minutes."

They walked side by side down a wide carpeted hall past glassed-wall offices to a conference room. No one else had arrived yet, though someone had placed manila folders about the long polished table. It was a large conference room, understated and formally arranged, full of light from a skylight and three walls of windows. From the windows that looked to the north one could see thirty miles off to the wooded hills, now ablaze with color, surrounding Dunham Lake.

Julia, looking around the room, said in a precise and earnest manner, "You're going to want the sun at your back."

"I want to be near the head of the table," Don said, smiling at her tone. He sat down, opened his briefcase, and began to spread out his work, setting sheet after sheet aside. Having looked through the sheaves of papers he had brought with him, he hurriedly began going through everything again. Then he leaned back and said in frustration, "I must have left my summation at home."

He looked off into space for a moment and, suddenly remembering, exclaimed, "It's on my bureau." Don got to his feet and stood, thoughts racing. He could not improvise.

"I have to go back for it."

Julia Brys stared at him across the table. "The meeting is in an hour."

"I'll be late then. I have no other choice." Feigning a gameness he did not feel, he winked at her. "Save me a seat."

In the elevator Don stood drumming on the wall, watching the lights descend on the control panel as he went down. When the elevator door opened, he ran to his car, threw his briefcase onto the front seat, climbed in behind the wheel, backed out and, bumping hard on the curb as he exited the parking garage, emerged onto the street.

By 9:15 traffic had thinned. The street was sun-dappled, starred with shadows. Running north, it curved and slanted, narrowing in places to avoid the orange barrels that had been set out to mark construction on the road. Don drove slightly over the posted speed, edging his way into the left lane, timing the lights. He had only to reach the city limits and the street would become unobstructed highway. In a few minutes, the smooth flow of traffic had calmed his mind.

And then, inexplicably, there came over him a nameless sense of dread. Instinctive, atavistic, like a child's fear of the dark, it gripped him and held him fast: Do not go there. The traffic was sparse, the light ahead green, and once he passed through the intersection, he would be on open road, heading home. Yet as he approached the light, he decelerated and braked to a stop.

A dark object flashed at the edge of his awareness; from out of nowhere, a black van shot into the intersection. The driver, intending to run the light, had, in the last instant, caught sight of the oncoming car. Furiously applying the brakes, he veered to the left, the vehicle spun three-quarters round and screeched to a halt, facing Don Shearer.

Don sat staring in astonishment, his hand on the wheel, shaking. Several yards from him, the other driver was sitting as if fastened upright, averting his eyes. Neither man moved. The light turned red and then green again. Other cars, arriving at the intersection, came to a standstill also, their drivers looking on, solemn and impassive, like watchers at an observatory window. On the sidewalk between a coffee shop and a supermarket a little group of passersby froze in place. A child began to cry in a doorway somewhere on the right.

Don was the first to stir. Overcoming the tremor of his hand, he moved tentatively out of the intersection and started on, slowly heading for the open road. Had he not paid attention to the strange premonition in the moment before…Only as he drove away, unwinding, did the sudden, stark realization of his near-death strike him.

—⚬⚬—

The BMW turned into the gravel drive. High among the dense firs, crows cawed raucously at its approach. Squirrels scampered noisily into a clump of late-blooming day lilies. A pheasant hastened across the grass. In a moment the house emerged through the trees. The gingko tree caught Don's eye at once. It stood in place at the back of the lawn, its yellow leaves dispersed beneath it.

An hour ago, Don Shearer knew, he would not have been having the thoughts that penetrated him now. He wound around in the driveway and looked at the gingko, recalling:

Man's days are like those of grass;
Like a flower of the field he blooms;
The wind sweeps over him and he is gone...

He parked and stepped out of the car onto his own land again. Driven by the need to find Kathleen, he hurried into the house and went from room to room, calling her name. When he could not find her, he rushed downstairs to search for her outside.

He passed through the wrought-iron gate into the garden, leaves from the surrounding trees strewn all about him. Now, walking along the path, he noticed everything about him with newly opened eyes, as if he were seeing things in his final hour—the last roses, the cardinals bathing in the little stone fountain and scattering as he neared, the wild ivy growing in the clefts in the rock, and at the end of the cinder path, the slender, dark-haired woman standing by the low stone wall, gazing into the distance, looking into the woods.

"Kathleen."

Before he said her name she heard his footsteps on the cinder path and glanced round. Story-book maiden, beautiful in the shade of a silver birch, more radiant in life than the image he carried of her in his heart, surprised, delighted, she came to him across the lawn in a swift, graceful run, orange-yellow leaves falling from her warm, lithe hands. Venus this, borne upon his poor shore.

"Kathleen."

Drawing near, Kathleen saw the tension in her husband's face, hesitated, then halted in mid run.

Don reached her. He took her hands in his and, looking into her eyes, said with emotion, "I have something to tell you, Kathleen." And he related the chain of events: how he had forgotten his summation, his decision to return for it, the traffic leaving the city, his coming up on the green light, the strange presentiment in the moment before he entered the intersection, the blur of the van, the flash of the driver's face and then the eyes of the driver turning away, and at last, the one thing that mattered to him:

"All the way home I had only one thought: that I hadn't had the chance to say good-bye to you." Sobbing with joy, Don gathered her into his arms.

"Kathleen, Kathleen, I love you so."

He had almost lost her, for to him his life and his love for her were inseparable. And now they were given back to each other, standing in the soft light breaking through the trees, lost in each other's gaze, forgetful of time, his left arm around her shoulders, his right hand caressing her breasts.

"Kathy, dearest Kathy," his voice among the leaves like a whispered prayer.

He knew they would talk later, when he returned home. They would walk to the woods above Dunham Lake at dusk, the last light touching the dark water beyond the trees, the day nearly done. When night came, they would lie down together and, for the first time in many weeks, allow themselves the time for leisurely, ardent love. And perhaps, because of the auspiciousness of the day, this time there would come from that union the living child for which they both yearned. As Don Shearer turned on the cinder path, his eyes promised all these things, and more.

Dunham Lake Road, before it joined the main highway, made a long, winding descent toward the lake. Massive spruce rose there and, in the fractured light beneath their arms, stood thin birches the color of bone. For fleeting moments—more frequent in autumn—the lake itself shone through the trees. On certain mornings, luminous objects rose in the neutral space: the sudden ascent of mute swans over the spruce could so startle a driver that his gaze was diverted to the right, off the road.

On just such a morning, Don Shearer approached the juncture of Dunham Lake Road and the highway. He carried with him his briefcase and the summation for which he had returned home, and he carried within him the joy of living fully in the present moment, awakened in him a scant hour before. A bright flash of light showed in the trees as he followed the winding descent of the road; startled, he looked to his right and, not realizing how far he had come, missed the stop sign. The oncoming truck that slammed into him broadside sent his car spinning in the direction of the mute swans, which, in that instant, were ascending over the treetops, blazing like white flames in the hazy azure air.

He was thrown clear of the car and lay facedown in a great pool of blood.

—◊◊◊—

Kathleen dropped the phone and stopped breathing. She turned toward the window and stood staring out. The sun had reached the garden and the golden light of afternoon was beginning to spread along the stone wall. Yellow- and red-veined leaves were fluttering to the ground. And everywhere the world was steeped in beauty. She looked on, not seeing, not believing.

—◊◊◊—

The sky was slowly going dark and the first stars were brightening in the Douglas firs. Where a path led into the woods, Dunham Lake lay blue and cold, unseen in the autumn dusk.

Stephen was sitting with Kathleen on the sofa in the high-ceilinged family room of her home. The room was as he remembered it: beautiful cut-glass lamps on the tables, Dyf paintings on the walls, Oriental rugs running the length of the polished hardwood floor. Glass double doors fronted onto the grounds where tall, leafless trees receded in the distance and, at this hour, a last gleam of light traveled through the woods.

"Once, everything sparkled here..." Kathleen said, her voice trailing off.

Six weeks had passed since Don Shearer had died and Stephen, concerned about his sister's state of mind, had come to spend the weekend of Thanksgiving with her. He was her only contact with the outside world; with him, Kathleen was agreeing to take her first steps away from a self-imposed silence and seclusion.

She sat slumped against a bunched sofa pillow, her eyes wide and trusting as a child's, folding and unfolding a small white handkerchief in her thin, trembling hands and speaking in a small, dull voice.

"How many more times are you and I going to sit like this, mourning another loss?"

"It's rough," Stephen answered, quietly, wanting her to talk.

After a long pause, she went on in the same subdued monotone, "One by one we watch those we love part from us and enter a circle bounded by the word *was*—the cruelest word in all of language—and now, it's Don who's gone, and tell me, where do I get the strength to go on?

"He was so good and kind, Stephen"—she glanced at him—"in a different league from me. Sometimes, when I think I can't bear up anymore, I want to ask you to tell me something mean and despicable about him so that I could hate him and stop feeling this terrible emptiness. Am I being horrible?"

Stephen put his hand on her shoulder. "No."

Kathleen lowered her eyes and fell silent. Having twisted the handkerchief into a knot, she began to finger a strand of her dark, fine hair. After another, a longer pause, she said:

"For neither of us, Stephen—children."

Stephen glanced at her from under his brows, fixing her steadily with his gaze, his eyes eloquent with feeling. She had stepped over a boundary, but that look said that he understood, he would not prevent her from going further. Suffering had brought her to a place of privilege. She could ask ultimate questions.

But she stopped talking suddenly and sat back into the sofa, drawing her feet up beneath her. She was cold. Removing his jacket,

Stephen got up and draped it around her shoulders. He offered to light a fire.

On the landing off the kitchen he found a stack of firewood. He selected several birch logs, returned with them to the family room, and set them on the hearth. The fireplace had not been used yet this fall and Stephen knew the last person to have laid a fire must have been Don Shearer. Kathleen, watching, was remembering. Stephen saw it in her eyes.

Placing two of the logs across the andirons, he overlaid them with small sticks of dry wood and sheets of newspaper he had rolled into tight tubes, put another log on top of the kindling, struck a match and lit the paper, then stepped back to see if the flame would catch. In a few moments the wood began to glow, there was a crackling sound, and the logs caught fire.

When the fire started to blaze, Stephen adjusted the fender and sat down again. They sat for a long time by the fireplace—Kathleen, wrapped in the oversize jacket, staring into the gathering dusk, lost in thought.

Stephen, too, was preoccupied. He felt certain that if his sister stayed isolated in this house, a six-hour drive away from him, she would deteriorate, emotionally and physically. Before the weekend was over, he would need to persuade her to leave the seclusion of her home at Dunham Lake and relocate nearer to the city.

Unexpectedly, as if she had sensed those thoughts, Kathleen turned her head and said to him, "Always before, when I looked out on the grounds, they seemed to hold such beauty and mystery. Now, they hold only mystery.

"I see each tree bereft, like a widow in a black dress. I see the path to the lake growing dark. I see everything my husband loved and that has outlived him..." She looked away, the strength gone from her voice:

"And his place knows him no more..."

—◊—

Stephen returned to the university. The days, the weeks passed.

A December night. Daniel Kress, S.J., saw the light when he came to the juncture of the main hall, and slowed his step. Turning to his right, he walked, slightly stooped but agile, to where light shone beyond an open door, his footsteps resonating long and hollow in the empty corridor.

From the doorway he stuck his long, gentle face with its thin, hooked nose into the room, grinning at the young Jesuit who was sitting alone at the desk, reading with total absorption.

"Say, Stephen, they'll be closing the building in a little while."

Stephen looked up, smiling. "Thanks. I'm running late. I'll be out of here, though."

Kress set his briefcase down. "Looks like we're getting our first snow tonight." Stiff-fingered, a bit awkward, he tucked a gray wool scarf into the neck of his black overcoat, raised the collar up high, and more firmly tightened the belt.

"I saw a former student of ours over the weekend," he said.

Stephen, directing his eyes over the desk in a wandering side glance, asked abstractedly, "Oh—who was that?"

"The gifted young woman who withdrew just before the end of spring term last year."

Stephen, taken by surprise and not wanting to show the look that he felt come over his face, leaned over the side of his desk and began to search through a bottom drawer.

"Mary Ainsley," Kress concluded.

Straightening up, Stephen laid a folder bulging with loose papers on his desk. He asked quietly, "How is she?"

"She seemed fine. I was in Detroit over the weekend and said the evening Mass at Saints Peter and Paul on Sunday. She came up afterward to speak to me."

"Did she mention whether she'd gone back to school?"

"No. And I forgot to ask. She wanted me to tell you hello."

"Thank you." Stephen looked across the desk and nodded. "Thank you for letting me know."

"Remember, another half hour and you're an overnight guest here," Kress chided with a smile.

Moments later, Stephen set his work aside and got up, preparing to leave. He closed his briefcase and placed it on the chair, flicked off the light switch, crossed the hall, and, with an effort he hadn't expected would be called for, pushed open the heavy outer door. Like the motion of an unfurling sail, a veil of snow, borne on a shaft of cold air, whipped into the hall. Lowering his head, he hurriedly stepped out, pulling the door shut behind him.

At the foot of the stairs he turned right, heading away from the Jesuit residence hall, taking the walk that led to the north end of the campus. Cold gripped his ankles, bit into his hands; bitter cold edged his collar. Snow descended on his shoulders and dampened his hair. He shook his head, releasing ice crystals into the wind; they reclaimed him at once, meshing into tendrils that clung, wet and raw, to his face and throat and along the back of his neck. Marshalling his breath in the sharp air, he rubbed his hands and forearms and checked his watch for the danger point in time.

As he walked he concentrated on a single image, saying its name to himself slowly and repetitively, as if for the first time, until his mind entered a state of meditation, emptied of all other thought—the single image of snow. To the farthest end of peripheral vision, into the deepest part of the night. Measured, like music, but soundless, as if in that vast expanse there were no ears, but only eyes, to witness the unbroken descent. And in the moment when imagination and landscape became one, he turned and walked back.

— ᨈ—

Kathleen spent the winter in a state of indecision. Then in early March she sold the house at Dunham Lake as Stephen had recommended, and moved to a two-bedroom town house in a condominium complex thirty miles away.

She was now forty-one, a beautiful young widow, affluent and independent. Don Shearer had seen to it that his wife's deep-seated need to feel secure and in control of her circumstances was not only met, but exceeded.

By late spring she seemed to be recovering, little by little, from her husband's death. The fear of loneliness from which she had suffered since her teenage years still was there, but she coped with it in her characteristic way, by immersing herself in one activity or another. Both to stave off depression and to reconnect with the familiar past, she decided she would go back to college and, perhaps, study speech again.

Then one afternoon at the end of June, Joseph Moore, Don's financial adviser and a longtime friend of the Shearer family, called her. He was retiring and wanted to recommend one of the firm's senior vice presidents as his successor, a talented investment analyst named Paul Brittain. At her convenience, Moore suggested, Kathleen should make an appointment to meet him.

"Mrs. Shearer." Paul Brittain spoke her name softly, introducing himself as they stood for a moment in the doorway before entering his office.

It was a baronial room of dark wood and polished glass and red armchairs, with a mammoth seascape by Montague Dawson on the wall.

Paul Brittain put a cup of coffee in her hands. "Sugar? Cream?" Kathleen declined with a smile. He had a deep, serious, precise voice with a bitter undertone. Like black coffee, Kathleen thought.

He sat beside her, spreading documents over a long mahogany table.

"Mrs. Shearer—"

"Kathleen, please."

"Kathleen."

Lifting her eyes, Kathleen looked steadily at him.

Paul Brittain was fifty-six, a tall, broad-shouldered man with lean, angular features, blond hair streaked with gray, and heavy, ungovernable eyebrows that grew down to keen hazel eyes. His mouth was thin and taut, with a small scar above the lip, and he had a slightly one-sided smile that lent him a wry, sardonic look.

His silk tie, beautiful manners, the tan that remained yearlong—these evoked Old Money, breeding, social standing. In fact, he was a child of divorce, on his own at sixteen, who had worked his way through school and risen to high position by relentless drive and resourceful, sometimes ruthless practices.

He had served and been decorated in the Korean War, and afterward attended Wharton. Ambitious, quick, and astute, he had specialized in investment banking, graduated with honors, received offers from all the major brokerage houses, and been hired as a junior vice president by his first choice. At forty-eight he had been made a senior vice president and full partner.

On this day in his office he and Kathleen went over all the holdings in her portfolio. There was no concern for any part of it. Together with Don Shearer, Moore had arranged everything in good order. Paul did have a few suggestions to make, ways to protect her equity, with hedges against inflation, for example. He wanted to show her how to write covered calls against certain stocks she owned, in order to augment her income. With Kathleen's permission, he would work up a few models for her to consider.

"Why don't we meet for lunch when I have everything ready?" he inquired.

Eight days later, over lunch, Kathleen met with Paul Brittain again. After eating, they sat for a long time in the half-empty restaurant and he told her about his experience as an investment analyst and how he perceived the complex world of finance. As he walked Kathleen to her car, he remarked on how much he enjoyed talking with her and told her he would call her if other investment ideas arose that he thought might interest her.

Kathleen looked forward to hearing from him, but six weeks passed before Paul Brittain called again. He wanted to discuss with her the initial public offering of a very promising company. When Kathleen explained that she was risk averse, Paul concluded that the investment would be wrong for her, and told her he would stay in touch.

One morning at the end of August, he called. The conversation was brief; he had a few recommendations for her. Also, he was going out of town for two weeks and wanted to know if she would have dinner with him before he left.

Kathleen did not know what to say. She had been a widow for only ten months; the invitation was sudden, though (she admitted only to herself), not wholly unexpected. When the silence became strained, Paul politely intervened.

"Perhaps another time," he said, "when you feel less pressured."

And when he called her next, in late October, Kathleen said, "You've been so considerate of me. I'm eating alone tonight. Would you join me?"

"Are you certain?"

"Yes. Of course."

—⚏—

Kathleen served a simple dinner of flank steak and salad, cheeses and fruit, with a bottle of wine. Afterward, they had coffee in the living room, the windows open to the warm autumn night. An hour earlier, there had been a light shower. Outside, the wrought-iron streetlamps along the drive glistened with rain and the drive shone glassy black, like a band of obsidian.

Paul chose an armchair in front of the darkened fireplace. Across from him, Kathleen sat on the small love seat where she read when she was alone.

Paul lowered his head for a few moments and regarded the palm of one hand. Then he looked up and said, "I'd like to know more about you, Kathleen. We've talked about my stint in Korea, my professional experiences, the stock market, options trading, the coming millennium, but very little about you.

"Where does someone like you come from. Well bred, innocent, so attractive..." His admiring gaze moved slowly across her face.

Kathleen sat holding a glass of wine in her hands. She did not answer at first. Her natural reserve, her love for her dead husband and loyalty to his memory, the undeniable appeal of this man, and the impulse to resist that attraction—all these feelings restrained her. She sipped slowly from her glass and then replied softly, unevenly:

"I don't know…I'd say that I'm a very predictable person. Life is less complicated that way. I'm one of three children, the oldest, the nonintellectual in an academic family."

"I doubt that." Paul smiled and extracted cigarettes and a silver-plated lighter from his jacket pocket. "May I smoke?"

"Yes…please."

Paul shifted an ashtray to his right before lighting a cigarette and inhaling deeply. He said, "Tell me about some of the forces that have influenced your life."

Kathleen's slender, nervous fingers, plain but for her wedding band, worked against the glass. "You know that I lost my husband a year ago…"

Paul nodded.

"He'd come home to get some papers he'd forgotten, and was driving back to work, taking the road he used every morning and…something distracted him." Kathleen was silent for a moment, then she made a slight movement with her shoulders and said:

"The irony in his death was that, twenty-four years earlier, my mother also was killed in an accident on that road."

"I'm sorry. That I didn't know."

"Afterward, my brother Stephen and I used to reassure each other that, if we could survive our mother's death and grow up psychologically intact, we could face anything life held in store for us."

Paul said, "You know, for some reason, I thought you were an only child." He asked reflexively, "What does your brother do?"

"Stephen's a Catholic priest."

"A priest?" Paul laughed. "No, you are not predictable!"

"Stephen is an exceptional person, very intelligent, good-looking, like our father. On the day he was ordained, I heard one of the nuns who taught us say to someone: 'Look at Stephen. Isn't he remarkable? There'll be no middle way for that young man. He's either going to become very holy, or he'll leave the priesthood.'"

Paul asked with his wry half smile, "How many years now?"

"Stephen's been a Jesuit for nineteen years, a priest for eight."

"I've never known a Catholic priest," Paul said. "No offense intended, but I've never understood men who don't have sex."

"My brother is such a gifted, sweet person, it's jarring to think of him in such reduced terms," Kathleen said defensively.

"I'm sorry. The remark was insensitive. Religion isn't a topic that comes up with much frequency in my conversations, unfortunately."

Kathleen's fingers tensed against the glass. She asked, "Does my religion make a difference to you?"

"Not at all. My personal history may matter to you, though. I've had two unsuccessful marriages, two divorces."

They sat for a moment without saying anything. The curtains blew softly in the night air. Beyond the trees, a car turned into a driveway. Then a car door closed and the heels of a woman's shoes clattered on a nearby walk.

Paul inhaled the last of his cigarette and extinguished it. He examined his palm again, thoughtful. At last he said, "Kathleen, I don't know where we go from here. You're too dear to me to want to stop seeing you."

A slender muscle at Kathleen's throat quivered. *Too dear to me...to stop seeing you.* Desertion in the same sentence as love.

Paul went on. "But you've experienced a great deal of hurt in life, and greater than my desire to see you again is my wish to protect you from further pain."

In his deep, serious voice he went on to explain that all his adult life he had been a very materialistic man, and that he didn't think he could change or that she would want his way of life. In the beginning, he said, he had been drawn to her—as had happened in the past with other women—by her beautiful appearance. But as he'd come to know her, he'd been affected by her gentleness and innocence, and that experience had been good for him. However, he doubted that he could fulfill her life.

"Kathleen, this is where I'm at," he said. "I'd like you to think things over. If you decide the differences between us are too fundamental, then I won't hear from you again, and I promise you, I will understand. I'll make certain to give your account to the most capable person I know. If, on the other hand, you think we can go on seeing each other, I hope you'll call me."

Pocketing his lighter, he rose to leave. Kathleen stood up, conscious of how pale she was. In the doorway she hesitated, her head tilted to one side. She was longing for him to hold her, not in a sexual way, but in the way a child is held: warmed, caressed, infinitely loved.

But Paul Brittain, relaxed and utterly composed, stood looking at her with an untroubled gaze; he was saying good night, he was saying good-bye, courteously, to the point.

—⚏—

For a long time afterward, Kathleen stood in her living room, staring into the darkness beyond the window.

She knew what she should do. Before it went any further, while he was giving her an acceptable way out, she should take him at his word and simply walk away. Yet she could not do that. Something had passed between Paul Brittain and herself.

She wished he were a stranger, someone she'd noticed while entering a room—"Oh, isn't he distinguished!"—and then forgotten as she moved on. Yet she wanted desperately to see him.

And running parallel to this stream of consciousness ran another current of thought, more disturbing, known only to her: the sense of life having come full circle.

—⚏—

When two weeks had passed, she set her doubts aside and called him. She let the greeting on his answering machine play twice before she called again and left a brief message. But he did not return her call.

She didn't understand what could have gone wrong. But as the hours and days went by, she began slowly to accept that, when he had told her good-bye, Paul Brittain had in fact meant just that. She would never hear from him again.

In the study, the grandfather clock softly chimed the hour. Kathleen sat in the kitchen, her arms folded on the table in front of her, trying to collect herself. She was ill at ease with silence. Silence held an expectation, a foreboding of ruin.

She recalled a young girl sitting alone by the phone in a darkened room. Down the hall, her brother absorbed in his work, farther on, her small sister asleep. Five hours before, her mother, in a brown cashmere sweater as dark as her eyes, had stopped in the door to say, "I'll be home by ten, or I'll call." It was now almost midnight and the phone had not rung. From the hall at the foot of the stairs came the faint chiming of the grandfather clock, striking twelve, and then the sound of a man's steps on the stairs. A voice called out in the night—her father's voice— and the world had gone wrong.

The images never dimmed. The bobbing path of light traveling through the moonless night. Running, stumbling in the dark, feeling for her father's hand, her hair tossing about, thistles scratching her skin. The grass black and grim, spattered with glass and blood. Ambulance doors slamming. The long siren wail dying away into eternity. Near dawn, passing a door. A teenage boy lying doubled over on his bed, sobbing and choking and gasping for air…She thought of her mother again—of her car, making the turn off Dunham Lake Road, and for the last time, heading for home. Kathleen lowered her head in her arms, and cried.

The phone rang.

"Kathleen? I just got back from L.A. this afternoon. Are you free for dinner tomorrow night?"

Stunned, Kathleen at first demurred.

"I think so…yes."

"What time is best for you?"

"Seven?"

"Seven it is. Wonderful news."

—∞—

In the bronze glow of a coach light, Paul Brittain stood in the entry, a bouquet of yellow roses in his hand.

Kathleen said, "Yellow roses," and murmured "Thank you" as their hands touched in the hallway.

He stooped to retrieve a fallen petal from the floor. "I hoped you would call," he said. "But I didn't know what to think."

Kathleen ran her fingers through her hair. She'd wondered if he'd seem different to her, if she'd seem different to him. She hadn't expected a change in herself, that she would feel so weak, so lacking in self-confidence.

"I wasn't going to call you," she said, utterly sincere. "I tried to stay away." The air in the room seemed strange and electric, as if they were surrounded by an unknown force field which, somehow breaking the laws of physics, at once separated and drew them together. She said very softly, "In spite of the negatives, I feel I'm falling in love. And it frightens me. I'm so afraid of being hurt."

Paul reached for her arm. "Come here," he said in a voice of both coax and command.

Kathleen felt lascivious waves move up and down her thighs and hobbled, stepped back. He was only an arm's length away. He was only a breath away. And then she was hearing her name said a new way, like the wind, low and wild, moving and calling through leaves—Kathleeen… Kathleeen…Kathleeen…And the leaves stirring and yielding and falling, falling from grace.

—∞—

For Kathleen, time took on a new configuration, its passage measured not in days but in intensity of feeling and experience. Thus, to her mind, the days and weeks passed by without differentiation, while the minutes and hours shone.

Within the month, Paul sublet his apartment and moved into her town house, turning one bedroom into his office. The move was the one significant change in his life. Kathleen's life altered interiorly, in deeper ways. What she was doing was not in character for her. Though she had reached adolescence in the 1960s, Kathleen had never been a member of the counterculture, had never taken part in the sexual revolution. Now she was violating the principles she had lived by all her life. She coped with feelings of guilt in the only way she knew how: by denial, and by reassuring herself that Paul would, in time, obtain an annulment of his marriage, and be free to marry her.

From the start it was evident they had little in common. Kathleen found herself in a different role from the one she had enjoyed with her husband and brother and father, men who had been emotionally open to her and entrusted her with their confidences. Paul Brittain kept his own counsel. His inaccessibility puzzled and worried Kathleen, who came to see it as due to a lack of something in herself.

What bound her to him was what happened between them in the dark. Paul's lovemaking had awakened in her more intense sexual feelings than she had ever known. In those hours she felt she had been released, and had touched some vital, elemental, unstinting part of herself.

And they were both, at heart, disillusioned people. But Paul Brittain was able to summon greater courage to meet the future than Kathleen, and, for this reason, too, she clung to him.

XIV

In the morning the weather report warned of severe thunderstorms moving in from the west.

At noon a high bank of cumulonimbus clouds darkened half the sky. A cold wind blew through the arboretum. Before the rain came, Stephen went to his office to write. There he worked for several hours on an article for the publication *Commonweal*, only leaving his desk to turn on the overhead light as shadows deepened in the room.

The storm broke out of deep silence, with a long thunder roll. At his desk, Stephen looked up to glance out the window. A sheet of white light dropped in front of the glass. Lightning flashed near the chapel bell tower, and the lights in rooms about the campus went out.

The overhead light extinguished, Stephen got up and, going to the cabinet behind him, searched through cluttered drawers for a flashlight. Finding the one he'd remembered, he sat down and propped it on a stack of books, balancing it so that its beam fell across the desk, and returned to his writing. But the makeshift lamp worked only to a degree. His work would have to be given up. At seven thirty he prepared to leave.

He had just snapped his briefcase shut when from the hall came the sound of footsteps nearing the door, then stopping, retracing their path, then turning back and coming to the door. In another moment, a tall, athletic figure appeared out of the shadows to stand silhouetted in the doorway, exclaiming, in pretended shock:

"My God! Even in the dark!"

Recognizing the voice at once, Stephen took aim with the flashlight and shone its beam playfully across the room and directly into the eyes of Matthew O'Malley, whose face, transfigured by the light, grimaced good-naturedly.

Stephen got up, saying, "Matt! What a surprise! What brings you here, in a storm?"

Reaching the building just as the storm broke, Matthew had been spared a thorough soaking. Because no one had been at the front desk, he had had to search from room to room through darkened halls to locate Stephen's office. He was about to turn around and leave when he spotted the faint glow of light from the improvised lamp.

This meeting was their first since Matthew's mother had died from a stroke two years earlier. Matthew was forty-four and distinctly hand-some, with his thick, sandy hair now prematurely whitened and his fine, clear features creased only by the vertical lines of concentration between his brows. One of those Jesuits who had adopted secular dress after the reforms of Vatican II, he wore an open-necked blue Oxford cloth shirt and a beautiful old Harris tweed jacket.

In the darkness the two men moved chairs over to the window and seated themselves so that they could look out over the north campus. Even with their faces barely discernible, they began to talk absorbedly with the trust and ease which were hallmarks of their friendship.

For three months the previous year, Matthew had volunteered at a hospice in his free hours and, sometimes, worked alongside his boyhood idol, the Jesuit Daniel Berrigan. Now he and Stephen talked about the days when Berrigan had been known for his writing—before Vietnam, the public protests, the destruction of draft card records, the time in prison.

"A saint with an FBI file," Matthew affirmed with feeling.

As he said this, the power unexpectedly returned, the overhead light came on, and for the first time the two men saw each other clearly.

Matthew gestured toward the ceiling and smiled. "And God said—"

They heard footsteps pounding in the distance. Someone was running through a downstairs hall, whooping and howling at the top of his voice. After a few moments he reached the front entrance and ran outside, banging the heavy outer door behind him. He could still be heard, yelling, until he reached the far side of the building and passed out of hearing. Matthew, glancing over his shoulder, laughed. "'It's spring, and the sap is running.' Remember that? Gerald Kaestner?"

Stephen recalled the dry wit of their dean of theology and smiled.

Matthew grinned. "I think Kaestner meant us."

They both laughed.

They were quiet for a while. Then Matthew looked at the desk and, indicating the writing materials with his eyes, inquired, "What are you working on, Stephen?"

"An article on Augustine for *Commonweal*, seen from this perspective: the self as the product of the autobiography."

Matthew fixed Stephen thoughtfully with his gaze. He asked, "What was it like to be Augustine?"

Stephen sat for a moment, thinking. Then he said, "It was to be many different things. It was to be involved in a long and painful search for truth and then, the quest fulfilled, to have one's life totally turned around. It was to be filled with a sense of urgency. It was to attempt to create order out of chaos in a high act of the imagination…"

Matthew sat listening quietly and seriously. When Stephen had finished he said, "Augustine was able to keep intact the purity of the first ideal. He never lost the convert's freshness of vision. I admire and envy him for that."

There was a long silence. Then Matthew asked, "Do you ever feel like you've settled for a life of mediocrity?"

"No. Do you?"

Matthew leaned forward in his chair and sat rubbing his hands. "When I was first ordained," he said, "I used to wake up each morning feeling that I could change the world—the way you do when you're a kid and life seems filled with endless wonder…Perhaps it's that I'm not at the beginning anymore. Now I'm facing middle age…Perhaps it's the result of having spent too many Sundays at teas, fund-raising…" Matthew smiled ironically, a sadness in his eyes. He looked down, then looked at Stephen. "Whatever the cause may be, that awareness of infinite possibility is gone from my intellectual life."

Moved by the admission, Stephen felt a sudden stab of memory. He recalled a May night, the grounds of the Jesuit seminary in spring, the path leading down to the lake, the dark woods, Peter and Alan beside him, and Matthew, walking on ahead, turning round to speak to them, the ring of his impassioned voice: "Carney lives on the edge: what men could be, if they would…"

Now that same voice spoke again, but in a muted tone. "As you must have supposed, Stephen, I didn't come just to visit. I came because I have something I need to tell you."

Stephen sat back slightly.

"They say," Matthew went on quietly, "that some men come into their own only after the death of their fathers. I don't know if that was your experience…For me, paradoxically, it happened with my mother's death.

"Colleen O'Malley believed that every good Irish family gives a son to the priesthood. From the time I was ten, she was grooming me for the Jesuits." Matthew paused, then he said:

"It would have broken her heart if I'd left while she was alive."

They exchanged sudden glances.

"Oh, no…" Stephen moaned audibly.

"I'm leaving the Jesuits, Stephen," Matthew said. "I wanted to tell you myself, not have you hear about it from someone else."

"Matt, don't. We both know there are some who live this life in a routine way. But you're not one of those. Your life is commendable."

Matthew looked away toward the black rectangle of the window, where a ragged spray of leaves had been affixed by rain, and did not reply. The remark troubled him, but Stephen knew his silence indicated tenseness, not withdrawal.

Dropping his voice, speaking very slowly, Matthew began to detail the chain of events which had led to his decision. It came down to the desire to live a different type of commitment, and the accompanying element of an obdurate, insensitive superior who had misinterpreted his spiritual searching for—

"—for narcissism. That bitter old man accused me of a failure of will, of being a chronic malcontent…Those were factors, Stephen. Important ones. But there's something else."

Meeting Stephen's gaze, Matthew said, "I've met someone…"

Stephen started, caught completely off guard.

"Her name is Deborah Allen. She's a nurse in the hospice where I volunteered. I was struck by her dedication, by how giving she was, from the beginning. She always maintained a distance. As did I. But over the course of the year, our work brought us together, and we became friends…I tried hard not to love her, but that became impossible. She was very adult, pleading with me to consider the seriousness of our continuing to see each other. But the more I thought of life without her, the more I realized there was no way in the world I could give her up."

Stephen started to say something, but at once changed his mind. He was aware that Matthew, though older, looked to him as a kind of role model, and that a slight sense of inequality had always existed in their friendship. To tell Matthew about Mary Ainsley, to relive that experience and the finality of its ending, would reinforce the impression and would benefit neither man. And so he said nothing.

As if he had read Stephen's thoughts, Matthew asked, "Do you see me as the seed which fell on ground 'that had no depth of soil'?"

"No, no…"

"What you think matters to me, Stephen."

Conscious of the weight of his answer, Stephen replied, "What can I say? I can't come up with words commensurate to the loss. The experiences we shared that made us brothers…your hunger for social justice that is an inspiration to me…the echoes of my own struggles that I hear in your words—all of these affect me profoundly, Matthew. I feel your sincerity and I must trust your judgment.

"I hope you'll stay in touch with me...I'll never forget you..."

—∭—

An hour later, Stephen left the building alone. The rain had ended, the night air cleared. Over the chapel bell tower, a white three-quarter moon lay in a thin veil of clouds. Where its light fell to earth, bright pools of water on the walks gave a hundred moons back to the night. The high branches of rain-drenched trees, if brushed by the wind, shed light showers that glistened like stars.

When he reached the low footbridge over the pond at the south end of the college, a breeze lifted clouds of white blossoms before him; they blew across the pond, gleaming on the face of the moon on the water.

An air of quiet beatitude had settled over the campus.

He walked home, thinking only of loss.

XV

That spring, Kathleen decided to give a party. For the first time since Don Shearer's death eighteen months earlier, she was ready to reenter the social world to which she had once belonged, the world she needed to be a part of in order to feel truly alive. Her guest list consisted of friends from high school and college with whom she had never lost touch, several of her former neighbors, and business associates of Paul's, and she decided to invite Stephen.

The party took place on a bright green Saturday in late May. Tables in the front rooms were festive with candlelight and fresh flowers—bouquets of lilacs and white tulips and green ivy—and Paul had lit a fire in the living room. At a buffet set to one side, a caterer was preparing to carve from a large cut of roast beef. A bar was set up in the den.

As guests arrived they were drawn to the balcony to look out at the grounds. The evening was aglow with the deep intense colors of the last hour before sunset. Beyond the trees to the north, the sky was filling with luminous tiers of soft, smoky clouds that drifted and receded into the distance for miles. Below, a narrow private drive curved away behind an arbor vitae hedge to a small stone gatehouse with a turret. Somewhere in the shrubs a red-winged blackbird called a long, liquid *ooh-ka-lee!*

Kathleen had on a boat-neck sheath in yellow silk shantung and had chosen not to wear jewelry. Her hair was loosely pulled up and back so that it spilled around her face in soft tendrils, and she had pinned small yellow silk mimosa flowers here and there among its dark strands. A glass of red wine in her hand, she moved through the softly lit rooms, shaking hands with newcomers, embracing and kissing old friends.

Amid laughter and conversation, couples stood on the white carpet in front of the fire and renewed former acquaintances or threaded their way from group to group, searching for familiar faces. Paul's business colleagues gathered in small clusters by the bar, smoked, drank, and talked among themselves.

Having made the round of the guests, Paul sat by the fire with a Scotch, surveying the room. He had little interest in the others. Kathleen's male friends were, in his judgment, cut from a privileged, pampered mold; they had the artificial manner of a country club set and approached life with a prep-school point of view. His business invitees, though a more worldly group, were underlings, there to curry favor. Bored and abstracted, he emptied his glass and looked about for Kathleen. She was at the other end of the room and did not see him. He had decided to get up and signal to her when he was suddenly distracted.

The front door had opened and a cool draft of air entered the room. A Catholic priest had come into the lighted hall and was standing in three-quarter profile just inside the door, talking with a woman in a red dress who had let him in. Though they had never met, Paul knew that it was Stephen Engle.

There, in masculine form, were Kathleen's dark eyes and dark hair and beautifully chiseled features, but without her quicksilver nervousness. The young Jesuit seemed to bring a stillness into a room. He had about him none of the grim, overanxious human concern to impress others or assert his own ego that Paul was used to seeing in men with whom he dealt. It was as though he had outgrown all that.

For a moment Paul sat wholly occupied with a man whom only an hour ago he had been prepared to dismiss, and as he followed Stephen with his eyes, Kathleen came into the hall.

She went up to her brother and hugged him tightly, then stood hanging on his shoulder, smiling at the woman in the red dress but not really seeing her, gazing up at Stephen, wanting his attention. She told him, "I want you to meet the man who's become so important in my life," and, glancing over her shoulder, looked round for Paul who, knowing what was expected of him, got to his feet and walked across the room to meet them.

"Stephen, this is Paul Brittain." Then, touching Paul's arm, "Paul, my brother, Stephen."

"Stephen, I've been wondering if anyone could live up to the advance notice," Paul said, shaking hands. Again he was impressed, but this time by how dissimilar brother and sister were. Kathleen was a good-looking woman and she was aware of her physical beauty; her whole being radiated the self-confidence drawn from it. But the handsome young man in the hallway, seen up close, was humbly dressed: his suit old, its nap worn down in spots, the cuffs of the coat sleeves slightly threadbare. And Paul Brittain asked himself, "What makes a man like this choose the life he leads?"

By ten thirty a third of the guests had left. Those who still remained gathered in the living room by the fire. Conversations continued, but in softer inflections. The evening now resembled those long-ago nighttime college sessions, familiar to all of them, that lasted until the early hours of the morning. At eleven, Stephen prepared to excuse himself.

Kathleen was sitting on the floor by the fireplace, her legs curled up under her, her back braced against Paul's legs, her body turned so that she could clearly see her brother, who was seated on an ottoman placed under one window. She looked across the room and smiled at him. She did not want this night to end. It was sustenance for her. Stephen's face, too long absent, was sustenance for her. She turned her head and whispered to Paul, "Please invite Stephen to stay longer."

Paul leaned over and spoke quietly into the dark strands of her hair where the shell of her ear showed through. He was thinking of something. Until that moment he had been looking for a way to end the evening. Now he felt his competitive instincts quicken.

"Stephen," he said in his rich, low-pitched voice, "I'm not acquainted with Catholic writers. But one that I have heard of is Teilhard de

Chardin, who was a member of your order. His views on evolution got him into hot water with Rome, I believe. What do you think of him?"

Kathleen glanced at Stephen uncertainly. Her eyes told him, "I didn't know he would choose a subject like this. Please...nothing controversial."

"Some of de Chardin's concepts were unorthodox," Stephen said, indicating by a barely perceptible nod of his head that he had seen her, and understood. "But, at heart, he was a highly creative thinker, searching for the imperishable, which he first understood in terms of the physical elements."

Paul took out a cigarette, holding it in one corner of his mouth while he reached unhurriedly for his lighter. When he had lit the cigarette, he settled back into the sofa cushion and said pleasantly, "That's an interesting progression. I'd like to hear how it came about."

Stephen looked round at the others. They were sitting, wholly content, listening.

"I'm not a scientist," he said, "I'm a teacher of literature, and so my answer comes from that standpoint, from an interest in the imaginative process."

He thought a minute and then he said, "Teilhard believed that spirit and matter are merely different aspects of one creation, and that all life, all matter, is not only evolving but also ascending, or, as he put it, is involved in a profound Becoming. What absorbed him was not matter itself, but the Absolute in matter, something in matter that hinted at imperishability. Please hold this thought in mind as I make a shift in perspective.

"Writing in his book, *The Hero with a Thousand Faces*, Joseph Campbell named the adventure of the hero one of the great central myths of Western civilization, and identified within it a minor myth: the call to adventure.

"To illustrate his points, Campbell referred to the Grimm folk tale of the frog king. The story, as you may know, tells of a young princess who has her lost ball reclaimed for her unexpectedly, almost miraculously, by a frog. This simple occurrence went on to alter her life dramatically.

Campbell saw the story as a metaphor for the human biography: specifically, for that moment in one's life when a new figure appears to mark a stage of transformation.

"Well, when you read Teilhard's biography with Campbell's insight in mind, something jumps right out at you. As a boy encouraged to love nature by his father, Teilhard became fascinated by the splinters of iron he found on their walks together. He kept a collection of shell splinters and other bits and pieces, convinced that he'd never found anything more durable, more wondrous than iron. In those scattered mineral fragments that lay about him in his childhood world he discovered a lifelong feeling for matter, a feeling that moved him to study science as a second calling. Iron had served as his 'frog,' if you will.

"Teilhard's intellectual passage, then, was from the child who delighted in what he called his 'God of Iron' to the scholar who would write that 'the merest chance reveals an unsuspected world,' and see all of creation moved and penetrated by God—'the divine milieu.'

"To my mind, the boyhood encounter with iron that led Teilhard to a lifelong feeling for matter is a striking instance of the mythical call to adventure. In his case, the call was to spiritual illumination. Whether you agree with his theology or not, as an example, the experience stands on its own."

Stephen sat back. A responsive silence fell. In the profound quiet the fire popped; a silk skirt rustled; someone set a china cup down on its saucer, delicately.

Paul ground out his cigarette in an ashtray and said, "Thank you, Stephen." At his feet Kathleen sat with her hands clasped loosely in a kind of silent clap, her dark eyes shining.

"You've won us," Paul added, smiling.

—ɯ—

They had another discussion a few weeks later, when Stephen came to dinner alone.

In the dining room, candles in crystal hurricanes gleamed at both ends of the table. A silver Revere bowl filled with apples and trailing green ivy shimmered in the center of a crisp white cloth. Paul was at the head of the table, a bottle of wine beside his glass. Kathleen sat to his right, looking very delicate in the soft candlelight. She lifted the bowl and offered it to Stephen. Nestled in among the apples were aromatic round green nuts with rough husks.

"Do you remember when we were children, Stephen, how Granddad took us down to the stream behind his farm to search for black walnuts and to show us the tree he'd planted for each of us?"

Stephen reached into the bowl, selected one of the walnuts, and held it between his thumb and forefinger, fascinated.

"Yes, of course I do. 'You plant a black walnut, not for a child, but for a grandchild,' our Grandfather Engle explained," he said, turning to Paul, "because it takes fifty years for a tree to mature.

"I remember the odors: the fragrance of fallen leaves, the bitter scent of the black walnuts, and how we, as children, thought that because our grandfather had taken us to see the trees, only we knew about them."

Stephen smiled at his immersion in the memory. "It's been a long time since I'd thought of it."

During the meal, Paul entertained them, recounting different stories: how as a boy he'd milked cows in the cold and dark before catching the bus to school each morning; where he had served in the Korean War; how after the war he had worked his way through college; how he had begun as a financial consultant at his firm and risen to senior vice president without any of the important connections others had had.

Paul paused to sip his wine. Then he said, "I've passed the fifty years it takes for the walnut tree to mature. With that passage, I've come to see the world with what I hope is clearer vision. I'm more confident about the future. We never thought the Berlin Wall would come down in our lifetimes, and yet it did. The Cold War is over. I think the next century will see democracy on the rise everywhere. If we can keep 'the

Butcher of Baghdad' in his place and settle the problems in the Middle East, we could see an unprecedented new era of peace and prosperity."

"Some things remain to be done," Stephen said amiably. "We still need to care for the brokenhearted, proclaim the good news to the poor, and freedom to the oppressed..."

"Then there will have to be more of you. Your ranks are thinning. Cause for concern?"

"Yes, of course. I have to acknowledge there's a very real need for vocations to the priesthood. But, I try to keep this perspective:

"At the end of his life, Lenin is said to have remarked that if he'd had twelve men like the first followers of Ignatius of Loyola, he could have changed the world. So perhaps, one day the Jesuits may come down to just a handful. But if that number consists of men like Francis Xavier and the others who became the first members of the Society of Jesus..." Stephen broke off with a smile.

"Those who know me wouldn't describe me as a religious man, Stephen. I'm very down to earth...realistic?" Paul was sitting back in his chair with his legs crossed, lightly and rhythmically brushing his knee with his hand in a posture he assumed when he wished to demonstrate authority. He continued:

"As I see it, life is chance, is opportunity, is loss, is tragedy, is recovery, is fulfillment: all fragmentary and impermanent. My ground for saying this is my own experience."

Stephen nodded. "Each of us sees a quality to life that, in Goethe's phrase, is 'like chance, since it evinces no sequence of causality...like Providence, for it hints at coherence.' So, where you see chance, perhaps, because of my faith, I see coherence."

"A beautiful quotation, but too otherworldly for me. I don't believe there is a way to substantiate religious faith."

Stephen ran a finger along the foot of his glass for a moment and then he said, "If those physics scholars who developed the unified string theory can assert that the elegance and beauty of the concept necessitate its being true—absent empirical evidence—why couldn't theology make the same claim?"

Surprised by the reference to physics, Paul surrendered an admiring smile. He said, "Well, you've made me think." He reached for his cigarettes, absentmindedly and perfunctorily offered them to Stephen, who declined, took one for himself, and lit it.

"You're a mystery to me, Stephen," he went on, snapping his lighter shut. "I've never known a priest before. Most men I've met are moved by the desire for money or power. I'll go further, and say that I measure success by the things I acquire, not by the things I relinquish. Do you mind if I ask you, do you ever think you made a mistake?"

"No, I've never thought that. I'd be a fish out of water in any other pursuit.

"But you want a substantive answer." Stephen was quiet a moment and then he said, "There are places in Scripture where we hear echoes of a historical event as it must have occurred. One of those instances involves the word *called*. *He called to him James, the son of Zebedee, and his brother John…and immediately they left their boat and their father and followed him.* We can sense in that passage the irresistible hold on others of Jesus of Nazareth.

"When those in religious life speak of having felt 'called,' they mean that they felt something like that original, mesmerizing attraction to the person of Christ. The commitment is to a man, not an idea."

"And that's enough for you?" Paul asked, rising. He had no further interest in the subject. Stephen's response left him cold. He had looked for thinking somewhat in line with his own but heard words that he considered meaningless jargon. He went to the buffet and opened a bottle of Scotch. "Would you like a different drink, darling?" he asked Kathleen, who sat, her hands folded in her lap, her glass untouched, listening.

Stephen looked at her and smiled, then, thinking of her, turned to Paul and said, "What matters in life, ultimately? When you think of the human personality—how man alone in the animal world will betray another for personal gain and will stand by a friend even if all he has is taken from him—what those extremes of behavior say is that we are a species for whom the word *relationship* is everything.”

“The world will be saved by love? Is that where you’re going?” Paul asked, returning to the table. “How many are capable of the kind of personal commitment you describe? Very few, I think. Most individuals fall somewhere between those parameters of behavior. If you want to know the truth about people, as I said before, ‘follow the money.’”

Paul sat down and waited for a reply, but Stephen’s only response was to give him a long meaningful look.

—⁂—

After three years at *Christian Comment*, Clare had earned the opportunity to write feature articles. The time spent honing her skills had flown by, filled with excitement and promise, and with some poignancy.

“When you’re young,” she remembered her Grandfather Shannon telling her once, “the years ahead appear to stretch into eternity, as if you were looking through a telescope at distant worlds. But when you’re old, the past seems very near, like a room you’ve just left, and are looking back into.”

Time hung in a balance between future and past for Clare Engle, at thirty. She wrote to Stephen:

> *You ask how my work is going, and if I find it fulfilling. I came to this position as a total beginner, but from the start, my editors have been very supportive and have encouraged me to write creatively.*
>
> *I’ve been asked to write an article for the feast of Saint Ignatius of Loyola, the subject of my own choosing. The story that has captured my imagination is that of a little-known Jesuit saint named Alexander Briant. Perhaps you know of him?*
>
> *Imprisoned in the Tower of London with Edmund Campion and, later, executed alongside him, Briant achieved his dream of*

becoming a Jesuit when the Fathers responded to his appeal, written to them from prison, and received him into the Society.

My theme—Seek the Lord, seek His face always—is described not by Briant's martyrdom, but by his acceptance of the will of God.

That wasn't always the way I saw things! Before, I think, I thought that sanctity consisted of always choosing the hardest path, in asking for suffering. But experience teaches how presumptuous that attitude is. Genuine holiness involves the death of selfishness, living life to the fullness of one's capacity—out of love for God— and leaving the rest to him.

It's hard, though, to achieve that simplicity of being. There is so much to divide the heart!

Increasingly, I feel pulled in all directions, when what I want is to be creating something original and lasting, to be doing the work I feel I was meant to do.

Distracted by the outer world, I turn to art, and it gives so much to me. Someday I want to go to Rome, to visit the churches— five in all—where the paintings of Caravaggio are on public view. His work caught my imagination while I was in the convent. One painting in particular draws me.

In the church of San Luigi dei Francesi, in the elegant Contarelli Chapel, taking up a wall to one side of the altar, glows "The Calling of St. Matthew."

With light and shadow and craftsmanship of almost photo-graphic perfection, Caravaggio captured a miracle: that moment when the transcendent breaks in upon time and space.

Imagine it: to the left, dressed like a sixteenth-century merchant and huddled over a counting table with four associates, sits Levi, unaware until this instant that all his earthly connections are about to be broken. A shaft of light illumines his face and the table on which rest the dull coins of the day's commerce.

To the right, by the door, veiled in shadow, barefoot and wearing the austere robes of the ancient world, Christ and Saint Peter have *entered the room, and Christ, in a magisterial gesture that hints at God the Father in Michelangelo's "The Creation," is extending his hand toward the table. Though the astonished Levi stares back, disbelieving, the finger he points at himself and the query in his eyes expressing both confusion and demur, Christ's feet are already turned toward the door, the decision made.*

In addition to its magnificence as art, the painting holds a personal meaning. At times I feel I live a kind of bifurcated existence, Stephen: I am a part of the world that is "too much with us; late and soon..." and yet, I have always yearned for that Presence in the doorway, and longed to rise with Levi and leave the darkened room...

The letter, with its tenor of spiritual yearning, its description of the call to discipleship, was a comfort to Stephen, who felt that it mirrored all life.

—⚬—

Just as on a stage where everyone is standing still a single moving figure draws attention, so, too, on a stage where everyone is stirring, a motionless couple attracts the eye.

Such a scene was taking place in the middle of a crowded city block where Kathleen and Paul were standing hand-in-hand.

The December night was cold and wintry and snow was falling over the city. Frost glistened amid the little white lights draped ivy-like on the street-lamps. From somewhere overhead a loudspeaker was blaring out a carol:

On the first day of Christmas...

Unmindful of the snowfall, Kathleen and Paul had been walking along a wide avenue, moving unhurriedly with the milling crowd. As they slowed to look at the Christmas exhibits in the lighted store windows, Kathleen's eye had suddenly been drawn to one display and she had gone over to the window to take it in. Paul followed her and they stood a few steps back to leave room for families who had also come up to the window. Parents waited in silence, chins tucked into drawn-up collars, while children pressed their noses against the pane, small rubberbooted feet shuffling on the pavement.

They were staring at the same scene that held Kathleen's gaze.

Centered in the foreground of the window, the tall, august figure of Father Christmas stared out through traceries of snow that had been hand-painted on the glass to effect a winter landscape. He was clothed in a long ivory cloak and heavy Icelandic boots and he had a garland of holly wreathed round his untamed hair. Behind him, in a clearing within a make-believe fir woods, waited an enormous sleigh laden with gorgeous emerald and ruby boxes. All about the sleigh, magnificent reindeer stood staring off into the distance or gently pawing the frozen earth, from which a white mist that made the display seem ethereal was rising.

Kathleen looked at the scene, transfixed, her fur-lined hood let down, her face upturned, rapt.

Paul was quiet a minute, then he laid his leather-gloved palm against her cheek. He asked, "What is it, Kathleen?"

"Nothing…nothing…" she answered softly. But she stood looking on. Don would have understood: it was the children. For an instant, she had had a connection with them and she couldn't make herself give it up.

She glanced at Paul and forced a smile. "What would you like for Christmas?"

Paul's deep, sonorous voice in answer was razor-edged in the bitter air, "Just you."

A thrill ran through her. "Forever?" she wanted to ask him but, gripped by the tension of longing to know and being afraid to know, was unable to.

She squeezed his hand so that he would read love in her grasp and turned her head away so that he couldn't see she was trying not to cry.

—⚊—

Miles away the street scene altered. Snow was falling heavily, drifting in sheets over the walks. Aging houses with snow piled up on unswept porch steps and small shops, their boarded-up facades blackened by the damp, sank together into darkness.

Down a quiet side street a door opened suddenly and from the recess of a basement staircase a wan shaft of light slanted upward. In a minute the door closed and Stephen climbed up the stairs and came out onto the street. He halted at the curb, looking around at the winter night, his face flushed from the warmth of the soup kitchen where he had been working below. With bare hands he turned up the collar of his coat against the cold and, walking quickly, started down the narrow, unplowed street in the direction of a distant traffic light.

He had the look of those who are poor—hatless, in a thin coat, head bent down against the wind: this strikingly handsome young man looking up fleetingly to glance at passersby, and in his eyes intelligence and goodness shone.

At a distance he had grown to resemble his father more, with the same suggestion of loneliness in his walk, though what in the father had been an isolation born of too great a loss was, in the son, the solitude of deep concentration, which is a different form of loneliness.

There was always about Stephen Engle the sense that he was moving away, as now, through blowing snow, he vanished from view. It showed here in a simple walk to the bus, the bearing that was ever the same: quick, focused, directed in response to some hidden claim on his urgent young life.

XVI

One evening in mid-August Paul told Kathleen that he had to go to New York. He said he knew the trip was sudden but he had to meet the client personally. It was a big account.

"I'd love to go with you," Kathleen said. "There's so much to do in New York, and we'd be together."

"Not this time. The hours are bound to be long. I should be back in forty-eight hours, three days at most." To placate her he proposed a pleasant diversion. "How about a trip of our own next month? We'll go to Hilton Head for a weekend."

Kathleen walked over to him, looked into his eyes, then laid her head against his shoulder and embraced him. Feeling the need to say it, she offered that if the appointment was that important, she would help him pack. Two or three days was not a long time to be gone; once he returned, it would seem as though he hadn't been away at all.

—∞—

On the evening of the third day, Kathleen was changing her blouse when she dropped an earring on the floor. The earring rolled under Paul's dresser so that she had to kneel to retrieve it. When her searching fingers could not find it, she bent over and laid her cheek against the carpet to look. She saw the earring and also something that had fallen behind the dresser and was lodged against the wall.

She got up and went to the back of the dresser and groped along the wall until she felt a folded piece of paper. It was a small blue envelope, addressed in a neat, controlled hand to Paul at his office. What caught Kathleen's attention was the name in the upper left-hand corner. Jan Brittain. There was something inside the envelope. Wondering, Kathleen opened it and with slightly trembling fingers took out a page of blue note paper. The page contained a single paragraph of seven short sentences. After she'd read over the paragraph, she read the third and fourth sentences again and then again. The other sentences didn't register at all.

"I know what you're doing, Paul. Does she know you still have a wife?"

She put the note back in the envelope and crumpled it in her hand. She felt chilled, as if a cold, wet sheet were being drawn over her from her toes to her eyes.

I've had two marriages, two divorces.

He had lied to her. Utterly composed, his words coming out slowly, a slight frown creasing his brows to emphasize his sincerity, he had looked directly into her eyes and lied to her.

—⚬—

It was drizzling, the evening vanishing in veils of mist.

Kathleen ran down the low flagstone steps at her front entrance and out into the soft haze, the crushed envelope shoved into the pocket of her unbelted raincoat. She wanted to run away, to be anyplace but where she was.

In front of her the dark band of driveway wound luxuriantly through treed grounds, circling them in a broad arc for three-quarters of a mile. She walked at a near run, scarcely aware that a man and woman entering their front door turned to look at her. She walked until she had to stop to catch her breath. When she glanced around she realized that she had come more than half the circle of the drive. Thirty yards across from her, beyond a neighbor's garden wall, she could see her town house through breaks in the trees, unnaturally large in the darkness. As she looked, a light came on in an upstairs window. When she saw it, a wave of nausea went through her.

—∿—

Paul was in the bedroom, his suitcase open before him on the bed, and did not hear Kathleen approach the door.

"Hello, Paul."

The low, thick quality in her voice caused him to look up quickly. They exchanged glances in silence. Standing with her back to the door, Kathleen put forth her hand, and Paul saw the blue crumpled envelope.

"Paul, is it true…you're married?"

He didn't answer at first, but stood grim-faced, flicking his fingers on the lid of the suitcase, his head lowered. Then he looked at her very deliberately and said, "Yes."

"And what am I…the affair, the girlfriend?"

"God, no, Kathleen." He walked over to her and took her hand.

She withdrew it and, with eyes beginning to tear up, backed away. "Then…why didn't you tell me about your wife?"

"At first? I would have lost you. You know that."

"Are you going back to her?"

"Never."

He told her a more complete story. After he and his wife had separated six years earlier, Jan Brittain had moved to Connecticut, and now lived in a summer home they had owned there, on Long Island Sound. They saw each other very infrequently, usually when money matters brought them together or, as this time, when his wife had learned of Kathleen. They had quarreled bitterly, but nothing had come of it. He had left with the status quo intact.

All the time he was speaking, Paul did not mention his wife by name but repeatedly referred to her as "she" or "that woman." Kathleen, who was listening only to the parts of the story that affected her, didn't notice the subtle, insistent depersonalization of Jan Brittain.

When Paul broke off, she said hurriedly, "Now that you've told me everything, and I understand...if you're not ever going back to her, you can get a divorce, and be free—"

Paul smiled slightly. "It's not that simple. Why do you think I've never pressed for a divorce? She would take me for every cent I have."

"But that wouldn't matter to me—"

"Oh, that wouldn't matter to *you*?" he said, and scoffed. "Do you think I'd let a woman support me?"

"But would that be so different from the way you're living now?" Kathleen asked, not realizing her implication.

His look cut her short.

"Paul, I'm sorry. I didn't mean—"

"We're moving."

"What?"

"We're selling this place and moving to one I provide."

"But this is my home—"

"Have it your way then, but I'm moving." He walked toward her and stopped beside her in the doorway. "If you want to come, come. If not..." He waved her off irritably.

"Paul, wait—"

Kathleen turned quickly and caught his arm. She pressed her face against the rough tweed of his sport coat and whispered fervently, "Wherever you go, whatever may happen, I want to be there, too. Always, always."

⟶

Paul's apartment was at the top of a historic downtown hotel, a two-story penthouse with lofty ceilings and an outdoor terrace that faced north toward the theater district. Though Kathleen missed access to the natural world—a private elevator to street level instead of the flagstone steps to the lawn—she made the adjustment quickly.

But they were arguing more now. Divorce was permanently out of the question: If they were to remain together, Kathleen would have to live with that provision as a freely accepted condition of their relationship. But this condition was exactly what she could not resign herself to. She suffered badly, and visibly. Increasingly short-tempered, bored by her moods, Paul began to spend time away from her. His absences, in turn, aroused in her the fear that he was seeing other women.

Once again, as had happened three years before after the death of her husband, Kathleen felt that she was somehow fated to lose everything of value to her. She could think of no way out of her predicament except to end the relationship, and that was the one move she would not consider. And then, just when she felt she was about to come apart at the seams, she thought of the resource that had been there all along, and made a decision that put one of her most treasured relationships at risk.

XVII

November. Like those seeking to do penance, the trees, shorn of their raiment, stood abjectly in gray, dissolving snow. The stone towers of the university campus rising out of the cold, autumnal landscape might have been images from a medieval world. Through the damp afternoon air came the sound of the chapel bell chiming two. She was a little late. Stephen would be waiting for her.

She found him sitting at the desk in his office, envelopes and loose sheets of paper in front of him, finishing a letter. When she tapped on the open door he got up at once.

"Kathleen." He walked over to her and brought her inside. Alone, out of the public eye, they embraced.

Stephen took her coat and pulled out a chair for her. He said, "You've moved." He added with a smile, "How do you like living in the city?"

"Oh, I love it."

Kathleen walked slowly around the room, studying her surroundings. She had entered a scholar's workplace, an earthen-brown room furnished simply with the essentials—a desk and a few chairs, bookshelves, a file cabinet, prints of Jesuit poets and saints on the walls. She stopped for a moment in front of the picture of a middle-aged man, a balding intellectual with a high, wide forehead, a short, neatly trimmed beard, and dark, intense eyes that seemed to penetrate the viewer's soul.

"Why does Saint Ignatius always look so grim?" she asked. She glanced over her shoulder at her brother and smiled. "Maybe he had too many advanced degrees."

Stephen laughed.

Kathleen moved over to the bookshelves. There were the classics of literature, many by writers she knew: Joyce, Eliot, Yeats; others by poets she had only heard of: Pushkin, Mandelstam, Milosz. Out of curiosity, she looked around for the one book constant in her brother's life, *The Poems and Prose of Gerard Manley Hopkins*, given to Stephen at his ordination by their father. It lay by itself on the inside left corner of the desk, the place reserved for the book a reader would reach for at the first opportunity.

She sat down then and looked across the desk at him: Stephen—whose face was as dear to her as her own. He was older now: touches of gray in the dark hair; around the eyes, fine expression lines that deepened into creases when he smiled. Still a face that—thinking now more of her own—she would term beautiful.

She became whimsical, telling him how brief the drive there had seemed, wandering from one subject to another, talking of nothing in particular. She thought of a former schoolmate of theirs whom by chance she had seen the week before, and asked:

"Do you remember Mary Ellen Newbert?"

"Sure." Stephen smiled at a memory that presented itself to his mind. "And all of her brothers. The nuns called them 'The Seven Deadly Sins.'"

"I saw her last week."

Stephen was quiet, simply enjoying her presence.

Kathleen looked at him wordlessly, her eyes searching his face. She wanted to say, "Stephen, help me. I'm floundering. No matter how I may appear to the outside world, in my soul it's dark night. You can understand. Give me a new baptism, give me a new name. I want to begin again." But she thought it was sacrilegious to use mystical language in relation to herself, and so she held back; instead, she turned to the past.

She said, "You know, when you first told us you were going to enter the Jesuits, Clare came to me one day and asked if I could enter the convent instead."

"Did she? That sounds like Clare."

Lowering her eyes for a moment, Kathleen said, "When I was a young girl, I used to imagine joining the Carmelites, like Saint Thérèse of Lisieux. That austere life seemed so full of high drama: sleeping on a straw mat, rising in the night to chant the Office, becoming consumptive and dying in a nimbus of glory at age twenty-four." She laughed softly. "Sounds rather silly now, doesn't it?"

Stephen smiled affectionately.

Kathleen looked down at the floor. Her thin, lovely hands smoothed the nap of her dark suede skirt. "Sometimes I wonder if, at the end of my life, I'll look back and think: it was all so short. Being a Carmelite and getting up to pray at twelve a.m. and then again at five wouldn't have been so bad, if when you died you knew you were going to heaven."

"There aren't any guarantees, I'm afraid."

Kathleen looked at her brother, surprised. "You don't think so? Do you mean Sister Irene—that witch I had for algebra—might not have a higher place in heaven than I will?" she said, smiling archly, and they both laughed.

As he listened, Stephen held a pencil in one hand, rotating it absently, eraser to tip, eraser to tip, on the desk in front of him. "I think I agree with your first example, Thérèse," he said. "She believed that in the end we go to God empty-handed, trusting in His mercy."

Kathleen looked off into space for a moment. "Paul doesn't believe in a personal God," she said. "He believes we make our heaven or hell here on Earth, and when it's over, it's over."

"What do you believe?"

"I'm not sure…I used to have such a shining faith as a child. I would love to have back the prayer life of a young girl. Everything was so tangible—so certain." She paused. Then she said, "Later, things seemed to tarnish."

Looking at Stephen, she asked, "Do you think we can lose our faith if we begin—imperceptibly—to make choices that compromise our values?"

"Yes, I do."

"But how do we know which is reality and which is distortion: the belief we had in the beginning, or the disillusionment later? Maybe the disillusionment is the reality."

Stephen asked quietly, "What's the matter, Kathleen?"

"I don't know," she said, at a sudden loss for words. Her face tensed. She asked, "Stephen, would you hear my confession?"

"Let's talk about it first."

"I can't."

"Just say one word about it."

"I've been lying to you—lying by omission—for over a year...Paul and I are living together."

"Why doesn't he marry you?"

"Because," Kathleen answered, her voice barely discernible, "his wife won't give him a divorce."

Stephen exhaled audibly, the pencil dropped, and he stared at her, disbelieving.

"I'm sorry, I didn't know how to tell you."

"What are you going to do?"

"I don't know. I love him. I more than love him: I need him." She opened her purse and took out a small white handkerchief and pressed it to her eyes. "I can't leave him, and yet, I can't live with the guilt any longer."

"Kathleen, I understand that you love this man, but I also know you're suffering. What kind of relationship is that?"

"Paul says the problem is with the Church. He feels the Church is inflexible and doctrinaire."

Stephen smiled faintly. "He has a career. He has a wife. And he has you. He has a great deal of flexibility."

Kathleen looked down at her hands and did not respond at first. At last she looked again at Stephen and in a low, dull voice said, "There's a road that winds its way along Dunham Lake, making a long, curving bend as it turns toward the highway. All of my dreams were shattered on that road."

Stephen unstrapped his watch and put it in a drawer. Whatever else he had to do that afternoon was tabled. Their shared griefs were coming forth. He said gently, "Go on."

"Stephen," Kathleen said, with tears, "after Mom died, I tried to be there for everyone. For Dad, for Clare, for you. I tried to do everything right. I prayed. I went to Mass every Sunday. I believed in God. I married in the Catholic Church.

"In all that time, I've never asked you for a thing. Stephen, just this once I'm asking you for something. Please, help me find a way to be with Paul and stay within the Church."

His eyes never leaving her face, Stephen shook his head. "There is no way, Kathleen."

"Please," she said, as if she hadn't heard. "Paul understands me, in ways that aren't possible for you to understand. He's given me back parts of my life that I thought were irretrievable. Without him, I have nothing. You must help me."

Troubled, Stephen looked at her in silence, thinking of how to respond. He was quiet so long that Kathleen, misreading what she thought was finality in his stillness, cried:

"I can't believe you. Where's your heart, Stephen? How can you be so cold?"

Stephen leaned forward, his eyes intent with concentration. "Listen to me. I am not cold toward you, or unmoved by your unhappiness. No one is more important to me than you are. But I'm bound by Church law and, in this instance, by civil law as well."

"Would you break a law for a higher good?"

"Yes, if my conscience allowed." Stephen doubted that a relationship with Paul Brittain worked for her or any other woman's higher good, but he would not say it.

Kathleen dried her eyes with the handkerchief again. "Everything has always been effortless for you, Stephen. Why am I the weak one, the one with the life going nowhere?"

"You aren't weak. You're very strong. You've endured losses that would have broken another woman in half. You had too much responsibility imposed on you too early in life. You took it on unselfishly. And because of that commitment, you never had the chance to enjoy reckless, carefree teenage years."

Kathleen considered his words carefully. After a moment she asked in a different, lowered voice, "Were you ever a reckless, carefree teenager?"

"I had a different temperament, a different way of looking at things."

"A different temperament, a different way of looking at things," Kathleen echoed. "Is that why life has always been effortless for you?"

"It's never been effortless, Kathleen."

Ill at ease with her tone, Stephen got up and walked away from his desk. He went over to the window and stood looking out at the grounds. A sharp wind was sweeping across the campus and the first traces of rain were falling on the walks.

Kathleen asked, "Didn't you ever have the longing to hold a woman in your arms, to make love to her?"

"Yes."

"I can't be the only one to bare her soul. You have to tell me."

At first Stephen did not reply. Then he said quietly, "It was during my second year here. She was a graduate assistant, and a student of mine."

Kathleen, startled by the disclosure, said the first thought that entered her mind. "What did she look like?"

In the manner of the shy younger brother of their youth, Stephen answered softly, "I try not to remember." He worked a loose floor molding with his shoe. "She was a very lovely girl."

"Was she in love with you?"

"Yes, she was."

"Were you in love with her?"

"Yes," Stephen said, and coughed to clear his throat. "I was seriously in love with her."

"Were you"—Kathleen halted for an instant, then asked bluntly— "were you physically involved?"

Stephen turned his head and looked at her steadily. "No."

"Well, the break must have been effortless then."

"No," Stephen said, turning his face again to the window. "It was very hard on her and very difficult for me."

An afternoon rain was falling, slanting rhythmically against the pane; the sky to the north was gray and blurred. Stephen stood gazing out toward the arboretum, his eyes far off and remembering.

"I explained to her that we couldn't continue to work together," he said. "She was very brave. She understood. I tried to convince her to remain in school but, tragically, she left...She was a student of such promise."

Stephen paused for long moments. Silence. Only the steady lashing of the rain.

At length, he said, "Afterward, I coped by intellectualizing, by working on another degree."

"God! How like you that is! You dropped her to study Greek!"

Stephen, still looking away, said quietly, "Her feelings were never a joke to me."

Kathleen immediately regretted the remark. It was totally inappropriate. Stephen had fallen in love, and the relationship had ended tragically. At any other time such a disclosure would have been astonishing. Upon learning of it, she would have rushed to his side to offer support; now her own neediness overrode any sympathy she might have felt for him.

She pressed him: "But what if you had become sexually involved with her? Would you have left the priesthood?"

"That's a hypothetical question that I can't answer. The situation would have been far more complicated and painful. But I hope I'd still be standing here today. I took vows that I intend to keep."

"Evidently, Paul and I aren't cut from the same heroic cloth."

Stephen, to deflect her sarcasm, looked at her and asked, "Kathleen, do you ever wonder—in a difficult hour—what Mom would advise?"

Kathleen started in surprise. "Oh, the irony of those words!" She hesitated for a moment, then she said, "I loved Mom just as much as you did, and I've probably never gotten over her death. But I couldn't talk with her about relationships."

Stephen looked at her inquiringly. He had caught the pause, the redirection in her thinking.

Kathleen avoided his glance to follow her own train of thought. "Mom doted on you," she said, her words coming out rapidly, bitterly. "'Stephen has great goals…Stephen needs money for books…Stephen should go to Georgetown or Boston College.'"

"You're laying some heavy burdens on me, Kathleen."

His unbroken self-control incensed her. "Do you want another one?"

Stephen tensed. Here it came—the reason for the pause. He lowered his head and watched the rain stream down the window in a long cascade. "Go ahead."

Kathleen spoke in a low voice, placing emphasis on each word. "Mom was having an affair when she died."

Stephen turned on his heel, startled.

"I don't believe that."

"Oh, it's true. I first learned about it one day when I picked up the phone and heard them talking. For days afterward, when I answered the phone, the person on the other end hung up. One morning, when Mom went out, I decided to search through her dresser. I found letters she'd kept, letters from the man she was betraying our father with."

"Why didn't you ever tell me this before?"

"Because of Dad. He knew, but he thought Mom was ending it. After she died, he told me he believed she'd been coming home to him that night. That was what he needed to believe. I never believed it. You and Dad weren't there when she left the house. I was the only one to see her. She wasn't tense or unhappy. She was excited.

"You never knew because Dad asked me not to tell you. He wanted our mother to stay perfect in the minds of her children. I would have walked through fire for Dad, and so I promised not to."

Stephen crossed the floor and sat down at his desk again, the chair facing out, his back to the wall. For a while he sat staring down at the floor, not saying anything. Then he said, "Kathleen, I deeply regret the mental anguish Dad endured. And how you've carried this burden alone all these years" – he looked at her and shook his head – "I don't know." He put his hand to the back of his neck. In a strained voice, he went on, "I need you to understand that it's difficult for me just now, with the pain of this disclosure so close to me."

Kathleen did not look at him. She said, "Mom died estranged from God and the Church."

"You don't know that," Stephen returned quickly. "I have memories of the night our mother died, too. She was conscious near the end."

"But what if she'd died instantly, without a chance to express remorse: Would you have forgiven her?"

"You know that I would."

"But you won't hear my confession because you know you couldn't give me absolution. The Church won't forgive me."

"This is very hard for both of us," Stephen said. "You know the reason. You're making a conscious decision to live in an occasion of sin."

"And she *wasn't*?" Kathleen returned in a hard cry that rang throughout the room. She stared at Stephen with a cold, trembling apprehension, fearing to lose control and go too far, yet not having the strength of will to stop herself.

"I don't know if I believe in God anymore," she said. "The God of my hypocritical mother. The God who took my husband away. The God who denied me children.

"You live here in your chaste ivory tower with the memory of your forbidden coed, whose face you dare not remember, whose name you dare not pronounce. I live in the *real* world, where men and women live together and go to bed together and struggle together.

"I hate the rigid, controlled way I've lived all my life. I hate the subtle, legalistic phrases that catalog sin and categorize sinners. I hate the Church and the way it imposes its will on people—" She broke off, shaking with anger, and sat in numbed silence, consumed by her thoughts.

Stephen was silent, too, his head lowered, his back again against the wall, his expression grave. After a long pause he responded. He looked straight ahead of him and spoke quietly into the room.

"The Church can't impose its will on you, Kathleen. The only power the Church has over you is what you as a believing Christian consent to give it."

"Then I choose not to consent," Kathleen cried. She slapped the desk with her palm, scattering the papers lying there. "I renounce the Church. And all its works. I do renounce them. And all its empty promises. I do renounce them. I'm done here, Stephen, permanently done here."

With a sudden, awkward gesture she reached for her coat, fumbling a bit with her things, stood, and started from the room. At the door she heard Stephen say her name.

His throat had tightened and he spoke with difficulty. "Kathleen. Don't close the door on us. In spite of what's happened here today, we love each other. Let some time go by, then let's try to talk again."

"No," Kathleen said firmly, "not a chance." But she turned to look back.

Beyond the window the weather had broken. Clouds glowed in the west, the wind had died, and the pane was beginning to clear. It was Stephen's face that bore the likeness of rain.

—⚭—

Paul lay, his head turned into the pillow, his arm pressed against her shoulder. When Kathleen was sure he was asleep, she freed herself from his arm and rolled onto her side and lay, staring into the darkness. Drained of anger, her mind returned to self-reproach.

Two months would pass and she would reach the age at which her mother had died. Always she had hoped that when she crossed that threshold she could define her life anew, and from then on, the years would be her own. But in spite of her highest, best resolve, when she looked now at the place to which she had come: she was her mother's daughter.

In her overwrought imagination she envisioned countless dark, intimate rooms as they were at that moment, with men and women gathering into one another. Except for her. She was the woman cast out, alone beyond the city gates.

—⁂—

The next morning, a Saturday, in the solitude of the cold, deserted campus, Stephen returned to his office, trying to collect himself. He pulled a chair over to the window, turned it so that it faced into the room, sat astride it, his arms extended over its back, and looked out.

Snow had fallen overnight. A cold, raw wind swept the last leaves down the walks. The long avenue of maples in the arboretum was now a trail of barren columns, a line of ruins. The scene made no impression on him, other than its general feel of desolation. He closed his eyes, overcome by memories.

It was Christmas night, the year he turned six. For most of the afternoon he had played outside with the glossy red sled his Grandmother and Grandfather Engle had given him, and come in, shivering and slightly feverish, just before dark. His mother had taken him upstairs at once. He remembered her leaning over him, putting him to bed, gently moving the covers about, touching his pillow, murmuring to him in her deep, honeyed voice (he was so drowsy he could scarcely reply), her face in the lamplight, her shadow at the door, the laughter of the grown-ups from the downstairs hall—the peace, the joy, the well-being of it all.

It was a spring day in the year he was fifteen. He was sitting beside a window in the kitchen, his schoolbooks spread about him on the table. A few feet away his mother stood, rinsing lettuce in a stream of water from the faucet at the sink.

"Stephen," she spoke his name softly as she dried her hands on a small yellow towel. Dinner was not ready, but she left her work and sat down at the table beside him.

In the same soft, intimate voice she said, "Stephen, someday, some girl is going to fall so deeply in love with you."

His face reddened and he lowered his eyes.

"Look at me, honey." She took his hand and squeezed it. "When you love her back, make certain she's someone who will be loyal to you, who will be true to you, who will never deceive you, or break your heart. Promise me."

He looked back at her, fixing her shyly with his glance. "Sure, Mom."

The following week she was gone.

It was a spring day in his thirty-eighth year. The golden light of late-afternoon sunshine filtered narrowly through the leaves and, coming in the casement windows, illumined the earthen brown of the office walls. His desk was falling into shadow and, beside it she sat, slowly folding and unfolding her hands.

He was standing by this window, his back to the glass, his voice breaking:

"I never meant to see you crying the way you're crying now."

A face down-turned like soft petals in rain. "I'll be all right, because always...there will be this love..."

She looked up.

An agony of feeling passing between them.

Mother, the irony of your words.

—⁂—

Christmas Day. In the college chapel candles were lit for Low Mass. A rough, dark wooden crèche stood amid banks of scarlet poinsettia inside the communion rail. Incense from Midnight Mass still sweetened the air chilled by the morning cold. A small crowd of worshippers—students who for one reason or another had stayed throughout the Christmas break—sat in the front and talked quietly among themselves, waiting restlessly for the liturgy to begin. From high above in the choir loft a young man's voice intoned the antiphon for the Mass of Christmas Day:

A son given to us...
A child is born to us

Wearing an ivory chasuble over a white linen alb, bearing his small bald head with its aquiline nose as erectly as a falcon on a coat of arms, a tall, heavyset Jesuit walked regally up the center aisle.

—◦◦◦—

Alone in a pew at the back of the chapel, dressed so as not to attract attention in a navy blue turtleneck sweater under a black windbreaker, the celebrant of the Mass at dawn knelt. Learning that he was present, students kept glancing round to look at him, but Stephen was wrapped in thought and did not see them.

For the first time in his life he had not heard from Kathleen at Christmas. Keenly aware of her fragile emotional state and unwilling to let their estrangement stand, he knew he needed to do something. Because of the weight of that undiscovered "something," he committed the early hours of Christmas Day to prayer.

All day the Jesuit residence resonated with the sounds of arrival and greeting. The comings and goings and general conviviality allowed Stephen to blend into the background, though many of his colleagues became aware that he seemed more reserved than usual, and somewhere else.

In midafternoon, the gathering thinned. Those who remained sat chatting in one of the front parlors or stood talking in the lighted hallway at the bottom of the staircase. When he sensed his timing was right, Stephen excused himself and went to his room to pack an overnight bag. He felt a sudden imperative.

The residence car was available and, obtaining permission to borrow it, he left the residence hall and walked out into the light snow descending over the campus grounds.

On the freeway he drove in and out of snow flurries for miles, the driving becoming difficult when night set in and the lights along the interstate thinned. Three hours out, the wind and snow swirled into a blizzard. He was forced to slow to a crawl. The snow came at him with incredible speed, flakes like thousands of twirling birds fleeing down long white corridors of air. For mile after mile the wipers beat it away. An occasional car passed as if moving through smoke.

And just as suddenly, the wind died and the snow turned to a fine powder. It was near midnight and Stephen had reached the Cathedral of Our Lady of Sorrows. Behind the church, at the end of a long, curved drive, stood a two-story rectory with a wide, deep-stepped, canopied porch. The rectory was dark, but a single light glowed in a downstairs window and, as Stephen parked the car, a lank figure passed across it. Stephen was removing his overnight bag from the backseat when the door opened and the gaunt figure came out.

Pale, elderly, dressed in a red plaid shirt and flowered suspenders, with tousled gray hair and wearied features, Monsignor Nathan Ryan, alone in a large house on Christmas night, had eagerly awaited his guest.

"Father Engle! Merry Christmas! Come in!" he exclaimed in a surprisingly deep voice. Then a few moments later, in a confidential tone, "You'll have a drink? You've had a long drive." He had a fifth of whiskey in his hand.

Coming in out of the late winter night, exhausted from the emotions of the day, Stephen wanted to beg off, but he had heard the urgency in the voice.

"Thank you," he said. "That's very considerate." He stamped his feet on the ragged mat in front of the door and, following Ryan into the dimly lit rectory, coughed without meaning to, catching a whiff of his host's Christmas cheer.

—⁊⁊—

December 26, the feast of Saint Stephen, the first Christian martyr, and his forty-second birthday. Stephen slept poorly in an overheated room, the window of which he found sealed when he tried to open it. Just before sunrise he awoke.

There was nothing to obstruct the view from his second-floor window. The sky was empty of buildings and trees, unpeopled, unmarked by traffic. All existence seemed to center on a rose-white light moving through the darkness along the horizon—the austere and beautiful dawn. It seemed to Stephen a gift. He offered 7:00 a.m. Mass at the cathedral's high white altar and then ate breakfast in the grand dining room of the rectory with the old monsignor, who was, at nine in the morning, subdued and somewhat forgetful, humbly grateful that the visiting Jesuit seemed forgetful, too, of the night before.

Leaving after breakfast, Stephen continued the drive, heading west to Dunham Lake and then on to the cemetery where his parents lay buried. It was a route he had traveled often and remembered well. The road wound through birch and evergreen forests, past wooded estates, past tracts of recently developed land with signs advertising "Lots for Sale" half-buried in the snow. Thirty more minutes and he reached the top of the slope where the snow drifted in great white banks down to the shore, and beyond a wide opening in the wall of firs, the lake lay before him with the same stark beauty as the earlier dawn.

Everything held that beauty: the snow-enveloped slopes, the high drifting clouds, the white birch forests, the dark firs. And here the air was brighter. Somewhere on the other side of the wooded hills a great light was growing: the sun came burning through the trees like the herald of a vision and, where its light struck the surface of the water, white released its colors and the lake shone deep and green and golden.

There was no other traffic, no one walking the road. There was only water and sky and woods. And there were birds: a gull soaring out over the unfrozen lake, crows haunting the forested hills, Cooper's hawks stilled in the highest trees.

Stephen slowed a little. He had arrived at the place where the road divided to follow the shoreline on either side. As he turned right, a flush of feeling came over him, for he was nearing the scene of his mother's accident. In less than a mile he came to the intersection of the highway. Making this turn, hit broadside, Elizabeth Engle's car had been sent into a Norway spruce, shearing off branches and bark and splitting the trunk so that the tree grew back in two sections. Stephen had never forgotten that tree and now, as he followed the long ascent of the road, he searched for it.

It was directly ahead, smaller than he'd remembered. Blanketed with snow, alone on a slight incline, the tree, fully grown into its strangely bifurcated form, bowed its two halves earthward, like a portent.

The cemetery was five miles farther on. It was a beautiful site, set far back off the road, and surrounded by towering white pines, with a high black wrought-iron arch to mark it.

Though no attendant was present, wide tire tracks in the snow indicated a truck had been there recently. On a cleared path Stephen walked along the outermost row of headstones, searching for the family plot. A little more than halfway down the row, opposite a cluster of handsome evergreens, he found the graves of his father and mother.

Lawrence David Engle

Five years have passed; five summers, with the length
Of five long winters…

The first lines of Wordsworth's "Tintern Abbey" ode, from which he had chosen words to eulogize his father, moved him with the sense of the moment perfectly defined and, eyes lowered, he prayed into the wind his deep need for wisdom like his father's.

Elizabeth Ellen Shannon Engle

Stephen brushed away the snow that covered the plaque on his mother's grave, as once she who now lay sleeping had run her fingers through a young boy's hair. "Mom…" *Thoughts that lay too deep for tears.* Straightening up, he saw the plot with the five small graves. Baby Thomas. Baby Michael. Baby Brendan. Baby Patrick. Baby James. Classic names. Saints' names. Names a mother had pondered, dreaming of the men her sons might be. One son had been given her, the firstborn.

Stephen walked along a narrow path, ascended a slight grade, and came to the largest of four polished gray headstones.

Donald Norris Shearer

His eyes followed the small line of vanished lives. Baby Grace. Baby Nicole. Baby Stephen.

It was beginning to snow again. Clouds obscured the sun. Now, as Stephen watched the heavy, wet flakes falling through the trees, a shiver not caused by the cold coursed through him. What had all this death done to these two women that he, a male, and celibate, could never comprehend?

In imagination he was standing in the doorway of a darkened room. The light from a full moon illuminated the broad, attenuated arms of the sycamore beyond the window, and moonlight and branch shadows broke into the room together and fell upon the bed where two youthful figures were kneeling in prayer. The voice of the older one came back to him, high and faint and distant as a star:

"In the name of the Father—no, you cross like this, from left to right—in the name of the Father..." she began again, whispering, her long dark hair falling like a veil over the small child's face. And the tender young voice in reply:

"In the name of the Father..."

Kathleen, at sixteen. Mother. The love required of her. The love denied her.

Retracing his steps, Stephen stood once more beside his mother's grave, looking down. Memory after memory of her passed in his mind, each more tender than the last, memories that the corrosive of disillusion could not touch. Tolstoy described this feeling in *War and Peace*, he thought: *All, everything that I understand, I understand because I love.*

Looking south, he saw he would be driving into heavy snow again. But the weather held no importance. Something had begun to take shape within his mind. The details had yet to come, but already he knew the theme.

All his life Stephen had believed in the transforming power of words; it was with the written word that he would try to reach Kathleen. With the written word he would try, if it lay within his power, to call her back to life.

XVIII

Standing at the door to her apartment, sorting through the mail, Kathleen saw the envelope with the vertical, artistic script and felt her heart race. She let her coat fall on a nearby chair and took the letter, unopened, across the hall and into the small golden-toned dining room off the kitchen. She needed desperately to be in a place where she felt protected, a place that was *hers*.

In this pristine room, filled with light from the midmorning sun, she sat at the table and opened the envelope, her nervousness evident in her awkward unfolding of the letter within. Handwritten on white stationery in dark blue ink, it was addressed to "My Dearest Sister":

As I write, darkness is falling; it's late; all but a few students are gone for the day. Unfailingly, at this hour there comes over the campus a profound sense of peace—but not here where I am, not tonight. Tonight I find myself pitched into inner darkness, and struggle with the realization that I may not see you again.

I think of the love that from childhood bound us together as a family. It was not an illusory thing, lacking depth, like seed sown on rocky ground that lasts only for a time, or a weak thing, irresolute and uncertain, like seed sown among thorns that bears nothing of substance. It was, in the great crises of our lives, a love strong as death.

Would you, remembering this, let me tell you how I see things? Would you believe me when I tell you that I've heard the very real, anguished, complex, and prolonged turmoil of mind and heart that you've carried within—alone and silent—for far too long? And would you let me speak from my own heart of what I believe about faith and love?

I know there are those who view human existence in terms of biological and sociological forces only, and believe we are organisms with higher brain development—a topping-off of nature, as it were—and no more. Yet, I look at nature—at the scope of it, the implacability, the inevitability, the sheer brute force and relentless, unyielding tide of it—and ask: Where does unconditional love, where does forgiveness come from? For nature is inherently economizing, intolerant of error. The feeling for the vulnerable, the opening out of self, the binding up of wounds, the rising from the ashes that literature and life attest to: these are marks of an altogether different order of existence. They define us as creatures who are drawn by values and ideals—qualities that belong not to the order of ineluctable nature, but to the dimension of freedom, to the realm of faith.

Tears filled Kathleen's eyes. She heard Stephen speaking, not in the composed, philosophical way in which he expressed himself as a scholar, but in the low, urgent tone his voice took on when he was deeply moved.

You know that I look to Christ as the historical figure in whom God's intention for humanity was realized perfectly. If His words are truth for me, then I must know how He defined love; and, when I search the Gospels, I find Jesus providing the answer in images of forgiveness so often that joy over recovering what was lost seems the great, moving theme of Christianity: the woman who turns her house upside down to find a lost coin, the shepherd who leaves everything to go after a wayward lamb, the father so prodigal in love that his son has only to set a foot on the soil of home and he runs forth to greet him.

Of all the priorities that have a claim on our lives, the first is forgiveness: the precondition of our gift at the altar, the standard by which we ourselves will be judged, the act upon which no limit can be placed—is forgiveness.

For years, Scripture scholars have debated the story of the sinful woman who came to Jesus in the home of the Pharisee and bathed his feet with her tears. Was her great love the requisite or the result of her having been forgiven much? Scriptural exegesis allows both interpretations. I tend to come down on the side of those scholars who believe the Gospel story should be read that she loved much because she was forgiven much, for it is always God who takes the initiative, whose prevenient love makes repentance possible.

Thus, forgiveness is ours at any moment; the new start is always there for us. We are not dumb beasts set upon an inexorable course, but self-transcending beings, capable of change, who can by our free decision, in any instant, become a new creation.

This is what Hopkins understood when he wrote:

> *In a flash, at a trumpet crash,*
> *I am all at once what Christ is, since He was what I am, and*
> *This Jack, joke, poor potsherd, patch, matchwood,*
> *immortal diamond,*
> *Is immortal diamond.*

Such a discovery is a form of faith: it triumphs over darkness; it gives meaning to life; it enables one to answer for one's life—not in speaking, but in living out—forgiveness.

Kathleen, two women need your forgiveness:

> *It is all we have left to give our mother.*
> *It is, for her daughter, the new start.*

And, in regard to myself, wherever you may be, wherever I may be, I hold out my hand to you.

Always,
Stephen

And so, Kathleen thought, on that fateful last day in his office, when she had looked across the desk at him, pleading with her eyes—*give me a new baptism, give me a new name; I want to begin again*—Stephen had heard her.

—◊◊—

What struck Paul Brittain first was a vague, generalized sense of absence. Then, fully aware, he took in the details. He walked slowly from room to room, disbelieving. Gone: the family photographs on the foyer walls, the silver-plated tea set with the footed tray, the hand-woven plaid throw on the sofa in the study, the striped sofa pillows with the jaunty suede ties, the Waterford crystal clock on the bedroom nightstand, the hand-knotted wool rug at the foot of the bed, the white terry-cloth robe on the back of the door, the enameled animal pins, the monogrammed silk scarves, the brown canvas French purses with the small LVs, the bracelets, necklaces, face creams, the bottle of Xanax, the shoes, dresses, suits—gone. She was gone and everything about her was gone, as if she had evaporated and had never existed in his life. Paul sat down, stunned.

"Jesus Christ," he said.

—◊◊—

Stephen was about to leave the confessional when he heard the door at his right open and the kneeler creak as someone came in and knelt. He pushed back the wooden slide and a woman, speaking in a barely audible tone, said the first words of the formula for confession:

"Bless me, Father, for I have sinned…" Then, in a clearer voice, she said, "Stephen…it's Kathleen."

Stephen started a little, surprised that she would be there.

"Kathleen…why, Kathleen, hi."

Kathleen covered her face with her hands and cried softly. "Oh, Stephen, you had to come to me."

"Why don't we go somewhere else to talk?"

"No. There's something I have to say to you, here, in the confessional. Is that all right?"

"Of course."

There was silence for a moment. Then Kathleen leaned toward the screen and said simply:

"Stephen, this sister of yours was dead, and has come to life again; she was lost, and has been found..."

In the semidarkness, through a wooden screen, had there been a hundred miles between them, she could see his eyes dampen.

—⚊—

As the year 1992 opened, Kathleen had reached a place of peace and self-acceptance. When she contemplated the future, she imagined a life different from the one she had lived in her twenties, thirties, and early forties. She thought she would go to work—as a volunteer, perhaps for an organization like CARE. Her only request would be that she not be consigned to a desk somewhere. She wanted to work in the field, with children. It seemed to her that in this way she might find a new purpose in life and, possibly, if she gave unselfishly of herself, become a mother at last.

—⚊—

And what of *her*? Kathleen would never ask him, not even her name. She and Stephen were closer now than they had been at any other point in their lives, but distances had been realigned, too, and out of respect for her brother's feelings, she would not mention the young woman again. But Kathleen could imagine her, from what she knew of Stephen.

She would have been a thinker, someone with whom Stephen could discuss Hopkins and Joyce, the world of ideas. She would have had a sensitive temperament, and there would have been about her a poignancy that hinted at great pain and great promise, stirring Stephen's idealism. The purity and refinement of a Bellini Madonna were what came to Kathleen's mind, and so, whenever she thought of the unknown young woman, she gave her the name of Mary.

And Kathleen knew the answer to her question, even if Stephen did not. If he'd broken his vow of celibacy, he would have left the priesthood to marry the young woman. He would have felt responsible for her: that was Stephen's way. He would have found work teaching at the college level, helped his wife obtain any degree she wished, and delighted in the intimacy of married life. With her he would have searched for a house like the Engle family home: old and two-storied and poetic, the walls soft with ivy, and the lawn bald in places where the maples and the sycamore cast long shadows. They would have filled their home with books, Stephen's on literature and theology, and hers—she would have loved literature, too—perhaps her books would have been the same. And they would have been intensely happy, for about a year.

And then one day, Mary (as Kathleen thought of her) would have awakened near dawn, and discovered Stephen gone. He would be at the 6:30 a.m. Mass and, afterward, would stay for the 8:00. As the weeks passed, and the pattern continued, a sadness would come into his eyes, a sadness that he would hide from his wife, so as not to mar her happiness. Then the headaches would have begun, and discouragement set in. With no one to confide in, he would try to repress the worsening tension, resulting in its inward deepening. In the end, he might have broken under the psychological strain.

So, whatever it may have cost him in physical and emotional pain, and whether he himself was conscious of the trajectory of events she so clearly saw, Stephen had taken the only course of action open to him. When she walked with him now, and when she sat alone, thinking, these were Kathleen's reflections, neither she nor Stephen aware how close each had come to knowing the other's thoughts.

—⚭—

And there was yet another irony.

That winter, Clare had become an assistant to the senior editor of *Christian Comment*. Restless in her old way, wanting to write a novel, thinking about it for months but, for lack of inspiration, giving up, she was assembling books to review for the summer issue, an issue dedicated to the works of promising new writers. Among the collections of poetry, biographies, anthologies, and novels, she came upon a journal of poems and reflections she recognized at once as the standout in the group.

Authored by a graduate student at the University of Chicago who, according to the Introduction, had studied for a time under the Jesuits, the book was written with the sort of radiance and intellectual seriousness Clare was striving for:

I read classical mythology and come upon the story of Medea, and in that tale hear a rumor from the ancient world that will darken the history of womanhood...

Clare was enthralled by the book, and she intended to send Stephen a copy of it, together with the review she would write. But unexpectedly, the senior editor came down with the flu, and when she had to choose someone to take her place at a conference on the arts at Notre Dame University the following weekend, she decided to challenge the skills of her assistant, and selected Clare. The book reviews went to another member of the staff and Clare, wholly distracted, forgot to tell Stephen about the luminous work by Carol Ward, whom the publisher identified in a cover letter as a young woman named Mary Ainsley.

XIX

Quietly, Stephen, too, had been writing. In the fall of 1992 he published a book of essays on the creative process he titled *Without Light or Guide*, from a line in *The Dark Night of the Soul* by John of the Cross. Complimented on the work by his colleagues, he replied with self-deprecating humor that the name gave away something about the author's methods.

Privately, Stephen considered the book a turning point in his intellectual life. In it he revised and extended his doctoral thesis, which he had always believed to be an imperfect work. This time he discussed the imagination in the ennobling light in which he had seen it all of his life, the way that Coleridge had understood it, as the supreme creative faculty, the capacity to see life in terms of its highest possibilities.

While he was writing he was always conscious of another imperative, a second incentive he had for immersing himself in the study of the imagination. Earlier in the year something had occurred within his inner life and, in writing about the imagination and how it functions to disclose reality, he was searching for its meaning.

"We can think of the imagination in contrasting ways," he wrote, "as an illusion, a dream, a fantasy, a shadow; or as the creative power, the means by which the human mind discovers—not sidesteps—reality. "Among the stages that are characteristic of the creative act are a ragged, unsatisfied feeling; an awareness of a new order to be discovered; a time of focusing on a problem; a period of struggle, hardship, and frustration that may last for months or years; a letting go; at times, an unexpected and fortuitous image; and then a breakthrough: the eureka moment, when everything makes sense, when all relationships are seen in their true significance, when one looks into a new world...

> *As he looked on, he was surprised*
> *to see that the bush, though on fire,*
> *was not consumed.*

"One of the great turning points in the history of religion was Moses's encounter with the burning bush, a psychological crisis the effects of which transcended the fate of the one particular man to involve the destiny of an entire people.

"To this mysterious event Moses brought the Israelites' highly developed spiritual sense, their history of suffering and oppression, and the stern details of his own experience. At the time of the revelation, he was living the solitary existence of a shepherd, minding the flocks of his father-in-law, Jethro, in the wilderness of a foreign land. These conditions have a metaphorical implication: they are figures for the arid spiritual state. It was in the wilderness, at Horeb, the mountain of God, that Moses saw the bush that burned but was not destroyed.

"Returning to Egypt, he disclosed to the people of Israel the revelation he had received, and the name of the One who had sent him. Literally translated, it is

> *I Am; that is Who I am.*
> *Tell them that I Am has sent you to them.*
> *That it is Jehovah, the God of their forefathers...*
> *This is my name forever...*

*The witnesses laid down their cloaks at the
feet of a young man named Saul.*

Acts 7:58

"The most striking example of the creative imagination's role in the act of spiritual conversion is Saint Paul. As the young Pharisee Saul, he was a vehement, vigorous persecutor of the early Christian Church. Because of his impassioned temperament, his conversion/call occurred not in a moment of quiet reflection, but in an overwhelming emotional experience.

"Everything in his background—his years of Pharisaical training as a student of Gamaliel the Elder, the zeal with which he pursued Christians, the instance when he stood, a witness to the stoning of Stephen, the disturbing effect of Stephen's commitment on the intense, imaginative Saul—everything culminated in that moment on the Damascus road when both blinded and sighted by light, he beheld all in the configuration of faith...

"From the first great Christian theologian to the second...

"Augustine's was a life also marked by inner struggle; but the context of his conversion was very different. There were, as with Saul, the years of study. . .Initially, he embraced Manichaeism, and later, Neoplatonism, and kept a concubine with whom he fathered a son. But he thought endlessly about first things: the purpose of life, the existence of the soul...

"The awakening of his soul to God took place in a garden setting, the single, striking image that occasioned it coming not visually but aurally. *Tolle, lege!* a child's voice called from a nearby garden. *Take and read.* Stephen wrote:

"Taken on the surface, the incident might not have interested another man. But Augustine perceived a design in the chance occurrence and, opening the New Testament to the Epistle to the Romans, came upon these words: 'not in reveling and drunkenness, not in debauchery and licentiousness...but put on the Lord Jesus Christ, and make no provision for the desires of the flesh.'

"They were transformative words. The conversion from worldly sensualist to committed Christian was cerebral and serene, just the sort of spiritual awakening that would befall a man of letters.

"The pattern holds true transhistorically, transculturally, and across disciplines," Stephen wrote.

"The German chemist Friedrich Kekulé spent years engrossed in an apparently fruitless search: he sought a scientific breakthrough—the formula for the benzene molecule.

"One after another his efforts met with frustration until one night, while he slept, he had a peculiar dream. He saw mysterious lines curving and looping, forming a configuration like six snakes writhing.

"Kekulé awoke, astonished. The formula that had long eluded the process of rational thought, the hexagonal ring of the benzene molecule, C_6H_6, had caught him unaware, through an image in a dream."

an image in a dream...

—⁄w—

In the spring of that year, Stephen had had a strange dream, so clear and detailed that it seemed to him, when he wakened, more real than reality.

He was on the grounds of the Jesuit seminary, walking the path that led down to the lake, at dusk. The woods at that time of day were dark and magnificent and absolutely still, but in the dream, mysteriously altered, charred and black and barren, like ruins from a fire. There was no way to tell who had been there, no sign to indicate what had taken place, until a child appeared, a dark-skinned, dark-haired, dark-eyed child with thin arms as frail as the frail arms of a bird. He asked her:

"Who are you?"

She answered, and the words unnerved him: "I am the ground of thy beseeching."

Then he saw that she was not alone. Out of the shadows behind her advanced other forms: dark, gaunt images in numberless succession, whether real or unreal he could not tell. In a world turned to twilight, these indistinguishable shadow figures stood gazing at him, as if waiting for him to respond. He woke.

This dream, startling in its strangeness, obsessive in its hold, haunted Stephen throughout the spring and summer and animated his work, for over him had come the certain feeling that he was being called to leave behind everything he had known up until then, and search for God among the dispossessed, the most impoverished of this world.

—⁓—

The provincial superior was seated at his desk, making a note to himself in an elegant, flowing hand. Kenneth Lynn, S.J., was in his early sixties, a large and vigorous man, handsome, with a ruddy complexion, a dark Vandyke beard, and brown-green eyes in which gleamed notice of everything about him. He finished his memorandum, removed his steel-rimmed bifocals, and sat back in his chair, reflecting.

After a while, he looked at Stephen and said, "You know what you'd be letting yourself in for? Seeing incredible poverty…doing manual labor…emptying slop pails…encountering debilitating diseases you've never heard of…" Lynn leaned forward, lowering his voice and enunciating his words carefully, with strategic pauses:

"That's a far cry from teaching English literature on a college campus."

"I don't have any illusions about the life," Stephen said. He paused to think. Then he drew on the world of literature, the source he had always trusted, focusing his mind on specific words, and an image. He asked, "Do you know the work of the poet John Keats, Father?"

"Not so well as you," the provincial answered. He smiled and waited for Stephen to go on.

Stephen shifted in his chair, his eyes searching Lynn's eyes. "In one of his finest poems, Keats, writing of his reaction when he read George Chapman's translation of the *Iliad* and the *Odyssey*, reaches for an analogy, and describes Balboa, whom he'd mistakenly identified as Cortez, in the moment that the explorer first sighted the Pacific:

> *when with eagle eyes*
> *He star'd at the Pacific—and*
> *all his men*
> *Look'd at each other with a*
> *wild surmise—*
> *Silent, upon a peak in Darien.*

"That heightened awareness, that sense that all that has happened in one's life has been leading up to this moment, comes close, on a natural level, to the feeling I've tried to describe to you."

The provincial responded with a nod, running his fingers along the narrow temples of his bifocals, his gaze faraway. He was recalling something told to him years earlier. A gifted young Jesuit had published his doctoral dissertation to great acclaim, and afterward, demonstrated uncommon modesty by declining public recognition and turning to a quiet life of study and teaching. The provincial remembered words used to describe that young scholar: "He would never make a moment be about himself." Kenneth Lynn had been a pastor in a rural parish in Illinois at the time, and that was the first he had heard of Stephen Engle.

Convinced by the memory, and by the story's central character, who for almost an hour had been opening his heart to him, the provincial stood and came out from behind his desk. Stephen, realizing that the interview was over, got to his feet at once.

Lynn looked into the younger Jesuit's face for a long moment. "You feel called to this, Stephen. I understand." Then he said, "Let me pray about it, too…It's Monday. Let's meet again at the same time on Friday."

—\\\—

For five years Stephen had belonged to a discussion group at the university which called itself "The Gang of Eight," a sobriquet taken from the infamous "Gang of Four" in the days of Mao-Tsetung. Made up of professors from the college of liberal arts, the law school, and the departments of physics and theology, the group met one evening a month in the lounge of the Jesuit residence hall. Its members ranged in age from Stephen, who at forty-three was the youngest, to seventy-eight-year-old Xavier Kerns, a professor of philosophy, with wisps of cinder-gray hair and a round, furrowed face that reminded one of the wrinkled surface layer of the cerebral cortex, as if the intricate whorls of wrinkles and folds essential for thought were etched upon his countenance.

Also among the eight was Alan Black, a novitiate classmate of Stephen's, now an associate professor of humanities. He was forty-five at this time, though his thinning face and receding hairline made him appear years older than Stephen, who usually sat next to him in the group.

When they met, the men sat together in an informal circle, each taking turns at introducing the topic for the evening's discussion. Interruptions were allowed, digressions were frequent, and the tone, though always cordial, could change from reflective to humorous to eloquent to disputatious and then return seamlessly to reflective again. Topics were wide ranging, perhaps the compatibility of faith and science, or the theme of loss in J. R. R. Tolkien's *The Lord of the Rings*, or liberation theology, or the Russian writer as the conscience of Western culture, or current films and their depiction of Catholics, particularly priests, particularly Jesuits.

Stephen was often the quiet member of the group, content to listen and reflect, joining in with a subtle, ironic interjection now and then—unless the topic of discussion was along the lines of the contemporary need for a poetic sensibility, or the loss of myth consciousness in the modern world. On those matters he would speak intently, and spontaneously take command of the dialogue.

On this night, as the members gathered, they formed "The Gang of Seven," since one of their number was absent, and immediately became the subject of discussion.

Someone said, "It's hard for me to picture a man as private as Stephen becoming a missionary." The speaker, Lester Stuart, S.J., who taught languages and Old Testament studies, evoked the image of a snowy egret: a small build and bent stature, a long, slender nose, a graceful plume of white hair gone wild. He went on, "If you'd told me he was leaving to join the Trappists, I wouldn't be at all puzzled. But Africa?"

"When I think about it," Alan said, "I'm not really surprised. Stephen's always been restless, in recent years going from degree to degree. But even when we were novices he unfailingly pushed himself to the limit."

A wrinkled smile distinguished itself among the many others on Xavier Kerns's face, and the old man said kindly, "That's a new side of Stephen to me. It's hard to picture the reserved scholar I know as a risk taker."

"No," Alan said, "that's not the meaning I want to convey. I'm suggesting the creative imagination inspires Stephen. I've known him for a long time, and have often had the sense he was reaching for something more. Perhaps he's found it."

—⁂—

Slowly, shyly, Clare turned. He was coming toward her not out of memory or imagination but out of the glare of the midmorning sun and, seeing him now, she felt a pang of both joy and loss. It seemed to her that, for Stephen and herself, life was lived in intense bursts of togetherness, followed by long periods of separation, and that he and she had missed out on the uncomplicated casualness that characterize other brother-sister relationships. Or, perhaps her perception of family bonds had been thrown off balance by losses early in life, and her relationship with Stephen—while unique—was marked by privation no more or less than was any other.

The three adult Engle children were meeting in the departure lounge of British Airways in late August 1993. A weekend together in July and now, an hour alone with one another before Stephen's flight, these would be their brief snatches of contact until Stephen returned for a week's vacation two years from this time.

To talk in private they looked around for a small, unoccupied place. They could not locate three chairs together. But outside a coffee shop they found a quiet space, stood to one side, and began to say their farewells.

That morning Clare had tried to steel herself for this moment by memorizing lines from a poem by Hopkins:

> *Give beauty back, beauty, beauty*
> *Back to God, beauty's self*
> *and beauty's giver.*
> *See: not a hair is, not an*
> *eyelash, not the least*
> *lash lost...*

Yet now that the time had come, she expressed herself in much humbler language. "All of my life I've been saying good-bye to you," she let slip to Stephen in a murmur. Feeling her throat tighten up, she pressed her face against the crush of his sleeve and put her arms around his shoulders.

Stephen, stroking her down-turned head, said gently, "And there's always a coming-together again."

Pushing her hair from her face, she nodded assent and summoned a smile.

Kathleen stood beside them, wearing the beautiful heightened color of a woman who was deeply affected by her emotions but fully resolved to preserve her self-control. Her total attention was focused on the practical details associated with helping Stephen prepare for the journey.

"Your carry-on holds mostly books! Do you have enough clothes? And more than one pair of shoes? If you get there and find there's something you need, let me know and I'll send it right away...I'll write every week, but I don't expect you to...and I'll send money, of course—to help with the school, the clinic, whatever you wish…and don't worry about us—"

There was a voice coming over the loudspeaker.

"Passengers holding tickets for British Airways Flight 189 to London, go to Gate Five for boarding."

Brother and sisters stood facing one another without moving, the significance of the moment registering in their sudden exchange of glances. Then, instinctively, they rushed into each other's arms.

Stephen was the first to break from the embrace, stepping apart as carefully as he was able, holding one of his sisters' hands in each of his, gazing first into one beloved face and then into the other.

Look at me last, Clare's expression entreated. And, as if it came about by the power of magical thinking, Stephen's eyes suddenly met hers in a glance unreserved, profound, utter, a glance that told her how very hard this parting was, for him as well as for her, and thanked her for letting go.

She and Kathleen watched him walk away, reach the departure gate, and quickly disappear into the press of passengers milling toward the counter where the bags were searched, then appear again for a few minutes as the crowd broke up and scattered, until he became a small, thin form at the distant end of a far ramp, turning back to wave to them one more time.

Part Three

I called to the Lord from my narrow prison and
He answered me in the freedom of space.

— Viktor E. Frankl, *Man's Search for Meaning*

XX

Stephen came to Africa in mid-August, before the start of the season of the small rains.

Midway in the journey of our life, he came, knowing Dante's vision, to a strange and dark wood. Intense, imaginative, poetic by nature, Stephen hungered to know the moment of which Scripture tells: Two disciples, traveling to Emmaus, met a stranger on the road and, afterward, marveling, said to each other:

> *Did not our hearts burn within us?*
> *Were not our hearts on fire?*

For this cause he put himself in denudation, emptiness, and renunciation of all that has significance in this world.

And thus Stephen came to this land of solitary wooded valleys, of boundless plains, of distant mountains veiled in mist, to the church of Mary, Queen of Angels, one of the poorest of the poor of the Jesuit missions. *Reine des Anges*, it was called in French.

———

Leaving baggage claim, he walked out through revolving doors into brilliant sunlight, separating himself from the little crowd of fellow travelers.

A driver had been sent to meet him, a lanky old man with very dark skin and bony cheeks, with large dark eyes and heavy gray brows, balding, except for a fuzzy clump of silvered hair that encircled the base of his skull like a sagging ring about a dark, knobby planet. He walked with a decided limp.

His name was Augustine Habanukwari, though he was known to everyone by the nickname "Mambo," Swahili for his favorite expression, "What's happening?" When he was ten, Mambo had been mauled by a lion in a violent mishap that had taken the life of his oldest sister. The accident had disfigured his left leg and made him lame. Unable to find work in a largely agrarian society, he had been hired as a handyman by the mission's superior, the Jesuit Jacques Cormier.

Now, leading the way across a four-lane asphalt road to a weathered hunter-green Land Rover parked at the edge of the airfield, he described the route he would take, speaking in French, with a marked accent. Stephen stowed his bags in the back of the SUV and the two men climbed in.

Behind the wheel, Mambo became another man. Weaving his way among buses, bicycles, and taxis, he lurched onto the highway and headed south, setting out at a speed that caused Stephen to give him a sidelong glance and smile.

The road led first through meadow and open fields and a vast interior of woods and streams and grasslands, past a wilderness scene of zebra and hartebeest, past groves of palm trees, past massive baobab trees whose astonishing, tangled branches resembled roots growing aboveground. Strange brown birds—hooded vultures—hunted high overhead. In the distance, herds of giraffes floated against the sky.

The road narrowed; the land changed. They drove upward into forest shadowlands. Giant hygenia, bearded with lichen and bearing ferns and orchids in their moss-upholstered arms, formed a parade line on both sides of the road. From their towers, trees released an enchantment of birds. A marbled seal-brown eagle floated down from tier to tier among the branches. Pale lanes of sunlight as wide as boards broke through the leaves to stand aslant the forest floor in otherworldly beauty, like a magic ring in a fairy tale or a pagan rite.

Leaning his arm on the sill and looking about him, Stephen thought of lines from Saint John of the Cross:

A thousand graces diffusing,
He passed through these groves in haste,
And merely regarding them as He passed,
Left them, by His glance alone,
Clothed with beauty.

The road curved west and opened onto grassland again. After a mile it bent right, winding up a long grade. To one side the earth fell away and, across a great bay of forest, gentle hillsides terraced with coffee plantations extended on and on as far as the eye could reach.

The Land Rover continued its ascent, driving on older, rougher road, going west into the glowing nimbus of the setting sun. Then a low stretch of wall showed over the brow of a hill; it flanked the road in a graceful arc, following the asymmetrical perimeter of the mission grounds. At times appearing, then vanishing, then coming fully into view, a series of long, grayish-white buildings emerged through the trees.

The mission was laid out in a kidney shape, with the church at the northwestern bend of the curve and, spreading out from that point, the Jesuit residence, the school, the clinic, the convent of the Sisters of Mercy, and a small guesthouse. Where the driveway entered the compound, it circled around an enclosed garden. A gray stone statue of Mary, Queen of Angels, serene and meditative among purplish-pink bougainvillea shrubs, stretched out her arms in welcome.

When the Land Rover turned onto the narrow road leading up to the mission, evening was falling. No one was on the grounds. Halfway up the drive, at the edge of a sloping lawn, a blue-headed lizard, startled, froze in place, then darted into the underbrush.

Mambo parked beside the long rectangular residence of the Jesuits and scrambled down from the driver's seat to reach for Stephen's things.

Surprised by the old man's agility, Stephen called, "No, wait—" and, jumping out and hurrying round the Land Rover, edged his body in front of Mambo's. He took hold of his carryall, then his briefcase, and swung them out and onto the lawn.

"I can't let you do that," he said, smiling. "I'll grow soft in my life here." He added, "You've driven a long way. Won't you come in?"

The Land Rover was his to use the next day and Mambo prepared to set out for home. "No, Father, thank you. I will see you tomorrow." He shrugged happily. "You have your family. I have my family."

Stephen said, "Tomorrow then," and Mambo, his limp leg trailing, clambered up into the SUV, waved in parting, and drove off into the gathering dusk.

Stephen followed the gravel path that led up to the priests' residence.

—◊—

The screen door was unlatched; he rapped once and waited, opened the door and stepped inside. The room he found himself in was modestly furnished, a wide reception area with a few black-and-white photographs on the walls, and a large wooden crucifix over the door that led into the priests' private quarters. In the far corner, beside an old-fashioned roll top desk, a very thin, almost gaunt, man in his midfifties was sitting, mending a book. A deep frown seemed to crease his forehead, but when Stephen came in he stood up at once, his face brightening with a look of expectation.

He was the French Jesuit Louis Joyeaux, a slightly built, plain-looking man with a long, lantern-jawed face and a hawk-like nose. Though he was not old, all his features seemed to have grayed: his ashen complexion, his thin, pale lip line, his once-dark eyes faded under sparse, grizzled brows, and his dust-gray hair, which was tied in a knot at the nape of his neck and fell over his shoulder like a small animal's tail.

Joyeaux's lips parted in a smile and he was about to say something, when the sound of a door opening on the right caused both men to look toward it.

First the shadow, then the sun.

With a brisk step, Jacques Cormier entered the room. Stephen recognized him at once from photographs he'd seen in Jesuit publications.

Cormier, now in his late sixties, evoked the image of Michelangelo's God the Creator, with a blown spume of white hair, two cliffs of cheekbone, and outspread, sinewy arms. He was tall and powerfully built, an outsize figure, a vivifying presence, and his voice, which was deep and distinctive, seemed to come from the outer reaches—though in this case, they were the inner depths—of a thickset chest. Extending his hand, he exclaimed in earnest French:

"Etienne Engle, de la Compagnie de Jesus. Allô! Allô!"

Without hesitation, Stephen stepped forward, taking the hand offered him. His hand was clasped at once by "God, the Creator," welcoming him to his new land, on this dazzling earth.

—ᴍ—

Few men are as dissimilar as were Jacques Cormier and Louis Joyeaux.

Intellectually, Cormier lived on an elevated plane: his was a mind that turned to the works of Augustine and Chesterton to probe ancient mysteries, an imagination that delved into the writings of Karl Rahner and Edward Schillebeeckx to awake to new understanding. Though born to rise to prominence in any role, Cormier would have worn the bishop's miter or cardinal's robes uneasily, his spirit imprisoned by the cathedrals and colonnades of officialdom. Instead, his wide and searching intellect had sought lodging here, in an impoverished land where, among the disregarded and forgotten, Cormier had found freedom in anonymity.

Before Louis Joyeaux entered the Jesuits, he had studied medicine. Now, years afterward, at the mission of Mary, Queen of Angels, he used his medical skills in the service of the sick who came to the clinic. He was a self-sacrificing, humble man, quick to blame himself if something went wrong. His asceticism found expression in the ordinary course of daily life: by declining the offer of water when thirsty, in selecting the least comfortable chair in a room, by refusing to repel the myriad gnats and flies that lived in the sleeve of air which swung above one everywhere out-of-doors. Adding to this regimen, he kept a detailed mental ledger of his acts of renunciation to lay open before God each night as he made his long, painstaking examination of conscience.

Thus, while both men were self-directed, one was as expansive in his thinking as the other was restrained, and they even moved that way: Cormier, eagle-eyed, with an open, purposeful stride; Joyeaux, eyes mortified, with a narrow, tentative step, slightly off-center.

—∞—

A pale, insistent dawn pressed through the night. The ragged moon floated in puddles on the marshes, like an apparition. In quiet backwaters, slender herons, stepping amid seaweed and sand, dipped and redipped their overlong bills into shallow pools. The first faint shaft of sunlight caught a glint of white: a gazelle stood, poised and still, in the green shadows, ears flicking.

Where the savanna began, crimson tipped the thin fingers of the high grass and the rank smell of a kill pervaded the air. Somewhere in a high branch an eagle screamed and, as if whipped by the wind, a flock of long-legged cranes lifted out of the wildwood.

Morning. Night crouched low in the brush, lying in wait for tomorrow.

—∞—

It was high and frail, the voice of a young mother singing:

> *"Sur le pont d'Avignon,*
> *On y danse, on y danse,*
> *Sur le pont d'Avignon,*
> *On y danse, tout en rond…"*

Stephen tapped lightly on the half-open door.

A French Sister of Mercy, wearing a modern habit with a starched white headdress, was sitting in a chair by the window, singing softly to a little girl she held on her lap. When the door moved, she reacted with a start: "Oh!"

Stephen held out his hand, palm up. "Don't get up, Sister. I don't want to disturb that scene. I'm just walking through the school to learn my way around. I'm Stephen Engle, of the Society of Jesus."

"Oh, I know who you are!" the nun exclaimed. She smoothed the girl's hair, saying quietly, "I must stand up, Chantal." The child leaned into her arms, searching Stephen's face with big dark eyes. The nun gently released her arms, set the girl down, and rose.

Walking briskly forward, Sister Margaret, the superior of the mission convent, smiled widely. She was petite and fair, and had a delicately boned face with high, rounded cheeks, freckles on the bridge of a small, refined nose, and luminous hazel-green eyes. A woman in her late forties, she was as slender as an adolescent girl.

"I'm remiss, Father," she said in a warm, personal voice. "I didn't know you were here yet."

"I arrived yesterday. And you're not remiss in any way. The school surprises me," Stephen said, looking about him. "It's bigger than I expected. And newer."

"I'd like to show you through it. And have you been to the clinic? I'd like to show it to you, if you have time. One of our nuns, Sister Genevieve, is a registered nurse. You've heard of Doctors Without Borders. One of them visits us monthly. But Father Cormier has told you all this, hasn't he?"

"Yes. I'm beginning to see how things work," Stephen said, smiling at her.

Sister Margaret turned round. "And you must meet the other nuns."

Stephen walked after her, saying "That's all right, Sister—"

But Sister Margaret had not heard him. Quick, agile, graceful as a gymnast, she left the room, the child trailing slowly after her, and walked swiftly down the hall, briskly clapping her hands together, like castanets.

"Vite! Vite! Pére Engle est ici. Répondez, s'il vous plaît!"

Reddening, Stephen composed himself, as from five different door-ways, excited sisters ran out. He was never ready for this: the veneration of the nuns.

—⚭—

Slowly he would become conditioned to the land and its exigencies: to the physical apathy induced by the heat and humidity; to the infinite variety of skin parasites; to the never-ending regime of malaria pills; to the routine listing of "lion injury" as the need for emergency care at the clinic. Harder to adjust to was the level of privation at which the people lived: an average life expectancy of less than fifty years; great poverty; and the certainty that, if economic conditions failed to improve, living standards would continue their steady decline. Yet, in spite of all, there bloomed among the people a sincere, living faith, a faith shorn of all expectations except the joy of its possession.

—⚭—

When he wrote to his sisters, Stephen minimized the austerity of the daily life with self-deprecating humor: "I'm a city boy, become a country boy, and the adjustment can be hard at times."

His letters were full of descriptions of the natural and spiritual beauty of his surroundings. In late September, he wrote to Clare:

Today I drove out into the brush in late afternoon. Spectacular life surrounds one everywhere there. With its flattened top, tapered thorns, and featherlike leaves, the thorn tree, the tree characteristic of the plains, resembles something out of a myth. Much of the land-scape evokes a sense of the surreal. A hundred yards from where I'd parked, a family of cheetahs stood watch from an acacia thicket, so straight and still the cats seemed carved with an engraver's burin. To the east grazed zebras, to the west, gazelles. High overhead, black-and-white Bateleur eagles described ellipses in the air. But this day it was the sky that held me, unforgettably.

A vast civilization of clouds advanced north, a boundless dominion in the sky: a civilization of great walled cities tinted ivory and blue, dove gray and silver; of moving terrain, mountainous and cratered, with deep valleys and unending plateaus and strange, distant islands; a civilization that pushed inland, invading the low-lying hills, dispersing far-flung colonies of mist and haze; overall, a brooding, ephemeral beauty, holding the earth in its thrall.

Toward dusk, an anarchy in the wind and undercurrents of disintegration. Then, as evening fell, the sky held out star after star through waning, attenuated clouds until, suddenly, the air cleared everywhere, and a thousand stars rose to the surface of the night. A new kingdom had emerged: star-swept, moon-swept.

And I think of you, the lover of dreams and legends and myths, the child who watched the night sky and searched for our mother among the stars, and I need to tell you how precious your life is to me.

Happy birthday, Clare.

At the close of a letter to Kathleen, Stephen wrote:

"Because of the simplicity of the life, it's possible to experience the quality of 'firstness,' that inner dawning which is the recognition of the seriousness of each moment...to live the biblical event of giving a cup of water in His name, and to affirm that such an act is worthy of the dedication of one's life."

—⁂—

In late September, before the short rains fell, the vast plains were devoid of green, the soil gone to near dust. Even the shiest animals left their habitats to throng around water sites. And then, in due season, thunder-clouds rose along the horizon, and the great herds ran.

On the last Sunday of the month, Stephen, having the afternoon to himself, decided to accept Mambo's standing invitation to drive out to the plains to see the running of the herds.

From the mission, he and Mambo drove east down the long arching road to a well-worn, rock-strewn trail that led through the woods. In the woods it was dense and dark, the air pulsing with mysterious, hidden life. Sunlight pierced through openings in the trees and floated before their eyes in moving patterns like aberrations in the visual field, or flickered like the beam of a dimmed lantern in the interstices amid the branches. A rain of leaves fell against their faces.

When the trail reached the place where the tree line ended, it narrowed and curved away into scrubland. They left it then, and drove off-road toward the low ground. Behind an acacia copse they slowed to a stop, parked the Land Rover, and hopped down into the tall grass.

They each cut an armful of branches and spread them over the roof and hood of the dark green vehicle, partially camouflaging it.

Then they stood together in the shade of the Land Rover, with the deep woods behind them and an immensity of land and sky before them and, farther on, in the remote distance, the blue haze of mountains.

Stephen lifted the binoculars, focusing them on the vanishing point of the horizon. His attention was drawn to a faint mist hanging over the long valley corridor that came up from the mountains to the west.

He looked round at Mambo, who all at once had put a hand on his arm. The old man was standing with his other hand cupping his ear and his eyes intent on Stephen's eyes. He said, "Listen…"

Stillness and yet not stillness. Like the roll of faraway thunder or the pounding of a far-off sea, a low rumble advanced over the plains. Materializing out of the air above the horizon, a concentration of low-lying stratus clouds seemed to rise and vanish, float and fall apart.

With binoculars, Stephen saw that the formation was, in fact, not clouds, but an ascending haze which, as it swept into his field of vision, released first one form, then a second, a third: a thousand furious fleet figures pressing on the hinge of sound. The sky darkened; he felt a wash of dirt and acrid air, and then the detonation of hooves: in herds by the hundreds, zebra, streaked with grime and foam, running in a stream of wildebeest and antelope of which there seemed to be no end, running as one, leaping and surging, stunning the air with the clash of their hooves, stirring the earth into a great vortex of dust. Then, all at once, like an immense heaving door, they swung east, moving in flux, held to a center, chasing the wind.

Stephen lowered the binoculars and stood in amazement. Dazedly, he remembered Joyce quoting Newman:

Whose feet are as the feet of harts and
Underneath the everlasting arms—

Thus caught up in thought he stood, breathless, watching the wild bounding creatures as they swept past, overleaping sound, returning to clouds.

—⁂—

In early October, with the beginning of the short rainy season, the weather broke. A thick white mist dulled the dark woods and thickets: the animals moved like ghosts through the trees. In the dark mornings, purplish-black clouds drifted across the sky to the north in great, towering masses, their thunder echoing up and down the hills. By early afternoon, the rains came, slanting through the woods in never-ending streams that turned the soil to bog. The wind was never still. Life moved indoors.

—⁂—

On his way out of the school, Stephen heard a melodious voice calling out to him. Sister Margaret, having finished teaching vocal music, was playing a refrain on the guitar for her students when she caught sight of him.

"Won't you come in, Father?"

Stephen paused in the doorway and looked about. The children were sitting in groups at tables around the room, with wide, shining eyes and folded hands and perfectly straight backs, listening.

Sister Margaret held out the guitar, her head tilted to one side, her eyes appealing.

"Can you play, Father? We need someone to teach us an American song. They are so eager to learn. Could you, Father? Anything…just some simple tune?"

Stephen smiled at her gentle ambush, knowing he would have to consent, though he hadn't held a guitar in years. He walked over to where the nun was standing and accepted the guitar from her, taking a moment to feel the weight and proportion of it. Then he ran his fingers lightly over the strings, tightened one of the pegs, and, tentatively, struck a chord.

He remembered a song from his youth, "Don't Let the Rain Come Down," which he had been able to play with some dexterity; it suited the season, and he played it once, and then he played it a second time when the children implored him, while they patted out the rhythm on the surface of the wooden tables, learning.

When he finished playing the last chord, Stephen turned to Sister Margaret, extending the guitar, but the children cried, "Don't stop, Father!"

He relented. He played "Where Have All the Flowers Gone?," "Blowing in the Wind," and "Guantanamera," picking out the melody and harmony of each song on the strings of the guitar and singing softly in French. Occasionally he glanced at the nun, who was standing at his side, gently swaying her head back and forth in time to the music, surprised and moved.

With "Guantanamera" Stephen became soulful and inward. The song evoked powerful associations for him. When he spoke the first lines:

> *"I am a truthful man from*
> *the land of the palm trees,*
> *And, before dying, I want to*
> *share these poems of my soul..."*

he recalled that the song had been an inspiration for Che Guevara, once an idol of his classmate Charles Cullen, now working among the poor of Guatemala.

When he came to the verse *"That the poor people of this earth are not to share my fate..."* he remembered the Jesuit Jim Carney, who had gone to his death in the jungles of Honduras.

And when he uttered the last line of the song: *"The streams of the mountains please me more than the sea,"* plucking slowly on a single note in the bass, he knew the words were true of his own soul.

Stephen stood in front of the desk, picking out the melody on the strings of the guitar and speaking softly in French. The children's voices rang out, lovely and pure, like a series of bells sounding on the morning air.

—⁂—

A storm in the night. Awakened, Stephen got up and went to the window. He saw lightning flash over the forest floor. Between the trees, a white crane. Vanished.

XXI

Natáre, the nearest city, was forty miles to the northwest, a picturesque country town set at the base of gently sloping foothills, its impoverished neighborhoods spreading out into the hillsides above it. Once a month, Jacques Cormier drove down to the Jesuit house and church located there. In early December, at the end of the season of the short rains, he took Stephen with him.

The approach to the town was beautiful, the road making its descent through dense forest in long, graceful arcs. At one stretch the road came out on a high ridge and, where the trees gave way, one could see Natáre below.

The town's charm lay in its variety and relaxed acceptance of discontinuity, for Natáre was an amalgam of markets and gardens, of aging churches and modern government buildings, of luxurious open-air restaurants set back on long, sunlit avenues, and grinding poverty hidden down close, congested lanes. On the outskirts, an old unpaved road leading in from the country intersected the main thoroughfare. This morning a line of dust like a low-lying fog rose slowly along it. Cattle were being driven on the road. They moved in a herd, negotiating their way amid the bicycles, antiquated taxicabs, and outdated European sedans bustling everywhere.

The road down which Stephen and Cormier drove crisscrossed narrow, winding lanes lined with market stalls. It was a market day; the air was aromatic with flowers and overripe fruit. Women wrapped in yards of flowing cloth walked up and down the aisles in slow procession, among them many who were very tall and lithe, Tutsi women of spectacular beauty, with slender, elongated bodies that looked like drawings by El Greco.

At the quiet end of the thoroughfare, infused with golden sunlight and a peaceful air of drowsiness, stood a pharmacy, a grocer's, a railroad station fallen into disrepair, and a redbrick wall, beyond which rose the Romanesque-style church established by the Jesuits fifty years earlier.

Cormier parked the Land Rover in the deserted lot that abutted the railway station and the two men walked the short block to the mission. Five young boys, clad in ragged pieces of cotton batik, followed them at a distance. Whenever the children came within the priests' field of view, they stopped to stare, or backed away shyly, their small bare feet kicking up clouds of dust that clung to their legs, like golden pile on dark velvet.

Glancing to his left, Stephen caught sight of the boys and smiled. In that moment, he noticed other movement on the street. Three men in combat fatigues and weathered boots stood facing away from the sun in the doorway of the pharmacy. Their voices carried faintly across the road, rising and falling so lightly they could have been the whispered exchanges of children. Smoking cigarettes and talking, the men seemed indifferent to the surroundings, but the flash of the whites of their eyes disclosed a sudden interest in the two Jesuits.

"Are the soldiers unfriendly?" Stephen asked.

"They're members of a militia trained for 'civil defense.' They patrol parts of the countryside. We notice them and they observe us." Without turning his head, Cormier gave the men a sidelong glance, and then he added with unexpected grimness:

"We circle the same star but with—we hope—very different orbits."

—⁂—

Mid-February came, and the season of the big rains. Now sunlight vanished and rain fell steadily and hard throughout the night. Snakes crawled up to the doors and lay inert, indiscernible on the sodden paths; water clogged the walks, rotted shoes. In those days, a priest had to count the pages in the missal the night before he offered Mass, for the pages, glued, not sewed into the binding, loosened overnight from the damp, softened, and fell out.

At dawn, mist moved in a silver wall over the land; strange veiled shapes tore loose, wafted across the roads, and fled into the hills like runaway mist children. First as blurred shadows, then as long dark blotches, the mission buildings emerged through breaks in the trees.

—m—

A Saturday in mid-March. The sun hung high over the horizon: round, pure, polished like a pearl, gilded with fire. Now it was enveloped by a dark cloud nebula and lost to sight. Yet even when concealed it was not obscured, but, making of the clouds a corona, streamed forth shafts of light that fell as fresh and bright as human song across the vast silence of the plains.

For the fourth time in as many months, Stephen was on the road to Natáre. He was going to deliver packages put together by the Sisters of Mercy for a small private school set up for "street children," and to see the school firsthand.

The school's director was Rebecca Talitha, the oldest child in a large, devout Catholic family, and the sister of a Jesuit novice named Peter Paul Talitha. A beautiful, unselfish young woman, she had won the title of Miss Natáre when she was eighteen, and attended the university on the scholarship that was her prize. Though European modeling agencies had courted her, Rebecca had found the thought of leaving her family and her homeland unimaginable; after graduation she had returned to Natáre. At age twenty-four, four years before Stephen met her, she had opened a school in an abandoned pharmacy, where she taught arts and crafts and tutored special-needs and orphaned children. Fathers held her up as a role model to their young daughters, and mothers spun such colorful, hyperbolic stories of her virtue that, had she not been so modest, warm, and fun-loving, Rebecca would have been despised by every girl in the province.

The sun had reemerged when Stephen reached the dark, narrow street where the school was located. He found himself on a crooked lane of small, two-story cinder-block shops, with discolored walls and dirty stairs winding round to the back, all identical in wear and drabness, except for one at the far corner. It was freshly painted honey yellow and had the French word *L'ecole* printed over the door in bright green letters.

With cars left everywhere, Stephen drove down the block a second time before he discovered a place to park. He sorted out the supplies, filled up his arms with boxes, and made his way across the cramped street. Pushing open the door of the school with his shoulder, he came into a small, square foyer. Here someone had introduced the beauty of a garden: intricately shaped branches together with seedpods and long yellow grasses were arranged in woven baskets on the window-sills; masses of white bougainvillea spilled out of terra-cotta urns placed about the floor. The walls were painted yellow, the ceiling a paler shade of the same color, as if to bring in the sun.

Stephen stopped at the entrance to a hallway that went into the back and rapped on the wall. From a room in the rear of the building, a woman's voice called to him.

"Come in, Father."

Following the hallway, Stephen went back.

Rebecca Talitha, wearing a brilliant turquoise dress with a turned-up collar, with white beads encircling her throat, was sitting with her back to a window in faint morning sunlight, embroidering yellow flowers on a white cotton blouse. When Stephen entered the room, she laid her work on the table beside her and stood.

She was as tall as he was and very beautiful. Her girlish oval face, bare of cosmetics, had the sensuous smoothness of a grape, and her complexion was velvety, flawless, and light as doeskin. She wore her long dark hair off her face, fastened with combs. Her lips held a gently ironic smile, cultivated to remind herself to lower the expectations of others upon meeting her. She existed, quiet, tranquil, and amused, behind radiant, almond-shaped eyes.

Stephen, seeing her for the first time, thought of the story in Genesis: Abraham, seeking a wife for his son, Isaac. An old servant had stood beside a spring and prayed for a sign, and near evening a young woman with a jar on her shoulder came out to draw water. She was exceedingly beautiful, the girl Rebecca.

"Father." Rebecca Talitha held out her hand.

Stephen took it in a gentle, loose grip. "I've wanted to see your school since I first heard about it," he said, speaking in French. "Do you mind if I look around?"

Rebecca smiled, looking into his eyes with the open, innocent gaze of one who had revered the Jesuits all her life.

"Please, if you wish. I know English, Father." She spoke with a slight accent, in a melodious voice that softened consonants and beautified vowels—"Fah-thair."

Nodding his head, appreciative, Stephen came into the room. It was a large room with wide windows along one wall; cupboards cluttered up with banana leaves, sisal, and bright scraps of cloth; tables, and an old pedal sewing machine tilted against a corner wall.

Saturday classes had ended, but three small girls were still seated at a round table at the back, their faces turned downward. They were barefoot and wore striped T-shirts with thin cotton shorts, and their slim brown legs, curled around the chair legs, had a taut, tender look like young branches have in early spring. On the table in front of the girls lay dark brown banana leaves, a pile of blue cloth, scissors, and skeins of white thread.

Following Stephen's gaze, Rebecca explained, "Two of the children are weaving mats and the other one is embroidering a dress for market day."

Stephen glanced at her. "Who can you expect to have as customers?"

"Women from the communes, tourists, visiting diplomats…" From beneath long, half-lowered eyelashes, Rebecca smiled at the formal, reflective Jesuit.

"Missionary clergy…"

Stephen laughed.

So that the girls would not understand her, Rebecca said in English, "These are children for whom the future holds little hope, Father."

"I'm not sure I understand."

In reply, Rebecca placed her hands on the shoulders of the smallest child and, speaking now in French, said, "Show Father your work, please, Renée."

The little girl patted the cotton dress she had been embroidering until she smoothed out its wrinkles, and then held it up, carefully, so that one sleeve partly covered her face. She was a delicate child with braided hair and lustrous skin and enormous liquid eyes, but her small, tense mouth was cleft by an ugly scar.

Stephen, just now glimpsing her disfigurement, rested his hand on the girl's slender arm; bending over and smiling gently, he complimented her on her needlework, careful that his tone did not exaggerate, did not express pity.

"C'est trés jolie. Merci, ma petite jeune fille."

The child whispered a shy thank-you and lowered her head, glancing furtively at her companions with ecstatic eyes.

"Children with deformities face a cruel fate," Rebecca said, speaking again in English. "When they are very young, many are ignored and die of neglect. Those who do grow up are often shunned. What I can do is teach them a skill, like to embroider beautifully."

Leaning over the child Renée, Rebecca gazed at her affectionately and whispered softly in her ear. When she looked up, her face was luminous.

"Renée has no family. She lives with me. I build her up. I'm Mama."

"How do you manage, against such odds?"

"What others call chance, Father, we call grace, no? Once, when I was a university student, I was invited to dinner in a diplomat's home. Did you know, Father, if you hold a piece of china up to the light, you can see small imperfections on the underside?" Rebecca nodded determinedly, as if answering herself. "Yes, it's true…At the dinner, I said to a lady sitting next to me, 'Look—flaws on this lovely plate.' Gauche, huh?" Rebecca shrugged her shoulders, laughing lightly in self-mockery.

"And she says to me, 'No, no, those are kiln marks from when the plate is fired on a pedestal…' and she informs me that the best china has such imperfections.

"So when I met Renée, I remembered this explanation, and told her that her beautiful face is like a piece of the finest china, and her scar is her kiln mark. And she smiled for me, Father. First time she smiled."

Stephen listened, deeply moved by the young woman's humility and innocence.

"Thank you, Rebecca," he said, voice low with admiration. "I think you have a gift with children, a gift near genius."

Filled with pent-up longing to share her stories and encouraged by Stephen's show of understanding, Rebecca began to tell him of other street children she had known: children who had been mangled by one of the big cats or, because of their disabilities, turned out of their homes, or orphaned, with no family to care for them. She told him how she had worked together with relief agencies to try and rebuild those shattered existences.

Unaware of how each of their lives would change before the year was over, she and Stephen stood and spoke of what the future might hold for such children, who were like beautiful flowers never allowed to blossom, whom fate had ground under its feet.

Then it was time for him to go.

Rebecca followed him down the hall with the soft ringing of bracelets.

"Will you come back, Father?"

Stephen turned to where she stood among the flowers and grasses in the foyer and looked at her thoughtfully.

"Yes. But it won't be often."

Glancing out the window, he felt a sudden jolt of apprehension. Behind the Land Rover he had left across the street, a military jeep was now drawn up and parked. Three men had gotten out and were standing looking up and down the street. They wore combat dress and dark boots and they had rifles slung over their shoulders. One man had opened a canteen and was taking a long drink; turning his head to one side, he spat, dissatisfied, the dark fluid streaming from his mouth like the swift, unfurling tongue of a frog. Another member of the group had gone up to the Land Rover and read its license plate, then walked around it, peering into the windows.

Rebecca gave Stephen a quizzical look and, following his gaze, glanced out at the street.

"Military, soldiers of war. Jesuits, soldiers of Christ. That's what Peter Paul says he will be, a soldier of Christ," she said softly.

Watching the street, Stephen was quiet, wondering: Did he only imagine it, or were these the same soldiers he had seen once before, on his first trip to Natáre? Ill at ease, careful not to communicate his concern, he turned to respond. He told her, "Your brother will be a fine Jesuit. But what you're doing here has enormous value, and calls for as much dedication as the religious life." He paused. Then he said, with a note of finality in his voice, "Now, I think I should go."

Saying this, Stephen stepped forward, reached for the knob, and opened the door.

Suddenly, on impulse, Rebecca started after him. "Father…"

His thoughts on the street, Stephen turned around so abruptly that, for an instant before she stepped back, disconcerted, Rebecca was caught within the curve of his arm.

Beautiful Rebecca Talitha, being watched from across the street, held in the arm of the American Jesuit in the doorway. Before the year was over, in the great civil war that would cleave her land in two, she would be beaten, raped, and mutilated, and bear her own "kiln marks"—machete scars—upon her face. The following year she would bear a son and be cast out by her own people, because the father of her child was a soldier of the enemy.

In her grief and shame she would cling to what the Jesuits had taught her: that beyond the external happenings of life lie great themes of meaning; that beneath everything and in everything is God's activity; that the birds of the air neither sow nor reap nor store up food, yet our Heavenly Father cares for them.

Was she not of even more value to Him than they?

—⚏—

The interior of the church was starkly appointed, stripped of all adornment for Holy Week, its statues shrouded with purple cloth, the altar covered with a plain white runner.

Because the Gospel that Sunday was the longest of the liturgical year, Stephen gave a short homily. He stood in the center aisle to speak, near the first pew of worshippers, looking from face to face with special focus.

"Throughout the centuries," he said, "theologians and historians—and ordinary men and women—have pondered the question, 'Who was Jesus of Nazareth?' His first followers, stunned by the miracle of the Resurrection, grasping for titles by which to identify him, reached to the farthest limits of literal and figurative language for names: Son of Man...Son of God...Prophet...Messiah...Savior...Christos...Kyrios...

"Now we have come to the start of Holy Week. The story told over the next five days is the earliest core of the Gospel narrative.

"And in it we discover him anew, as the One foretold by Isaiah:

He is despised and rejected of men;
a man of sorrows, and acquainted with grief...
Ours were the sufferings He bore,

ours the sorrows He carried…
He was pierced through for our faults,
crushed for our sins.
Like a lamb led to the slaughter
or a sheep before the shearers,
He was silent and opened not His mouth.
Oppressed and condemned,
He was taken away,
And who would have thought any more of His destiny?"

Stephen Engle, S.J.
homily for Palm Sunday
1994

XXII

The Lord then said: "What have you done!
Listen: Your brother's blood cried out to me from the soil!"

— GENESIS 4:10

When searched for on a map of the world, it is a country so small that it
can escape the eye; when seen up close, it is a land so lovely that it can
lay claim to the title "The Switzerland of Africa."

Belgium colonized it after World War One, controlling the citizenry
by pitting its ethnic groups against one another.

The minority Tutsi became the privileged class, favored by the
Belgians because their tall stature, lighter complexion, and thin lips
evoked the European ideal of physical beauty. The majority Hutu—
shorter, dark-skinned, thick-lipped—suffered the social and economic
humiliations of those consigned to an inferior status.

The imbalance of power caused wave after wave of civil unrest
until, in 1962, Belgium abandoned colonial rule and established a
republic.

Still, the years that followed the hard-won independence were pervaded with social upheaval. As the Hutu rose to power, they lashed out
at the once-privileged Tutsi, and the hostility often exploded in violence. Belgium intervened in the early 1990s to call for conciliation and
reform. But the critical moment had already passed.

Throughout March 1994, forebodings of disaster hovered in the air. Eerily paralleling events that had occurred at Medjugorje in Bosnia-Herzegovina, the Virgin Mary was said to have appeared to young visionaries in the hill country, warning them of severe afflictions in the days ahead. Other stories were told: in one, a local seer dreamed of rivers of corpses floating from cove to cove amid the inland islands.

In the capital, the attention of passersby making their way through the congested streets of the open-air market was distracted by a mud-spattered truck parked flanking one sidewalk. Young men, bare-chested and in khaki cargo pants, were working in the back of the truck, pushing crate after crate to the fore; on the ground, other young men lifted the crates, balanced them in their arms, and stacked them—over forty in all—so that they formed a kind of low wall along the curb. And the passersby wondered, with some trepidation: long months before the harvest, what use could anyone have for so many machetes?

And then it was April.

Returning on April 6 from UN-sponsored peace talks abroad, the country's president was murdered by unknown assassins, his plane shot down on landing. A nation stunned by the killing was all at once overwhelmed by other, even more horrific acts.

Within hours, extremist politicians seized power, commandeered the militia, and roused the Hutu people to a long-suppressed, now openly sanctioned, common undertaking: to utterly destroy the Tutsi people.

Within days, death squads went forth throughout the country, hunting down, torturing, raping, and murdering Tutsis. They struck with guns, knives, axes, and grenades; they used spears, machetes, and the *masu*, a club studded with nails, which they called *nta mpongano*, "show no pity."

People from all walks of life took part. Members of a man's own household turned on him.

Slow to react and observing from afar, the Western media described the crisis as a tribal uprising, one more problematic episode in the historical record of that sorrowing continent. World governments averted their eyes.

Yet of such vast scale was the devastation in those terrible days that the story of that suffering people and their tragic fate transcended the particulars of time and place, and once again,

A voice was heard in Ramah, sobbing and loud lamentation;
*   Rachel, weeping for her children, and she would not be comforted,*
for they were no more

By mid-April the capital had fallen, and the northern half of the country plunged into chaos.

—⁓—

Mountainous landscape and immense forest lay to the southwest. But the fear that reprieve from the killing would be short-lived advanced everywhere.

That alarm was what filled Jacques Cormier with such urgency as, one morning in mid-April, he made the three-hour drive to see the governor of the southern provinces, taking Stephen as his companion.

The process of painting the administrative offices had been interrupted because of the societal disorder, and the governor had been forced to make a room in the courthouse his temporary workplace.

Stephen and Cormier reached the courthouse as the doors reopened for the afternoon. They were asked to wait for a few minutes, though no one else was in the anteroom. After about an hour, a clerk appeared and motioned to them to follow him. With stony-faced efficiency, he led them down a narrow hall to the main chamber at the back.

The governor was sitting at a table in the center of the room, reading from a stack of documents the thickness of a Bible and chatting quietly with an army captain seated next to him, but he lifted his head as Cormier and Stephen walked in.

He was an unattractive man, huge and balding, with a sloping forehead, a prominent nose, hooded eyes, and loose folds of aged and leathery skin—features that gave him the look of a bored but attentive iguana. Hedonistic and self-indulgent by nature, he considered the black-garbed Jesuits with their psychological attire of celibacy and restraint the embodiment of gloom. He greeted them with perfunctory courtesy and then, aware that the officer seated next to him knew Cormier, directed the priests' concerns to him.

The captain hung over the papers he had been studying for a while before he looked up.

Jean-Baptiste Dhavée was the son of a Hutu father and a Tutsi mother, a tall, powerfully built man with sensual features and a brooding restlessness in his dark, pensive eyes, wearing a military jacket, with a spotless pair of white gloves precisely folded at his right.

His profile exposed to view the long, misshapen nose and weak chin that—when seen from certain angles—lent him a hungry, adolescent look. To ward off the impression, Dhavée had cultivated an earnest, formal bearing, addressing others with his shoulders squared, his neck bent slightly, his face thrust forward, his eyes fixed and intent—a pose that gave his head a weighted, authoritative cast.

Cormier knew him from the days when Dhavée had been a talented but unfulfilled youth in the mission school. He was a boy from the communes whose father had died from rabies at thirty-eight, and left the only son of nine children lonely, poor, and steeled for disappointment.

In his late twenties, at once idealistic and cynical, burning with a desire to remake his world, Dhavée had abandoned the Catholic faith of his childhood and replaced it with political radicalism.

Drawn to the dramatic, single-minded, self-absorbed, and ambitious, he had found a calling in the military, where he became an eager, but moody and unpredictable leader. He was one of those men born with a defiant and resolute temperament, and who are capable of undergoing martyrdom—or of inflicting it.

Now Dhavée got to his feet to welcome the Jesuit he knew, saying in a voice rich with husky, sensuous undertones:

"Father Cormier."

Jacques Cormier stepped forward and looked at his former student with a softened gaze of wonder. "Jean-Baptiste..."

Dhavée extended his hand and asked politely, "How many years has it been, Father?"

"Many, many," Cormier answered gently, shaking hands.

The two men exchanged looks and handclasps in silence. The silence lasted for several moments. Then Dhavée dropped his eyes, withdrew his hand, and stepped back.

"You've come all this way, not to see me," he said laconically, "but for other reasons."

Cormier gave the governor a tactful look, but the governor, seemingly engrossed in his reading, did not look up, and the Jesuit turned again to Dhavée. Cormier spoke of the tragic loss of innocent life, the fear felt by the people of the southern provinces with whom Dhavée himself had grown up, stressing the desperate need for intervention.

"Of course I'm aware of all you're telling me," Dhavée responded. He was quiet a minute, checking his watch, touching the papers in front of him. Then, shaking his head in commiseration, he said, "It's an ugly business. Let me explain why restoring order is so difficult.

"The killings are often the work of mobs who prowl about the countryside and strike at random, without warning; afterward, they simply disperse into the population, and disappear."

Dhavée leaned across the table and fixed Cormier with a solemn stare, like a man being forced to reveal to another the worst news of his life.

"Still more dangerous are the paramilitary groups. They are highly organized. Their strategy is to enter an area nonviolently and lure those they've marked for destruction into confined areas. When this is done, they go to work with ruthless efficiency. First, they disable the men by cutting the Achilles tendon. A machete blow to the hip can cripple a man totally."

Dhavée illustrated his account with a stark, theatrical gesture.

"Before they kill the women, they rape them, sometimes with great brutality," he said, then waited and said, "Have you seen the stamen of a banana plant? How stiff and pointed like a spear it is? They penetrate the women with those stamens." Dhavée shook his head reproachfully.

"It is monstrous," he said. "I apologize that I must tell you of such things.

"In the end, they dispatch their victims with guns or machetes. Death is most merciful for those who don't put up a struggle.

"The mobs move in afterward. They torch the houses, pile up the bodies, then bury them in mass graves."

Having said this, Dhavée shifted his chair and sat down, his weak profile evident in that off-guard moment. "I have heard these reports from trusted sources," he concluded. "I have no doubt they are true."

During the description, Cormier had stood listening in disbelief, his face pale with shock and pain.

"How is it that Christians are behaving in this way?" he asked dazedly, as if murmuring to himself.

"You ask me that, Father?" Dhavée answered with a peremptory wave of his hand. "How naive you are! You don't see the hypocrisy of the Church you represent? Pleading for the restoration of social order, when for years it went along with the injustices that gave birth to the violence? What are the Jesuits, but an adjunct of European colonial rule?"

"How have the Jesuits wronged you, Jean?" Cormier returned wearily. "Who gave you your education, fought to save your father's life... looked after your mother and your sisters when he died?"

Dhavée did not reply. Instead, he turned his attention to Stephen, who stood a few steps behind Cormier.

"You're American, aren't you, Father?"

"Yes."

"I've never met an American before."

Guardedly polite, Stephen nodded his head, meeting Dhavée's eyes for a moment, and then looking ahead, a little to the right of the captain's face.

Dhavée stiffened. That well-mannered slight, that hint of mistrust masked by a veneer of civility, aroused within him an acute feeling of animosity and with it, a strange envy. The elegant-looking Jesuit with his reserve and patrician bearing was the kind of man he most resented and yet of all men the kind he wished most to be like.

Dhavée looked down a minute and then, pursing his lips, said sardonically, "Perhaps someday you could teach me American ways, Father."

Dhavée leaned forward, spreading his long-fingered hands over the table, touching the papers in front of him, angling them slightly, as if by accident, so that their contents invited the eye.

From where he stood, Stephen could see that the pages consisted of columns of two- or three-word lines. They were lists of names. He knew that with a barely perceptible effort he could read several of those at the top, but, determined not to respond to what he sensed was a contrivance, he deliberately ignored them and continued to look directly ahead.

Dhavée thought for a moment. He slowly stroked one cheek and looked at Stephen from under his brows. Then, with an air of mild condescension, he turned again to Cormier.

"In regard to your concerns, Father, why should you be worried? The West is pulling its people out. It's we who are left behind who will suffer."

"From the beginning," Cormier said, "we came to minister to the people. That is our agenda. That simple."

"Can you bear the suffering that we must bear?" the deep, sonorous voice answered back. "Can you drink the cup that we are going to drink?"

Struck by the choice of words, with their reference to Christ, Stephen glanced at Dhavée in surprise. His reaction escaped the captain's notice, for Dhavée was staring fixedly at Cormier.

And, whether because of a memory that had suddenly surfaced in his mind, or because of an unexpected stab of remorse for the callousness he had shown toward a man he knew to be authentically good, or because of simple moodiness, something within the temperamental officer softened.

"You have been forthright with me, Father. I will be frank with you. When you start back, take a different route from the way you came."

It was a break in his attitude, a momentary return to a time when he had been a shy, lonely child from the communes, and the burly old man in front of him a teacher at the height of his powers, who had known how to bring out what lay dreaming in a young boy's heart. Today, except for the warning Dhavée had just given, everything was feigned. Yet it was this pretense which held the world together. Without it, chaos could erupt at a moment's notice. Both men knew that now they were enemies, but understood that accepting pretense as a principle of behavior allowed them to communicate.

As Cormier and Stephen turned to leave, Dhavée, with the air of a man who has authority over others and over events and their outcomes, called out to Cormier a last time:

"May all that is good come about for you, Father."

The two Jesuits walked out of the courthouse in silence. When they had reached the street, Cormier, a faded Tolstoy, said:

"Stephen, share your impressions freely with me. What did you think of Dhavée?"

Stephen looked down at the pavement and shook his head slowly.

"He's a hardened, shrewd, complicated man."

They walked on for a few moments without speaking. Then, turning his head so that he looked directly into Cormier's eyes, Stephen added:

"When he described the mass killings? I felt I was listening to an eyewitness account."

—◊—

Following Dhavée's instructions, Stephen and Jacques Cormier headed back to the mission by a different and more circuitous route. It was an old two-lane road which, taken to the end, wound through the northern gorges to the lake country. An hour out, it forked right, going through woods and meadow corridors, then made the ascent into the hills.

Little by little, the wilderness transformed into a landscape culti-vated for human existence. Yet the small thatched huts the two men passed were uninhabited; the farms deserted; the newly sown crops laid waste. A jarring sense of isolation swept over the land.

The sun was low over the horizon, an orange ball behind dark, scud-ding clouds. In the pale band of sky to the south, vague shadows were moving, flying slowly in one direction and then turning in midair to fly back in the other. Cormier inhaled deeply and said, "Vultures have found something."

Ahead of them, over a rise, a thin cloud floated strangely near to the earth. By the time the Land Rover reached the slope of the hill, the cloud had transmuted into a blur of ash and smoke, drifting on the wind.

They had come to the remains of a devastated, burned-out com-mune. Stephen slowed to a crawl and cut the Land Rover's engine and he and Cormier sat and looked about them.

The dwellings had been leveled. Flaring up from time to time, the serrated flames of dying fires still worked among the wreckage. Along the perimeter, beyond the smoldering ruins, there were fresh gashes in the ground where the earth had been crudely tilled. All was quiet. Only the vultures were impatient, retreating stiltedly from amid the detri-tus as the Land Rover approached. Uttering soft hissing noises, they pounded up into nearby trees and fretted among the branches.

Leaning his arm on the windowsill, trying to calm his mind, Stephen raised his eyes toward the sky in the distance. Near the horizon the clouds were night black, trailing dark tentacles through the foot-hills where rain, ink-like and streaming, was blotted up by the brush, absorbed by the earth. Soon it would reach them. Merciful rain.

—m—

The next afternoon, Stephen attempted to answer the stack of mail that had accumulated on his desk, first and foremost a letter from Kathleen, together with his half-written reply. He sat looking over what he had said so far, but after a few minutes, restless, unable to concentrate, he pushed back his chair, stood, and went to the window.

The mists that veiled the trees were thinning, and the sun, glowing through blown plumes of gray clouds, hung like a gold coin over the woodlands. The earth was about to explode with the glory of spring.

His thoughts ranged back through remote ages of time. Deep in human history, when catastrophe had befallen the people of Israel, their prophets had defined the experience as God's chastisement: historical ordeal as divine punishment, calling for repentance and the renewal of moral vigor. And throughout the centuries, men had stood as he stood now and wondered how to interpret events when tragedy felled the innocent, as in this April it had these people, these humble Christians.

Long moments later, he heard a soft tread, one foot dragging slowly behind the other, and turned from the window to see Mambo standing in the doorway.

"What do you think, Father?"

Mambo's question was intended to elicit an opinion on the unconfirmed report that the UN had decided to reduce its presence in the country and not intervene to stop the killing. But Stephen, lost in thought, had understood the question as, "What are you thinking about?" and answered:

"American Catholics know the writings of Thomas Merton, a gifted Trappist monk. Not long after Merton entered the monastery, his brother became a casualty of the Second World War. In memory of him, Merton wrote a poem of haunting eloquence. Certain words from it come back to me now: 'In the wreckage of your April Christ lies slain...'"

Stephen glanced at the desk, at the half-written letter, then looked back at the old man, holding his eyes.

"Thoughts like that, Mambo..."

—∿—

It was the last Saturday of the month. A light rain at dawn still hung in the suspension of glass-like beads that sparkled in the giant spider-webs stretched across the bougainvillea along the mission wall. Stephen crossed the drive to the tree-lined path that led to the convent of the Sisters of Mercy, moving along the edges of puddles, skirting a tortoise the size of a boulder.

At the entrance to the convent, before knocking on the door, he paused to wipe the mud off his shoes with a towel he had carried with him.

Seeing him from a window, Sister Margaret walked quickly to the door to meet him.

Uncharacteristically, she was alone. The other nuns had gone to the school to prepare to close their classrooms. At the direction of their motherhouse in France, they were evacuating the mission.

"Sister, have I come at an inconvenient time?"

Sister Margaret wiped her hands on her ribbed cotton apron. "Never, Father. Come in, please. I'm cleaning cupboards. It would be nice to have coffee. And a pleasure to share it with you."

Stephen stepped inside and closed the door behind him.

"You know we're leaving?" the nun asked as they walked through muted, airy rooms. "As soon as Tuesday…"

"Yes. I've come to say good-bye. And to ask you how we can help."

"Thank you. But we'll be ready. Please, won't you sit down?"

In the little kitchen, with its cast-iron stove, the window was partly open. A mild air, permeated with the green smells of wood meadow grass and wet earth, drifted into the room and a pile of loose papers on the floor by the broom closet rustled in the breeze. Stephen pulled out a chair from the table for the nun so that she could sit facing the window. Nothing stirred on the paths outside. The day was slightly overcast; through the mist the sun shimmered with an almost mystical beauty. *All is fleeting*, Stephen thought. *In a moment, this scene, too, will be gone.*

Hastily opening and shutting doors, Sister Margaret was searching in the cupboards for something sweet.

"There's no more fruit," she said, turning around. "And I'm out of cookies. I have so little to offer you."

Stephen smiled. "That's not necessary, Sister."

A cup of coffee in each hand, the nun came over to the table.

"I wonder which is older," she said, "the code of hospitality, or war?"

"War, I'm afraid."

Sister Margaret handed him a cup. "Please," she said, motioning to the chair opposite her.

They sat down together, and Stephen asked, "Are your plans definite?"

"Yes. Yet I have doubts. Running away from adversity is not in my nature. We're abandoning the children here. I keep wishing we could find a way to stay. Should we? What do you think?"

Stephen nodded his head in understanding, but other thoughts absorbed him. The night before, the Jesuits had learned of a brutal attack at a Catholic mission in the northeast, and he would not tell her how the nuns there had died. He said only, "I think the decision to leave is the right one."

Sister Margaret stared off into the distance for a long moment and then gazed at Stephen. She fingered the cup in front of her and began to speak in the dreaming voice he remembered from the day when he had first seen her, when she held a child in her arms.

"Not far from here grows a kind of morning glory that opens after dark—so fast, you can see it happen. Sometimes, I think that if it could, it would recoil and refuse to unfold and that the animals, too, must study us and wonder: who are these creatures that they behave toward one another with such brutality?"

Slowly stirring his coffee, Stephen lowered his eyes and said quietly, "I have those same thoughts."

Sister Margaret looked at him with the candid gaze of one who has lived through perilous times with another, who has for that other a deep, enduring, and selfless regard, and who was now about to be parted from him, knowing they would not see each other again.

"You read Saint John of the Cross," she said.

"Yes," Stephen said, surprised. It was one of the most personal facts about him.

"One day—not long after you arrived—I was working in the sacristy, and I found your books on the counter. I thought: how wonderful! Father Engle reads Saint John of the Cross!"

"Would you like to have the book until you go?"

"Oh, no! Thank you, but Saint John of the Cross is way over my head."

She reflected a moment and then she said, "When I was a child, I wanted—as so many French girls did—to grow up to become a Carmelite, like Saint Thérèse." She tilted her head to one side. "I visited Lisieux once. You'd be so disappointed. Very bourgeoisie...stuffy...suffocating...Still, a great saint came from there, and I wanted to follow her example."

Sister Margaret laughed gently. "Ah, Father, you're wondering: how did she end up *here*?"

Stephen smiled. "Something like that."

"It was in my teenage years that I began to think: if Jesus was to be the center of my existence, then I must pay attention to where he said we should look for him. This meant I had to read the Gospels carefully. And when I did, I found this:

"'I was hungry, and you gave me food; thirsty, and you gave me a drink; a stranger, and you welcomed me; naked, and you clothed me...' And so, when I was seventeen, I entered a missionary order, and now—here I am."

Stephen looked down at her hands where they lay extended near her cup. They were small and slender and graceful, chapped from washing dishes and scrubbing floors, cracked from being exposed to the sun and from digging in the earth; the nails were broken and soiled underneath. His eyes wandered across her face. It was said of Saint Thérèse of Lisieux that in the last days of her life her face had taken on an exceptional beauty, the translucent pallor of those in the final stages of tuberculosis. He gazed at the pure brow, the fair skin, the luminous eyes of the woman who thought she could not understand Saint John of the Cross.

"I knew another Margaret once," he said, "a volunteer at the school where I taught, the first year after ordination. You are so like her—the fine impulses."

"Father Cormier was the first Jesuit I'd ever worked with. He has always seemed to me to be the embodiment of the ideal Jesuit: learned, disciplined, high-minded."

The nun lowered her head and fell silent. When she looked up, her eyes held tears. She asked:

"Do you think the mission will survive?"

Stephen did not answer at once. The question caught him off guard, but only because someone else had voiced it; in the silence of his own heart, he asked it repeatedly.

"I honestly don't know," he said at length. "My hope is for something positive to occur, for the intercession of some governing body that would establish a truce." To himself he thought, it couldn't happen again, not after Auschwitz.

They were both silent for a minute. Then, Sister Margaret said:

"Forgive me. I want to ask you a personal favor."

Stephen gave her a thoughtful look, answering with his eyes.

Sister Margaret asked, "Do you know the story of Lidice?"

"The name sounds familiar, but no, I don't recall it."

"During World War Two, Lidice was a village in occupied Czechoslovakia. Its story is one of sad irony. In reprisal for the murder of a high-ranking Nazi official, Hitler ordered German forces to kill or deport to concentration camps Lidice's entire population and obliterate every sign that the village had ever existed.

"But what happened afterward was like a miracle. People all around the world renamed their villages Lidice so that its memory wouldn't be erased.

"I'd like you to tell Father Cormier that I make him this promise: if the worst happens, wherever I go next, I will ask if the mission's name could be changed to *Reine des Anges*, so that the work he began here won't be forgotten. Would you tell him this for me, please?"

Deeply moved, Stephen lowered his eyes and nodded. "I will tell him." After a long silence, he said:

"Viktor Frankl saw this kind of mass killing and thought of Lessing's words: 'There are things which must cause you to lose your reason or you have none to lose.'"

Stephen meant to continue with that thought but interrupted himself, reminded unexpectedly of another, more personal memory. Leaning forward, his hands around his cup, he said in a voice at once reflective and tense with feeling:

"When my father was in his last illness, I sat with him that final morning, reading from the Book of Kings, the scene where David lies dying and, calling Solomon to him, says, 'I am going the way of all mankind.' The dignity of that death, and this—" Stephen's voice broke; suddenly, involuntarily, his eyes filled with tears and he did not go on.

Over his face came the ravaged look that accompanies intense emotional suffering.

"Father," Sister Margaret spoke his name softly. She said:

"You came here at such a singular time. This is my seventh year, and I have memories of so much that was beautiful. But you—you are experiencing the worst that can be imagined, without any balance..."

"Last year, I attended Easter Mass at the cathedral. Everything was so lovely—the soft white clouds overhead, the bright green fields, the street scenes on the drive through the capital, the altar banked high with lilies, and, at the end of Mass, the children's choir, singing a cappella—like this—"

Sister Margaret leaned back and, tossing her head lightly, as if in defiance of the outside world and any ability it had to touch her, she intoned in Latin: "*Regina caeli, latere. Alleluia.*"

Her voice was high and light and frail, like something winged that could not make it to the window. Stephen recovered, collected himself, and joined her. His voice, lower, deeper, stronger, lifted both, carried them out through the window and beyond, into the yard, as they called out from the little convent kitchen into the freedom of space:

"Quia quem meruisti portare.
Alleluia.
Resurrixit sicut dixit. Alleluia.
Ora pro nobis Deum. Alleluia."

Queen of heaven, rejoice. Alleluia.
For he whom you merited to bear. Alleluia,
Has risen, as he foretold. Alleluia.
Pray for us to God. Alleluia.

—〰—

Three days later, the French Sisters of Mercy left *Reine des Anges*. Walking down the driveway in the half-light of sunrise, Stephen heard a horn sound behind him. He leaped to one side to allow the mission's van to pass by. From the front passenger's seat, Sister Margaret leaned out, called to him, and waved.

"God go with you, Stephen Engle!"

God bless you—Stephen mouthed the words in French, smiled, waved back.

—〰—

A single voice pervaded the afternoon—an old man's voice—calling out beside the mission wall.

Tall, gaunt, balding, with a withered face that looked like it had been penciled on onionskin, the speaker stood in the thin crescent of shadow just inside the gate, where a crowd had gathered. His demeanor was pained, his cheeks and eyes twitching, his gnarled hand raised in the air, like a witness. He recounted:

"When Dhavée came with his men to our village, he called all the people together. Many were frightened. Some of the women were crying.

"But Dhavée spoke to us from the Gospels. 'Don't be afraid,' he said. 'What father among you would give his son a stone if he asked for a loaf of bread? Or a scorpion, if he asked for a fish? I've come to help you.'

"Because he had grown up in a commune and his parents were remembered by many, Dhavée could summon trust.

"He encouraged most of the village to go into the church. Only my family was left behind, for a purpose.

"Did those who were led away feel a grim foreboding? I was there; I saw: some were shuddering, as if suddenly cold.

"Soon after the church doors were closed, a van full of soldiers arrived. Dhavée, who had remained outside, gave orders to the soldiers. They began to run around the outside of the church, pouring gasoline from large red cans all over the ground until the church was encircled. They did this again and again.

"Then, all at once, the great door of the church opened and a young man stepped out and looked around. When he saw the soldiers he was confused at first, then his face contorted with terror, and he came out, running along the path. Dhavée raised his arm and brought it down. One of the soldiers fired his gun. The young man fell, though his legs and arms kept twitching. The soldier fired again, and he was still.

"Other soldiers set the rings of gasoline on fire and ran back, hurrying to get away. Some of those who were in the church had come to the door, but the flames rushed together and made a mighty fire...and they disappeared.

"We who survived watched in horror. When the flames flared up above the trees, we felt their heat and shivered..."

The speaker broke off, his eyes going from face to face as if searching for someone, or as if afraid to alight. His listeners crowded close together in dazed attentiveness. They might have been huddled figures painted on the walls of caves in ancient times, ageless depictions of fear and suffering.

With an intensity that reflexively caused his voice to quaver, the old man spoke again:

"Dhavée came up to us. His face showed nothing. He said in the cold, bitter voice of one who threatens to deliver a stone, 'Your lives have been spared so that you may bear witness to what has been done here. I mean to spread terror throughout the land.'

"He came into our midst like Christ, and he left as a fiend."

—∭—

When Cormier, Joyeaux, and Stephen learned of this behavior on the part of Dhavée, they fasted for a day. Too appalled by the fall of his former student to speak, Cormier went off by himself, turning his reddened eyes away from the eyes of the others.

Stephen, dismayed, read the Psalms, Isaiah, remembered Blake:

> *When the stars threw*
> *down their spears,*
> *And water'd heaven*
> *With their tears...*[1]

He went alone to the church to say Mass in private:

"Behold the Lamb of God who takes away the sins of the world," he prayed before receiving Communion.

—∭—

---

1 The lines are from "Tyger! Tyger!" by William Blake. *Tyger! Tyger! burning bright/In the forests of the night/What immortal hand or eye/Could frame thy fearful symmetry?...When the stars threw down their spears/And water'd heaven with their tears/Did he smile his work to see?/Did he who made the Lamb make thee?*

If concern for Dhavée and his actions weighed heavily on the Jesuits—and, in the case of Cormier, preoccupation at times reached the level of obsession—the Jesuits themselves absorbed the thoughts of the captain of the army.

The experience of killing had radically reshaped Dhavée's inner life. Soon he participated in each aspect of a massacre. All the powers of his soul were concentrated on his victims' reactions. In their frenzied attempts to escape, in their anguished cries, in their torment and despair, or in their heroic valor before going down under the machete, Dhavée united imaginatively with those he was about to slay, as a dreamer is himself each of the characters in his dream. This illusory encounter with the final moments of life had become for him a kind of conquest of death.

The act of killing invigorated him with creative force, allowing him to break into the life story of another like a god and bring that story to a transforming end. Alone among human acts, administering the death blow gave him the sensation of transcending the banality of the everyday, clarified reality with the certainty of an absolute principle, and, in time, satisfied his need for human intimacy. Dhavée knew that what was said of him—that he killed indifferently and without soul—was not true. He had discovered that the commission of murder could be an intensely spiritual act: he was the last and only one to see a man's soul revealed in his dying eyes.

And, of all men, none fired his imagination so fervidly as did the American Jesuit: Stephen's aloofness at the courthouse in the provincial capital; his intent dark eyes with their look of silent reproach; his rapport with Rebecca Talitha—and, as he recalled what his men had told him of Stephen's visit to Rebecca Talitha, Dhavée, embittered, spat; the ease with which Stephen moved among a people who were not his own, looking as he did, yet not governed by the desires of the flesh. All this coalesced in Dhavée's mind as he considered his next meeting with the Jesuits.

From his seat in the rear of a military jeep, the captain of the army looked south, toward the hill country, in the direction of the Jesuit mission of *Reine des Anges*. A surround of weighted lead-gray clouds hung low above the dull green fields, like a mountain chain inverted over the whole earth, and the sharp morning air smelled of rain.

Dhavée smiled inwardly. "A little while and you will not see me, and then a little while and you will see me again," he said quietly aloud, in deliberate and sacrilegious mockery of the words spoken by Christ to his disciples at the Last Supper.

—m—

Evening. A violet light had closed over the earth and out of the distant hills a white moon was rising. Stephen entered his room without turning on a light. The last on the floor, his room faced east and looked out on the courtyard and the path that ran down to the clinic. The walls were ivory and bare except for a wooden crucifix over the bed. The other furnishings were a table with a lamp, a bookshelf, and a desk and chair next to the window.

Soon after his arrival, Stephen had simplified his intellectual life to *The Poems and Prose of Gerard Manley Hopkins*, the slim blue volume with gilt edges now worn away, given to him by his father; the works of Saint John of the Cross; and two copies of the New Testament, one in English, the other in Greek. They rested on the desk next to the paper he set aside for his writing.

While the light lasted, he sat by the open window meshed with mosquito netting, reading Hopkins's "The Windhover"; of the collected works, it was Hopkins's personal favorite. Stephen had begun a commentary on it for the Jesuit magazine *America*, intending to finish the article by the weekend.

When darkness fell he gave up trying to work and, without undressing, lay down on the bed and fell asleep. After an hour he woke, thought of getting up, but drifted off to sleep again. Dreaming, he watched disturbing images rise in his imagination and, all at once, from "The Wreck of the Deutschland," he heard that dying scream call through the night:

Christ, Christ, come quickly…

Stephen snapped awake. He sat up. Gripping the edge of the bed, he looked around, his every sense alert. The air was chilled. All was silent, still. Then he understood: a bat had screamed. Impinging on the wall outside, it hung now, quivering, upside down in the window, caught up in the netting. From the darkness, its blind eyes stared into his.

—⁂—

It was morning, the next day. In one corner of the residence kitchen, where the range was lit, a harsh red light glowed. The rapid bubbling of boiling water and a gentle ring of glass were the only sounds.

Their faces misted with steam, Stephen and Louis Joyeaux stood beside a table, filling glass jars with sterilized water and arranging them along the counter under the open window.

Since mid-April, the normal flow of life had been severely interrupted, and the basic necessities of ordinary existence—unreliable even in the best of times—had been seriously degraded. Even such a common staple as salt, essential in the treatment of dysentery, was in painfully short supply. Whatever water was available to the mission now was unclean and had to be strained through filter bags and boiled before it could be bottled and used for drinking.

For long minutes, Stephen and Joyeaux had been working in silence, emotionally drained, by necessity alert to the rising violence in the outer world, absorbed by thoughts they found more and more difficult to bear. Intuitively, the mission's three Jesuits felt their spiritual values were being profaned and called into question. Instinctively, they looked to each other for psychological support. Each needed the others to remind him of what was real, absolute, indestructible.

Louis Joyeaux, educated in the medical sciences, not inclined toward literature or the arts, suddenly felt the need to understand events compelling him to turn to metaphor and myth. For the third or fourth time that morning, he paused to wipe his brow and glance timidly at Stephen. After several minutes of internal debate he overcame his reluctance to express his most private thoughts.

"Stephen—"

Stephen looked up at him.

"Suffering and death on this scale…which of the great literary figures could tell of it?" Joyeaux asked, enunciating the unaccustomed names slowly and deferentially. "Homer…Virgil…Shakespeare?"

Stephen could see how stirred the French Jesuit was and could imagine what he was feeling. He paused and thought, looking out through the half-open window, north, across the mission wall to the distant mountain slopes. Then he shook his head and answered quietly:

"Dante. He envisioned these terraced fields and hills."

—∿—

In those intense days, they prayed, worked, and slept, and did little else, except that Stephen wrote. Sometimes he penned poems or penciled thoughts on the backs of envelopes or in the margins of his books. At other times he shared his reflections in letters. Paraphrasing Hopkins, he wrote to his seminary classmate and university colleague Alan Black:

> *Now, just as when the dying Jesus stared out upon an indifferent earth from Golgotha, the world looks the other way and, again, Christ suffers "in ten thousand places…in limbs…in eyes not His."*

To Eugene Dowd he wrote:

Death takes many forms here: the destruction of the social order, the spiritual disorientation, the horror of mass murder. Everywhere we witness the emotional reaction Augustine described as "the death of the living upon the loss of the life of the dying."

I confess I find the dark elements are not countered by any ascendancy of spiritual feeling or thought on my part. In the absence of that inner state there is instead darkness, silence, anxiety, fatigue.

When I was in graduate school, one of my professors remarked that Godot *is a drama which asks the question, "My God, my God, why have You forsaken me?" Not grasping the full implication of his meaning then, I understand it now.*

I protest against the void with such a small thing: the word yes. *Yes, to silence; yes, to fatigue; yes, to an unknown future; yes, that God is here, present in the dark spaces; yes, that sense will be made.*

I haven't forgotten that it's spring at home. I can picture the maple tree on the lawn of my parents' home as the shadows lift at daybreak. The branches will be putting forth red buds now; by month's end, leaf out, soft green; burst into flame in autumn, then still, as if for a portrait. "There lives the dearest freshness deep down things…"

Your loving son in Christ, Father,
Stephen

—∭—

In late afternoon on the twelfth day in May 1994, Bernt Dolmark, a senior staff member of CARE, made the long, last turn in the road and pulled up before the entrance to the mission grounds.

Dolmark was Norwegian, a youthful-looking man of fifty-eight, with dark, leathery skin like that of all those who spend their lives out-of-doors in the African sun, and light brown hair the sun had bleached palomino.

At the edge of the drive, beside the low wall, he stopped, idled the engine, and sat for a while, immersed in thought. The air was mild and still. A soft haze was turning into a drizzle, imperceptibly. Somewhere through the mist, a wild ibis called. Dolmark, looking on, could see, beyond breaks in the trees, the low, curving line of buildings—the Jesuit residence, the school, the clinic, the convent with its gardens, and the church at the center—the sight which, from the first time he had glimpsed it, reminded him always of the monasteries built throughout Europe in the Middle Ages. Knowing he was parting from it irrevocably, he gazed long at the scene, moved by its beauty: the unself-conscious beauty of simple, timeless objects.

Minutes later, he drove onto the grounds, parked by the grotto and, leaving his jeep, crossed the driveway and headed toward the Jesuit residence. At that moment, the door of the clinic opened. Jacques Cormier, wearing black clerics and with his collar undone, came out and walked swiftly up the path to meet him.

"Bernt," he said with a pensive smile, "you have news. From the doorway, I saw it in your face."

"I'm sorry, Father. I'm afraid I've come to say good-bye. I'm leaving tonight."

Cormier looked searchingly at him.

"It's reached that stage…even for you?"

"The entire country is in a state of collapse. Paramilitary groups seem bent on destroying everything. They've seized the international airport and mounted machine guns along the runways. There's no safe way to travel now. Roadblocks are going up everywhere. Soon traffic on the main roads will be stopped."

His chest heaving with emotion, Dolmark excused himself and took out a large white handkerchief, unfolding it and pressing it against his face, which was moist with mist and sweat. He asked:

"And what of the three of you? Surely you know how vulnerable you are? Surely you're making plans to get out."

Cormier shook his head. "No. If I were to go, that action would convey a sense of hopelessness to the very people who are most traumatized by the violence."

Dolmark looked off into the soft gray haze for a moment and then gave the Jesuit a sidelong glance.

"You aren't aware, are you, that Dhavée arrived in Natáre yesterday, and has set up headquarters there?"

"No!"

"He has a list of foreigners he intends to kill. My name is on the list. Tonight, a convoy of relief workers is leaving the country. I'll go in that group."

Dolmark broke off for effect, then said pointedly, "A paramilitary unit could be here within a few days."

Cormier stood with squared jaw and half-lowered eyes, his arms folded across his broad chest. "I was a boy during World War Two," he said. "My parents worked for the French resistance. They helped rescue downed Allied fliers, often at great risk to their own lives. They didn't have to do it; they offered to help because they believed one must live one's faith." He looked up at Dolmark. "But who am I to instruct you, who in your own way are so committed to human need?" Cormier smiled sadly with this last remark, and fell silent.

Several moments passed. Then Dolmark asked, "What about Father Joyeaux?"

"He is staying, too."

"And Father Engle?"

"Yes. He wants to remain with us."

Dolmark looked at the Jesuit fixedly. A note of frustration, but also of resignation, came into his voice.

"Realistically, Father, what can you still do here?"

"Be a witness to these events...try to protect whomever we can."

Grateful to the Norwegian for his solicitude, Cormier held out his hand to him in a firm clasp.

"'Let us thank God that we live in perilous times,'" he said gently in parting, quoting words remembered from childhood. "'It is not permitted to anyone to be mediocre.'"

There was no way to deflect that singleness of purpose, Dolmark saw, and thus no reason for him to linger. But he had to struggle to take his eyes away from the French Jesuit's face, and looked on it movingly, as earlier, on the road, he had stopped to gaze a last time upon the mission grounds. He was picturing a younger Cormier, the tall, striking cleric with a moral radiance shining in his translucent blue eyes and a seemingly boundless self-confidence, who had distinguished himself even among the Jesuits for his dedication to the poor, and who had come with two companions to this forested hillside where he founded the mission he named *Reine des Anges*, Mary, Queen of Angels. Over the years, his colleagues had been transferred and replaced, but Cormier had remained. And now, he stood like Peter, an old man on the road to Rome.

As Dolmark turned to leave, the other two Jesuits came out of the residence and walked over to greet him.

Louis Joyeaux, whom he had always found a pain-filled, inhibited man, one of twelve brothers and sisters, the others left behind in the south of France.

And the American, Stephen Engle. What would those who knew and loved the younger Jesuit think of him now, in these days, when it seemed that his soul had come into his eyes, suffusing his expression with a tenderness and suffering reminiscent of the luminous faces of saints in the stained-glass windows of old cathedrals.

Bernt Dolmark parted from them then. He drove out of the mission grounds slowly and, reaching the main road, turned right, heading west. As he made the long wooded bend, his eyes were drawn to an unexpected spectacle spreading over the hills. Emerging only now, with the coming of evening, the sun shot through a phalanx of silver-gray clouds, as if it were fire flashing through smoke. The light flared out; it fell on the dark rock pinnacles, on the wooded valleys, on the distant lakes and mysterious islands, on the solitary mountain trails, on the blood-drenched countryside where the whole earth had become a tomb, groaning under the weight of the numberless dead.

—∾—

An hour later, Stephen entered the small dining room off the residence kitchen. Jacques Cormier was sitting alone at the table, scrawling notes in a large cursive hand on the back of a long white envelope. He looked up at Stephen with a kind of absent musing, as if reluctant to leave his inner world.

Feeling he was intruding, Stephen stopped a few steps into the room.

"Jacques, would you prefer to be alone?"

Cormier shook his head, indicating with his eyes the chair beside him.

"If you hadn't come, I would have been looking for you soon. Sit down Stephen…please."

Stephen pulled out the chair to his superior's right and sat down. It was growing dark in the yard. A faint red light filtered through the trees and hung a crimson afterglow on the far wall: the lamp of the sun going out.

"Stephen," Cormier went on, focused now, "I've been struggling with a decision…"

"Do you want my input, or would you prefer that I just listen?"

"Just listen," Cormier said with a rueful smile. "I already know what your input would be." He ran his fingers unsteadily over the envelope.

"Dhavée is in Natáre, with a contingent of men. I've decided that Louis and I will go there tomorrow to ask him for protection."

Stephen stared at him in disbelief.

"You're right about knowing what my input would be!" he said, exhaling the words softly in a single breath, as if speaking to himself.

Cormier looked away for a minute, preparing his response. Then he said, "You didn't hear Bernt when he first arrived. He's a conservative man, not prone to overreact. So when he describes events as dire, I listen. And I know I must take some kind of action. I must go to the source and reason with him, and that source is Dhavée."

Cormier sat bowed over the table, his arms folded in front of him, explaining in a low, meditative voice why he believed his plan of action would work.

Stephen listened in silence. He was remembering Dhavée that day in the capital: the nimble, long-fingered hands moving across the table, the careful angling of pages, and the written columns meant to be enigmatic that he was now certain contained names of those singled out for death.

In the deepening shadows Cormier seemed aged, his features grayed, his forehead furrowed, the wrinkles around his lower lids deep and distended.

"I knew Dhavée as a boy," he offered simply.

Stephen looked with heartache at the selfless, deeply burdened man beside him, with whom he was about to differ, and spoke with determination.

"Jacques...you don't know Dhavée anymore. The man's personality has been ravaged by violence. He's become a psychopathic killer."

"Faced with a moment of truth, he wouldn't harm one whom he knows has meant him nothing but good," Cormier said, and for a moment retreated again into his thoughts. His mind seemed to wander off. When he came back to himself, his voice was grave:

"The mission, its people, are doomed unless we take some kind of action."

"We can go underground," Stephen urged, for the first time expressing the thought that had been forming in his mind for days. "We can gather everyone together and make our way to the border..."

"Take the elderly and women and children into the bush? Over twenty miles of rough terrain, where, at any time, around any bend, they might encounter militia?"

Stephen did not answer. He sat looking at the blurring outline of the mission wall, pondering each possible course of action and its inherent risks. He wanted to say, "If you must do this, then let me go with you," but he understood that Cormier had chosen to leave him, rather than Joyeaux, in charge of the mission if the trip ended in failure, and would not put his superior in a position where he needed to state it. Instead, he broke the silence by saying:

"If you're right, there's someone in Natáre whom I hope the authorities would help to get to safety."

Cormier raised his brows, listening.

"Rebecca Talitha. Together with her family and a child named Renée."

"Rebecca Talitha," Cormier said sadly. "Rebecca Talitha, with her little school for children no one else wanted."

His voice thickened so that he was almost unable to speak, he pounded his fist twice on the table, then looked away.

To calm himself, Cormier turned to the chest behind him and opened a drawer, removed a half-empty box of cigars, and took out a veiny, blunt-ended corona. In his unsteady hand the cigar shook perceptibly. The struck match flared up like a thin torch; for an instant it illumined the older Jesuit's face in a halo of light, then went out. The gesture, the light scent of cedar, the red burn of the cigar brought back to Stephen's mind the memory of Eugene Dowd, and an agonizing wave of loneliness passed through him.

The sun had gone down. It was a little past eight, the hour of darkness. Beyond the wall a hyena howled, a call wild, violent, protracted, timeless.

> *Night belongs*
> *To the wild beasts now*
> *To the silent, listening trees,*
> *To the far-removed, indifferent stars:*
> *The witnesses*
> *Of our desperate memories.*
>
> *Stephen Engle, S.J.*
> *May 12, 1994*

—◊◊—

The next morning, Jacques Cormier and Louis Joyeaux set out for Natáre.

Rising before dawn, Jacques Cormier had offered the 6:30 Mass at the church's main altar. Afterward, he finished a letter he'd begun the night before, in order to mail it in town. Joyeaux slept little. His pattern that morning was the same as on every other morning: he said Mass at one of the side altars and then walked briskly up and down the length of the kidney-shaped compound. Before departing, the two Jesuits had a light breakfast together.

At nine, the silver-gray mission van drove out through the trees and down to the gate, Stephen trotting alongside it. As the van neared the approach to the road, it slowed and then stopped. Louis Joyeaux, his eyes humble and poignant and his thin mouth working, sat behind the wheel, staring out into the yard.

"I plan to be back this evening," Cormier was saying, "tomorrow afternoon, at the latest." He reached out the window to clasp Stephen's hand. Silently the two men looked into each other's eyes. They had lived for a month now with the heightened awareness of death, and knew that no parting was any longer casual. Certainly this one was not.

With his right hand Cormier traced the sign of the cross over his young associate. Tears of affection welled up in his eyes. In a voice rough with tenderness he said,

"Look after all...look after yourself..."

"Jacques...Louis..." The emotion of the moment was almost more than Stephen could bear. Dropping his hands, he stepped back.

Joyeaux shifted into gear and the van lurched forward, heading for the open gate; picking up speed, it veered out onto the road.

Just as the road began to bend to the right, before the van reached the first trees of the woods, Cormier turned around to glance back, and Stephen, standing in the very spot on the mission grounds where he had first stepped down nine months before, looking across the low wall with its purplish haze of bougainvillea, in a profound and awful silence penetrated only by the far-off four-note call of some unseen, unknown bird, saw his companion's face one last time.

—⚭—

As Rebecca Talitha leaned over the little group of giggling girls, tracing the graceful curve of the letter *S* to write out the name of the youngest child, Salama, she heard her own name pronounced in a way she had never heard it spoken before.

"I have long been desiring this meeting, Rebecca."

Jean-Baptiste Dhavée stood leaning one shoulder against the wall as he addressed her, six of his men wedged in the narrow hall behind him. All wore drab olive combat fatigues and bandoleers, with rifles slung over their shoulders and machetes hanging from their belts.

Shaken by the sudden arrival of the soldiers, not wanting to show fear in front of the children, Rebecca placed her hands on the shoulders of the girl beside her and steeled herself to face the captain of the army. With her eyes she pleaded:

Let the children go.

And as if he were a schoolmaster excusing a dance class, Dhavée stepped courteously aside and dismissed the children: five little girls, barely up to his waist, in white T-shirts and dark tattered shorts, two of them limping because they were lame. The last child, a very small eight-year-old with enormous brown eyes and a disfigured mouth, would not go, and stood, staring back into the room, until a soldier brandishing a pistol chased her away.

Dhavée came into the room and walked about, holding a pair of white gloves in his right hand and slapping them softly and evenly against the palm of the left. He passed by a counter lined with rows of jars and painted gourds and paused for a minute, tidying it up. Glancing over at his men and laughing with cold scorn, he brushed everything away with one sweep of his hand and watched the glass shatter on the floor. Afterward, he stood for a while in silence, drumming with his fingers on the edge of the counter, his eyes fixed on Rebecca. Then all at once, he crossed the floor to take her.

In the last hour of her doe-eyed, girlish beauty, in the moment before Dhavée reached her, Rebecca Talitha covered her face with her slim, lovely hands and told herself over and over that no matter what happened, there was a part of her that could never be despoiled or corrupted, as, with an effortless flick of his long, nimble fingers, the captain released the metal buckle of his cartridge belt and his men filed quietly into the room and stood barring the door, their bandoleers unfastened, and waited.

—m—

It was after nine and the street was dark when the child Renée slipped back. She stood at the entryway, a little girl with enormous listening eyes and a small misshapen mouth, peeking in. The school was silent and empty now.

She turned to go, when from the door she heard a woman moan, and halted. Carefully, she tiptoed across the little foyer, warily felt her way down the blackened hall, with her sandaled foot bumped into something lying on the floor, and found Rebecca.

XXIII

They call to me from Seir,
"Watchman, how much longer
the night?
Watchman, how much longer
the night?"
The watchman replies,
"Morning has come, and again night…"

— ISAIAH 21:11

Two days had passed since the morning when Jacques Cormier and Louis Joyeaux had left for Natáre. On the third day, Stephen, having waited until midafternoon and having heard nothing, felt he must look for them, and knew he would have to go to the town.

He was certain the road that led directly down from the mission was no longer safe. But three miles out, it was bisected by another, less frequented, gravel road. To the right, that road wound north through forest and dwindled to become a mountain trail. To the left, it ran through the hill country and in one place forked, and switched back, following the lines of the hillsides and approaching Natáre at an angle. Setting out by this route, Stephen came upon the town from above, at a slant.

He had to park the Land Rover off-road, climb down a wooded slope, and, keeping to the shelter of the trees, make his way to an acacia copse. There he found a perfect vantage point.

A thousand feet below him and more than a mile off in the distance, Natáre, discovered by pale spears of sunlight, emerged out of the neighboring foothills. With the naked eye, Stephen could see the graceful mix of avenues and gardens, the terraced restaurants covered with dark tile roofs from another time, the hospital, the Jesuit cathedral with its great towers, the steep, narrow backstreets with their small square shops, one of which housed the little school run by Rebecca Talitha.

Natáre on this radiant afternoon in mid-May had a transcendent, timeless look. Brushed with gold and shadowed by dispersing clouds, it evoked an image from art, Vermeer's "The View of Delft." And, like a painting, all was silent and stood still.

Using binoculars, Stephen took a closer look. And now the image altered. The air was alive with birds; ravens, disturbed by something, flew among the rooftops, cawing wildly. At the far end of one avenue, an abandoned fire was dying out in the open doorway of a restaurant. Stephen trained the binoculars on the cathedral and its surrounding area. Around the grounds ran a formal redbrick wall, to the right of which grew a large mango tree covered with dark, shiny foliage; beneath the tree a metal object glittered in veiled sunlight—the silver-gray hood of the mission van.

Adjusting the glasses, Stephen concentrated on the Jesuit residence, trying to get a better look at the windows. Nothing stirred. If Dhavée and a contingent of his men were down there, he wondered, why didn't they have a presence on the street? It was Monday, a market day. Where was everyone? The town, which only moments before had seemed imbued with an unnatural loveliness, was distinguished now by an eerie quiet, a sinister unease heightened by the strange crows flapping fitfully over the doorposts.

Even now, as he stood hidden in the brush, Stephen had an uneasy sense there was awareness somewhere. Though he wanted to drive into the town and continue the search for Cormier and Joyeaux, every instinct told him to take a different course. Leaving the slope reluctantly, he returned to the Land Rover and climbed in, then backed up to the road and headed home to the mission.

Twelve miles out of Natáre, a fourth of the way back, his side-view mirror caught the sparkle of low afternoon sunlight off the windshield of a distant car. To the right and far behind him, at the summit of a hill, a low haze was rising off the road. As long as the road ahead of him continued to follow the steep incline of the hillside, he was safe in the shadows. But soon the road would straighten as it crossed a stretch of open grassland. Then the Land Rover would be clearly apparent to the eye.

He decided to take cover. He veered to the right in order to conceal the dark green SUV in the growth of the trees that lined the road. He parked, got out, and, pulling up long grasses and fallen branches, covered the tracks the tires had left in the earth. Then he made his way to the road. When he was a few feet from the shoulder, he crouched in a dense thicket and concentrated his whole attention on latticework openings in the leaves through which he could see whatever passed, and waited for the car to go by.

It was a military vehicle. As it approached, Stephen could hear the harsh whine of the gear changes and the tires churning up the gravel, and men's voices reveling and murmuring on the evening air.

Four men were riding in a military jeep. Stephen recognized Dhavée at once. Though the others wore combat fatigues, the captain was dressed in an officer's uniform, with epaulets and white gloves, and he had a sidearm on his belt. Sitting in the front passenger seat, he posed, imperious, his head held high, his long, bent nose protruding—a falcon's, a vulture's profile.

As the sinister spectacle of Dhavée and the other soldiers passed by, Stephen felt a chill run through him. It was the men's demeanor that unnerved him. They drove slowly, leisurely. There was a peaceful languor about them. They batted at one another playfully with their hands and stretched their arms lazily in the descending dusk, crooning and laughing softly together. Bronzed, lordly, spattered with dried blood, they were like young lions preening after the hunt, the kill, the long feeding in the high grass.

—⟋ɯ—

Never in his life had Stephen felt such a sense of vulnerability as on that thirty-six-mile drive, which took him hours, running without lights, pulling off the road now and then to sit for half an hour at a time and watch for other traffic, not knowing whether somewhere ahead the military jeep lay in wait.

When he reached the mission cicadas were drilling in the trees around him. Faint noises reached him from beyond the wall. There were rustlings in the darkness near the Jesuit residence. Feet shuffled on the gravel path. From the doorway came the sound of voices talking in anxious whispers. But they were voices Stephen knew.

He drove onto the grounds and parked, then got out of the Land Rover. Six men from the mission council walked down the lawn to meet him. When he glimpsed their astonished faces, he realized they had not expected to see him again. He explained that he had gone to Natáre, but only to the outskirts, and why. He had seen Dhavée with soldiers on the road: these men needed to know there were mere hours, not days, to protect themselves and their families.

Stephen was exhausted from the stress of the day and, glancing about the yard now brightened by a kerosene lamp, he felt strengthened and consoled by the presence of the others. But the relief lasted for only a moment. In the men's tense, guarded looks he recognized an unmistakable meaning: the wish to spare him. He said tersely:

"You have news of your own."

The others nodded. Someone murmured, "Yes."

Stephen looked uneasily from face to face. "Of Fathers Cormier and Joyeaux?"

No one answered. Eyes lowered.

"Are they all right?"

One of the men crossed himself. "They were…all of the Fathers… were killed."

Stephen stepped back, shaken. "All?"

His arms hanging helplessly at his sides, he listened as by degrees the council members related fragments of news they had learned concerning events that had taken place that day. They spoke of how soldiers had been marauding throughout Natáre for days, and recounted the story of a surprise attack on the Jesuit residence the night before last, while the priests were at supper, and how Dhavée was present to supervise the murders of the Jesuits.

Stephen broke in with a terrible clarity of tone:

"How?"

"Father Louis and the others, with machetes," came the muted response. "They say Dhavée himself shot Father Cormier."

The six men stared nervously at the lone Jesuit survivor. Another one of them, a handsome old man with a curved spine that caused him to lean on a cane, was about to say something, but Stephen spoke first. His eyes had a blurred, stricken look and his voice broke with anguish:

"Dhavée shot that good, gentle man who taught him when he was a child?"

The lamp flared up. No one spoke.

Stephen made a gesture to excuse himself and left the group. Once alone, he walked into the shadows along the side of the residence. There, overcome with desolation, he leaned against the wall and broke down and wept.

He returned over and over in his mind to that fateful last conversation with Cormier, losing all sense of time, conscious of nothing but the tragedy that had befallen his lost companions.

The first faint rays of morning grazed his hands and then, his hands withdrawn, fell upon his eyes. The long, anguished night was over. Stephen looked up to watch the approach of the dawn. Along the entire length of the sky the tranquil upper air was renewing, a vivid azure blue. The kind of sight that once stirred in him the question:

How is it men say
Thou art absent?

———————

They would go now. Forsaking home, country, possessions—all that they had—now the people of the parish would flee into the bush, hoping to make it to the Rift Valley, the border, and safety.

Stephen, too, made plans to leave, all the while knowing that unless everyone connected with the mission agreed to go, he would return once the others had reached the road leading to the border. How he would manage to do this and how he would survive afterward on his own, he did not know. He would work that out when the time came. For though he longed with all his soul to get away, and outwardly went through the motions of attempting to leave, inwardly he felt that he had come to the Gethsemane of his life and, abandoning himself to God, would do what was expected of him and accept without question the outcome and his fate.

Stephen returned to his room in the Jesuit residence and crossed the floor to his desk, stumbled, and went down on his knees. He was unshaven, spent. Sleep forced its way.

He was awakened by voices. Outside his window, up and down the circle drive, men, women, and children were milling about.

Hurriedly, he changed out of his black clerics into chino pants and a blue cotton shirt. He smeared insecticide on his neck, arms, and ankles to safeguard against ticks and flying insects. Then he bundled his breviary and sacramental stole in a backpack along with rehydration salts and antibiotics retrieved from the clinic. His books and writing he packaged in a cardboard box which he shoved under his bed, forcing it until it bumped against the wall. There was no need to carry the keys to the mission buildings with him; he buried them in the bougainvillea beside the convent, together with the keys to the Land Rover.

Many from the small neighborhoods of farms, afraid to go unarmed into the bush, chose to remain behind; others, clinging to the "delusion of reprieve," believed they would be spared, and elected to endure alone. But those who wanted to risk the journey—over fifty men, women, and children in all—set out.

—⁓—

As they went along the way, they met an image of human pathos standing in the road: a gaunt old man with dark yellow teeth and the long wild hair of a soothsayer, barefoot and dressed in rags, one of those too weak to make the journey. Coming up to Stephen, he raised his hands and cupped Stephen's face within them, his fingers frail and stiff as a bird's legs, his eyes distraught and painfully interrogative. Swaying slightly back and forth, he asked in a weak, hoarse voice:

"Father, will you come back to us?"

Stephen, seeing that the aged figure seemed close to giving in to despair, looked on him with compassion.

"Yes. I'll come back. I promise you."

Speechless with emotion, the old man embraced Stephen and kissed him.

—⁓—

The dry season had come early that year. Except for the morning of Bernt Dolmark's visit, the weather had been fine and clear for almost two weeks, and benign winds had hardened the mountain trails.

Behind the mission a narrow dirt path led into the woods and wound gradually uphill. It was the natural route for travelers to take. Sometimes walking two abreast, sometimes going single file, young men led the way, their wives and children following after, then the grandparents.

Toward the end of the ragged procession, Mambo with his slight, aging body, shuffled along beside his wife, who was dragging a heavy pack. For those who were older, for women with children, for one who was pregnant, the pace had to be slow.

The path thinned until it vanished; for a long time they climbed up and down gentle slopes on their own, always bearing west.

In late afternoon they came to a small footbridge and stopped to rest. The bridge, a narrow framework of wooden steps and waist-high rails, was built over a little ravine; beneath it, wrinkling like a ribbon of green silk, a slender stream wound through the trees. From the upper woods came a dull, short "tick" alarm note, the only sound there. The evacuees crossed the bridge and stopped again to look back over the trail. Out of sight, far to the left and six hundred feet below them, the mission lay silent, dark, and undisturbed.

It was cool and peaceful in the forest. Moss as thick as carpeting clung to trees and hung in giant webs between the boughs. Great hygenia rose out of the earth, wild and magnificent trees with orchids blooming in their cushioned arms. Delicate flowers burst forth like stars on the mossy floor. Overhead, black-and-white colobus monkeys, elusive as coils of smoke, twined among the branches. For a while the evacuees changed pace and walked slowly, dazedly.

When they came out onto a small bluff, the sun had almost gone down. Dragonflies were floating on the evening air. An advancing dusk of bats streamed across the sky toward feeding grounds. Hyenas bayed in the woods below.

They climbed another forty feet to a deep glade carpeted with thick grass. There they set up camp. As night moved in, the far-off caterwauling of a great cat could be heard and, like children in need of a mother's touch, young and old curled up close to one another for reassurance against the dark, while above the trees an ascending white moon lit the southern sky.

Stephen withdrew a stone's throw away to pray alone. When he returned, he found the others already asleep. At the edge of the path, before entering the encampment, he stopped short, struck by the beauty of the scene in the glade.

The thickets of trees, the sleeping silhouettes beneath them, were backlit by moonlight and illumined, as though hand painted or placed under an enchantment. The vulnerable prostrate forms seemed archetypical in their repose, evocative of all those who throughout history, myth, or legend have been cast off into darkness, abandoned in streams, or left in a woods, and whose special fate it is to be protected by the Providence of God.

Stephen found a place to rest close by. He leaned back against the burled trunk of a great hygenia and looked out over the dark shoulders of the hills to watch the moon rise. After a while he closed his eyes and tried to sleep, but his thoughts were too active.

Image after image presented itself to his mind, like the passage of a universe of mysterious stars, eternally welcoming, eternally irretrievable: his mother and father; the child Kathleen on long summer nights, hunting for walnuts in the woods behind their grandparents' farm; the grounds of the Jesuit seminary in spring; Clare and her dreaming eyes; the bridge over the pond at the south of the college; Mary Ainsley turning around in the doorway; Eugene Dowd in the evenings at Saint Aloysius; Louis Joyeaux, his nervous, working mouth, his sadness; the tender, dignified face of Jacques Cormier.

With a sudden pang, Stephen remembered the day he had met Dhavée and the conversation with Cormier afterward, on the road back to the mission, when Cormier had confided his apprehension about his former student's cynical indifference to murder. Again Stephen saw the French Jesuit's pained, compassionate eyes; again he heard Cormier's worn, moving voice, quoting Dostoyevsky:

"'Love a man even in his sin, for that is the semblance of divine love and is the highest love on Earth.'" And he realized that Cormier had had a premonition then that the brutish officer might have a hand in deciding his fate, but he went to see him in Natáre anyway, because he had already forgiven Dhavée in his heart.

Stephen's eyes grew heavy. Unaware, he slumped to the earth. For hours he lay in a deep sleep; then, in the middle of the night, he awoke to noise. The very air seemed to have come alive. Lying on his side, his head on his arm, he listened to the night voices of the forest: the cicadas' high-pitched, insistent drilling; the low murmur of a distant falls; the dry, guttural croaking of frogs in far-off dark lagoons; faint hyena cries; an indefinable screeching from the slopes above; and everywhere about them in the darkness, the din of a hundred thousand insects trilling.

A canticle of praise? Warring cries? Or only sounds? They seemed to Stephen in that moment to be a metaphor for the mystery of human existence.

He slept again.

Morning broke.

Waking before him, many in the makeshift camp were witnesses to two dawns: the scarlet flush of light brightening the eastern sky, and a preternatural pink discoloration enveloping the horizon line and its surrounding woods and fields.

A man rushed by, running along under the trees, saw Stephen, and motioned to him frantically: "Fire!"

Jarred from sleep, Stephen instinctively sprang to his feet, stumbling at first on a great gnarled root that grew aboveground, then, regaining his footing, ran through the empty glade toward the sound of voices.

The others were crowded together on the brow of the hillside, staring at the sinister radiance below. Smoke blew over a far-off valley and through its dark foothills. There were fires in some distant place, either in a commune or its coffee plantations.

Families watched, spellbound. Women shielded their children against their bodies. Full of fear and confusion, the children clung to their mothers and cried.

In the midst of the disorder, a young man and woman, gripped by a new imperative, suddenly broke from the group and ran toward the woods. Without thinking, the others retrieved their scant belongings, and followed them.

They wandered among the trees for hours, resting each time the older adults or the children tired, until the woods deepened and the landscape changed, and they came to the most difficult portion of the journey.

A great, stern hill rose up more than two thousand feet in the air, in places almost at a forty-five-degree angle. This rising ground stood in the way; to reach their destination, the evacuees had to scale it.

Brambles punished their flesh; they stumbled among tangled vines and struggled to see through low-lying clouds. But far from deterring them, the ordeal of the climb revived their numbed emotions, restored their flagging spirits, and drove them on.

In late afternoon, the group reached a long meadow corridor, with an unbroken wilderness of gorges, streams, cataracts, and thickly wooded heights visible off in the distance. A little more than a mile ahead, on the right, unseen beyond a stand of great cypress, ran the road that led to the border.

The people spread out as they came up through the brush. Their joy and relief were palpable. Women and men looked at one another in astonishment and cried when they realized they had accomplished the harshest part of their flight.

Stephen walked alone, behind the others, studying the landscape and picturing the trip back. Because of the slowness of the pace, after all this time they had come only eight miles. On his own, he calculated, he could make the return trek in about three hours.

Evening was approaching and they were in the meadow. The sky above the hills in the west was layered for miles like drifts of sedimentary rock: stratocumulus clouds massed in paradisal bands of orchid, gold, and orange, russet and faded rose and deep crimson, behind which flared the setting sun.

To compose himself, Stephen walked out onto a bluff facing west. And just as had happened the night before in the moonlit glade, the sky held him. The surpassing beauty of the clouds—beyond all human power to create or to revoke or to corrupt—seemed to render ineffective

the cares and assumptions of the worn earth below, as if he were standing at the intersection of the timeless with time, and all the opposites
of the world had melted into oneness, and that oneness of an order
utterly sublime and wholly other. He experienced there—for a fleeting
instant—a feeling of such intense joy that tears came to his eyes and,
unbidden, a line from Nietzsche pierced his consciousness:

All joy wills eternity—
wills deep, deep eternity.

—⟶—

Almost as one, at daybreak everybody was up. While the men and older
children gathered wild berries in the bush, the women took out loaves
of bread, broke them into pieces, and set them aside for the Eucharistic
meal.

Stephen opened his backpack and, going from one family to another,
apportioned the precious contents of antibiotics and rehydration salts. As
he drew near to Mambo, who stood watching him with troubled eyes,
fearing what might be about to happen, he prepared to say good-bye.

Many of the others had not foreseen his leaving them and, when
they learned of Stephen's intention to go back to the mission, they
swiftly formed a protective circle around him.

Anxious voices called out from the crowd:

"Militias may be searching for you, Father."

"They're through with the area around the mission now," Stephen
said. "They won't be looking there." A smile breaking softly at the corners of his lips, he added, "And you've taught me how to hide in the
bush. They won't be able to find me."

A woman's voice entreated, "Stay with us, Father. We've been
through so much together."

But Stephen, lowering his voice in a tone of closure, said, "Thank
you. But I gave my word. I have to go back."

There was an uncertain silence. Then a young woman in a green patterned shawl came up to him and asked him to hear her confession. Stephen, as if he had anticipated just such a request, went to his backpack and took out his sacramental stole. Draping it around his neck, walking from family to family, he made the sign of the cross in the air, giving general absolution, pausing to hear the individual confessions of the many who asked.

One after another they approached him, their faces expressing grief and confusion mixed with an innocent trust in the sacrament, emotions so nobly constrained that no one articulated anything other than his or her offenses in soft, broken phrases. Stephen listened in silence, saying only the words required of him by the sacrament, while with dark, expressive eyes he searched the faces of each of the men and women who came to him, understanding, remembering.

In the meadow corridor, below a piebald-blue sky, Stephen celebrated the Eucharist, using a wooden bowl as a chalice, and the broken loaves of bread as hosts. The scant meal was shared by all.

Then they were ready to go. By hiding in the bush, by foraging for food wherever they could find it, by walking throughout the day, they would reach the border by evening of the next day.

Just before they parted, Stephen and the evacuees met a search party from the International Red Cross traveling on the road, going in the other direction. Stephen spoke to the senior member of the staff, who told him that when he and his coworkers finished their work in the area, they would try to make their way north and meet him at the mission.

XXIV

On a dark night, kindled in love
with yearnings—oh, happy chance!—
I went forth without being observed,
My house being now at rest.
In darkness and security,
By the secret ladder, disguised—
oh, happy chance!
In darkness and concealment,
My house being now at rest.
In the happy night,
In secret, when none saw me,
Nor I beheld aught, without light or guide,
save that which burned in my heart.
This light guided me,
More surely than the light of noonday,
To the place where he (whom I well know!) was awaiting me—
A place where none appeared.
Oh, night that guided me,
Oh, night more lovely than the dawn,
Oh, night that joined the Lover with his beloved,
And transformed her into Himself!

— SAINT JOHN OF THE CROSS, *DARK NIGHT OF THE SOUL*

Following the faint path worn in the grass, Stephen walked back through the meadow corridor until he reached the opening in the brush where he and the others had come up the day before. At the brow of the hill, he paused for a moment and looked about him.

In the early morning light the great forests stood half in shadow, half in glowing color. The sky was deep, deep blue, with high white clouds; flurries of birds rose above the escarpments from the woods below.

Looking on, Stephen felt something stir within his soul. On the trail, Mambo, speaking out of fear and desperation, had put a question to him. "Father, Jesus promised the Kingdom. His life ended violently. Is the world any better? Did life really change?" And Stephen, answering from the core of his being, had said, "Yes. Christian hope. The hope that in the end our lives have meaning." That conviction now bound him to a course of action.

Because of the steepness, he would have to descend the hill backward, with his face to the rock, as if he were climbing down a ladder. He checked his watch and studied the angle of the sun: as he went north the sun would move left and cross overhead. Kneeling, he adjusted the backpack.

Shelter me, Lord. I place myself in
Your care. I place my trust in You.

The binoculars dangling from a strap around his neck, he lowered himself over the edge, grasping a handful of heavy vines and searching with his shoe for footholds in the earth.

It was not hard to climb down at first, gravity now working for him. However, a third of the way down the slope, he stepped into a hollow, his foot caught in a web of tangled vines, he stumbled, lost his balance, and fell.

He clawed at the earth, trying to catch hold of clumps of the undergrowth. But the brush slipped from his hands.

The line of his fall brought him within reach of a long, arching branch. Near the limit of his endurance, Stephen strained for it, grasped it, held on, and broke his slide. Yet the backpack with his breviary, his sacramental stole, and the canteen of water had torn loose and rolled into the dark abyss of the underbrush, lost.

Moving sideways, he worked his way down the hill to a level ridge, slid to the ground with his back against the rock, and sat gasping for breath. He was laboring hard from the fall. His face and arms were scratched and, where the strap of the binoculars had whipped his neck, the skin was abraded and sore. But these were minor afflictions. His most urgent need was water.

To his right, the ridge curved back, then reappeared in a broad sweep to form the first in a series of stone ledges, over which cascaded the narrow falls he had heard sounding from the glade two nights earlier. Below the shelflike projections, water splashed and eddied in four ankle-deep pools. Stephen climbed along the ridge and scrambled over boulders, moving down through low scrub to the most accessible of the pools.

In the soft earth surrounding it, he found only the faint tracks of small wood antelope. He lay down and lowered his head to drink. The sudden cold instantly revived him. Dropping to his knees, he plunged his hands into the pool, splashing water on his face and throat, rubbing it into his hair and along the back of his neck.

When he felt stronger, he stood up and continued to move downward. His path followed the descent of the falls until they broke again two hundred feet below him, then dropped in a long straight ribbon through the trees.

After an hour he reached level ground again, leaving the rocky heights for the thickets and groves of the woodlands. Staying within the shelter of the trees, checking the direction of the sun, he made his way to the great forest of their exodus.

Bathed in a strange half-light, the forest trails had a fluid, otherworldly beauty. Small, shy animals stirred in the underbrush. The wandering, flutelike whistle of indiscernible birds came from the high trees. Pale shafts of sunlight floated through the leaves like the polished spears of warriors shimmering in a blurred dream.

At the edge of a little ravine, patches of sky appeared through gaps in the trees, disappeared, and appeared again. The sun was crossing overhead. He had come more than halfway. Bending right, Stephen pushed through the underbrush. Ahead, something like a horizontal ladder cut among the trees. A small footbridge stood out over the ravine, and he gazed at it gratefully. He had found the bridge he and the others had crossed two days earlier.

For a mile he followed the trampled path by which they had made their escape. Then he decided to change course. He could return to the mission by the path through the woods, but he was wary of doing so, in case Dhavée and his militia had tracked the evacuees to where they had left the grounds. Instead, he backtracked on a narrow trail that curled down through scrubland and came out above the mission grounds.

When the trees thinned, Stephen stood before an open field perhaps a thousand yards in length. It was a little after noon; predators would not stir for several hours. But to cross the open plain, unarmed, was perilous at any time, for on foot he was prey. He stood behind a screen of trees and studied the landscape, training the binoculars on a distant scene.

Far to the east, a herd of zebras was grazing near a waterhole, and beneath a dark acacia shrub, crouching low to the ground, long tail flicking slowly, a lioness was watching. The pride's attention was drawn to quarry. Stephen stepped out from the trees.

He walked in the open, moving fast, at times at a trot, heading north, to where an acacia thicket appeared upon a rise. In fifteen minutes he was on land familiar to him. Four miles ahead ran the gravel road that he and Mambo had taken on the day they had gone to watch the running of the herds. High, thin clouds drifted slowly through the sky in the east where once, as he drove through the brush, a glowing embankment of stratocumulus clouds had inspired a letter to Clare, written in a September that seemed to him now a thousand years ago.

Turning left, he brushed past rough shrubbery and reached the road where it began its descent to the mission. Just in front of him, the long, low wall that bounded the mission grounds emerged through the trees. As Stephen neared it, he caught sight of the Land Rover. It had been pushed off the grounds, rolled over on its side, and left lying in the brush, its wheels stripped, its windows shattered. Stephen advanced uneasily. No matter how thoroughly he had steeled himself to face what lay beyond the wall, he was overwhelmed by a feeling of foreboding.

He released the latch and pressed against the gate; in that moment a solitary thrush called out, a piercing, sweet *eey-o-lay*, and Stephen entered the mission grounds.

He heard a man's voice call out, a strangled cry: his own voice.

"Oh God, no, no..."

The grounds had been totally deserted when he had seen them last. They were crowded now. But reality had transformed into the grotesque.

The mission grounds lay before him like an emptied sea that had given up all its dead. Everywhere—on the drive, on the gravel paths, across the lawns, in the doorways, in the bougainvillea along the walls—human remains were strewn over the grounds. Wherever one turned, black swarms of flies rose and descended in ever-shifting columns, seeking blood, while high overhead, vultures, scenting death, described spirals above the horizon line.

Stephen wandered the lawns, dazed, the grass beneath his feet slick with blood. The killing had taken place within the past few hours. Bodies still had warmth. *How many were there?" he wondered. "Four hundred? Five hundred? Hundreds more?* One did not have to imagine the scene as it must have unfolded here. The bodies and faces of the dead revealed all, fully and profoundly. The killing had been pitiless, skilled, and thorough.

Young women, stripped of clothing, sexually profaned, lay stretched out on their backs beneath the statue of Mary, Queen of Angels, staring up and beyond her, eyes crazed. Mothers lay doubled over the bodies of their children, who had been torn or chopped from their arms; their husbands sprawled on the grass around them, clubbed or chopped or knifed to death. Stretching past the church and all the way up to the clinic were rows and rows of bodies of the dead who had been machine-gunned in masses and collapsed facing the clinic door in a hideous caricature of patients queuing up at the dispensary.

Against a background of forest and sky was all this red—

Stephen went from body to body, kneeling down again and again to feel a wrist for a pulse, murmuring, "Know that someone was here and grieved for you."

In that act his eyes were drawn to an eerie sight. In the well of shadow beneath an olive tree lay the partly dismembered, naked corpse of a man, which his wife or mother (it was impossible to tell which, for her face had been battered away) was bracing with her arms, bearing his whole weight upon herself. The awkward embrace, the blows that rendered the features void, the youth's hammered body, his severed arm— in death, the desecrated human forms had taken on the appearance of Mary and her crucified Son in Michelangelo's last *Pietà*.

Stephen could not take his eyes away from the scene. *Then those in Judea must flee to the mountains, a person on the housetop must not go down to get things out of his house, a person in the field must not return to get his cloak. Woe to pregnant women and nursing mothers in those days.*

His mind sagged. This was the landscape after the apocalypse: the anonymity, the indifference, the stillness of death. Going slowly and carefully from row after row of the dead, he made the sign of the cross, giving general absolution. He knew he had to hurry. Soon vultures would arrive. The ferocity of the proceedings that had taken place on this site had kept them at bay thus far, but at dusk they would arrive by the hundreds.

When he had finished praying over the dead, Stephen searched in the storeroom of the clinic for a shovel. There was one propped up among the stepladders and cleaning buckets; returning to the grounds with it, he began the near-hopeless task of digging graves.

The day wore on. A vast silence lay over all, a silence made more intense by the incessant droning of the flies, Stephen's ragged intakes of breath, and the dull thud the blade made in rhythm with his labored breathing.

Along with silence there was perfect stillness, except in two places.

Like the spiraling winged seedpods of the maple tree, four vultures floated lazily down from the sky and stood atop the roof of the school, spreading dark wings.

And there was something white that moved among the trees: the long wild hair of an ancient figure resembling a soothsayer, who had bought his life in exchange for another's.

Toward evening, thirsting, lonely, aching, shivering from exertion, Stephen secured the front doors of the church and followed the left-side aisle up to the open door of the sacristy off the main altar. He was so exhausted that he needed the wall for support as he felt his way along, and had to pause for long intervals every few steps to recover his strength. Inside the small room, he sat on the floor in one corner, his legs drawn up, his arms folded on his knees, his head bowed. Intellectually, he hungered for a copy of the Gospels; emotionally, he longed to clasp some object that was unstained and beneficent and unrelated to the anguish of the day. But he had left his books packaged in his room in the Jesuit residence, and his legs would carry him no farther. After a few moments, he lay down on the floor, his head on his arm, and drowsed off, insensible to his own exhausted groaning.

In the morning, he planned to forage in the woods for berries and other fruit, work again, hide in the brush at any approach. He felt he could endure for days, for weeks, this way.

—�—

The strict and brittle snap of a stick in the darkness.

Stephen awoke.

The lone window was partly open; the air was mild and still, a smell of beginning decay coming from outside the wall. Around him the grounds were dark and silent.

Footfall.

Someone was running stealthily in booted feet over the lawn.

There was a sudden loud, insistent banging on the door at the front entrance to the church and, without warning, rough, discordant voices began intoning the word *Jesuit* in French.

Stephen got to his feet, dread washing over him.

The voices, gathering and intensifying, called out in rhythmic sing-song, chanting the word *Jesuit* in French.

His eyes accustomed now to the darkness, Stephen looked quickly about the small room where he had vested for Mass each day, knowing in advance there was nowhere to hide. Yet even as he absorbed the desperateness of his situation, a resolve was forming in his mind. He would have in this moment what Viktor Frankl has called "the last of the human freedoms"—to choose one's attitude in a given set of circumstances, to choose one's own way.

He turned inward, and summoned forth in his imagination those Jesuits who had trod the path that lay before him. Their images rose in his mind out of a long record of dark nights and anguished cries, a cortege of black robes steeped in scarlet.

Isaac Jogues, canonical fingers severed, headless body floating in a crimson wash in the autumn leaf waters of the Mohawk River.

Straining to control the trembling of his lower jaw, Stephen began to pray:

"Body of Christ, save me..."

The brusque voices had entered the church and echoed now from the nave, their measured chanting in grotesque counterpoint to Stephen's impassioned thought.

René Goupil, lying bound on the dank earth, listening to the cries from the longhouse, waiting for dawn, and his turn.

"Passion of Christ, strengthen me..."

A white light glimmered suddenly beneath the door; it flickered along the uncarpeted floor, illuminated the shelves above the bare counter, disclosed the gray metal crucifix suspended over the lintel. Feeling for the wall, Stephen stepped back into the shadows, his eyes fastened on that crucifix.

"Jesus, hear me. Within Your wounds, hide me..."

He felt weak, cold, estranged from everything around him. He could not remember what day it was, or what he had intended to do tomorrow. The structures of time and place, like his life, were coming undone. All that was left to him were the images he groped for in his mind; they were darkening and receding, but he would not let go.

Edmund Campion, asked by his executioner how he felt, tortured upon the rack: "Not ill, because not at all..."

"Don't let me be separated from you..."

What would be said by those who found him in the days ahead: that he had been alone and defenseless, that there had been no means of escape? Could anyone know that, in the most ultimate of meanings that would not have been true?

The chanting reached him from the sanctuary, now demanding and boldly hostile.

"At the hour of my death, call me..."

The door fell in soundlessly, amid an explosion of voices.

"So, Jesuit! Waiting for us?"

The machete struck his left shoulder, severing the bone. Stephen clutched his arm instinctively, and fell to his knees. A look of confusion passed over his face.

And it came to him that once he had been a child like Samuel, sleeping in another room, when someone had called his name; and he had answered then, as he answered now, through blood and air, half whisper-moan:

"Here I am. You called me..."

Dhavée, the first of those present, struck him on the side of the head with the barrel of a rifle and spat on him, saying, "Yes! We called you!"

The crowd closing around him laughed in an uproar.

Then a white-gloved hand cut an arc through the air, and one by one they descended on him in a blur of spears.

When they had killed Stephen, they dragged his body up the center aisle and left it lying in the doorway at the entrance to the church.

—⁂—

Morning. Stillness.
A scurrying wind along one wall
Stirred only flies
And scraps of dark cloth,
Flapping, flapping.

Where,…in what desolate and smoky country,
Lies your poor body, lost, and dead?

— *THOMAS MERTON, O.C.S.O.*
FOR MY BROTHER: REPORTED
MISSING IN ACTION, 1943

June 9, 1994
Dear Mrs. Shearer,

    On the morning of May 18, I met your brother, Stephen, and was, I believe, one of the last persons to speak with him.

    I was a member of a small convoy of relief workers distributing food and medical supplies in the field that day. About 9:00 a.m. we came upon a group of men, women, and children who were fleeing the area and making their way to the border.

    Among them I noticed a slender, dark-haired white man with very handsome features; he was wearing a blue cotton short-sleeved shirt and chino pants and had several days' growth of beard. His sense of presence, his bearing, were remarkable. He simply leaped out at you in a group. At first I thought he was European but, when he came over to speak to us, he introduced himself as Stephen Engle, an American priest and a member of the Jesuit order.

    He was intent on knowing if we had been in the area of the Catholic mission that lay seven miles to the north. I told him that we'd come from the opposite way and only now were progressing toward that location; thus, he and the others had the most recent knowledge of its status. On learning this, Father Engle gave us an account of a fire they had witnessed the day before. He was concerned about individuals who might have sought sanctuary in the church and was about to leave the group he was with to go back to assist them. A few minutes more, he said, and he would have missed us.

    Barring unforeseen circumstances, we agreed to meet up with him at the mission within forty-eight hours. Unfortunately, because of military action in the region, we were not able to keep our commitment until six days later. At that time, our path crossed that of a group of UN inspectors who had arrived at the site the evening before. They informed us of what you already know: that your brother returned to the mission alone and there, sometime on the night of May 18 or early morning of May 19, he lost his life.

It will not leave me: that last glimpse of him as he turned onto the mountain path to begin the journey back. A part of me vowed unequivocally, "I would not undertake what that man is setting out to do: leaving the ninety-nine in the wilderness, as it were, to go back after the one." Yet as my eyes followed him, another part of me said quietly, "That is the kind of human being I hope to become."

I am grateful to whatever accident of circumstances and time took us to just that road at just that hour and gave me the chance to meet him.

My most sincere condolences to you and your sister Clare.

Very truly yours,
David Penn
Senior Staff
International Red Cross

—ɯ—

Kathleen had gone up to the Jesuit main house with the others attending the memorial service, but Clare stayed behind to look back for a last time across the grounds.

Everything there—the soft firs, the lawn that sloped down to the lake, the path along it, the water, silver blue and half-hidden in the trees—Stephen had loved.

She stood just outside the chapel doors in the shade of the blue spruce trees, an intense, imaginative sequence of thoughts passing in her mind.

"Is there a ritual that can take us back to the beginning again? Or is it all fated from the beginning, fated the way the Greeks understood the word: that character is fate? And so, from the moment Stephen took his first step away from us, his life was lived on a line that led always to this day.

"In one of his novels, Dostoyevsky has the hero's young protégé ask, if Jesus 'could have seen Himself on the evening of the crucifixion'—not the still-beautiful body of a man cut off in his prime, the way He would be painted by Rubens or Velázquez, but the bloodied corpse of a man 'wounded, tortured, beaten,' in whom there was no longer any outward appearance of beauty or dignity, the way He would be depicted by Hans Holbein the Younger—if Jesus 'could have seen Himself on the evening of the crucifixion, would He have gone up to the cross and have died as He did?'

"It's the question behind the question friends asked when they first were told of Stephen's death, trying to comprehend it: Why had he left the group and returned to the mission on his own? He could have continued on with the others and still have shown solidarity with the victimized.

"Some wondered if he was motivated by what he felt Father Cormier would have done. Others suggested that, having personally experienced how devastating the loss of a parent is for a child, he went back out of concern for children who might have been orphaned.

"Those theories are all credible. But, at heart, I believe there was another, even larger, purpose for his decision. I think Stephen wanted desperately to *do* something. But he had no worldly power; he couldn't take up arms. He had the spiritual power of a priest, and in his inmost soul, he knew that all he could set against a monstrous evil was this one pure act."

Epilogue

The next evening

Clare looked up. The light was out. Kathleen had finally gone to bed. She leaned over to unlock the door of her car.

Footsteps.

A man was walking toward her down the sidewalk; by his step, a young man. Without a streetlight she could not see his features, only that as he passed, he flashed her a smile. He was wearing a white scarf, which, when seen from behind, formed a narrow white band along his collar line. He reached the corner, looked both ways, then turned to the right. As he walked away, he began to whistle.

A whistle so pure and piercing and joyous.

A whistle that went right up to the stars.

So, should I never again
Be seen or heard of on the common-ground,
You will say that I am lost,
That, wandering love-stricken,
I lost my way, and was found.

— JOHN OF THE CROSS

Attributions

In Part One, Chapter Four, elements of Gerald Kaestner's talk are based on the teaching of the great Jesuit theologian Karl Rahner (1904-1984).

In Part Two, Chapter 15, Stephen Engle's words on the call to follow Christ gives voice to thoughts I learned in the class "Poets, Mystics, and God," taught by Justin Kelly, S.J. Later in the same chapter, Stephen Engle's description of the word "relationship" was taught to me by my friend and mentor, the late Dr. Bruce Danto.

In Part Two, Chapter 19, Stephen Engle's book, Without Light or Guide, develops themes I learned in the class "Theology of the Imagination," taught by Justin Kelly, S.J.

In Part Two, on page 124, Stephen Engle's comment on the John Updike short story, "Pigeon Feathers," is from material learned in the class "Theology of Death and the Resurrection," taught by Justin Kelly, S.J.

Acknowledgements

At the end of *To The Lighthouse*, Virginia Woolf describes her character, the artist Lily Briscoe, turning to her canvas:

There it was—her picture. Yes, with all its greens and blues, its lines running up and across, its attempt at something. It would be hung in the attics, she thought; it would be destroyed. But what did that matter? she asked herself, taking up her brush again. She looked at the steps; they were empty; she looked at her canvas; it was blurred. With a sudden intensity, as if she saw it clear for a second, she drew a line there, in the centre. It was done; it was finished. Yes, she thought, laying down her brush in extreme fatigue, I have had my vision.

Isn't this the way every artist feels, finishing his or her painting? The way every writer feels, concluding his or her book? However elevated or humble the work, it began as a gift they were given, and they spent themselves for its sake.

This book grew out of an awareness, a kind of waking dream, I had in the fall of 1994. In my imagination I saw a young nun, a novice, talking with her mother superior. The young nun had had a strange and wonderful dream. Describing it, she said, "I saw a priest alone in a darkened room, and I had the certain sense that he knew he was about to die. And he spoke to me. He said, 'Don't let me die here alone. Tell my story.' And then, he was just shot through with light, as if he'd been engraved out of diamonds and lit from behind. And then, he vanished.

What could it mean?" The older nun advised the young novice to put the dream to a practical use; perhaps she might like to write a series of articles on Christian martyrs.

From that beginning came Clare Engle, this novel's heart. Over the years the book came together, piece by piece, the way a mosaic does. I wanted to put into it everything that I loved: Velázquez and Caravaggio, Monet and Vermeer from the world of art; Yeats and Hopkins, Joyce and Keats, Eliot and Pushkin, towering figures of literature. Because, as Cleanth Brooks, author of *The Well Wrought Urn*, wrote so beautifully, "Poetry is the lesser mystery, religion the greater," here, too, are Saints Augustine, Ignatius of Loyola, Francis and Clare of Assisi, Julian of Norwich, Karl Rahner, Viktor Frankl, Thomas Merton, and the great Carmelite saints, Thérèse of Lisieux and John of the Cross.

I am grateful to the friends who supported me throughout the years that I wrote.

I would like to thank Monsignor Patrick Halfpenny of St. Paul Catholic Church in Grosse Pointe Farms for his kindness in reading an early draft of my manuscript.

I owe so much to my professors of literature at Michigan State University, at Wayne State University, and to the late Sister Mary Aquin, S.S.J. of Nazareth College in Kalamazoo, Michigan. They were the people who opened my mind to literature's beauty and truth. Excerpts from papers I wrote for their classes are in the novel.

Thank you to Justin Kelly, S.J. of the University of Detroit/Mercy from whose wonderful classes -- "Theology of the Imagination," "Poets, Mystics, and God," and "Theology of Death and the Resurrection" -- I drew a depth of knowledge that has stayed with me all my life and that I have tried to share in these pages.

Thank you to my readers, Cherie Warzyniak, Joan Kaltz, and JoAnn Foster-Floyd, gentle critics and reassuring confidants, who with me took the long journey toward a finished work.

Thank you to the late Jeanette Piccirelli, who from 2011 until her death in February, 2015, was my editor. Her attention to detail was flawless; her encouragement, invaluable.

Watching over me like a guardian angel was my first editor and cherished friend, the late Gladys Garner Leithauser, a mental genius and a genius, too, in bringing out the best in others. This book would not have been written, but for her.

Thank you to my indispensable typist, Nancy Goodrich, for her patience, her professionalism, and her friendship.

Last and above all, I thank John, my husband, who had the perspicacity to see that Alexander Pushkin's line, "Not all of me is dust," was a fitting title for a book about belief in eternal life lived in the face of death.